Previous novels by Kathleen Bryson

Mush
Girl on a Stick

The Stagtress

The Stagtress

Kathleen Bryson

With best witchy wishes!
Kathleen

fugue state press
new york

ISBN 978-1-879193-30-7

Library of Congress Control Number 2019944325

Manufactured in the United States of America

Published by Fugue State Press
PO Box 80, Cooper Station
New York NY 10276

www.fuguestatepress.com
info@fuguestatepress.com

For my childhood friends and fellow girl-witches Alanna and Janice: in remembrance of magic spells cast in the wild, especially those charms that used beach-found Japanese glass fishing buoys as crystal balls. And therefore for all grown-up girls who preferred witches to fairies as kids.

Chapters

Illustrations

The Stagtress

Part I

The Velvet

Once upon your spacetime there was a house in the woods, the house in the woods. That woods would eventually disappear, that woods with a house in a valley stuffed with trees. In the future the valley would be called Haca's Ey, by way of either Sourditch or Dedrlaf's Farm, and then it came to be christened Hackney – timely, as that was when the Christians triumphed. The woods in which was found the house grew many things: bushes and moss; little stags and large rodents; other houses amongst the brush, cottages like smallpox stipples, bumps of construction and stone. And then, reaching maturation, the house in the woods became a veritable town in the woods. The town was called the Hamo de Herst, quite literally the town in the woods, and then that word slithered into the word Amherst, the surrounded grove, and then Amhurst Grove, the grove of groves, the doublegrove, a grove on top of a grove, a leaf-furry ouroboros eating its knobbly, budding tail.

But your once-upon takes place smack in the middle age of that. There is no town. There is only the woods, so the concept of a grove itself is ridiculous, for it implies that a town reigns sovereign and after all once upon your time it was the woods that reigned. Like the Horned God herself, a female stag holding court amongst brown leaves, dead leaves, crumbling leaves. Nevertheless, there was a house and let us at last begin with that singular shelter. The roof was made of green leaves stitched together with red-blonde threads of hair. The filaments could have been from a rus-set golden retriever dog, had those particular canines been bred to gilded glory back in those post-Haca's Ey days, which they had not. The filaments could be from a flaxen neo-Norman Anglo-Saxon. That is at least chronistically correct – and rhymes, as well. The freshness of the leaves meant that they must have been sewn into a thatch-quilt recently. Perhaps that very morning. Yes, maybe in the ante-meridian hours a young Englishman was still unton-sured, and a sapling still full bloom in its green blush. There was no meridian back then; there was no Greenwich but a Grenewych (though it was both a mean and cruel time) and there were no cityscapes to speak of, and there were no thermonuclear bombs, so why couldn't a roof be woven of locks and leaves?

    Now, though, along an empty road, in a mustard-coloured landscape, after the bomb has gone off, after the bomb, a stripling walks hand in hand with a sapling, man and tree are friends at last. The human is bald and the tree is bare. The man and his tree fuck on the bare sand; get radioactive dust under their bark and in their eyes and beget nothing, I said nothing. Above them the suns are bright; there are one, two, count them, three suns in the sky. Where do the man and the tree go? They're going away, but eventually – in order for hope to work – they must go towards something as well.

The young man has baroque dreams when he lies down in cold night with his tree, dreams working against the bright minimalism of day and dark chalkboard of night, against branch and flesh and dirt.

The young man dreamt of carrying phosphorescent jars of cold blue honey and fireflies, of sugar tasting of violet and vaginas, of stenograph machines whose metal recordings could be scraped away at least one hundred times; he also dreams, and sometimes even hallucinates in day, as a mirage, the melting of German lead in spoons and the casting of it into cold water to tell futures that way. But what can he say to console his walking-stick: You will bud again, you will burst in spring, you will bloom. The tree could say: Dear Martin, you will love, you will beget and smile, you will burn with whiskey and you will skin fish.

The tree also dreams extravagantly, of the indescribable pleasures of tightening sap, of the wound one time by which a pair of lovers assaulted it via their initials, of its favourite bird from 33 years ago. That bird, that season, was particular. The bird gave lay to jewelled eggs and Russian nesting dolls, Christmas-tree baubles and baby teeth. Everything hatched. Everything grew back.

The forest is silent on the matter of who exactly took its leaves to coat the house. Forests are too quiet, often too quiet, don't you think? Close your eyes as you read this and think of a forest. How do you see it? It will be particular to you. Is your forest blue or green? Maybe purple. What quality does the light have; is it a singular sol that leaks through the underbrush in unexpected, unrepeatable filigree patterns, or are there clean starbursts from three stars on high drilling through the trees, chlorophyll-coloured tricksiness?

Keep your eyes closed. What do you smell? Woodsmoke, just damp moss and comforting decay. Maybe you have a cold and detect little. And what do you hear in this forest of yours? Try again. All right, close your eyes tighter and try again. You hear nothing, my beloved. As I told you.

Will you knock on the door? It is, after all, the only house for miles. What will you do, what will you do? Will you turn left or right? Will you turn away? Will you turn into a bird, one that is cawing from the tree to your left, one that is flying past and dropping a diamond-and-garnet egg on your exposed, too-broad forehead?

The bird is acting very aggressively. You ignore the bird and then you knock, you knock.

As I told you that you would. You were always going to.

***

The fruit trees that surrounded the cottage bore grey fruits who would change colour according to the mood of passersby, to soft appleish reds or bright venom purpures in the case of angry or excitable people. In the morning, when it was quiet and the sun streamed down and no people or animals walked by to shift the fruits, they stayed a comforting dove grey. It was never clear whether such trees were tame or feral.

Near the cottage was a dangerous lake. There were seven yards of barbed wire underneath, and it was also rumoured that there were moving spiked grille grates that sluiced through the water, silently, and you never knew until they stuck you and held you underwater until the last. There was also rumoured to be a bed of nails.

The cottage was surrounded by a brick wall that had been painted white so that shadows showed up easily against it. The shadows from the trees that bore the grey fruits were curliecued and impressive shadows. In the cottage, in the woods, a little girl lived, along with her parents and her three little brothers (triplets). Her eighth birthday, the day before, she had received her first jack-knife from her father with her own name chipped into the wooden sheath in curlicue letters – F-L-O-R-E-N-T-I-N-E – and that was also the day that she had stepped outside the house and headed towards the lake. The lake was a pool and the lake was a mirror. It was the dangerous lake. Do you remember the dangerous lake? I do. She had looked down and the surface had been something solid, like silvered glass. A looking glass for Florentine, she had peered down and it was then that she had seen, rather than felt, the two bumps on top of her head, velvet buttons, rather like the vestigial horns on male dehorned family pet goats. Oh deer, was she going to turn into a goat, too? Though the velvet was indeed doe-a-deer, not wether. Her brothers had not yet been castrated, but she was experienced with the term wether *vis-à-vis* the alpine caprines; such goats had been in her family for a long, long time.

This night, or more properly early morning, she woke up to what she thought was a knock, but then heard nothing more. She sneaked out into the alcove behind the back of the house, where the logs were stacked up. She crouched down and tore off the leaves of spirch bark, revealing the damp rot. No. Nor the grey-bumped shroud of bruce bark, similarly sodden. Florentine stood up. Her pulse was rummy and rapid, all the way down to both wrists. Mouth dry. The wood wrong. Oh, not that on some logs there were buds both spirch, both bruce. That was odd, but manageable. No, everything had turned wrong. That exact night before, Florentine's brothers had transformed into goats, three small ones. Their horns were nubbins. Their hide was smoke and white and still fluffy, almost chick-like in its sweetness. When it happened, on her very eighth birthday, Florentine immediately had wanted to pet and stroke them with kindness, for they were still her brothers. Since their parents were forest-farmers, they were tight-lipped folk, and Florentine and her brothers had not deemed it sufficiently relevant to analyse this new snowy hide and horned experience, though it was a bond that, as it happened, would wind them tight like a witch's white wool together.

*

Florentine returned inside from the wood pile. It was dark. Her mother and father and little brothers all slept this night after her eighth birthday. The sun would rise, soon the sun would rise, soon the sun would rise. She went and lay under the wooden table on which they ate their breakfast, and waited for an act to happen.

But right when she did this, there was a knock on the door. Florentine rose up and bumped her head. She sneaked a look over the alcoves where her family lay, but they all still snored.

Time passed but not much of it; her family began to rise and make breakfast, but no one noticed that Florentine went to the door and answered it.

It was you.

"How do you do," you said to Florentine, "I am looking for a man with a walking-stick, or perhaps for a jewelled bird. Have you seen either?"

Florentine looked at you and the bumps on the top of her head began to grow; they expanded like a tree unfolds to its maturity; they stretched out like fingered hands until they reached antlerhood.

You merely looked at Florentine, the little girl with stag's antlers. You had never seen anything like it before.

"Where are," you said, "where are Pret a Manger sandwiches and Prada shoes and Campbell's Tomato Soup Low Sodium and Spud-21 missiles and forget-me-not flowers?"

Florentine observed you with a curious expression

on her face. "We have forget-me-not-flowers behind the log pile, on the edge of the woods," Florentine said. "We cast their seeds in springtime and tell the future from them."

"I am from that future," you said to her. You did not want to break a young girl's heart, not even a young antlered girl's heart, a girl who looked like she could gouge you quite easily with a single horn. What could you say to her?

You said: "We have deserts of failed crops; do you know what crops are?"

"Yes," said Florentine.

You said: "We have landscapes poisoned by bombs." (She looked confused; you continued.) "I'll backtrack a bit to what we had after you. We had defaced angels and pussywillows and prickwillows. We had a king who lost his head and foot-and-mouth. We still have 16th-century graffiti on cathedrals. We still have the River Ouse."

"The River Ooze?" said Florentine. "Does it move in that strange manner?"

"The River Ouse. We had the people's princess and then Facebook and we've had printed advertisements for quite a long while, but we still love each other."

You gave Florentine a hug.

She said to you: "We have the sallows and the mallows and a walking-stick shaped like a snakehead. We have people who tread around the marshes on stilts. I've heard that. We have blackwaters and Greek fire, and villages set alight, and a spiney abbey. All of which I have heard but not seen. From my parents, from an occasional uncle or peddler.

Past the forest, of course, where there is the world. We now have no Pest. We are a beggary people, with innocent trades, such as iron and soap. We have pitchforks, heaps of stones. We have florid names, but old customs. After winter, there is thaw. We have bog-oaks and peat."

You and the girl with antlers stared at each other.

"We're not so different," she said, "look at you." She pointed to your scalp. You put a hand up, and you felt your horns as well, a deep surprise. "We're not so different, you and I," she said, "you from my future, and me from your past."

The sun was rising.

"Come inside," she said at last, "sit down and eat breakfast with my family, and we can talk much more."

You followed her through the low door, and in the dawn light you remembered to duck low enough and subtile, so that your antlers only scraped the wooden frame.

You next went wandering in a field filled only with blue leaves, for petals are leaves too; they are just softer and more tender and, let us not forget, more colourful leaves. Primroses and wild blue violets and bluebells and forget-me-nots. You are not sure whether this flower memory matches either the truth of wildflowers or geographical or indeed temporal accuracy, but nevertheless this is what you recall of that morning.

Your promenade in the blue field took place after your breakfast with the little girl's family. Throughout the meal you had smiled and nodded at her parents and her three little brothers gruff. Throughout, throughout, throughout this entire meal you had been steadily aware, as you complimented the mother on her feastly griddlecakes and smiled alongside her father as you both attempted to grab the last morsels of spiced *chevon* and *chevreuil* (which the little brothers and your girl host did not touch) and the father deferred them to you, throughout, throughout, throughout these genuine affectations of hospitality, you remained singularly aware of your own new antlers. They were horns, really, like those of a moose or caribou. They were not as helix-delicate as the fragile jewellery of a stag.

You gingerly took the opportunity to touch one of your horns while the mother poured out a flask of hot beer for you. Your fingers brushed lichen; yes, your horns belonged to a land mammal of the New World. You had a sudden, overwhelming sense of difference. You were from a different continent (and so were your antlers).

Here, the New World had not yet been discovered! You were sure of it! You drank the steamed froth – it was not beer then, nor exactly cider; it was a liquor made from the strange grey fruits, you thought, you surmised, you wiped your lips – and smiled round at the other six, and you knew then, suddenly, with a flash of near panic, that it was paramount that you left this constricting little shelter. You knew that your antlers would grow too big, otherwise. In fact, you experienced the certainty that your horns – like pubertal reactions, you were not quite sure how to control these new sensations – would grow so large, like plastic flapping hang-glider wings, that you would never again be able to leave the cabin!

Of course, this was not what was actually occurring; it was just what you feared. Nevertheless! You smoothed off the griddlecake crumbs from the corners of your mouth politely with your sleeve.

"Thank you much for this delicious repast. And would you mind terribly if I stepped outside for some time? I find myself suddenly lightheaded."

No one minded at all.

So now there you were amongst this chaos of blue flora. The romanticising of the stiff blooming weeds and the drone of bumbling bees and chipper dragonflies, all saturated with the honey glow of early morning, made you think nostalgically of former lovers. Even in the midst of amnesia recovery, you had always been one to want to make great love in such flowery fields, but none of your lovers had ever been willing or wild. Perhaps you had read both *Lady Chatterley's Lover* and *The Wonderful Wizard of Oz* at impressionable ages.

Nevertheless, nevertheless, nevertheless here you were on your own again in just such an expansive field and it appeared that you had no such urge to have sex with yourself, and so in the end, even you had proven to be an unwilling and unwild lover unto yourself.

Yet. You sat down amongst the vegetables of this pastoral heaven, nestled yourself into the sheaves of lily-green grass and bluebells, and you knew that you were hidden from all eyes now; that is how tall the bluebells were. And you *were* wild now really, weren't you? You had the proof of it; you had horns. You checked right then, and the rest of your body was still human-shaped. Still, you felt you had more right to be here, cosseted by Nature, answerable to no one, than you had ever felt before unantlered.

Even if only a smallest percentage of your moosey or cariboued self was manifesting itself so peculiarly. More agency than on tender little park walks through Lunden's ersatz wilderness, where even there you had felt spooked, your phantasies of sexual congress in wild fields aside. Here, perhaps for the first time ever, you felt straight connected.

O, the clouds above you were no shapes in particular, and this was fine with you; you had no need to force artifice and patterns onto Nature. Not now that you were part of Nature.

The breeze whistled a little as it skimmed your horns; it sounded a little like the rush of a creek. The early sun hot gold molasses rapture on your cheeks and you balanced the weight of your head and you shook your moose-antlers a few times to vary the tone. Your fingers and bare arms touched thick uncut bushels of forget-me-nots – O, forget-me-not, you whispered to yourself, I will never forget this moment. You felt such jubilee.

This was the first time that you met the Stagtress.

*

There are fireflies in the air, and they are lightning bugs of a variety of colours, no mere little electric white bulbs, but blues and roses and greens and purples too, holiday twinklers.

He lies in the field on his back with his walking-stick beside him and he looks up at the sable night. A night punctured with stars and these pretty fireflies. He has come to this place; ended up at this destination towards which he has been drawn, with its strange fructed trees and a dangerous lake, and he has knocked at the door, but no one has answered.

Now he has resorted to drinking badger-soiled water from a creek and at present is flat on his back in a flowered meadow where, as it is night, he can't even make out the colour of the surrounding flowers. But he presumes them to be various, perhaps even night-cacti, similar to the flickering orange bugs skimming past the ruby-red bugs, and the blue bugs, and the silver bugs, and the bronze bugs, and the bottle-green bugs, and the golden bugs.

All insects are beautiful.

All insects are always beautiful.

*

Before we return to more subsequent times, let us take one last glance at Florentine and her brothers, two seasons after you lay in the blue field. It is winter. Or perhaps we should say it was winter. It was winter.

Winter was always going to be blissful. Winter in a

forest is always going to be blissful. Only six months ago, the night after you had been there, Florentine and her three brothers had snuck out of the cottage, while their mother was snoring and their father was experiencing sleep apnea, and snuck out to the same field of flowers where you had lain, and they had observed the shape you had left behind, a bowl of human-pressed crushed grass. Then they had found, to their surprise, another pressed area, where someone else had watched the fireflies.

That was then. Now the winter night was soft wintry pink even in the gloaming. The snow was white and slightly rosy. This time Florentine and the three billy goats boy stayed out shivering until the alpenglow faded and the stars came out and Florentine's cheeks grew frostbitten and the goatpelts' texture slate and stone in the bitter cold. Autumn had been difficult for the triplets, for the little gambolling caprines had been foretold, soberly, that they would face a menacing act in the late spring. An act that always took place when the May buds unsticked themselves.

That was then. Now the four siblings – foreboding scratching at their ears – exchanged glances and gretel and multiple hansels alike looked one last time at the warm house and the still-burning stove (*perhaps* it was a 1742 Franklin stove), and then they turned their respective backs to the heat and faced the snow.

The snow lay in folds at the edge of the woods, cruel eiderdown. Beyond the ice-gnawed stalks and old blue trunks were pockets of darkness and beyond even those all was unseen. Florentine and her three brothers went further out in the snow past the first fringe of season-gutted deciduous trees and dulled-down evergreens, past the unknown patches and then past the uncharted altogether. They were there (they were here) and they lay down in the drifts. It was so cold. It was probably January. Most likely to be January. All the stars were out. They were dressed in snow-apt clothes and heavy boots (fourteen boots in total), but the skin on their faces felt brittle and chill. It was so silent.

"Look up at the stars," Florentine said to her three brothers. "If you just look at them and try to drift away, you can feel nothing and then it will feel like you're floating. If you concentrate really hard."

Florentine could feel herself floating, as in a lake (a non-dangerous lake). Afterwards all three brothers announced that they had felt it too. But Florentine was wrong and it wasn't like floating; it was more like they were being swallowed up, and there was only silence – Florentine inside her head, the cold outside and quiet. She could not remember summers and years later whether they had closed their eyes or not. This would have been perilous to do since they were in the middle of nowhere, and at least within the middle of the woods. Florentine thought later that they had closed them. And then they would have opened them. All eight eyes open. They lay five foot-lengths away from each the other on their backs. The spaces in between. They looked up at the stars. The sounds went out. Eventually, the sky went out. Thud, heartbeats, breath and cold. That is how Florentine would remember it. It was intense yet impersonal. It was not like hypnosis. Clearly, they were each in control. When Florentine and her brothers got up and brushed off the snow, they didn't say much to each other as they trudged back to the warm cottage, but they did admit to each other that they had enjoyed the experience.

The boys entered the house first, and Florentine hung back, and that is when she saw the Witch.

The Witch was a grown woman and she was a pretty woman covered in unseasonal leaves and she was standing barefoot in the snow. She did not want to be let into the house (as you yourself had desired, remember); Florentine understood this instinctively. The Witch instead wanted Florentine to stay *outdoors*.

The patina of hard diamond snow crunched in the weight of Florentine's footsteps even as she stood there, trembling. The base of both antlers felt suddenly warm, melting the chill on her scalp. Florentine's palm on the door latch, the red heat from the wood-smoke interior warming the far tips of her hand.

The Witch crooked her finger towards Florentine. Come here, come here.

***

On a desert night, on a hot sand's night, after the bomb
goes off, after the bomb, on a desert night it is said to be
cold. Once the sand cools, it is cold; the sphinx's nose falls
off from frostbite. On such shiver nights, people want owls
descending in swoop in a dark navy sky; people want the
violence of the owl's mouse-murder, the red crush of blood
that lets folks know that they themselves live whilst others
die, as when former pets killed. Then we said, No, bad kitty,
bad kitty, poor mouse, poor sparrow, poor earthworm on our
doorstep.

Poor city, poor nation, poor planet. Radiation-gutted,
pounds of black dust that is in actuality radiotrophic fungi,
powder-drifts of nuclear waste. Poor Martin, here along
a road, in the desert with his walking-stick, one moment
dreaming of lightning bugs in gladed summerwood nights,
now putting one foot in front of the other, then boring the
hole in the desert sand with his stick, three impressions
followed by three dragging impressions, footprint-footprint-
hole, footprint-footprint-hole; when he looks behind himself
he sees the way that he has journeyed but, when he looks
in front of him, there are no tracks.

I said it was a road that that Martin walks, but in fact
there is no path; I said there was a noseless sphinx and yet
there are no sphinxes, pyramids, camels; there is only flat
toxic night sand, and Martin and his travelling stick are the
first to walk this direction.

Martin has been having the most phantasmagorical dreams, dreams where he is waking up in places crowded with people, locations called King's Cross and Berlin and Kodiak, dreams where he is waking up in nature-blessed fields full of rich-coloured little fireflies. In every one of these dreams he has his walking-stick, and in every one of these dreams he woolgathers that he is waking up, and so he has been finding it so very difficult to distinguish when he actually *does* rise up in the morning into the luminous present; he has had it hard distinguishing between a sleep and a reality.

(Once upon a time, before the untrod path, before the bomb, before the bomb, Martin watched a programme about an ancestor called *Australopithecus afarensis*. For scientists had been so lucky to discover footprints stonefied into volcanic ash, proof that near-humans had stepped on the Tanzanian Laetoli site (three individuals, one of them walking in the footsteps of another), and then that these three individuals had moved on; kept walking. This then spurs Martin to recall another programme, one concerning a later kinfolk type, *Homo sapiens neanderthalensis*, and the Neanderthal handprints found in the depths of Spain's El Castillo Cave, old paint fingers-and-palms still as raw as new wine.

In both cases, Martin remembers, these were exam-ples where the ancestor had still been living when they left their mark – *Here are my hands; here are my footprints!* – as opposed to the yellow-pale bony skull and teeth of toddler australopithecines or crumbling maxilla of *Homo antecessor* – depressing when you considered the topic too much, easier if you could avoid thinking of a grieving australopithecine mother – no, these ancestor-cousins were *different* and had marched into immortality by forever remaining alive! By their marks, their intentionality, not by their bones (inevitable as those bones would have been, of course!).

The desert night is forest-cold and Martin finds himself in a kind of delirium, whispering shiverish platitudes to his walking-stick. The sky has grown meconium-dark now – babyshit dark, the pre-birth of our souls – too dark to see the footprint-footprint-hole marks on the sand that the two of them have been leaving in their wake.

Martin ruminates over these dark unseen indents as he makes himself move forward, and thinks about how, barring unscheduled volcanic eruptions, the marks that he creates will likely never petrify with the proof that he has been there. Wind will blow over the triplet-tracks; birds will eat up such a hansel-and-gretel trail; the birds will be the wind. If birds there would be, which there be'n't. Perhaps his bones will remain, however, his bones and the stick itself (already the bone of a leafing tree). Perhaps lie there as proof of his walk on this earth, like any common garden-variety Neanderthal museum specimen. So, not for him the starry artist production of footprints on stiffening ash or red palms on cave walls to claim: I carry on, I carry on.

Bones then. He accepts it. And not another human to ever walk the earth again and see those bones. This is a so-sorrowful thing, the thought much more slicing than just the desert doing its good work to melt one's carcass down to fossil.

*

Eventually, the darkest hours fade and the desert stops dreaming. It warms. In three-quarters of an hour, Martin and the stick will halt to sleep (the stick will dream of autumn on this occasion, of dissolution). It has to be some old night-travelling instinct, the urge to foil nocturnal predators and the suns' blistering by dozing down at dawn and twilight. Except there are no predators anymore ever again.

So Martin walks on in cool dawn, with the light of three suns just starting to curl and imbue the generally flat, only occasionally valleyed, sands with a blue husk, a purplish tone to the sands and sky that will warm to garnet but not yet warm to garnet. (How opportune that each star rises and sets with the other two, most opportune.)

As he walks on, Martin begins to notice things, things that shouldn't be there. Off to the left is an oversized pineapple, glowing faintly. It is isolated, set alone like a museum piece, and he passes by a hundred feet away from it.

In front of Martin and his stick is another object, although it is impossible to discern its shape until they are nearly on top of it due to the still-grainy, nighty blueness of the world. It is a moustache, over-grown, stretching out over five feet from end to end. The moustache is nothing so flamboyant as a handlebar, and it is not attached to a face. The giant moustache is made up of dark, oiled clean hair, combed and pubic. Martin and the walking-stick look at it, circle it from the right, and then walk on.

Then the zippy light begins to sky across the distant sand, just little spottings of wine-light, red low clouds, pinky flickerings that give more than they promise (cornucopia-like) on the horizon.

Finally, also on the right, they pass by a flowing faucet, a tap as if for a sink, though this faucet is suspended in air, a ewer with no visible method of plumbing. The tap is made of tin and emits cold, delicious water directly into the sand, which is soaked up immediately. The waterstream appears normal and it looks as if Martin will be able to loll his tongue round it perfectly for a drink. This strikes Martin as a far-too-convenient mirage/oasis (though when he blinks and when the walking-stick widens its knotted eye, the floating faucet is still there). Martin wets his hands in the pouring stream, fills up a dry canteen for later, in case he changes his mind regarding its suspicious provenance, and moistens down the walking-stick too.

The suns are hell-red now, beautiful ladybug slots across the lower eighth of the sky. Then a few seconds and dawn entire hits; the desert turns gorgeous-gold and even more remote. Illuminators. Rubricators. One can see for miles. Martin decides to forgo his intended sleep. Then he sees something and his heart clicks, a living human being in the distance, the first other breathing animal he has seen in twelve good years.

It's you.

2

Snow Hill

Florentine woke up the next morning having dreamt of a
witch so beautiful, a barefoot witch who offered stalactite-
icicle treats that Florentine had politely refused, reasoning
correctly that glacé glossies would not keep her warm in
winter. The Witch had been covered by a dress of green leaf,
and that sight – even in the dream – had been shocking and
other-worldly, the alarm of seeing living spring in a season
where all's silver, white; and grey and sable and brown.
The image of the Witch's leaf dress stayed with Florentine
throughout the next morning, when she helped her mother
spin flax and watched her brothers tease each other, butting
and braying throughout the hearth-heated room. A dress of
leaves. A dress that stayed alive when it should by rights be
dead.

Did the Witch mean death itself? Had she *been*,
in fact, a dream? Florentine was not sure. Her parents
had always described Death as a man hobbledy-gobliny,
a sheathed man with a cowl covering his features, a man
with curling crescent knife who dabbled in plague and
pox, a heartless man and at times a capricious man, which
led Florentine to suspect that Death indeed had a sense of
humour, and so perhaps it was entirely possible that Death
showed up as a silver-skinned witch, female, in a dress of

green leaves. She had discounted the experience as a dream; now she understood that she had done this in order to cope and that it now was time to accept that the experience had indeed been real.

"Mind the wheel!" her mother snapped at her, for Florentine was wandering.

Florentine put her mind on the thinning puffs of wool again, and thought bitterly how her goat-brothers never had to do the spinning. Perhaps her parents considered it enough that her goaty siblings contributed the wool in question.

"And the flax!"

And the flax, too, Florentine should take care with that, too.

Florentine glanced out the window while the thread blossomed from her fingers, while the movement of its creation skimmed across her palms. She stored the new twine by looping it round her antlers, as she proceeded. She could see the fruit trees, the tiny orchard that ringed this cabin. The fruits on the trees had become hard shells in the winter season, nuts that revealed no emotion, for, as mentioned, in spring through the autumn, the fruits changed colour with the mood of all who passed by. But here in winter it was impossible to circe out the real truth of one's sentiments. One was hidden even to one's self.

Her mother was chattering. Her mother kept chattering. Florentine nodded at the right times, but her thoughts stayed outdoors, beyond the glass window frosted up with iced shadows. Her thoughts soared up to the grey sky outside, to the heavens. There had been the man who had arrived, the man with the antlers who wore peculiar clothes and spoke peculiar words. Florentine hadn't liked him much, but she had spoken kind words back to him (she had good manners and had been brought up properly). Perhaps they would have been friends if they had got to know each other better, over a span of weeks rather than the breadth of a day; they had the antlers in common, after all. Regardless, that man had walked away, and seemingly laid down in Potter's Field, for she and the brothers had that evening come across the bowl he had carved out for himself in the grass, the space he had left behind. The lightning bugs buzzed and frivolous that twilight; everything quite gay. But the man had left and he had never come back. They had found a second area of crushed grass, too; it appeared that the man had not been content where he first had laid his head, and had, at some point, made a shift.

Spindle, loom, thread, loop. Her mother beaming at her. The snow falling outside, covering up the Witch's tracks, if they had never been there in the first place. Two people coming into her life, touching its periphery, and then disappearing just as quickly. That was the dreamlike quality. That was why it felt like a dream. The Horned Man had not been a dream. The Witch had not been a dream. The snow outside was a dream, however. This house was a dream and this wool was a dream. Outside the glass, the snowflakes fell soft but grew stiff over days in drifts, hardened like whitened bruce sap.

The Dead trees outside. Through them a witch walks in a leaf dress. She is a witch and so she does not grow inordinately cold; if she is frostbitten then so it goes and so it warms up later. The scraped bare spirches with their dark knorls. Death is everywhere. One day, even if this Witch does not die, you will. You will and your mother will and your father will and your brothers will and the fruit trees will, even though they are longstanding and empathetic trees, even the fruit trees will die.

"Take your fingers more slowly round the wool," said her mother, "and the thread will go slimmer as well." By the fireplace, the goat-brothers were playing an involved game of knucklebones and betting buttons against each other's skill. Her father was nodding off, nearly sleeping in the heat, and his fingers were slipping from the jack-knife and current branch at which he was whittling.

Where are you and what are you?

Where is Thy sting, where are the bumble corpses and hornets falling stripèd from the skies? Where are gutted stags and the gasping trout? Where are the expiring single-season flowers, only to be outdone by smug perennials? Outside the snow falls and the forest floor welcomes the new layers. The tree leaves will die, and death floats down from the skies, and death falls white on the mounds and the roots, and death closes the buds and makes them sterile, and death has its branches stilled and barren, and death has clouds passing through it and death freezes up in ice that cracks in spring, *¡Viva la Muerte!*

Inside the house, the spinning was finished. Her mother
put away the distaff and the tools, and unlooped the fresh
spools from Florentine's antlers. Her brothers stirred ever so
slightly by the fire.

Are you a barefoot woman in a leaf dress, rebelling all
by surviving your exposure? Are you the Witch?

"We are having owl for supper, Florentine," said her
mother. "I've repeated myself three times now, my love.
Please prepare yourself."

But Florentine started to cry every time they ate owl
and had always done so, and her mother knew this, thus the
warning. Her three brothers and her father were already
waiting, stools pulled up tight, hands and teeth ready to tear
in.

She could not bear to see it served up there on the
wooden table, with its feathers charred with barbecue and its
eyes glassy, cooked like meat, solidified.

Winter is a hard season, and this was winter in the
house.

It was then, right then, as Florentine stared with antipathy
at the chargrilled owl cooked up with rosemary and shal-
lots, that the entire family heard for the first time the baying
Horn of the Hunter.

Florentine's mother dropped the piece of fowl she
was chewing on and Florentine's father went ash-pale. They
both stared at Florentine's antlers, a feature not often dis-

cussed nor even widely noticed as unusual in that particular family.

"No," murmured her mother, moving already in front of her daughter to place her body between her child and the door. With the Horn echoing through the woods outside, past Snow Hill, out behind the shroudy spirch trees and the bruces, way back in the part of the woods where no one sees or can guess what is there, way back into that Unknown, where the Witch walks, too. All the family, all six of them, could hear the hounds howling, and could hear the musical kind of Horn bellowing, as well. The sound filled the single room of the house and bounced against the walls, the sound that meant danger and danger and danger.

"No," repeated Florentine's mother.

***

The figure approaches Martin while Martin stands still, which delays their meeting to some degree. As the suns continue to rise high and smear the whole sky red, it becomes clear that the human approaching Martin (at not too fast a speed, neither a menace nor a dawdle), as the suns continue to rise high and rise red, it becomes clear that the human approaching Martin is male and bears an antlered headdress.

There have indeed been two male signifiers in the hallucinations Martin and his walking-stick have left in the sand behind them – the thick moustache, the pineapple (perhaps) – though the faucet had been female Freudian, no argument. (Martin swiftly turns around and can still see it trickling behind him, now practically a normal-sized faucet due to perspective).

With Masculinity thus in mind, Martin observes the man – Caucasian, 33ish, dressed in formal jeans and T-shirt wear – draw even nearer. Lord of the Hunt, the male Stag, a big Buck, the Trois-Frères cave paintings of a horned shaman: a dozen images and phrases from countless old programmes fight their way for recognisance in Martin's mind, then in some sense all merge together.

The man keeps approaching. Martin can't see his expression yet, but he feels suddenly uncertain at the looming sight of the head-dress atop this other human's head; it seems so aggressive a countenance to offer to what was perhaps the only other form of human life on earth. Or maybe merely a clothing choice borne of enforced cheminage or, god knows, isolation and insanity; not that Martin has any room to judge; he converses regularly with his walking-stick and is conversed back with as well, the walking-stick being quite the chatty little twig.

Martin's feet on the sand; *the footprints would stop here; perhaps this would be the end of all footprints*; the other man twenty-five feet from him now. Martin raises his stick, not in an act of aggression. Though maybe it is a subconscious dickametric. He takes care to smile at the same time. He raises it up and with both hands holds it pointing up vertical from the top of his head, so that his body now with prosthetic is over ten feet tall.

The other man's antlers – *Alces alces americanus*, moose, thinks Martin – are wide but not as tall as Martin + stick. The other man stands directly in front of Martin now and the horned man smiles in a hesitant manner. Martin slowly lowers his walking-stick to the ground, now convinced that this other survivor has *not* donned a bull-moose-themed headdress as an act of aggression.

Not unless organically growing a pair of bull-moose antlers from the base of one's skull can be considered an act of aggression. Who knows, perhaps it can.

Uneasy lies the head that wears a crown.

*

Marry, fuck or kill.

You had been dreaming again, but this was a new one for you. No pastoral symphonies of branch and twig and firefly, some pre-Lapsarian proto-England that your brain cooked up. Complete with a Pippi Longstocking, a sparky little girl and one with antlers at that. You have figured that one out; she is clearly your *anima*, the horns gave it away (horns always give it away; they are hard to avoid). No New Jerusalem, all Kate Bush and Celtic cross-quarter days. No inner Wickerwoman or English real ale, Angela Carter, William Wordsworth or sacrificed goats or maypoles or Grimm's fairy tales, mixed in with a little Cold War history. Your previous dreams were as predictable as politics. You were obvious. You were an easy one to work out; your therapist (and several exes) always said so.

This was a new one for you. You were in some post-apocalyptica, a landscape where everything looked dead and felt dead too. There was nothing but sand. You still had your antlers. The suns (yes, plural to three) were rising or setting; they were glowing red. You waited a few minutes to ascertain which, after which point you were clear it was dawn. You were dressed like you normally would be. You ran your right hand over your jaw. You didn't have too much stubble, so you were aware that even your dream-self had enough self-oomph to get up and shave in the morning, a trait you didn't always share in real life. You stopped thinking about your clothes and your scruff; you didn't like having to look so scrutinisingly at yourself; you were tired of daffodil mirrors.

In a lucid dream, it doesn't matter what you do, for there are no consequences. You can murder or fly or rape or shoot heroin or breathe underwater or have sex, because it doesn't matter what you do. Traditionally, in those nights before your dreams turned into nuclear fairy tales, you usually chose to orgasm. Who wouldn't? Sometimes, though, occasionally, there was a state of lucidity where you were entirely *aware* that you dreamt, and yet where you had no control. You just experienced, such as in an ergoline trip. Perhaps you were just passive or had no imagination. It doesn't matter. You now were caught in this tussle again, not leaf nor green meadow rushes scratching at your cheeks, but instead endless hot sand and look, what was this here, someone was walking across the sand, walking towards you. So perhaps something would happen to you after all. Something was going to happen.

You started to walk towards the person. Yes, you did. Since your only power in this dream seemed to be normal human locomotion and an awareness of your breathing process, you wondered, horrified, for just a split-second, whether this meant that this dream was actually real, since (moose horns atop your bonce aside) this interlude followed all normal good rules of physics. You pinched yourself and didn't wake up. You didn't have a lot of choices, then. You kept walking.

When you reached the other at last, you saw that the other was a young man with a shaved head, naked except for a rucksack. His prick was "happy to see you." He raised the stick that he carried up onto his head, mad bodger, and he grinned. A lunatic. You were going to die. You smiled a little, for what could you do? This was only a dream. What will be, will be. You were passive inside it, remember. You could bend down and charge him like Bullwinkle the Moose, but somehow you were resigned that this wouldn't change a thing.

"I'm Jack Candle," you said. "Who are you?" (You didn't know where you pulled that name from; it seemed like a *Mother Goose* rhyme or from something out of the *Domesday Book*. Still, this was a dream and, while you could not fly, you could still break a few rules and *lie*.)

The younger man lowered the stick. He was trembling. His fists on the wooden stick were shaking. He tried to speak for three minutes and all the while the suns rose higher in the sky. You got the impression that he hadn't spoken to anyone in a very long time. Finally his voice was like a tree with wind: "I'm Martin." So faint. "I haven't... seen... another walking soul for twelve young years."

Despite his odd phraseology, your dreaming brain noted the use of the word "twelve" and approved. You had always liked the number twelve, perhaps because it too, like the *Domesday Book* and *Mother Goose*, was old-fashioned and irregular in congugated speech, no mere binary-offshoot of the teens and all those that follow – into *infinity*, "Jack," into *infinity*! The brain cannot even *conceive*! – twelve is the last real English number. This inclination likely pointed towards your Green and Pleasant Land dreams with the little antlered girl, some manifestation of your own Ludditity. Lucidity. Ludditity.

"Where are you off to now, Martin?" *Where are any of us going? Do you know way to San Jose? What are you doing here? What does this mean and why have I grown a pair of horns?* Et cetera and et cetera. You resorted to small talk.

He gripped the stick again and you glanced down at it. It was heavy. Martin's eyes weren't quite trustworthy; there was something rapid about them, and even though you were in a dream – nominally safe – your heart heated up and your pulse raced. Danger? Or love? "There is a cave back the way you came from," said Martin. "I've seen farseer programmes about it. I know it's there. Did you not see it? Did you *come* from the cave built into high rocks in the sand?"

You told him the truth and he seemed to accept it, though you never would have if you were him: "The sand's been all I know so far. And now you." (In *this* dream, anyway.)

"Of course." He smiled and there was sand crusted into the premature, sunburned furrows on his face when he grinned, because he was not too used to the expression. There was something heartbreakingly raw and yet still overcooked about him; he reminded you of yourself in your late 20s, both man and still-boy. Perhaps he is an *animus* too (with detachable stick; the mind boggles!). Yet if you had such Freudian control over your dreams, jung man, you'd be in some elysium paradise fucking up a storm by now, and you are not.

You suddenly felt wistful towards Martin, tender.

"Are you coming with me, towards the cave?" He turned towards you, in a rush, his stick still in hand, and you could not tell if he was threatening you or cajoling you, and your throat turned sour, and your heart felt like cracking into love. The stick was high in his hands again, in the air.

What do you do now? Do you follow Martin towards the cave and throw your fates together, a union? If you follow Martin into the cave, keep reading what follows and eventually find yourself at the beginning of Chapter 4,

then skip down to the third section you see.

Do you say No, let's sleep, and you then carefully set aside the stick and lie down next to Martin and kiss each other brotherly, or perhaps more David-and-Jonathanly, for Martin has, after all, been bereft of touch for many a year? If you cuddle Martin, keep reading what follows and eventually find yourself at the beginning of Chapter 3.

Do you grab the stick from Martin's hands and bash him to the ground, ruby carnage slipping hot bracelets down your arm? (You must protect yourself, after all, and he is, most likely, an enemy. He is certainly a stranger.) If you murder Martin, turn to Page 1.

If you cuddle Martin, keep reading what follows and eventually find yourself at the beginning of Chapter 3.

If you murder Martin, turn to Page 1.

***

Jack was sitting on a chair during the session, trying to avoid starting the conversation, but the analyst was from the psychodynamic approach and believed in keeping uncomfortably quiet until Jack himself felt compelled to speak. Or not. The therapist would consider it an interesting development if Jack instead chose to keep quiet throughout the session too. He was an optimistic man, the therapist.

Jack took a drink from his latte. His head was cloudy. The word cloudy reminded

Jack of the sky and the suns.

"Jack," said that therapist finally (or, rather, *didn't* say the therapist, since we know that "Jack" is not "Jack"'s real name), "Jack," (*unJack*), "you appear to have something on your mind."

Jack stared at his only-moderately wrinkled hands (the hands of a peri-middle-aged man, a man of around 33 years, by his best reckoning) and thought of the notes he had pinned up all over his flat, notes telling him what to do, which decision to make, how to deal with the future. Destiny was weighing in, but in a very slapdash way. No one desires to see psychic predictions labeled out in Post-It notes all over one's apartment. Particularly if such admonitions and advice are accurate. It messes with a fellow's feeling of Free Will and it also makes one feel that one's personal fate is rather an afterthought since it has been jotted down on frigging Post-It notes. Jack had left his flat this morning and aimed quickly for the nearest Starbucks. Starbucks had started an irritating procedure of asking for customer names for latte/espresso/filter/Americano identification, a revelation Jack felt quite too personal, and so Jack was prone these mornings to naming himself Persephone or Crazy-Split J for the purposes of Starbucks.

The therapist cleared his ancient throat.

Right then. "I have *many* things on my mind."

The therapist raised one old eyebrow (the bastard, Jack envied him the ability too much for words or contemplation). "Last week you were saying that you suspected that you were a passenger pigeon, the last of your breed. A government psychic put out to pasture, was that how you put it? You definitely mixed all your metaphors."

Jack nodded and took a sip of his latte. Good, the Starbucks drones had remembered to dose up His Lordship Emmeline's beverage with sufficient amounts of vanilla syrup this time. In his heart, Jack knew baptism by coffee was company policy and not the fault of the drones.

"Ex-CIA, you were saying?" said the therapist. "Or something like it. You're American, anyway. Or Canadian. I can never tell the difference, *ay*? You were convinced that you were leaving notes to yourself from the future, because you can't remember anything these days but your dreams and your recent present. You can't remember your wife or your daughter or your job. But yet you recall a little Horned Child - we'll talk about the implications of *her* later, shall we -" Jack could see the Jungian was excited about *that*! "- and a bald younger man with a walking-stick. And your beleaguered, also-horned self, of course, the poor ex-psychic. Am I remembering correctly?"

Jack was unnerved. He was pretty sure therapists weren't supposed to be sarcastic, and that jab about the "poor beleaguered ex-psychic" certainly sounded mocking to Jack's ears, and the lowering of the therapist's voice on the second time he pronounced the word "horned" implied cuckoldry. There was, after all, a professional rivalry between psychics and psychologists. Jack rallied (the analyst doubtless a spook plant any-way, at best): "I *do* remember my dreaming life with greater detail than this endless battle with fake coffee names and Post-It notes." (He observed the therapist writing down something about Jack on a yellow Post-It note right at that very moment and found it doubly irritating.) "Yes, I *do* recall my dream life. However, it's not just the antlered girl and Martin and the stick. I *do* recall other… impressions. Two of them un-antlered and un-sticked most particularly."

"Oh?" The analyst leaned forward. "What are the other dreams about then, friend?"

("Friend"? What was that about? Jack was not a frigging Quaker.) Jack rubbed at the back of his left hand, suppressed a desire to glance at his watch (an impulse that the therapist was not on his own part suppressing, terce plus one plus twelve) and took another sip. "Let's see if I can recall. I was walking around with an almost-forgotten lover. We were visiting various stagings set up in some sort of sex theatre variety show." (Ah, *now* he had the analyst's attention!)

"I cannot recall the bulk of the goings-on, but the last display," continued Jack, "that last display was a group of kabuki-white-faced females dancing quite violently on stilts to loud trance or perhaps the term is trip-hop. The females were wearing kimonos and eventually, when their breasts were bared, they each had a chain that connected the nipple of one huge breast - larger than their feline heads - to the nipple of their other, very tiny breast -

(still a woman's, not an adolescent's) –
chains that were in turn connected to rings
upon their workman's hands that gripped the
stilts. It was very disturbing and erotic at
the same time. Like the most fucked up bur-
lesque you could imagine. They were totally
powerful. My ex-fuck buddy, she was very
uncomfortable. I thought of Melanie Klein's
good breast/bad breast psychological theory
when I woke up. What does it all mean?"

The therapist was blushing. The heat,
the potent heat of the vanilla latte, rolled
down Jack's throat.

"What was… the other dream?"

Jack had control of the session now.
"Perhaps we should call it a *story*."

"What was the other story?"

This is the story that Jack told his shrink:

*You always went hiking in forests when you
were young. You would dawdle; your little
feet would pitter-patter behind your parents
(you were the eldest; all this must have
been while you were still enjoying the Pre-
Lapsarian bliss of an Only Child).*

This is what Jack told his shrink, more or
less:

Your parents disappear. There is only you. The greatest forest in all the earth. This story of yours takes place in a forest. Just green trees and blue sky. The trees touched dirt and sky. Trees were fed at both ends, rank dirt planet and the blue-blue-blue of air. Air is clear when you are inside it. You can't see blue. So much blue it's invisible when you breathe it in. Just like the globe is flat when you stand on it because it's so big. Just like how these trees were endless when you were in the middle of the oldest, biggest forest of all, the forest that grew on top of the earth.

This is what Jack told his shrink (a psychodynamicist of a Blakesian-Jungian bent, which should come as no surprise):

When you were young, the world was infinite but it was also small, because what you experienced of it was so small. Once upon a time in the greatest forest of all. There lived a _____. No, that would be telling. You can't say what once lived there. It would give the game away. So you can only refer to its ghost. The ghost of the _____ that once lived. You'll call it the ghost. That's what it was for you. The ghost was easier to see under the circumstances. Just like flatness is easier than a round planet. Just like blue air is easier than clear air. The truth is that you live on a globe and that you breathe in clear air, however,

once upon a time a ghost lived in the forest, the woods. This forest was so huge that it covered the curved blue planet, which actually looked like a flat, brown and green planet up close. The ghost had lived in the forest for so long that it actually forgot the thing it had been in the first place.

The ghost drifted through the bruce trees.

The trees grew denser and denser and darker and darker and the ghost began to forget all of its previous life; it forgot the words for things like _____ and _____. The trees began to crowd out the clear sky, and it grew so dark there that sometimes the ghost couldn't even see itself, especially when it snowed. People sold postcards of that joke, blank postcards rubricked "Where is the ghost in this postcard of snow and milk?", blank postcards entitled "Ghost in the Snow."

One day the ghost thought to look up

into a sky which was no longer blue. It was grey. It realised, to its horror, that the light was gone entirely. It wanted light back, because when there was light the ghost remembered old things and old words. The ghost was able to name things. That made its ghostly life easier. And so it did something.

You can't say what it did.

You have a difficult time talking about what the ghost did.

The sky got darker and darker.

It was night.

The ghost somersaulted up into the air and the ____ were like diamonds there in the dark sky. Do you like sparkle? The ghost liked sparkle. It liked it very much.

It did something up there.

When it got back down again, it was light. Things had names. There were *Prada* shoes and *Campbell's Tomato Soup Low Sodium* and *Pret-à-Manger* sandwiches and *Spud-21* missiles and *forget-me-not* flowers. There was so much of ____.

You can't say what it was.

There was too much of it.

You can't say where the ghost is.

Where is the ghost in this picture?

Jack's therapist was either very intrigued or sexually fantasising about something else, for there was a curious fixed and intense expression on his face. Jack gave a dramatic pause (he was nothing if not a generous performer), and then continued:

Now, as you can see, there are parts missing in this story. So here is the story all over again and yet entirely different. In the beginning, in the very, very beginning, there was being and there was non-being and there was none but the clear force of the universe, nowhere and nowhen, long ago and once upon a time, and all that, there was a ghost. It was your ghost.

Forest all around your ghost, all around it, tall bruces and small bruces, pale spirches with knots like bruises and scabs, the darkness around such trees that meant you couldn't see the green on anything unless the sun was there.

This forest was so huge that it covered the curved blue planet, which actually looked like a flat, brown and green planet up close. The ghost had lived in the forest for so long that it actually forgot the thing it had been in the first place. Imagine the ghost drifting through the bruce trees.

The trees grew denser and denser and darker and darker and the ghost began to forget all of its previous life; it forgot the words for things like viola longsdorfil *and* vaccinium alaskaense. *The trees began to crowd out the clear sky, and it grew so dark there that sometimes the ghost couldn't even see itself, especially when it snowed.*

There were three things then that showed, only three things, and those were the suns. It was the suns that the ghost looked at all through the day and that the ghost pined after all through the night, the three beautiful suns that shone through the ghost and made its vapourousness shimmer like a veil, like suns through water, like suns through a cloud, like suns through the strange wispy folds of a vapourous ghost.

The suns, though, the suns were stars so brilliantly shiny that they soaked up all the ghost's thoughts and they made the ghost think about them all day like the ghost was in love with them and even their heat would tickle at the ghost, although generally the ghost was cold the way a breeze is cold.

The ghost began to daydream about the suns, even when it wasn't directly look-ing at them, which wasn't a problem for the ghost because the ghost no longer had any retinas and it could stare at suns for as long as it wished. When it wasn't staring, it daydreamed. The suns seemed far away but they also seemed close, yet whenever the ghost had tried to float up through the air to them, it realised how far away they were, and then it would grow depressed, because it knew it would never touch the suns, oh god, it would never have them, never.

At night in the suns' absence the ghost began to weep, and its tears evaporated for they had no real substance, and soon even the re-appearance of the suns every morn-ing in the east, the pink threads of morn-ing in the clouds that preceded them, the chill then warmth, the light, all the light, light, light, was no solace at all.

The ghost hung itself over trees like a cloud and wept and wept with heartbreak, and the huge, yellow, prism-studded suns dispas-sionately rose, and set, and rose, and set.

But then the day came once while the ghost was floating up there above tree-level that something flashed past its eyes, a slice of cream-white in the blue sky like a cloud with wings. It was a bird. But how many things fly like that? A bat, an airplane, a man o' war jellyfish, a pterodactyl, an angel. A winged stone lion guarding a Czech memorial. UFOs. A fly. A butterfly. A bubble. A balloon.

The white bird had a blue mouth. The ghost wondered whether all of the inside of the bird was blue, too, guts and every-thing. The ghost stared at the bird's blue mouth for seconds, seconds, then at its white feathers, and the mouth's afterimage shadowed on the wing now looked red, and it looked red, which is the same shade as the rays sometimes were at sunset. And the wing looked white, which reminded the ghost of the suns again.

If the ghost could have spelled out its love for the suns in skywriting, it would have done so. It would have laced the clouds with an alphabet. The letters would have spelled out the words _____ and _____. Well, you can't say everything, can you?

What should you do?

"I think we're about at time now," said the therapist of "Jack," and Jack glanced down at his own watch, and saw that it was indeed ten minutes to eleven o'clock. It was an old-fashioned analogue watch, a book of hours that also showed a metal sun/moon

waxing or faltering depending on the time
of day. Just one single sun, not three.
Three would get you a wrong answer on the
Montreal Cognitive Assessment test if you
drew a clockface that way. For a moment,
Jack closed his eyes and thought so hard of
an analogue watch that showed three metal
eclipsed suns on its watchface that he could
nearly feel the trio burn into his wrist. *I
am the ghost. I am the spook.*

He rose and chose not to look at the
analyst as he exited.

For his second coffee of the day, thirteen minutes later, he chose the pseudonym
Tinder Eyewear Chicken.

***

On Snow Hill the flakes are old; there has not been a fresh
snow for weeks. The crust is getting dirty, squirrel-track and
urine and dust and leaf-crumble; the forest has been waiting for something. The air is cold and so tight and winter is
oppressive in this way, but still the world waits.

*

The horn sounded again and the horn sounded again, and
terror was melting in Florentine's mouth and she could no
longer swallow the sour down, terror as her mother gripped
her shoulder in a show of comfort – would her mother ever

be able to protect her? – terror as her father hustled the brother goats beneath the space under the trundlebed and bade them quieten – would her father ever be able to save any of his children? – terror –

The horn, loudest now, just outside the door, and then its failing, and only the sounds of the hounds' quick panting and their nipping, and of horse steps clocking, just outside the door.

The snow outside, everywhere. The snow covered the forest trees and the orchard trees (feral, tame); the snow covered the house and the lake and the woodpile where Florentine used her first jack-knife, and now it was being stomped by hooves and pissed on by dog vulvae, penises, and just the sound of the hot breath of the horses then, while the world listened.

*

She was running through the cast snow and past the frozen orchard trees, whose fruits were still seasonally emotionally unrevealing (the fruits have never been genetically sequenced by scientific taxonomy, whether ash-fruit as they appear or as apple or as greengages or as wholly newly particularly greylike fruitmeats), she had not seen the Hunter nor the hounds nor the clopped steeds when she had darted blindly from the house, pushed past her mother's screams and anguished clutching arms, past into white sleet for now it snowed anew at last, now the snow was coming and now it was pausing again, so fast her exit never could have happened so quickly, never could have happened so blindly. But now Florentine was running barefoot on the old snow and the skim of new snow (like the Witch had) and the Hunt followed her and her family would be safe as she was leading the Hunt away; yes, her family would be safe.

The snow on fire, her feet on the red flame that pierces so only when ice, her same feet not pausing long enough to melt the snow but only long enough to burn her soles. She ran upright, upwards, uphill. The snow, the lake, the horn round-sounding behind her.

Was it the Witch, or perhaps the grown man she had met, the Horned One like herself? Florentine's mouth was sour and crisping in the cold; her feet frozen lumps now to the knees, lifting and pounding ahead again, the snow surrounding her and only whiteness ahead of her and only the scent of blood behind her; she did not know how much longer she could last. A Horned Witch? A pack of dogs wailing. Florentine the animal, too.

She dashed round a corner with the very last of the strength in her numb legs and saw a low-branched tree, its bare boughs within a leap's reach.

And so she leapt, and when she did so her horns entangled into the branches above, ice-wood and cartilage fusing and, though the strength in her hands failed, her horns held her up, dangling from the boughs while the Hunt rushed on below, unaware that she hung above them, antlers caught, feet trailing, the talented noses of the hounds seemingly fallible. The rush past lasted forever. She closed her

eyes so that she did not have to see them below. The heat of
them, the noise, the spat-up snow from their chase. She did
not see it.

Florentine hung there.

The woods were silent again, but the echoes were
still in her ears and her heart was beating violently, violently. She began to kick herself free, to establish a swinging
motion to loosen herself, and could not do so. Panic set in
again. The Hunt could come back at any moment and this
time they would see her.

She could hear the bay of the instrument again, the
call, and yes, the dogs that sounded like wolves. They were
coming back. The ones she had not seen were now returning.
Florentine tried her strongest, her best, to free herself, but
the baying horn grew louder and more dangerous and her
own horns, the antlers which had saved her, stayed fast; did
not wiggle. The cold snow, her body on the drifts, and muzzles smeared with bright blood. She kicked, and nothing.

The Hunt closer.

She thrashed and threw herself around, and nothing.
Nothing. The sound of dogs biting at each other now, and
soon the unimaginable vision of whoever it was who led the
Hunt.

She had it in her pocket where she always had it,
even slept with it. Her birthday gift and the one with her
name. She drew it out, unpopped it and then began to cut
away at her scalp, severing her link to the tree.

In the end she tumbled to the ground, weeping with

pain and bereft, truly bereft, some sense of her self with her antlers still hanging in the tree and the two bloody stumps on her scalp, a terrible unlocking, but she was free.

She put her jack-knife back in her pocket and she began to run faster than she ever had in her life, this time ignoring the burn cold on bare foot, and the snow no longer taint but so pure ahead of her, and the crown of her head dripping blood to lure the hounds, and her first antlers still hanging in the tree.

*

The cottage (the cabin) bordered by snowed greyfruit trees, past the lake (past the dangerous lake), was injured even from a distance.

Florentine was still running, but she hadn't heard the Hunt for quite some time now and she knew she had outrun them, miraculously escaped them.

But the cottage, the thatched-roof home of her family, was wrong.

There were dog prints and other tracks – cloven? human? It was hard to say – outside the house where the Hunt had stalked her down and waited for her to appear. The snow was dirty there. There were the bodies too there of her mother, and her father, who had with apparency followed herself-Florentine out into the cold to restrain and save her, and their throats were torn out by dogs but the blood that coloured the snow had stopped running some time ago. How long had Florentine been away? It had been her fault. It had been she whom the Hunt had sought, and she whom her parents had strived, fatally, to protect.

The door to the house was open.

*

A mile away, on Snow Hill, old antlers swaying on a branch.

*

Inside the house all was as she'd left it, the dead owl still glancing upwards from the servingboard, and also not as she'd left it, for the room was an odd combination of temperatures from the open door that let the snow fall in, the cold air in, and the heat from the hearth still burning. One was cold in some places in that room and hot in others.

Florentine moved to the trundlebed and looked under it, and there she found her three brothers, shivering. They were in a cold place in the room.

3
Imaginal

They are still lying in each other's arms, but Martin is awake. He feels the heat of Jack's upper limbs; can see in close-up the fine and coarse hairs over the other flesh and his own. He watches the great man's antlers, and the moon's lux picks out figurative vines and sticks in sharp relief on the sand.

Jack groans in his sleep, and in sleep pulls Martin closer to him, and Martin feels his heart explode into a fourth sun, red and hot and beautiful inside him. He can barely breathe, he feels so happy, as he overlooks Jack and instead looks up at the night. He has no clue what will transpire, but now he has a human companion, a Jack. A touch of guilt glazes his mind, and he reaches out towards his walking-stick and pats it a few times consolingly. He sees, miraculously, that from one of its sterile knots there is a greenish, pinkish bud, which almost looks ready to spill over into the shape of a leaf.

There is a lushness to the desert. Unexpected. The absence of tangle makes space into a concentrate form, where sandgrains become glitter and so much of it. These rising suns mean that there is that red velvet charge to the air again, the *milieu* Orientalist and full of the promise of luxurious tents if not the hope of green fertile oases.

Into this peculiar lush/lack warmth wakes Martin again and his Jack at last, cuddled and sticky. They detach from each other; they stretch; they yawn; they chew their cheeks for lack of food and wet their lips from Martin's canteen, and then at last they walk, for they have no morsels and no chances to secure them. In silent and undiscussed agreement they head towards the Cave, from whence Jack has come (though he cannot remember), and the Cave, which Martin has never seen.

*

You had 6.1 Adventure Points left and a Class 3 Mace that you had exchanged for a wooden staff. The Cave was before the two of you. You had by now become amused and were taking stock of all easy referents: maw, dentata, fear of the Monstrous Feminine. Someone – god, the ghost, your giggling self – was peppering your subconscious with in-jokes.

The younger man touched you lightly and indicated the Cave with a jerk of a chin. It was a question, so you answered.

What was your answer?

Well, you both entered the Cave together. Plato? you wondered, Or some half-remembered *Choose Your Own Adventure Book* from the liminality of late childhood, early adolescence?

The inside of the Cave was a bird's mouth, the tint of chicken tongue. The colour deeper than sky-blue because it was Turkish-tile blue and lagoon blue. Were there stalactites? Why not. They hung down and were menacing, their points riskily close to your and Martin's faces. In fact, as the two of you advanced forward in the blue light, you had to portion out each step and dodged and ducked to avoid stickings from the encroaching blue milkteeth. And you were in fact trying hard not to think of *v. dentatae*, which was nearly as difficult as trying not to think of *v.* themselves.

You took each other's hand. You kept walking. Eventually the stalactites whittled down to blue nubs, and soon the cave interior was smooth cerulean blue: more mothering, far less Turkish. And who knew where the light was coming from? Further you went, the two of you, holding hands. Your touch was not that of lovers, or friends. It was not that of enemies, or of family. You were the two last human beings on earth and you wanted this connection of palm to palm very badly. Martin went tip-tip-tip with his walking-stick in his other fist, poking out the trail in case your steps went wrong in the salty sea light. He stopped to wonder once at handprints on the cave wall, which he insisted were red, but you could not believe this without proof as these handprints, once-upon-a-time dipped in paint and then splayed, these handprints were dark grey in the blue light. Your brain was recalling that the toilets in King's Cross nightclubs had blue lights so that addicts found their veins with more ease. But weren't veins blue on white skin; wouldn't this make them melt into the undersides of white forearms? You had associated heroin addiction with Caucasianism. You were confused and ashamed by your own racial profiling.

You travelled this way with Martin (and his stick) for weeks and you rarely felt the need of water (Martin had a full canteen, but it was a mere formality) or food, despite the fact that you had silently agreed that you would survive and surviving meant eating and sleeping and drinking water. You never slept.

In the centre of the Cave, when you had travelled as far as you could without being en route *outside* the Cave, the two (three) of you came to a lake (a dangerous lake, or so muttered Martin). You turned to Martin, but he appeared a little shocked at the lake, and this filled you in turn with some unease. Martin, of course, should not have appeared shocked in any way; Martin was a cipher and this was some allegorical dream-trip, through the only-too-obvious depths (see: Cave) of your subconscious, but Martin indeed looked scared and this was troubling and irritating. There was a grate beneath the water.

"A sluice," said Martin. "A dangerous lake," he mentioned yet again.

You didn't have the slightest clue of what Martin spoke. But here you were, the two (three) of you, and your blue path had disappeared behind you, and there was no longer any path ahead of you; there was only the lake. And now you were going to have to make some choices.

Do you grab Martin's walking-stick and use it to topple Martin into the water, so that you can indeed test his theory regarding a grille-studded and dangerous lake, one which might, for all you know, contain many pre-historic and piranhic, blind-eyed, sharp-toothed water beasties? If you want to topple Martin, turn to Page 1.

If you ignore Martin's of-recent irritating traits, and make a pact with your Martin-companion that you will dip in and swim the cave lake together, to whatever end on the other side, since, after all, you have few options, keep reading what follows and eventually find yourself at the beginning of Chapter 4, and then skip down to the third section you see.

If you sit down on the edge of the lake and the both of you wait, in stasis, keep reading what follows and even-tually find yourself at the beginning of Chapter 4.

***

"You are walking through the woods, your Lordship," said the psychologist, "who are you walking with, your Lordship Emmeline?" A lie. The psychologist actually called him Jack. Twice.

Jack put his hand up to his hair. "I am all alone. I am walking in a desert. I have a walking-stick with me and that is all."

"No, not the Cube game. I said the woods, and not a desert."

"Oh," said Jack, "sorry."

"And then, while you are walking in the woods. You see an animal. What kind of animal would that be?"

"It's a bird."

"Well, can you describe the bird?"

"Well, I don't want to describe the bird, but I will." He really did not want to describe the bird. "It has a blue mouth."

"As in your ghost dream."

Jack ignored the interruption and continued. "It's up in a tree. It sits on a nest made of pins and needles. There are pale green eggs there with fragile shells, but the pins and long needles prop them up; hold them secure rather than pierce. There are jewelled eggs and Russian nesting dolls, and in each doll is another doll, and in that doll there is an egg, and in that egg you'll find a seed, and from that seed will grow a tree, and on that tree you'll find a branch, and on that branch there is a nest, and in that nest there sits a bird, and under that bird there lies an egg, and in that egg there is a doll —"

"'*Ro, ro, the rattlin' bog*', and so ad infinitum. Back to that blue-mouthed bird. Your account of infinity is dispassionate, Jack — how do you *feel* about the bird? What interaction takes place between you and the bird?"

"This is cheap."

"What do you mean, cheap?"

"*Cheep, cheep!*" crowed Jack. "A cheap psychological game for a psychologist, party tricksies."

The therapist leaned ever closer, menacing. "Jack, you're walking deeper into the woods. There is a clearing —"

"Like in the movie *Snow White*."

Jack's interruption was ignored by the therapist, which concerned Jack, as *Snow White* very well could have been important. It had all the major psychological iconographies such as poisoned virgin sexuality, frigidity à-la-glass-coffins and a lovely but evil older woman.

"You enter a clearing and lo and behold, Jack, before you lies your Dream House. I want you to describe it to me."

This part and these details came easily

to Jack and he didn't know why. In his head it looked like Snow White's forest home. "It's a log cabin. It's surrounded by a moat in far-North London – Cockfosters, let's say, though some historians are arguing for Amhurst Grove in Hackney – but it looks rustic Alaskan. It has a woodpile outside one wall. The roof is thatched with hair and leaves."

The therapist swallowed hard. Perhaps he was swallowing a hairball. "Human hair?"

"Oh, yes. Red-blond human hair."

"Were you –" the therapist gave a surreptitious glance at Jack's hairline "– ginger as a young boy? Or perhaps –" daringly "– *bald*?"

Jack didn't answer. He couldn't remember.

"Is this dream house of yours surrounded by a fence?"

"The only fencing is deep inside the lake. There is a moving grille therein, a spiky one."

"Lake, hmm? Fabulous. With spikes made of, I'm assuming now due to your medieval setting but wouldn't want to influence you unduly, wood. We'll come back to that lake in a bit. Let's say you're now inside the house. You're in the dining area. Describe the table. Describe everything on it."

"Owl *cacciatore*."

The therapist looked disgusted once again, but he was a very stubborn therapist so he continued. "You exit your dream abode and you see a vessel lying on the grass. Describe the vessel and what you do with it."

Jack was alarmed; this seemed like it would be far too indicative of hitherto unrevealed erotic tastes. He point-blank refused to answer.

Strangely, Jack's refusal seemed to energise his therapist – "You walk now to the edge of the grass, and you're standing before a body of water. What type of body of water is it? Wait, shut up," said the therapist as Jack started to answer, "you said it was a lake; you can't change it now. How will you cross the lake; how will you do it?!"

"Well," said Jack, "I think I'd most likely –"

"I'm changing tack," said the therapist. Jack knew he would say that. A betrayal, after being strung along so and then abandoned, as it were, in the woods.

Cognitive-behavioural blue balls. His mind faltered, reaching out for dream-disappearing threads of cabins twined with red hair and twig floss, and missed the cords themselves. His cheeks were wet. The therapist did not notice.

"Go back as far in your memory as you can," said the therapist. "How old are you?"

"I'm four."

"Imagine that you are your four-year-old self. What's going on for you?"

"I'm a little girl."

The therapist paused, then recovered. "Okay. Now have your four-year-old self look even further back, into your past. What do you see?"

"Darkness, redness, swirly paisley in my corneas. I feel fine about it all."

The therapist looked pleased but surprised. "Let's jump ahead a little in time. When would you like to go?"

"I'm eight years old exactly."

"Fine and good. Now, *Jack*, what I would like for you to do is this - imagine yourself as this eight-year-old boy. Or girl, of course. Or whatever, of course."

Jack shut his eyes tight and imagined.

"Now, what I would like for you to

do is for your eight-year-old self to look back to that four-year-old self that we just explored. What would your eight-year-old self like to say to the four-year-old?"

Berries. Greenness. Clouds in the sky and faceless trees. A sense of protectiveness towards the younger child, as if towards a little brother or small animal.

"You're very unforthcoming, Jack. But that's okay. We don't always need to say everything out loud. It's enough that you think it.

I'm thinking it.

"Now pick the next major turning point in your life."

I'm nine.

"Say nine or so. What does your nine-year-old-self say to your eight-year-old self?"

You have those horns on your head, little self. But they'll be gone soon enough.

The therapist's timeline was moving faster and faster, and he barked sharp little Pekinese orders to Jack's subconscious.

"What does your nineteen-year-old self say to your nine-year-old-self?"

Can you swim?

"What does your twenty-four-year-old

self say to your nineteen-year-old self?

Leaves. Buds. Unfolding ferns and tongues tasting bruce sap. Sweet and smoky resin in your mouth and on your limbs, your face, in your hair, in your brain.

"What does your twenty-nine-year-old self say to your twenty-four-year-old self?" The therapist was narrowing in.

That's quite a rack you have.

"What does your thirty-three-year-old self say to your twenty-nine-year-old self?"

Her kiss is perfect when it happens, but no one remembers a witch's kiss the next day. No one except you.

"What does your forty-one-year-old self say to your thirty-three-year-old self?" A wider jump, which made Jack's heart jump too. He stopped, shocked. There was nothing in front of him. There was nothing there.

"I can't do it," he said aloud.

"Why can't you do it?"

"I'm only thirty-three *now*. How can I talk ahead of myself to my behind-the-future self? How can I know?"

The therapist cracked two knuckles and then a noisy third, clearly exasperated. "That is the point of this entire exercise. We envision potentialities, and then we follow them. And, in any case, we have had a huge success! You have categorically identified and defended yourself as thirty-three, exactly, whereas you have always hedged your bets before. Progress. I'm asking you again. What does your forty-one-year-old self – and the dental records I secretly requested from your dentists assures me that this is indeed the case – say to your thirty-three-year-old self?"

But Jack's mind couldn't burrow in there; it was even more opaque than that nebulous time between birth and four, full of squiggling but warm and kindly paisleys. He wondered suddenly if he was destined to die shortly in the future before he hit forty-one; that perhaps could explain why he was entirely unable to look eight years back to the present. The thought gave him a chill and he tried harder, but there was only blankness and _____.

"What does your forty-one-year-old self say to your thirty-three-year-old self?"

Jack shook his head. "I can't do it."

A big sigh from the therapist. Jack sneaked a look at his watch, and confirmed the count by wall-clock, and they had at least ten minutes to go. The therapist was struggling to fill the time now too, an adversity and hypocrisy that he dealt with in far more blaming terms than Jack's own inability to lock down words. For a moment it seemed as if the therapist would suggest that they finish the session earlier, but then the therapist rallied. "Fine. Word association, then."

"Surely now you are just grasping at -"

"Not yet the final straw, Jack. But speaking of straws…"

Jack knew the drill and now he sighed too. "Jack Straw."

"Excellent!" The therapist beamed. "Excellent, Blairite or rebel peasant. I'll be choosing some nouns that you have mentioned in our journeys together, and you may find this a little triggering, but I want you to know that you are entirely safe with me. *Fireflies*."

"Bugs."

"*Mother*."

"Fucker. No, daughter - daughter! Mother-daughter!"

"*Winter*."

"Nuclear winter. Apocalyptica."

"*Brilliant*, Jack, really exciting." The therapist was beaming. "*Really* exciting stuff. *Really* exciting."

"*In*-citing."

"No, we've stopped now. Stop."

"Go."

"Stop."

"Go."

"Stop."

"Go."

After his successful therapy session, Jack headed towards Starbucks in Crouch End again. He traversed the pedestrian zebra crossing after dutifully waiting for the Green Man to appear to let him know that it was safe to walk; the Green Man all glowing green and dripping leaves from his cock and helping little old ladies to cross the street, since that's the kind of good old-fashioned neo-Pagan deity he was. The Green Man turned as red as blood. Stop. Go. Stop. Go. Stop.

There was an ominous twitch to the huge
newsbroadcast screens up at Manor House Station *en route* home, little murmurs about
inconsequential wars and rilings-up and middle easts and middle classes. Ever since the
Ebola scare, Jack had ignored all such murmurs as he always did these days, for such
breathless worrying never played itself out
to be ultimately influential within his own
life, or at least had not proved so far to
be the case so since the Ebola scare, and
Jack was nothing if not a rational man.

By the time he returned home to his
diminutive bed-sit and had unlocked and re-
locked the latch door, he could see that it
was very clear that there were more Post-
It notes than usual strewn around. This
time the entire flat was dotted with sunny
flaps of paper; it looked very cheery. Someone had done their work. Over his takeaway
dinner, Jack read a few missives from himself about his purported "wife" and "little
girl" before giving up and going to sleep;
in truth he found these Post-It warnings as
influential and life-changing and effective
as those Manor House screens that doomsaid

war and pestilence; that is to say, not very much at all these days.

*

Jack woke up late that next day and made himself a tasty yet tarnished omelette from the previous night's curry takeaway leftovers. Adding sunflower seeds did not improve its virtuousness quotient. The omelette had the taint of the bedsitter about it and the sunflower seeds felt desperate.

He sat at his small table drinking Fair Trade cafetière coffee (a similar effort to block out domestic truth) and he flopped up the yellow Post-It stuck to his mug, heretofore unnoticed.

"It's Jack," read the note, "I can prove it. You have a light-brown mole just to the right of your left nipple, looking downwards of course." It didn't prove a thing. The Post-It didn't say anything else on that side, but there was an arrow drawn indicating that the reader should continue on the other side and so Jack did. "You have forgotten your family," said the Post-It note, "and the shame is all yours." By this, Jack deduced that the writer was North

American, as was Jack himself, for the Brits more often said "You have forgot," and did not usually accustom themselves with the retention of the Middle English "gotten" form.

Jack had forgot(ten) many things. So sue him. He finished his breakfast, and eventually made his way out to Green Lanes, on the Haringey-not-Hackney side of Seven Sisters Road.

Green Lanes high street was mainly empty, although he saw a dog. He tucked himself into a Tesco supermarket when it started to rain, but couldn't find a cashier. He found the egg section, though, and he cracked up three dozen free-range Happy Eggs until a beam of diamanté rather than the gloop of sun and mucus gleamed up from one brown shell. The gem was ovoid-cut, Jack saw, once he had kneeled on the quiet tiled floor of Tesco and peeled back eggshell and membrane. He checked it against his teeth, hard ice, but knew he'd never have a comparison so facet was fact as far as Jack was concerned. He was willing to pay for the egg and the mess he'd created, but there were no till attendants there, nor any managers to speak of, so he shuffled home.

He placed the glittering diamond egg in a clear glass tumbler, waterless, and set it on his bedside table before he fell asleep, in case he wanted to look at its shimmer in moonlight or to touch it in the dark if he woke up in the middle of the night, which he did not.

That night he dreamed of his putative daughter, the jewel of his loins. But firstly he was back in his very same tiny bedsit, having a little difficulty with the carrot, as he always knew there would be. In the end, in order to mine his salad crisper, Jack had to take a spoon to it and dig out that puppy. It was odd how the carrots always produced the warm-coloured jewels (garnets, topazes and so on). On this occasion, a fat little ruby.

Jack set the ruby aside on the counter, and then he looked through the rest of the refrigerator. It was not cumbersome to open as he was not wearing bull-moose horns in this particular dream. The only awkwardness was the paucity of eggs. He had cracked and disposed of all eggs five days back. So how about that bottle of milk (semi-skimmed)? It took some doing, but Jack drank down the whole bottle, drained it dry and then spat out three creamy diamonds into his palm. Dreaming, Jack's heart enwarmed at the thought of his future wife. Someone was going to be getting a pretty engagement ring on the morrow.

He rinsed off the diamonds under the tap and managed to do it just in time before the liquid turned molten silver (ouch). Jack glanced over at the egg-shaped diamond in the water glass near where the sleeping Jack lay lightly snoring, his head tossing back and forth beneath the cage of his moose-horns, but then hornless Jack turned back to the basin.

He held the trio of diamonds tightly in his right palm and watched the stream from the faucet for a while, as one watches a river or the ocean or any moving water, really. The tap seemed bigger than it was. Jack could have collected up the molten sil-ver in a dish as it steamed out, but he let the metal spin down the drain. He knew that when he eventually would call the plumber that the plumber first would be pissed off, but then upon cranking open the pipes, that the plumber would turn jubilant and tight-lipped. That is how plumbers make all their money, actually, through siphoning off and then reselling the detritus of alchemical situations; not many people know that.

After a while, Jack tired of watching the silver flow and he was in a different dream and in a different time, though still in his bedsit, and his gaze turned to the kitchen table, with that pretty rose in the vase that his daughter had placed there. He drew close and put a finger on it, pink-quartz crystal; the leaf fell off, a chip of emerald.

Jack's daughter entered the room then. He ran to her, hugged her, all ten fingers. She turned gold and stiff all over, the way a teenager usually does with hugged. Jack had forgot. Ten.

***

Now that winter was ending, and now that winter was ending, Florentine found herself taking care of her goatlings, quite literally, her kids; she allomothered them by spearing fish and stewing mushrooms and mopping fevered brows; and aloefathered them with tender leaf ministrations for their scrapes and pains; and sistered them as best she knew how, the lessons she had learned, from before.

They had simply been her brothers before, but now

that she mothered them they had taken on personalities. The lastborn and runt, Percy (*né* Percival), was especially sweet, and it was he who would help gather mushrooms and thus earn himself extra stew helpings on the Fry Day. Eldritch for his part had newly noticeable French Alpine markings; had a fine little tuft of white hair proud and saucy that stood up over his anus from which dropped dark and belligerent pellets, whereas Brother Beaman followed the Toggenburg side of the family: a light beige scan mapped on in parts to his snowy pelt, Beaman with his grandfather's mischievousness in his rectangular eyes.

On Moon Days, Florentine would add a punch of powder of the jinxing mushrooms to the lunch stew, the jinxing ones scarlet and snow-spackled, and in the evening on such days the four siblings would sit before the fire, their pupils swelling from compressed lines and small dots to squares and eclipses. They would talk excitedly of their strange and wonderful late afternoons, and they all felt that Spring was coming, green and fresh and snowy and dirty. Spring was coming, with scaled branches soon a-fur with leaf, with the islands of tarnished snow cupping the tree bases growing smaller each day. And Florentine had a new set of antlers budding forth too, in time with the season. At the moment she looked like her brothers, tomboyish with just the nubbins of horns.

There was one time. There was one afternoon. Florentine went back to Snow Hill once on her own, when her brothers were ice-trouting at the lake (the dangerous lake). She saw her old antlers swaying in the tree, nearly covered up with the new tender-green leaves that grew on the real branches around them, as if they were branches themselves.

***

The next morning Jack woke and was faintly alarmed to see that there was nary a yellow Post-It about - for he had come to expect them; it was true. Exactly as he had come to expect the complex and emotional dreams. But now in truth here he was, stuck in cold mundanity with no whisper of mystery or magic, an empty waterglass on his bedside table, in a cold part of the room, with yesterday's dirty socks still crusted to his feet. He rose and tried to recognise his own face in the mirror, and was still not successful at this. His hair was brown. Your Lordship Emmeline Crazy-J Tinderbox, thy hair is brown. He was out of mouthwash. He hoped he'd recall the yellow mental Post-It note he was currently making to purchase a new bottle, but chances weren't good.

The calendar segment on his watch said that it was the first of the month. Always good for a new beginning, particularly when you were a fellow with no actual clue who you were being.

Jack had no responsibilities that he could recall, aside from the alleged spouse and daughter, and those ones seemed figment. Having seen the therapist only a day before, he assumed he was not due for another week; he might not remember his life, but he could remember standard operating procedure of the therapist-client relationship, which suggested to Jack that he might have been in receipt of therapy for a very long time to have the SOP placed square in the middle of such an instinctual cognitive pattern. Likely before whatever was the cause of his current amnesia. In fact he guessed a precise 3 months and 1 day.

For a moment, Jack stood frozen with fear, and nearly dropped his filled French press from the shock. He had been assuming — his therapist *also* had been assuming — that there indeed had been one singular incident or series of incidents that had "turned" Jack this way, but what if there hadn't been? What if Jack had always been like this since birth, lost halfway between a past and a future? The notion was too horrific to consider, and Jack shivered, and sat down to drink his ostensibly stable coffee with a shudder.

Still, with no responsibilities, Jack ought to go out of his bedsit and see the world. But the world was grim. But he still ought to go out. But North London felt dirty. But he still ought to go out, breathe fresh air. The neighbourhood was grey. But he still ought to go out. He at last stepped out onto Green Lanes again, dodging a burnt-out car shell that was still smoking. The fumes were acrid in Jack's throat and would probably set off an asthmatic attack later; dandy, he thought, fine-and-dandy. *Loved plum cake and sugar candy.*

There were a few corpses gutted before the Turkish grocery on the right, but he stepped over them and made his quick way to the bus stop. He waited a long time there for a bus, but no bus came. The only working form of transport seemed to be the army helicopters churning above overhead in the sky.

***

Florentine had been having terrible dreams every night of a hairy witch. The buds were opening and the cottonwood poplars were stinking up the forest with their musk. She grew unsure of her parenting, though she made sure her brothers were oiled and curried and brushed and fed and amused, and wondered whether that was enough, and sometimes wondered whether that was how all parents felt, how perhaps her own parents had felt. The ice over the lake was nearly all melted, except for the frail chips at the edges still. There was no time for any of them to grieve. The four of them, Florentine and her brothers, ate and slept and bickered and pissed and shat and laughed, and not in any of those actions was there any time for grieving at present.

Florentine knew even dreaming that hair itself is suspect as it covers things; one cannot see if a human has pox-scars or even fresh buboes just as her mother had told her burst from folks' faces the year Florentine was born and the year her parents had escaped into the woods when the first rumours came. Hair, a frightening thing. Her brothers had hair. Hair could be tightened and woven, and laced across rooftops in thatches in deep night. So that no one could see the deed done.

Then the fateful morning came when there was a hum in the air and Florentine had again dreamt of the horrible hairy one. When she went outside in the morning sunlight with her brothers, the tree sap was seeping and blooming over, spilling out, and snow was found only in fluff-spots, like on the tails on her goat-brothers. Her new horns were almost an inch long now and had started new offshoot prongs on both sides. She watched her siblings kick high their heels in the haze and she was hearing a sound, perhaps animal, but not again. She glanced at the greyfruit trees; their crusts had melted; they showed her the pale green of their fruitmeats; she was not sure what that meant. But her brothers were still cavorting, too close to the lake (the dangerous lake).

She was standing in the terrible spot where her parents had been gutted last season.

"Percival, Eldritch, Beaman!"

She herded them instead into the forest, away from the danger. Gamine Percy laughed and bit at Eldritch, who ran ahead through the fresh moss and sticky aspen leaf-buds. Florentine followed: lonely, wistful. She could not name the emotions and wished that the greyfruit trees were in sight so that they could name such feelings for her. Her brothers giggled up ahead, as seen through twigs. Her nostrils were filled with the scent of white lichen and her heart felt cold. There was no birdsong. There was the sun-filled woods and cottonwood perfume and a mulch made up of dirt and small boney animals.

Through the trees, through the new-green trees, through the fresh trees. The four of them pushed ahead until they were at Snow Hill, and that was when Florentine looked up and saw her first antlers, still up in the tree.

Surrounded by tender leaves, they continued to look like branches themselves.

They went further in.

They went further into the deep woods, further than they had ever gone before. Audacious. The brothers were cheerful, but Florentine not. The sun was cheerful. The little sap-clusters were cheerful. They continued on. They went further in.

From up above them, far above their heads, as there had been antlers which looked like branches, now there were branches that looked like antlers. Florentine heard the gristled call of a bird. It was more like a growl. She looked up but she could not see it; she could only see its terrible blue mouth. Then she saw it and it was white and endless; its feathers snowy and its mouth sky-y. She gasped, and her brothers looked up too, and cowered. Her heart was beating like it had when she had been Hunted last winter. In his fright, Eldritch let loose a little stream of pellets, dung that turned immediately to diamonds, and Florentine did not give a shoot, for her brothers' lives were in danger, and she let the gems lie there; she would shepherd her brothers backwards. They began to move away, all four of them, and only made very quiet rustling noises, but somehow the bird heard them. Its mouth opened terrible and blue. Florentine's face went white too, and she froze, her hands stilling her brothers' movements. The little brothers began to shake at their knees in fright.

The bird soared downwards through the trees,

its feathers scraping against the treetop branches, and it occurred to Florentine again that they would have to run back to home and to the lake, which did not seem so dangerous at all now in comparison, for now – *right now* – came the revelation that here in the forest was where the Hunt had come from and *now* they were hunted once again. Through the hoary moss, and scratches on her pale white arms and their ruffled snowy fur were red vines trailing; the haze of morning sun still in the air, already their panicked return. She went last, and they all four ran back the way they had come, with a desperation, and overhead the bird cawed, and growled, and spat out pearls that stung when the pearls hit their flesh, hailstones and buboes. Past her own antlers, their retreat, how could she shield them, so fluffed and innocent? Even now they laughed, even as she spurred them. The sound of the growl spread; it covered everything, the whole horizon.

The soft brown cocoon shells falling off the bruces. Everything easy but this. The witch would get them all, with her fur and long claws, the witch would get them. The sun made them glow and sometimes even cast a green sparkle to them as they ran. The season smelt like young pears. There was a growl.

They ran back to the house, and the buds were snapping and popping their scent as the paler new green ones burst. Overhead the great white bird was growling, a terrible roar, and it dropped pellets from its dungy cloaca, opals the size of chicken-eggs, crazed rubies and rouged tourmalines and, as Florentine ran and pushed her brothers past the grey trees as they returned, the greyfruits flashed an immediate bright red, blood and garnets. The growling was louder now; if they could only make it to the reeds at the shore of the now-not-so-dangerous lake;

The bird lowered itself from the sky, a white pterodactyl, a sonic boom, its mouth everblue, and Florentine intended to push her brothers under the rushes, and then herself and they would all breathe through snapped-off reeds, and then be safe.

There was a rent. Red and flesh. The brothers were snipped by the awful blue beak and left with maws, bleeding holes aside their penii and worse the shafts themselves, such a terrible, terrible thing; their cries were pitiful and mewing, their tears worthless gems in such pain. And Florentine had not been able to stop the witch bird, not been able to stop it at all. Grief hit her. Her impotence. The bird flew away. And still she pushed them under the water to guard them further and they all four breathed through straws, blood dissolving in the water and marking their presence anyway, until it would be safe to come up –

She had not saved her brothers from their fateful spring, after all.

When Florentine arose dripping from the water, there the Witch was.

She was not truly hairy, but she did have a stripe of fur along each cheekbone, and a patch atop each hand, and she was extremely pretty. She had night-black hair flowing from her head.

"Your bird!" growled Florentine herself, shaking water off herself, defiant and desperate for her brothers, "you are cruel!"

The evergreens bent with the weight of their smouldering fresh needles. Everything was expectant, ready to crack.

"That was not my bird," said the Witch. The leaves turned greener. She stretched out a hand to Florentine. "Come out of the water. I am taking you, all four of you, away from here. Children should not live on their own. I am taking you away from here."

The scent of spring was in the air now. She was not a dark bad witch or a white good witch, she was what most of us are, grey, though most of us are not witches. Florentine looked at the Witch's face, which was enchanting and perhaps her hair was fog-coloured, smokey, though the Witch's face was bright, and Florentine looked there in the Witch's face for her own – Florentine's – emotions, but could not see them there. It was not the same experience as with the grey-fruit trees at all. Florentine stared further at the witch but stayed waist-high in the lake. Her brothers were still breathing underwater. Blood in the water, spring exploding out in buds on the branches. The Witch crooked her finger.

"Come here."

4

The Rest of the Green Men
Have Reasonable Voices

You waited at first, but then you and Martin and the stick dove into the lake. You were always going to.

*

Martin tumbles, rolling in an underwater twist. He surprises himself. He has not previously been aware that he was capable of such feats. He needs to hold his breath in this lake (this dangerous lake), and he needs to hold onto Jack, too. Air burns and curdles in his lungs, as the two men dive deeper in to the blue claire water. Or so Martin imagines the water colour and clarity, though his eyes are closed, and one hand of his clumsily dog-paddling due to its grip on the stick.

The stick, being wooden, is trying valiantly to rise as the two men try equally valiantly to dive. Their bodies touch and strain. Martin opens his eyes despite the sting resulting. And first, seen through the push of the water pressure, the under-lake is just as blue claire as he has supposed. But at second. For then Martin sees something green and lush flickering through under-lake, a glimpse of something leafy.

*

You always Chose Your Own Adventure. You and Martin

were underneath, since you had made that decision fast. You swam while holding hands, and you had a sense-memory of plunging beneath big waves and surviving. You knew you were from North America – were you perhaps from California? Or Florida, Hawaii? Or the colder climes of Oregon, with a wetsuit? The depths swallowed you and you both kicked forward, blind frogs.

You were the froggiest. Oh, this water amnesiac and amniotic, the fish bowl (the ewer, the hanop) holding the two of you snug and holding as well other possible nessies and water insects (*all insects are beautiful, all insects are always beautiful*) of the lake, this water amphibian and amphoric as it held you then spat you out like bad frog wine; you were both moving forward; you were both swimming towards an underwater cavern, and for both of you there was daylight at the end of the tunnel.

The water was a dreamy water, for this was a dream, *remember*, you remembered, and your swum journey seemed slow. You were beginning to have flashes of what might be your waking life again, your life as the spurious Jack Candle. This was the longest dream you had ever had. You had been dreaming for months. You saw for a moment in the water a man swimming in your direction; leaves alone costumed him; leaves covered his face and arms and torso; leaves bound his legs so that he was only a sodden nine-foot evergreen cone. He could not kick nor swim. He sank. You and Martin paddled on but it was likely that soon both of you would have to come up for air. Perhaps it was likely.

This was, after all, a dream. Everything was equally likely and unlikely.

The water was littered with green men. Serpents flowed within the water. Garlands sank to the depths, and rogue single flowers – violets, roses, bluebells – floated. This lost liquid world enseeded in cavetown, in hot sand apocalyptica. It made even you nostalgic and this was your first experience in the lake (the dangerous lake). You had never tip-toed into this dream before.

You swam past Pucks, masqued satyrs, dunked green georges, pre-pubescent cernunni with antlers or twigs growing from their scalps – it was hard to tell which – Lords of May and transvestite Ladies of May, hairy wild men, festooned chimney sweeps, oak-apple garland-kings, vegetable bogies, greenwood knights, hood-robins and goodfellow-robins and burry men; swam towards the underground tunnel whence came the daylight, perhaps your only escape. Puck was silent; the other-Jack as well (your quiet Jack-twin, the sinking leafy cone) emerged and now bobbing. The rest of the green men had reasonable voices.

Your self was in the water tyne, but there was a story in your head and you did not know why you thought it now. The timing was very peculiar. You were reminiscing something from your living and wakeful past; perhaps it was a clue to *you*, Jack Candle. You were recalling small children telling their parents that they remembered other lives. You were remembering these children saying things like "That was where I used to live with my other father, before the fire and before I came to you," creepy things, statements like "I used to have a little brother, before I was born." Such tales gave you goosebumps even in the water, for there was the tunnel like a black hole with the light at its end, and perhaps you were just here in the nether, perhaps that was what this place was, the neither and the both before birth and perhaps death, though you did not know this for a fact because you could barely remember one life and definitely not multiple existences. You gripped Martin and his stick, and you moved forward and ignored the sultry eeriness of the underwater with its dead or alive green men; you moved forward towards the light.

You saw as you approached the submerged tunnel that your skin had a green cast to it, as did Martin's, and that the stick was budding forth a sprig an inch now long.

Martin watched this transformation of his walking-stick too; like yours, his eyes had been under-open, and he was startled, even when he had not been surprised by the previous swimming procession of archaic pagan greenies. Perhaps Martin also had been distracted and submerged with uncanny thoughts. Perhaps Martin also had been recalling how green men, coned up with leaves and cel-ebrated, were thrown as mock sacrifices into ponds and lakes and rivers and seas; perhaps, like you, Martin also had touched upon the older, uncastrated (or perhaps more literally castrated) traditions, how the Jack-in-the-Greens were first merry gods, then their fate lower than dirt expend-able. But you had no idea what Martin had been recalling;

that was not your qualia nor, truthfully, your business. But now here in what passed for reality, and such labels were difficult in dreams, Martin was not so insouciant; Martin coughed in panic as he viewed the sprouted stick, and as he saw his own and your limbs turn green as fact. And now Martin is writhing and drowning, and thrashing and splashing, and now you have to act.

Do you and Martin both start to drown, but then, at the last moment and in unforeseen ways, save each other? (If so, keep reading about Jack and his Starbucks and when that's done, then skip ahead to the section that starts with "You had 0 Adventure Points.")

Do you dive and brave the tunnel, dragging Martin and his stick along with you? (If so, keep reading.)

Do you say adios to Martin, leave him to drown, swim to the surface, and try save your own skin right pronto? (If so, turn to Page 1.)

(If so, keep reading about Jack and his Starbucks and when that's done, then skip ahead to the section that starts with "You had 0 Adventure Points.")

(If so, keep reading.)

(If so, turn to Page 1.)

***

Ding-dong and knock, knock and ding-dong, the children on fire, the therapist gone.

Jack kept pressing his finger on the doorbell buzzer at his therapist's Crouch End practice, but there was no answer. He took out a crumpled bit of yellow paper from his pocket and read the notation – today's date, today's time: not terce, not sext, but nones. He had confirmed both measurements in the morning with his sun-moon watch, and seven days since he had last been here, but now no therapist. The rain came down to curd the puddles. Into all the gutters. Actually, now that it came to that, there was no one here on the street either, but there was quite a lot of litter and many people seemed to have decided to let their pets run stray.

Jack crossed at the green man again. The pedestrian crossing box showed neither leaf nor blood; it had been clicked off by an unseen hand. There were no cars on the road, so everything was working out cheerfully for Jack anyway.

There was the Starbucks. Jack gingerly angled his way through the shattered front glass door. What a fine day, a day where a gentleman didn't even have to worry about doorknobs. Strangely, the Starbucks was deserted. There was the acrid odour of spoiled cappuccinos and there were the split and spilt foil bags of ground coffee all over the floor, making the business much dirtier than it would otherwise appear.

Jack slumped down at one of the empty tables and sighed. He had been rather looking forward to using a name he'd thought up on the way to the therapist's office, "Fergal." It was a name both ugly and Celtic-attractive, *beau-laid*.

As Jack sat there, he became increasingly sensitive to the lack of noise. Over the last week, he had become accustomed to the sounds, heard even through buildings, of the sombre military vehicles overhead in the sky, but now even the black helicopters were gone.

Jack felt lonely, yes he did. He fingered a small yellow packet of saccharine that someone had left behind on his table and came to the conclusion that he would try self-therapy. Who needs therapists, after all. Jack recalled the therapist trying to regress and then proceed him, but how the therapist had been unable to move him past 33 years old. Yes, that had been good work on the part of the therapist. He was definitely 33 years old. He had dreamed of a body of wavy water last night, but that was the best of his recollection. Jack drummed his hand on the Starbucks table. A rapid memory came, a TV documentary where creepy small children freaked out their parents by casually mentioning previous lives and other

mothers, then would generally shut up about
it all by the time they turned six or so.

Where had he watched such a TV show?
When had he watched such a TV show? Why had
he suddenly thought of it now? He labelled
it TV and not telly, so this was more fodder
to his suspicion that he was North American, from some place with waves. He even had
a grip on the demotic. Fuckin'-A. Hurray.
Hurray.

***

You were the force. It was you who propelled Martin and
his stick and yourself through the tunnel's lip, and the water
turned from swimming-pool green to aquarium, to black,
and you swam last, pushing Martin, free carl that he was,
blindly across rocks and juts. Thou didst hold thy breath
(informal), but you did not know if you could dream and
drown (formal). Was Death a foregone formality, and did its
set include you (thou) in this state? Ya kept swimmin'.

Through the underwater tunnel the three of you
twisted, and then from the vice you were born into the
world.

You swam into a tree. You were sitting in a tree canopy, high above the world. Your rump on a bump. A bump
was a branch. *Rattlin' bog.* You scanned the green horizon
that touched the blue sky; looked out for sand or for the
mountain where you had entered the cave or for your likely

symbolic natal tunnel, but you saw only trees. Well, you were also seeing Martin and you would also see his stick were it not camouflaged by other leafy sticks. You reminded yourself that you must ask Martin why his stick had started budding, but this was not the time. The only protuberances peeping out over the tree canopy were your respective heads, and overhead three yolk-hot suns did shine.

You and Martin stared at each other, then smiled. He was going to say something.

I love you, you thought, *I-love-you-Martin*. (But *did* you love Martin? This seemed unlikely.)

"I love it when you smile like that," said tonsured Martin, and his eyes twinkled as he reached out to touch your shoulder before withdrawing his hand back, and oh, you did love him, you did. Something about being up here amongst the gnats — life! — and trees, with his stick a part of the trees, with himself a part of the trees, with yourself a part of the trees. Something about that.

"Thanks," you were about to say, but that was when cameth the bird.

It was a huge white bird, and straight on its arrival it showed you and Martin an entire blue mouth. It hooked its claws onto a top-limb not far away, and it started chewing on some softer pinecones that it had found, looking every now and then with suspicious eyes.

It was a terrible bird and the suns shone hot on this terrible bird. You quickly looked to Martin, who was peering at the animal while he stroked his stick, which is not as obscene as it sounds. Nor was it as obscene as the terrible toothless mouth of this white bird that opened blue to swallow pesto pinenut pitch, all the seeds of the world; this mouth that smelled of carrion and the cries of young boys. It dripped seeds from its mouth and these escapees fell through the canopy, through the tree branches a thousand feet below where they buried themselves in the earth and grew up as empathetic greyfruit trees, with fruitmeats that did change colour did. The bird spewed pods and still ate the pinecones and still sputtered and glared at you both and splayed its blue mouth like labia towards you, provocative and spittle-wet and old raw pain.

"Simorgh, simorgh... Simorgh..." Martin had called it something now, a name; Martin was whispering to the bird, but it would not pay attention.

Do you close your eyes and think of anything else that you possibly can? You do. Skip the next section and turn instead to the section that begins with "This was the bird's" and see where your brain takes you, as you sit aloft the tree canopy and dream that you sprout feathered white wings and Martin mounts his stick like a witch and you both sail over the tree canopy, downwards, Simorgh left behind.

You will land in a desert. You have lost your white wings. Your bare feet will have the bees of stinging sand on your soles. Your moose horns are weath-

ered yellow, newborn lemons, turned canary from wind and desert (yes, you had forgot[ten] about your moose horns, hadn't you?). But you have not grown wings. Your eyes are closed up here on the tree canopy and you understand that you and Martin operate like twins.

I told you to skip the next section and turn instead to the section that begins with "This was the bird's." Why didn't you do so? Do it now, before you wake up and the bird takes a bite from your nose.

*

Was that how it went? Maybe it went like this.

You had 0 Adventure Points left and 0 weapons. You were gasping. You ever get the feeling that this jig was up? Well, this was that, down you went towards the silt of the lake bottom, endgame. You had expected – okay, hoped – to see your life flash before your eyes, giving you at least a Facebook timeline photo album clue to what your life might have been, but this did not happen. You were strong, but you were drowning. We'll be fine without you, you'll see.

     A hand had your hand and was pulling you up, and that hand's body was dragging you like cargo as you were draped over a long stick; that same body was swimming you towards a shore, and once you'd been spat up on said cave-shore motte that same body was giving you mouth-to-mouth (no tongue) and you choked back into life, both thankful and resentful. Martin was grey with his efforts, and now it was your turn to resuscitate him (also no tongue, but not necessarily *no homo*). You were both tearful, then rallied. You both backed away the way you both had come into the lake area; reversed back into the etymologically turquoise Turk's eye (they always have the prettiest blue-green ones) tunnel; you both returned in minutes when it had taken you both weeks to get here; why, it was anarchic as a dream, it truly was; you were both back to the ol' desert himself (his name was Sandy). You were both still cough-ing from the lake. You both looked behind from whence you both had come and the entrance to the cave was sealed shut, no matter how many open-sesame-seed hamburger buns you both cajoled it with. Here you both were. One of you with moose horns. Back with Martin in the desert. And so the both of you (in every sense) started to walk the sands again.

*

This was the bird's eye view. You had an uneasy mood as you walked the desert with Martin, an instinct that you had trod this sand with him before, in exactly the same direction, at exactly the same time of day, with exactly the same pace. Your gait was casual, for that matter, and, as you and Martin and the blooming stick progressed, Martin mumbled of large moustaches and faucets and pineapples. Martin was truly dog-mad. Maybe you should never had saved each other; you both had rescued only the crazed.

The sand was hot on your bare feet and the weight of your horns truly heavy in a heated desert. But each step you raised then sank, and on the three of you went, step-step, step-step, hole-hole. Oh, do the hustle. The pattern seemed strangely wrong. You turned your shoulder and you had come some distance from the mountain holding the cave; this was hot new territory for all concerned.

"Pineapples," continued Martin, "moustaches." You ignored him.

It was peculiar; there were statues of cactuses ahead in the sand. Cacti, you meant, with Latin logic seeping into your dream. Tumbleweeds. Juniper bushes. (Were you from California? Was it the Mojave Desert you were remembering?)

Simorgh, blue and white, watched you all from atop the tree canopy, all in leaves. On the ground was a series of blank yellow Post-It notes, laid out before you in a trail; you were off to see the wizard. You and Martin stepped hopscotch upon the Post-It notes, which led you to the sculptures, which were cacti, you had been right, but cacti that had been sliced and shaved into depictions, a zany desert topiary; you had been right again. There were cacti that bloom only at night that were flowerless now in day. There were bluebells and prehistoric ferns. There was a saint-like figure surrounded by smaller cactus animals, canine fellows the wolf and the fox; a boar, a stag, a toad, a badger. The empty Post-It notes blew away in a suddenly light desert wind. You understood how Hansel and Gretel must have felt. You touched what had to be Saint Francis.

"Ow!" Seminal cactus features had been retained. A few blood drops ran down your wrist; you were the queen of toads.

"Ow!" Martin, never one to learn from the examples of others, had done the same. He too was bleeding. He was the queen of toads with ruby eyes.

You shook off the blood. The cactus statue did not, after all, depict Saint Francis and his beasts (were you once *Catholic*?), but instead, as the letters carved into its plant-flesh base told you, Saint Ciaràn of Saguaro. Wait, not saguaro but saighir. Who was this Saint Ciaràn? Perhaps you had not been brought up Catholic after all; you were not familiar with the details in the book *Lives of the Saints*. And, do we not burn, chew and swallow stag and boar and badger and wolf and fox and toad? For all his P.E.T.A. rhetoric, Saint Francis had not been protecting his "friends" very well, in that case.

You looked down at Saint Francis-*cum*-Ciaràn's spiky cactus pets, amongst them the wolf and the boar and the badger rendered gentle by God, and decided against petting them. *You* learned from your own mistakes and sometimes those of others.

It was a moot impulse, anyway. Martin was doing something violent now with his walking-stick. He was bashing down the saguaro Saint and its animal companions, ripping them open until they were pulp. Then he knelt to drink, watermelon and aloe vera, thirst quenched in a biblical desert, and ate the prehistoric fern, and you did the same. You were an accomplice. The cold liquid in your throat. *You are walking through a desert on your own and come to a vessel lying on the ground; what do you do?*

All around you there were sprigs pushing up from the sand, as far as you could see, not weathered and dusty and Joshua-tree, but green and rich and moist. The night-cacti, *Selenicereus grandiflorus*, were flowering. Queens of the night. Primroses and roses. A bluebell broke open from one such plant. Wild violets on another. A forget-me-not shrub. Soon this would be a glade and not a desert. As you scanned the blooming desert, you saw spirches grown in the sand, their roots churning up loam and rot. The perfume surrounding you was life, whether living life or dead life. Martin's stick was blossoming green, with two branches now jutting out at the top. Now things were really starting to bloom and sprout.

What do you do, which page do you turn to?

You continue. That's what you do. You have no choice.

I would like to recount briefly what happened next. It all may seem a bit sudden. Perhaps there should be a sentence or two preceding, more of a build-up. But life does not work that way. A bomb went off. Everything exploded. There were other humans than Martin and you here at last in this world, but now these survivors were lying dead in the meadow, in a field, their green legs and arms splayed in impossible positions. They were burnt from the bomb glare, lying dead in a primrose field. The beautiful insects and the greyfruit trees were lying dead in the field. There had been a flash, a flare, a *fata morgana*. Now you were all lying dead in a field. This greenery would falter and shortly turn back to radioactive desert. All of you lay here, in what once had been a green and pleasant land. In addition, your horns had been blown off.

Do you _____? You can't. You don't know what to do.

Do you dust Martin off, tell him it's just a dream and not _____, that his pale skin, burned in places, is false? You can't. You don't know what to do.

***

There was the glade, and there was beauty in the glade's paled green in spring, forest pongs in summer, orangeness of autumnal leaf, winter silver mess. There was admissible beauty.

The oaks were fine sturdy trees, vast tents, with motherly branches that dog and person felt relief for when rains came. The oak boughs were more impressive than the bruces and spirches that had surrounded her little cabin-cum-cottage back home, back home by the dangerous lake. When Florentine looked up at the sun, a sun with whom she fell in love anew each morning, there was that green chandelier of leaves and diminutive multichromatic dazzlers of filtered daylight. Any sane and thoughtful being understood that these oak trees, heathen with gravitas, were objectively much more impressive than the bruces and spirches and occasional cottonwoods and aspens and dwarf greyfruits back home. Anyone understood it. Yet it was her native trees that Florentine craved, not these acorn factories with their Druid taint of a State Religion, old magisters that slit throats for their gods, the ultimates in churchy values, reichwing as Putin-compromised USA Republicans as they exercised their seized dominion. The spirches and bruces were weeds in comparison. She liked weeds. Oh gods, Florentine knew it now for *sure*. She liked weeds.

*

Like the trees, the School too was foreign in every way. She was surrounded by girls, whereas before she had always had brothers. There existed therefore no kin-link and, under the best prescriptions of Hamiltonian evolutionary fitness, Florentine felt herself caring less for these maids who did not share at least 50% on average of her exact genetic makeup, give or take, heads or tails on a witch's tossed coin. The coin falls in the water. The golden coin falls to the lake depths, trailing blood.

The Witch would take Florentine's injured goat brothers to a place of sanctuary, the Witch had told Florentine, to a Spital. And in near-Spring, amongst the tears and frantic grabbing between four siblings, the Witch had led the three gossons away as soon as she had deposited Florentine at the Blue School, the school with no roof set amidst the oak trees.

Florentine and her brothers had kissed and waved to such each other, and then her brothers' white pelts had disappeared between the windows of branch and leaves as they were drawn further away from her, and then they were gone.

*

That same afternoon, the little girls, all fifty of them, sat cross-legged in two circles, one inside the greater other, and listened intently to their instructor. Florentine was surrounded by strangers. She could not distinguish one from another, even though she knew they had different hair tones and eye colours and heights and weights. They all wore the same face. Florentine had tied her brown hair up, and the bundle hid the short branches of her new antlers. She squeezed her hands together in a clasp and tried very hard to understand what the teacher was saying.

She couldn't concentrate. The girl sitting next to her, who had freckles, was drawing something in the soil with a stick. Florentine had freckles, too, not as many. Florentine admired her for her naughtiness. But for herself she resolved to stare straight ahead at the teacher, and to try her very best to listen.

The instructor, a female like the girls but one in early cronehood, had a young unrooted – still kicking – oak tree as an example in the glade, clasped in her grip like a snake, for the instructor held it with authority and there was no plan in any heaven that this tree would ever choose to sink its fangs in her.

The little girls, and now even Florentine and the naughty girl beside her, watched rapt.

"This sapling," said Mother Blue Cap, "this piece of forest and this tree, audacious in its fertile rooting and Bolshevik in its fruiting and growth-spurting, this tree bows down to us."

"Oh," sighed all the little girls around Florentine, "we see, we see."

"*This tree is for us to use as is every bark for us to use* –" after these words, the other little girls, except for the naughty one and Florentine because she didn't know the words, began to chant, too –

> "*Every bark for us to use.*
> *Every fish for us to gut, then use.*
> *Every storm for us to drink, for use.*
> *Every log for us to burn.*
> *Every root to dig, then eat, for use.*
> *Every beast to skin, then use...*"

With each line, Mother Blue Cap tore a leaf off her examplar tree, to show its usefulness.

The word use had become a nonsense word in Florentine's head through over-use and through the irregular s/z alternation and, as the others continued chanting, the word seemed sinister as well. She glanced briefly at the bad little girl sitting next to her.

> "Every bird for us to pluck, then use.
> Every stone for us to mould for use.
> Every stag-horn shell, for us to use.
> Every river's stream to drink, thus use..."

The freckly bad girl was drawing a tree in the soil, and each time the teacher tore a leaf from the real tree, the bad girl drew a new leaf on her sketched tree, in blasphemous unison.

She looked at Florentine and she smiled. Florentine didn't smile back. Florentine didn't chant along. As the tree was shorn, the drawing bloomed. Florentine's clasped fists were hot and sweaty. She could feel the pulse of both of her new baby-antlers on her scalp. Was she just a thing to be used as well, with her stag-horn shells, an object that the whole world had decided to claim for its worldly own?

The young oak tree was stripped and the older woman stood there triumphant, her lesson having gone just the way she planned. It was the Religious Studies requirement and it was an integral component of the Blue School curriculum, for how else would they grow up to be good little pagans, if they did not claim straight from the very start their birthright dominion over flock and fowl, shrub and hoof, tree and stone, sky and pool. How else would they fight off amongst each other one day, rival bee queenlets, to be a Lady of the Hunt, to cajole and swallow their Lord, to appease and bend their necks before the mere sight of his mighty horns. Nature worship has its rules, understand. Religious Studies was of prime importance to the Blue School. Everyone was now getting to her feet. The freckly girl erased her drawing in the dirt with her shoe as they stood up, and she winked at Florentine.

The fifty little girls were to be led back into another glade to practice whirling, but Florentine looked back, remembering the occasions when she had looked back to see her own antlers hanging, bloody in the tree leaves.

What is glory? There is glory to the reveal of a cicada turning imago, clear breathless hope at the sight of green translucent wet wing revealed to be beating, the corpse body left behind, and yet in the latter there is deep grief too, for extreme change has as its charge loss no matter how beautiful the metamorphosis. All insects are beautiful.

But now she saw this poor leaf-stripped oak, thrown horizontal on the ground, its once-moist roots drying in the hot sun that pierced through the chandeliers of green and twig above. An insect had left its shell on the bark and flown to a new beginning. The wood was rotting, but did not know it yet.

She and the other forty-nine girls trooped dutifully ahead to Glade No. 14. Glade No. 14 seemed, to Florentine, to be full of promise. The other girls were whispering of evening sunlight and dancing. The first lesson had not been to Florentine's liking; far closer to her hating. She was not eager for future lessons; she was a reluctant student. Mother Blue Cap was distracted as Florentine held back towards the rear of the throng. It was hard to be inauspicious with horns.

"Blue Mother," the wicked little girl who was now Florentine's friend was saying to the teacher in order to divert, Florentine realised, "Blue Mother, do the stones and sticks use *us*? Are *we* for them to use? Do the stoats and stags use *us*?"

Florentine slipped behind a tree and hid herself, and no one noticed, for they had turned their ears to the quizzing of Mother Blue Cap, who was annoyed by the tone of the questioning and merely shook her head, while the bad freckled girl continued. Though the Mother and the other students had not noticed that the inquisitor gave Florentine a wink just before Florentine slipped behind the tree.

"The birds and boars, do they use us as we use them? The fish and fowl?"

The group was moving slowly away. Florentine could barely hear the freckly girl now. Her voice trailed away. "Do they use us, the creeks and crags? The roes, reynards, do they use us...?"

Silence.

Florentine walked back to the area where Mother Blue Cap had instructed them. There was the uprooted young tree on the ground. It had no leaves left. There was soil clinging to its roots, but that was all. She felt sorry for it even though she didn't, on principle, like oak trees. This tree had been killed for a metaphorical (she hoped) lesson; what good was that? She picked up the dying tree. There was sap on it but that would soon dry. The tree was fresh flowers in a pot; it appeared alive but the sun was moving fast through the day; it was doomed, like infection before the outbreak. Her mother – it made her very sad to think about her mother – had said that the year that Florentine was born was still safe, but that there had been infection already and the blue sickness came full on in later years, through noxious breath and difficult planet alignment and cats.

All that withstanding, it still made her disheartened to look at this specimen examplar tree. It wasn't the tree's fault that it had been chosen out for Mother Blue Clap. It was doomed, but some Pest survivors had been too, and they still lived to walk today.

It had no acorns yet; it was too young.

She gripped it; it was less a bough-tree and more a staff, but she took it with her and backtracked for many steps back into the forest, far and far away from the Blue School. There was a dip in the forest floor there and not many oaks. Less competition, she reasoned; maybe that would be better. There were still many snow drifts here, further in. She dug a hole in the loam and coaxed the tender roots into the spread and then patted the soil up against the base again. She did not look back at the young tree as she left it and returned to her School; there was nothing more she could do for it.

*

Glade No. 14, a beautiful glade with sunlight coming through
the trees and real stumps for chairs and real feathers for
quills and real charcoal from campfires for pencils, and all
the while the wild sun beat through and dappled the glade
green, for Spring was coming, and the dancing little pools
of blue little girls twirled. The girl with the freckles paused,
grinned at Florentine, then joined the crowd again.

The Blue School's fifty little girls wore their smart
frocks cowl-necked in the medieval, monkish-style, blue as
the sky or of a human's blinded eye: true-glow blue were
their costumes. The fifty little girls, ranging in age from
what appeared to be seven to thirteen, were proud of such
garb, and whispered to each other that they were necro-
mancers, sorcerers. They twirled their blue skirts and blue
armlets and blue hoods around unto each themself and there
were many such preoccupied little whirlpools when Florentine entered the glade that evening.

She stole away from the group for a second time; they
would not miss her; she was too new here. She climbed up in
one of the hated oaks and hid herself.

There was a bird up in the tree, but it flew away,
and Florentine climbed hand over hand higher up in the
branches. She looked up at her fingernails and there were
black moons from the soil inside them. Her hair had come
loose but, if someone saw her from below, she would be
just a normal unantlered little girl, for to this extent did her

horns blend into the brown branches. I will grow leaves from my antlers, thought Florentine, I will grow leaves on my stag-horns and I will live my life up here and no one will ever know. I will never come down again unless I want to.

Leaves bright green on antlerhorn. The girl is a tree. The girl can stay as a tree forever and forever, through spring, autumn winter summer. I will run through the meadow at dawn when no one is there; I will be laughing as I run, and I will grow leaves from my antler branches, which in turn grow me, a little girl, from their base.

It was dark sullen twilight turning night and through the flaming, between the trees now dark with day's end, trees with the faintest trace of snow clumps clinging to their terminal branches, between such trees there were smears of glowing blue, smudges of glowing ghost-girls, on their way home. Whitened phosphorus, the type of fish-bait you lure trout with, floating ghosts and clouds.

5
Venatrix

The Apocalypse has come. Martin rises to his feet. There are dead bodies everywhere. He is the survivor. Moosehorn Jack is deceased from this desert blast, stretched out on the sand, and so is everyone else deceased. Snow begins to fall. Martin is the King of Nuclear Winter. The snow is also ash. Not in the way of trees. Martin looks at his walking-stick. The leaves that were so new and brave – have fallen off. There is a patina to the stick as if it has been deadwood for decades. Polished. Frosty. Martin begins to walk the desert again. He wants to walk it; he desires himself far away from all these bodies.

The cave is now ruled out; his new friend Jack is definitely "ruled out." So Martin's run dry on opportunities and, sadly also, hope. Gotta keep truckin', buddy. Keep on truckin', buddy.

The snowflakes come down. Martin thinks of leaves newly fallen from his stick, and of the night-flowers. Since when does winter follow spring? Every unique, special, backwards snowflake.

*

The snow comes down all through the night, though it is not a heavy fall. The stick has new frost creases running vertically down it now and Martin is shivering blue himself.

His feet are numb, as are his emotions concerning Jack – but he needs to keep moving, otherwise it will very well get worse. He has a sense memory to this effect, straight through from the soul-palms of his feet, but no source for it. And eventually the stick balks and refuses to spike on further, and Martin will sleep after all. He burrows himself in a clump off a drift and I'll give the story away right now to reveal that he does not in fact acquire hypothermia on this particular night.

Martin dreams something uncanny that early morning as he sleeps somewhere out in some snowy reaches of some desert landscape, something uncanny and unwelcome. In his dream, what surrounds Martin is entirely dark, so it's impossible to tell of which stuff, exactly, the dream world is made. Martin is on his own. No Jack. No stick. Some pre-universe, icy but dingy, some space-time long before the Norse giants started licking ice cows to form the worlds, or perhaps that was the other way around.

When an object eventually does appear, it's very clear to Martin that it's a snake, and a red one at that, a blushing Worm bigger than himself, taking up most of the space before his eyes. The snake begins to divide itself, or be divided, into sections, sliced vertebrae into chunked steaks (they taste just like chicken). Invisible hands guillotine its flesh and then do it again. The bloody sections quiver, stand alone and vertically separate from the snakehead, yet keep their form. Dreamed, raw meat.

Martin wakes to the snowy desert, and rubs his re-found stick companionably, though it is cold, so cold. The snow has been coming down the entirety of his nighthorse. Delicate weather fills the space. A shaken snowglobe out to all horizons, glass or not. The snowflakes melt on Martin's arm. They do not melt on his stick. Is it in fact Martin's stick? Maybe he is the stick's Martin. The snowflakes do not melt on Martin's stick and that is proof that it is wood and he is not.

Once upon a time, there was no Jack-with-moose-horns. There was only Martin and the stick, so why should the loss now matter? He just has to move his mind back to how it was before.

The snow comes down thick and fast, like rain. The drifts cover dunes, make them into white people's flesh, blue veins and freckles fading fast into antarctic; snow that freezes even such pale skin. Milk. Delicate semens, not necessarily from Caucasians; milk and snow towards cum and frostbite. When the snow comes, everything else is forgotten. Jack is forgotten. Like the world's locked jism un-licked by ice cows, the snowdrifts mean intrigue attributed to a desert where there was no mystery before. Under the snowdrift, under the snowdrift, anything can be found now: forests, cities, planets. When spring comes towards sum-mer, a universe will be created. But spring has not come, but snow has come, snow is come, winter is icumen, loud do not sing the cuckolds.

***

It was an abominable dream, with a sense of dispassionate foreboding. The horror of its suspense did not dissipate from start to finish, nor did the impact of its imagery recede for Florentine upon awakening. The general feelings it evoked reminded her of the bad-hairy-witch dreams, before the somewhat-good-somewhat-hairy witch came to save her and her siblings. That rescue only one day ago, though it seemed like years had passed, and the somewhat-hairy witch had been recognised thereforth as something less than monstrous. Yet this latest dream, with its slow, initially methodical fearfulness, was all kinds of monstrous.

Florentine dreamed of a chopped-up snake who still wiggled even though Florentine could see the spaces between the slices. A horrid view made more horrid by the fact that it had reminded her now, upon waking into her first morning in her wardship at the Blue School under the dapple-sun branches, of one of her mother's fairy tales; it reminded her of the best fairy tale that her mother had ever told; it reminded her of the retrieved friendly conversational timbre to her mother's voice, and memory made Florentine's throat swell dry. That fairy tale of her mother's had been about a snake, of course, a white snake that had been chopped up and put into a stew, and the cooked stew smeared upon the over-curious lips of a servant, and then the servant had understood the languages of birds.

Florentine sat with her legs crossed, in some emotional pain, before she fully rose from the lean-to wherein she had slept, walked once round the slumbering, snoring camp, and then returned to her bed anew. She wanted present her mother, her father, her goaty brothers. The pierce-needle of their absence. She didn't want to understand the bird's language. She didn't want its feathery syntax or a translation of its talon evil. Her eyeballs flickered left as she recalled blue on white, perverse reverse, a cloud on sky. Foreboding. Dread. Ugly anticipation. Very worst of birdy all, unbeaked expectation.

*

There was a dream, there was a dream where her brothers were falling from branches, and she reached to save them; stretched her grasp towards the white hair tufts on their necks, but their young beards tore and down they went falling. There was a dream, there was a dream where the man who knocked at the door was there; he was trying to send her a message; he knew something in her world that he did not know in his; she could not understand his message.

Florentine caught the freckle-faced wicked girl's eye as they both yawned and stretched and exited from their respective personal lean-to of stacked spirch branches and sweat-damp leaves. These lean-tos all the little girls make each their own every new night, and then dismantle with the corvid crow each morn, then build anew at moon.

Florentine drew closer to the girl. "I'm Florentine," she offered, in a shy voice. She missed Beaman especially, and was not used to making friends. She scuffed at the forest carpet with one toe.

She learnt that the girl's name was Eglentyne, and she learnt that nettles make good soup but bad friends, nettle-knowledge of which Florentine was already in receipt but politely did not mention, and she learned all of this before they reached Glade No. 1 for lessons in avoiding rocks and puddles whilst undertaking trail processionals. She learned that Mother Blue Cap was also called Brigid, and that Brigid stood there with two assistants, one of a middle age named Breesha, and one called Bríg, a younger woman who bore a white hood. Breesha had a mean face and she kept a beady eye out for any fidgeting, which small young females were wont to do.

The fifty little girls formed four straight lines of twelve-and-a-half girls each. They looked up expectantly at Mother Blue Cap.

"Which are our three Holy Trees?" intoned the blue-hooded priestess.

"The Yew, the Oak, the Greyfruit Good," chanted the fifty little girls in chorus. Florentine tried to follow along.

"Which wood did we anoint just two days yestern?" Florentine had missed that lesson.

"The Yew!"

"Yes, the Holy Yew, the wood of visions! And which wood did we anoint just one day yestern?"

"The Oak!"

"The Holy Oak," specified their teacher. "Our Council of Oaks. We tore its leaves and branches, one, two, three." The air around them was moist. Florentine felt Eglentyne wince beside her.

"Do not fidget! Heed Brigid!" rhymed out Breesha, glaring in the direction of Florentine and Eglentyne. And so then when Breesha turned away, Florentine whispered to Eglentyne a fact, a fact that she had not confided in Eglentyne previously to this moment, a fact about how Florentine had rescued and re-planted the stripped tree, deep in the woods, and that it had therewhence a chance to grow. Eglentyne grinned so widely Florentine feared her face would split, and she gave Florentine a quick squeeze of the hand.

"Do not smile!" shouted Breesha, as Eglentyne beamed away. There was the smell of violets in the air, and new, cramped weed blades. From far away in the distance, Florentine could hear a chicken cooing.

*

On Imbolc, the day of sweet ewe's milk, also called Groundhog's Day, more commonly celebrated these days in supermarkets as vacuum-wrapped packages of high-quality feta cheese; on Imbolc, the hag goddess the Cailleach trembles her nose out of her abode. Such a day will be sunny, so she can gather her sticks for her firewood. Winter stays for weeks when sunlight thus hits the Cailleach. Imbolc means the budding pregnancy of ewes and goat does. Imbolc is not for bucks or rams. And if the Cailleach is lazy, or if the weather is unsuitable poor, she sleeps through the sun-filled haze, and winter is near its end.

The Cailleach is also known as Brigid. Brigid's mother is a poet. Brigid is also Dagda's daughter, and Dagda is the Father of us all. Dagda has a pig ever-roasting on a spit, and a piglet ever-growing towards its own inevitable roast. Brigid is our Blue Sister and, surprisingly, also our Blue Mother. Don't ask. Brigid has two oxen, the king of boars and the king of wethers, be they wethered sheep or wethered goats. Dagda has spread the greyfruit tree orchard across the lands; he carries seeds when he travels and down go the seeds. Dagda's penis drags to the ground and it is necessary for him to have a little wagon with him always, to carry it. Brigid is a huge bird, some will say, and she carries her firewood sticks in her mouth. Perhaps she also spills pod on pod, fecund seed-parts crumbling from her mouth onto the fields, onto the valleys, onto the glades, onto the forests, floating atop the waters, as she does swoop her heavens. Come in from your flights, Brigid, thy bed is ready. *A Bhríd, a Bhríd, thig a sligh as gabh do leabaidh.*

In other places, every ninth year nine male animals from nine different species, including humans, are sacrificed to Brigid at Holy Wells, but that is not how she does things these days. These offerings have always been a little pre-sumptuous on the part of those sacrificing – take Moses, for example – assuming that you know a god's, or indeed even another human's, inner thoughts.

Humans; pigs; horses and donkeys and mules; dogs; cats; chicken and geese and ducks; sheep and goats; cattle; mice and rats. Or, owls and other wildfowl; deer and moose and elk; boars; badgers and wolverine and weasels and ferrets and martens; crows and ravens; wolves and foxes; bears; lynx; squirrels. Or, mosquitoes; bees and wasps and hornets; spiders; house flies and fireflies; ants; ladybugs; crickets and grasshoppers; caterpillars-cum-butterflies; termites.

Things that slip and slide between environments: toads and frogs and snakes; freshwater fish and saltwater fish; seals and sea lions and walruses; beavers and otters; bacteria and viruses (controversial); lice; whales and dolphins; octopuses and squid; crustaceans.

Things undreamt of and exotic: elephants; lions; apes; skunks; raccoons; scorpions; jackals; coyotes; armadillos. Or, scarab beetles; penguins; toucans; coral; venus fly traps; cougars; mammoths; snow white tigers; monkeys. Or, dinosaurs; llamas; guinea pigs; parrots; crocodiles; alligators; kangaroos; sea anemones; jellyfish.

Sometimes there are flames in forests which are spontaneous. They merely start aglow, with no source. They are naturally occurring fires. These natural flames must be attended and Brigid is the one who does so.

Brigid is the patron saint of serpents, poets, holy wells and all our early springs. Spill her libations with early milk; it seeps into the soil. Spring might be coming, and spring might not be coming. We do not know. We do not know. Winter or spring, spring or winter. Black, white,

white, black. Bird, crone, crone, bird.

The Holy Wells of Brigid are important. They are visited at Imbolc. The wells are dressed with tied scraps of cloth, each torn scrap a prayer. The petitioners circle the wells, sunwise, also known as clockwise. But suns are older than clocks. Never withershins. It was always sunwise. It was always sunwise. *Fertility, please Brigid. Life and not death for my plagued children, Brigid. Let my livestock serve and foal, my Brigid.* She has a white wand all of spirch and she touches it to dead stumps and they burst in buds; they leaf and flower; polypody ferns grow new curly roots beneath the earth. Everything will re-green. When Spring is coming. But sometimes Winter stays. Spring. Winter. Sometimes stays; sometimes goes. The pieces of cloth are now blessed and sacred and are gently touched the rest of the year through.

Sometimes wind blows through the pieces of cloth hung in branches, or through small pieces of hanging bronze, and this branch-music is the oracle.

The water from these wells is holier than ewe's milk. These wells are holy ground. Take off your shoes. Take off your shoes. Now fly.

*

It was only late in the afternoon that the young students of the Blue School reassembled. They each held hands solemnly with the girl on either side in their standard rows. The cloudy sky suggested rain; neither Mother Blue Cap nor

Breesha nor Bríg in her white hood – that was actually grey with dirt – did smile.

There were so many thoughts in Florentine's head: the owl, her missing wounded brothers, the stripped oak perhaps secretly growing, her parents (the compulsive red pain of that loss now starting to dull just a little), her new friend holding her hand.

They watched in their rows as Blue Mother Brigid washed her old feet in ewe's milk, and then bid Breesha and Bríg and the little girls too to wash their own feet – to purify – in the cool milk before they all approached the bonfire lit. The rows dispersed and once clean then all females gathered, circling the open hearth in the centre of the glade, the eternal coals sputtering and taking spark already. The round was intimate, with the smoke scent pungent in nostrils, and now with many of those present smiling, even Breesha, their cleansed feet and ankles still shivering and dripping milk. The tongues of orange flame rose high as the wood snapped.

Now Brigid too rose to her feet, with her left palm clutched around an unseen object. She was nearly grinning, and nearly beautiful, for there was something needling to her strictness. Florentine felt a lump of admiration despite herself. She squeezed Eglentyne's hand, but there was no response this time, so she put her attention again to the Blue Mother and to Breesha and Bríg. In Florentine's nostrils was the cheese-sweet smell of ewe's milk. Her feet were chilled, though dried now. The pop of the twigs, turning in the flame. And now Brigid, imposing, standing before them all.

"The greyfruit trees," intoned Brigid. Her eyes were fixed upon the sky, up towards the trees.

"The Greyfruit Good," returned the little girls. Florentine had no idea what would come next, but Eglentyne's hand had grown sweaty in her own.

"Two days yestern, we did spike, and Breesha and Bríg and I did suck, the Yew. The sap runs within all three of us, and all of you, one day. You will bend your heads and bare your necks for juice. You will learn your lessons well. There are hedges here in the glade that no men can cross."

Florentine sensed what she thought might be irritation in young Eglentyne beside her. But Eglentyne didn't waver her head to look at her friend and instead stared out at Mother Blue Cap. So Florentine's gaze, too, returned.

"One day yestern, we did strip the Oak. We exploit and sunder, rive and tear. It is ours. All is ours."

"All is ours," intoned most of the little girls, breathlessly.

Brigid released the fingers on her palm, and the circle leaned forward. "I have here five seeds from the Greyfruit Good." Five long pods, grey-brown and silent, rested on the older woman's flat palm.

"Ooooo," said most of the little girls.

"They are seeds dropped from the Tree itself, life-acorns, full of sentiment. Love and rage and lust and tenderness and shyness and melancholy and jealousy and affection, all here, all seeds and pods and kernels and pips. Pop, pip," said Brigid.

"Pop, pip," answered the crackling twigs in the bonfire.

"The Holy Ash is wide in air where its boughs touch night stars spangled, and the Holy Ash is wide in earth, where its roots span out to worms and grubs and termites and moles. The Holy Ash is an embrace. A hug. A clasping-to. The green falls, then dies, then rots, then feeds, then blooms, then falls, then so on," continued Brigid.

"The Tree is the first of all gods. Dendrolatry the purest of all faiths. We nail and hang rags and charms on our trees as prayers and we do wish. To the unschooled, wishes do feel weak and waffley in comparison to robust prayers, but this is not the case; wishes are hardy. Wishes are the oldest custom. We do this still, in multiple aspects; the tannenbaum and yule logs do not grow alone; there are glades of such wishes and such practices; forests. Forests that cover the entire world, first-forests."

Brigid curled her fingers round her seeds again and raised that fist up to the sky. She spoke loudly: "O Holy Ash, yggdrasil, we pay tribute to your oxhorn stump, saglagar, tannenbaum, dodana, wacah chan, gaokerena, bo-tree, eden, bodhi, asec, nuin, banyan, peepal; we suck juice from your leaves and elixir from your fruit; your branches drink the very air from our mouths and we both thrive immortal in our mutuality. Your sap can cure our dead. Your late-budding leaves divine our shaken futures and slap poultice to our wounds."

Brigid peered through the fire at the other woman

and at the little girls; she was looking from the other side
of a blazing sunbeam or its opposite, a shadow. It was nigh
impossible, impossible to read Brigid's expression.

The ever-flicker fire was impossible too, sunset and
eternal flames, guarded by maidens.

Everyone else was attentive to her raised closed hand.
Everyone seemed to know what to expect. Eglentyne would
not meet Florentine's eye. Brigid's palm with sweated seed-
pods clutched within it. The other little girls were watching;
they watched with their shudders.

"This is your third lesson," said Brigid to all the little
girls, "this is what the greyfruit trees will teach you.

"Little girl, step forward," said Mother Brigid, and a
little girl did do so. A little girl drew up to Brigid. "I want
you to tell me what you feel." Brigid's free hand smoothed
her charge's cheek, and displaced a tear.

"I feel frightened," said the little girl. "Anonymously
and secretly, I do. Anonymously, I feel frightened."

"So you do," said Brigid, and she pressed her closed
palm against the little girl's hand. The girl recoiled but her
fingers curled round the gift. "Throw that seed within the
flames," Brigid said.

And the little seed was parquered into the fire.

"This is your lesson," Brigid said, as the seed
exploded in a burst of terror. Fear was a thing so raw-shock-
ing to see in the fire and the little girl trembled. Her fright
was at its peakest. The shadow-orange-red of the burning
flickered out through the ceiling of even the tree canopy's

range in that glade. The volunteer's expression became much worse. What that little girl felt was the greatest fear she had ever felt, and that fear's proxy was popping and cooking in the fire, and the emotion itself was for a breath-span in her lonely head alone. Yet they all felt the fear soon enough; they all felt it then. There was a nihilism to it all that Brigid was coaxing forth, a push to destroy, to throw the seeds in the fire, death to potential hope, very punk-rock desperate.

"Little girl, step forward," said Mother Brigid, and another little girl did do so. A second little girl drew up to Brigid. "What is it that you feel, child?"

This little girl glared at the Blue Mother, and Florentine admired her for it. "I feel wrath," the little girl spat out. She had angry sable braids beneath her hood.

"So you do," said Brigid. "This is your lesson." She handed over the second greyfruit seed-pod. The second girl hesitated not at all. She propelled it into the fire with a heady anger. *Crash! Despair!*

The seed exploded with rage and a brightened blue flash. The angry child disappeared back into the horde, and said nothing further. They all watched, angry, and then their hearts slowed back to peace.

"Little girl, step forward," said Brigid, interrupting the tranquillity, and Florentine tried to dodge so that she was not seen by either Brigid or by Breesha or Bríg. And relief: another third cowled child did step up to feel the flame heat upon her neck and cheeks and backs of hands. This child was beaming and sunny. Florentine had the distinct impression that Eglentyne was rolling her eyes, but by now Florentine stared straight ahead herself and could not confirm this.

"What emotion do you feel, which sting?" asked Brigid of the newest little girl. Then she continued to talk. She smiled at the rest of the girls and at Breesha and Bríg, to show them that she could read even this emotion accurately. "It will be no surprise, girl, for you are doubtless happy."

"I *am* happy," said the little girl, "I feel happy; I've been dancing all day. It's been beautiful and sunny and per-haps – as you know – perhaps spring is coming."

Brigid did not mirror the laughter. "You confirm your state as a happy one."

"Yes, it is."

"Then that is your seed," said Brigid, and Florentine observed how Brigid appeared disgruntled, and maybe dis-appointed, and Brigid pressed the fourth little seed into her recruit's hand, the wee pod. "Throw it into the fire," she said to the little girl, "throw it into the fire."

"And I'm going to go throw it into the fire now," said the little girl, and such joy spread over her face.

"And now," said Brigid, "do it now."

It was a green flash of happiness exploding but it was nothing like happiness previously known. It was like every-thing better, fruit-running joy. A green apple.

And so what happened was what had happened with the other small seedpods as well.

It was then that Brigid registered Florentine. Eglen-tyne immediately dropped her hand. "Stop," muttered

Eglentyne, "don't look at her; don't make eye contact." But Florentine had already made eye contact.

"Florentine," said the Blue Mother, "come through, come through. What is it that you feel?"

Florentine could feel her own eyelashes scraping her face as she looked downwards.

"She feels grief," Blue Mother Brigid announced to the crowd.

"No," said Florentine, though her legs had stepped her forward, almost involuntarily, so that she was standing in front of Brigid and Breesha and Bríg, catching the sizzle off the fire. "I do not feel grief. I don't feel a thing today. I do not want to feel it."

"How is it that you do not want to feel the grief?" asked Brigid, and she pulled off Florentine's hood, and Florentine's small horns were revealed to all. The other little girls, with only few exceptions and amongst those Eglentyne, began to wickedly laugh and smirk. They pointed at Florentine's antlers and the Blue Mother did not stop them.

Florentine felt her hood gathered at her neck. The sun hit her antlers. They were there; they were visible. It was not exactly shame. They were there regardless, whether they were shameful or not.

Brigid looked at Florentine's horns, shown there in front of everyone, and all the other little girls looked at Florentine's horns as well.

"Venatrix," said Brigid, mocking. "The horned huntress girl, ahoy.

"Or perhaps the hunt-*ed* with your velvet popping out anew. Is it not grief you feel, Florentine?" Brigid asked again.

"I suppose that it is grief indeed."

"Then if it's grief," said Brigid, "then you must address it. Throw the seed into the fire. Here is your seed. It will test you. We will see if it is the grief, or not."

Florentine's tears begin to roll down her face and the other children, she could see, were already disturbed as well. But what could she do, but look up through the tree canopy, and then look down again? Her small antler prongs burned on her scalp, good twins.

And Florentine looked at the fire. Arson. "My goodness," she said, "I feel it. I feel it all."

"Stop it!" Eglentyne yelled then at the other girls. Eglentyne had pushed herself to the front of the line and was staring all of them – Blue Mother, Breesha, Bríg and forty-eight other little girls – down. Some of the other little girls had tears already running down their cheeks. "Stop staring at her horns!"

But Florentine was somewhere far distant from that. The seed, the fire. And Florentine began to feel it all suddenly. She could feel first the Pest, that thing she had never known but which had left so many gaps in her world, the thing, the thing, the bullies and the cavities of that sickness; her brothers, the deep holes on them; and then the blood-soaked holes where she'd knifed off her own stumps, not knowing they would bud out again as they were doing now, which seemed of cold comfort at the moment; her horns and then the greyfruit tree orchard by the cabin, the woodpile outside the house sprouting both spirch and bruce at once; her parents and her horns and the dogsteeth and the dogs-teeth again and the dogsteeth and the tears came running down her face.

"There," said Brigid – "Shut up!" screamed Eglen-tyne at the Blue Mother, but she was ignored – "there," said Brigid, "all of you see the possibility now, girls; it is grief; it is grief indeed. These five pods are the entirety of your new knowledge submitted. This is your lesson from the greyfruit good, grief-fruit good. Grief is good or grief is not good."

Grief is not good, thought Florentine. Grief is good.

"You all must feel these things," said Breesha, finally speaking now herself to the crowd, and in deference to Brigid. She was slightly nervous, as if it were the first time that she had done this. "It is important that you feel these things and do not let them spoil inside you." Grief is good. Grief is not good.

Florentine, shaken, retreated back to Eglentyne. Her friend hugged her. "There may be some truth in this," Florentine whispered to Eglentyne, "like the lancing of pustules, but why must they be so strict? Why must they monitor our emotions; why not in all natural good time? My father always said all feelings rise in broth at the end, whether you will them or not."

"The Hooded Mothers want to stop it," hissed Eglen-tyne back, spitting so angry so that Florentine shuddered for fear of what Eglentyne's anger-seed-pod might have looked like. "But they can't. They fear they can't. They want to try to stop the re-emergence of the blue sickness. Of the Pest. We have to be strict. They have to be strict. They say so, for else comes the blue sickness again and that we cannot have a little of that. Even a little of that will kill us. But they cannot stop it. None of us can stop it."

"The greyfruits," whispered little Florentine to little Eglentyne, "where do the greyfruits come from? As I have not been listening. How do the seed-pods know our hearts?"

"Their tight claws over all nature. Their extreme May castrations and their smouldering fires with the insistence that sacrifice means that fewer shall die." Eglentyne was speaking so quickly, wretchedly. She was talking on some entirely other subject.

There were some words that she had said that Florentine had recognised, however. Her brothers' castrations had not come in wether-season May. Their losses had come at the early wrong time. There was never going to be a right time. Everything was wrong. Everything askew.

"Yes," said Eglentyne, and this time she did not lower her voice but it made no matter for the crowd was dispersing and no one took any notice of them anyhow and all save them were drawing away from the low, still-flaming fire. "I'll tell you what actually is going on with their saintly greyfruits, oaks and yews. What's going on is that we have survived the tree of life. We have survived. We're all orphans from the plague, every one of us girls – I am guessing you too, Florentine? – we are but little orphans. The Pest could not be stopped and that's why their juju is all pointless. My own *parents*! My parents rotted in their plague beds, black and sore, full of sad, stricken wounds, and I had to run away. My dear, sweet dad; my brave, domestic mother. Florentine, the greyfruit seeds that grow the trees are spilled from the Tree of Life itself, called Yggdrasil. But the Holy Ash will not help us keep our lives. It will not save us. Nor will the Oak. Nor will the Yew."

The next morning, the little girl scraped through the ashes. All the others in the school could hear her lament from far away. Eglentyne heard Florentine's lament and she came to her. She helped Florentine to scrape the ashes.

Their fingers were forks. The day after Imbolc, the tradition; you scrape the ashes and see what message Brigid has left for you. Their fingers were forks in the ashes and they tried to see scripts there; they divined nothing. It was not like tea leaves. They were on their knees on the ashes. The wind blew through the glade and made the cloths and bronzes whistle; the wind blew away the ashes; the ashes were gone.

My grief is not gone, thought Florentine. She wondered if the smiling girl of yesterday's lesson was still smiling. Eglentyne looked angry and still stubbornly scrubbed at the soil for a vanished, missing message.

"I personally like your antlers," she muttered to Florentine at one point, rather bitterly. Eglentyne's fingernails were half blacked and rich with earth and cinder chalk.

The happy girl's happiness likely was not gone. The ashes were not gone. The ashes were here. It was a chilly morning. It started to snow again. It was snowing. The Cailleach had seen her shadow. She had seen her shadow. It was snowing there in the glade, by the shell of a holy flame, with the winter. One cannot make bleak readings from late snowflakes any more than one can from cooled ash. The winter sky dropped; the air was threaded with cloudy strings and those knots of snow kept falling.

6
Ladywell

This is what I would like to add. That night, Florentine sneaked out to where the young oak had been sowed. The snow had come back in parts and she went out into remnant drifts and out into the springy marsh-moss that had been developing. It wasn't precisely a surprise to her, for she had hoped for it, but she saw then that the salvaged stick was not dead. That it was in fact there upright on the ground planted, and with a fresh bark to it and perhaps a bit of greenery too to some browned nubs on its branches, which she saw as a good sign.

At its base, she scraped the newfallen snow away and patted the soil above the roots; made sure that such whiskers were covered. The young tree was difficult to see in the gloam and there was a crescent moon in the blue sky, the grey sky, the sable sky. But she knew herself that the tree was doing better than might have been expected and so she smoothed said roots and willed it strength and resilience through the final season. She trusted softly. She could not water it, for the snow would do that. Horticulture was senseless. It was not a garden plant or even an orchard tree. Though feral or domestic, that distinction had never been clear with the greyfruit orchard trees of her home. This stick – oak tree, really – was not a plant that needed tending; it was more like those grown objects gathered by her parents the forest-farmers: scrounged fungi and fiddlehead stump and more. Plants who muster. The oaks were wild things. I will be back, Florentine thought, I will be back and I'll probably come soon.

*

There was just enough room to sit up fully from the waist with her head branching the top sticks. She would remember to build it taller as she grew through time; to select longer support sticks each night. It was warm in her shelter from her breath and massed clothes – and still cold-wintry outside. There was not much snow at all left now. Still, she was disinclined to step outside. She had been at the school three weeks altogether, and it was a Sun Day at the end of Solmonath, Mudmonth – the month that followed Wintermonth and preceded Springmonth. She had a deep disinclination to be chilled.

She could go wake Eglentyne; they had become fast friends by now, but it was the kinder gesture to let her friend sleep that little longer. The sun gave spark and beam to the diminishing snow clumps within her view; from not so far, she could smell the breakfast fires starting and soon would clang the bell that called them to wake up and then at some time not so long after that would clang the bell that called them to eat. Then they would bear out that night's lean-to sticks in their arms, stack them near the fires for burning and would gather, yawning, shivering, sleepy-eyed. The sun was merry even on this cold morning, and caught the edges of what could be new buds on leafing trees in the forest as seen from her vantage in the lean-to, but were not quite yet new buds, or not since winter had chosen to fold in on itself again for six more weeks and only three of those six had passed. Not a choice, really. By Brigid's order.

Into the lean-to's entrance popped suddenly a bird, smack into the sunlight that tapped through the trees and through the shelter's leaves and twigs and through her eyes and through her mouth. Her lips were dry from sleep. This little bird was a bright blue and she tried to be wary of it, categorising it as she must with the terrible blue foul/fowl attacker, but Florentine found that she could rally no fear towards this little one at all.

Blue is a most beautiful colour when blue is not being an attacker and yet there was that association which was not a comfortable association.

It was so wee.

The blue bird would not leave the lean-to, even though the lean-to's front was unbuckled to the sun. The blue bird behaved as if it were trapped within the sticks even though it truly was not. So on this morning Florentine did not dismantle the lean-to for the fires in order to build it afresh that night, but rather let it stand.

"This way," she told the blue bird, "this way you can peck for worm and seed and yet be assured of shelter."

She left and a short time later returned with a small

wooden bowl of water. In the back of her head was the knowledge that all she had to do was un-pick the lean-to and the bird would fly free as the stick walls vanished; but it was also true that all the little blue bird had to do was fly out the open sunny entrance and it would be free too, which was something that it did not do.

Florentine set the entrance sticks ajar and went off to practice whirling with the other little girls that day.

And then the next morning, the little bird had turned yellow. It was all feathers. Sunny. Florentine opened one eye as she lay on the stale leaves of her unchanged nest and looked at it.

"Lemon-bird," she said. She brought it seed-crumbs that day from their griddlecakes and brought it as well water and it hopped. It was not a pet, though. It was wild.

The third morning, when Florentine woke up, the bird had turned the colour of blood. It was a venous, deep red. It did not appear to be wounded anywhere at all. Florentine had not told any of the other little girls about her bird, not even Eglentyne, and would not today relate the tale of a red bird, either. The bird was her secret.

The next morning, the fourth, she heard the bird cooing before she opened her eyes, and she wondered what colour it would be. And she wondered, were its chirps due to hunger or of thirst? Because she had fed it and watered it. Yet this day the bird was black and Florentine went around in despair that whole day throughout the incense lessons and faking-of-natural-fires-in-glades lessons, even though the bird itself did not seem terribly depressed that it was night-coloured. Eglentyne did not choose to play with grumpy Florentine and ran off to practice natural fires with Ermintrude instead, Ermintrude being the girl with the black braids of the angry greyfruit seeds.

All night in her faltering, mildewing, wilting lean-to, of olde tightening wood that was shrinking, unfresh, Florentine tossed and turned and wondered anew what colour that the captive bird who would not fly away would next be. The bird had taken her mind off her grief, which was a good thing. It was a good thing. But a bird changing colours might not be a good thing. What colour would it be, what colour would it be? Perhaps when she woke up, the bird would be gold and that would mean she was an optimist and that might mean her grief was gone.

The morning bird was green. It had green feathers. Leaf-bird. The bird was entirely green on this fifth morning. She looked upon it.

She pushed open the entrance again, as she had done each time on the previous four mornings, and this time the green bird hopped up to the hinge of leaves and flew away. The bird let her stay there in the lean-to. She let the bird fly away. The bird green. It was leaving the lean-to for green leaves, or at least for a future of green leaves once the remaining snow, melting, had vanished. It was leaving for the green leaves. It was green. It was beautiful. It was beautiful and the blue sky.

Jack's therapist had once introduced him to a Japanese psychological game known as Kokology. This had occurred back in the second year Jack (*un*Jack) had started coming for counselling sessions.

An *un*orthodox therapist, to be sure, and although as previously mentioned of the psychodynamic bent, the therapist spent most of his sessions administering a variety of widely sourced mind games. Just like his policy against revealing a surname, the counsellor had made reticence and mystery a feature on his website – so this methodology hadn't been exactly a shock, and indeed Jack had found it an attractive world-view. Jack remembered all this whilst he lay in his bedsit bed, therapist-less.

Then one day a little bird came to Jack's window. It was a blue bird, but it was a blue bird. Jack retrieved a Post-It stuck to the window-latch. It said: *Let it be*. It had now come to this. Living the famous exploratory mind-game of The Blue Bird in real-time, accompanied by Beatles lyrics. This development would fit with the recent Martin episodes and the little girl with antlers, too. What should Jack have done with such a bird; shooed it out? It didn't matter. The blue bird would refuse to get out. The entity writing the yellow Post-It notes had implied that Jack should welcome the bird in and Jack was feeling obedient.

Jack ate the last of his Ebola crackers on a trencher with some dill pickles, and then thought to offer the blue bird a glass full of three gloopy egg yolks and some diamonds. The bird was grateful and drank it all up.

" 'A touch of cannibalism'," said Jack, aloud. Yet he left the window open. Blue drone didn't fly out. Jack thought of drones; the concept had come to him easily. Drones had been everywhere recently – then had gone extinct as of late, like the black helicopters. But this drone looked very much like a blue bird. This drone was a bird. It was not a male bee; it was a bird. It was not extinct; it was a bird.

The next day the bird had turned a different colour instead of being blue. It was now yellow, which was a further interesting development. For Jack, yellow would always mean egg yolks and Post-Its. Happy-Jack observed the bird and set to drinking his coffee. It was instant coffee, also leftover from the Ebola scare. There had also been a bag of rice, in which he had been surprised to dig up a mobile phone. He had turned it on; it had beeped into an apple but caught no signal. He still had his coffee and he looked at the yellow bird. He left out some cracker crumbs for it and some more water. It partook. Which was good. Because therefore he knew it wasn't going to die before the next morning. Instead, it was going to turn into a ruby-coloured bird the next morning. Was it now a cardinal and not a bluebird or canary; did colours shift species? This was all unclear for Jack. He knew what would come next, according to Kokology, but the nuances of everything - *everything* - were tricky.

He knew what colour the red bird would be the following fourth morning, too. This was because he had at one time committed the entire Kokology game called The Blue Bird to memory. It was black. It was a bluebird then a canary then a cardinal now a raven. What did it signify that the feathers were currently black? Was sable a bold colour or a defeat?

Those were not the questions that mattered, as the kokological shrink had always said; the question that mattered was what colour you thought the bird would be on the fifth and final morning. Would it stay black, or turn back to blue again? Would it turn white or even gold? Those were your choices. If it returned gold, that was potentially beautiful and transcendent. Staying black perhaps indicated that you were a depressed person. That was never nice. Yet the memory fragments of the rules were nebulous. What if the bird just plain went missing before the fifth day, as the shrink had done? Jack, despite his hubris, could not *really* remember the significance of anything.

Predicaments are all very well when they are games, purely suppositional, but when a predicament is real for you, as it was for Jack right then, things feel entirely different. He had no theory, for example, as to whether he had a wife and daughter and was a CIA spook, as the yellow Post-It notes kept insisting. He had no theory as to where his therapist had trotted off to, or why it was currently difficult to get a signal on his mobile phone. He had no

theory – *absolutely* no theory – as to what
colour the bird might be the next morning.
As opposed to the game, he would have to
experience his life rather than choose it.

The next morning, the bird was a bright
green, which had not even been listed in the
options.
UnJack stared balefully at the green
bird, even though he was secretly fond of
it. He sipped with deep meaning from his
bitter instant coffee, then went over to the
window sill again to reassert that he had
left it open. Yet the green bird did not fly
out. It winged its way to Jack's shoulder.

*

"*The Blue Bird*

One day a bird suddenly flies through a win-
dow into your room and is trapped. Something
about this lost bird attracts you, and you
decide to keep it. But to your surprise,
the next day the bird has changed colour
from blue to yellow! This very special bird
changes colour again overnight -- on the
morning of the third day it is bright red,

and on fourth it turns completely black.
What is the colour of the bird on fifth day?

The bird doesn't change colour at all;
it stays black.

The bird turns back to the original
blue.

The bird turns white.

The bird turns golden coloured.

Key to The Blue Bird

The bird that flew into your room seemed like
a symbol of good fortune, but suddenly it
changed color, making you worry that happiness would not last. Your reaction to this
situation shows how you respond to difficul-
ties and uncertainty in real life.

1. Those who said the bird stays black
have a pessimistic outlook.

2. Those who said the bird turns blue
again are practical optimists.

3. Those who said the bird turns white
are cool and decisive under pressure.

4. Those who said the bird turns golden
can be described as fearless."

[This Abridged Compilation and English
translation is copyright © to the I.V.S.

Television Co., Ltd., and Yomiuri Telecasting Corporation in the year 2000.]

*

The green bird. Well, it flew away eventually, out through Jack's window. In the event of this colour, Jack had broken somehow, somewhere, the rules.

***

She would never forget heroic elderly ferns that grew in the secret glade near her oak. Orange and gold and yellow were the old dead ferns, tending flat towards the ground, rusted up on their driest, most frail edges. All revealed by the melt. She had forgotten what dead ferns looked like and now it looked like she was remembering. These old ones had fed her tree and she would never dismiss their sacrificial gift. Her tree had several leaves now and its bark was tough. It was going to survive.

She ran back through the woods to Eglentyne. Strange Anglish forest scents, trees all of which with she was not familiar; she liked the fragrances. No lichen on these other trees; did this mean these local trees were not healthy? *A stag, a buck, a hart, a doe. Deep in the forest, where the bad ones go.*

She reached Eglentyne, who was twisting rosemary braid-stalks in the fire for extra-curricular incense practice.

Florentine's cheeks were flushed. "The tree is going to live!" she told her friend, and there were shivers down her back. "There are two leaves upon it!"

Eglentyne threw down the rosemary braids and grabbed Florentine and they whirled around in a short dance. She put both hands on Florentine's shoulders and impulsively kissed her friend on each cheek in turn. "Wonderful! Wonderful!"

"I know!" Florentine grinned back. All the way through entrail-divination practice (frogs, sorry to say; not unknown in American high school biology classes either), all the way through entrail-divination practice that day they would catch the other's eye and grin for the secret joy of it.

*

The tree came loose at times, and went walking with her in her dreams. It had roots that were proving fast now and and yet its roots moved like feet.

It was the next year. It was the next year. She was nearly nine. There were few days where she did not think of her parents and her brothers. Yet some persons were salvageable and some no longer were.

One night she creeped into Eglentyne's lean-to, which was very cramped. "I am walking to find my brothers," she said, "will you come with me?"

Florentine and Eglentyne set off in the late lauds, or what would have been a late lauds if they were not at a school with a state-certified pagan curriculum.

They first walked the woods, which was easy for Florentine, as she was wholly more familiar with forest ways. Eventually the trees grew sparse and there were more glades, and space opening up. Florentine was terrified and excited; she had never left the forest, it had been her entire world, though both her parents came from outside the trees. Eglentyne, on the other hand, came from a town, and she had spoken often of it, and she was familiar with the ways of field-farmers.

"We will have to steal eggs, and possibly take pies from windows," she informed Florentine confidently.

They came to a hamlet. Florentine's eyes grew wide – cottage upon cottage, cabin upon cabin, perhaps even a dozen or more!

(Dozen is not a Anglish word, not at *all*. Not like good old-fashioned twelve. Dozen has the etymological whiff of the Norman, with their onzes and their douzes, all the way up in ol' *base-dix*. You knows hows it goes, *mon seigneur*. *You* knows hows it goes.)

Eglentyne had walked this hamlet before and she named the streets for Florentine as they slipped through the alleys in early morning when only the bakers were up: Ladysmith Street, Holywell Street.

"For indeed *ladies* can be blacksmiths, too," Eglentyne

told Florentine, with some authority.

"And what is a blacksmith?" asked Florentine.

Eglentyne sighed and patted her friend's hand. "Now we must steal a strawberry pie," she said. "Where did you say your brothers were?"

"The Witch-lady said she would take them to a Spital."

"And after we steal a strawberry pie, we will pay a visit to the Spital."

*

"There's the Spital," Eglentyne pointed out to Florentine, her mouth still full of fruit and pastry.

Florentine had never seen a building so huge. And look, here was what Eglentyne was now naming to be a tended and organised "garden," far different than a forest glade.

"Yes, look at the statues too in this 'garden'," Florentine whispered back to Eglentyne, testing the new word. There were depictions made in both stone and also bush, topiary and granite carved sharp that fringed the walkway up to the hospital. The bushes and chipped rock slabs were of beasts and heroes – King Arthur and several saints, all of whom Florentine recognised from her mother's fairy tales; a Satyr and a Nymph; and beasts her mother had referred to as "improbable," including a dragon, a unicorn, a tiger and a sphinx.

Further back was a pond, equally manicured. A dangerous pond? We shall see.

Florentine and Eglentyne tread up the walkway and arrived at the locked front gate. And it was then and only then that Florentine saw the waiting others, five in total. These three men and two women were dressed in rags. One of the women had her jaw bound up in an equally filthy sling, stained dark red and yellowed.

"Leprous," whispered Eglentyne, as she took her friend's arm. Florentine had heard of such illness; her mother and father had named it something fearful like the Pest, except sometimes you lived after all and sometimes you lived most wretchedly. Florentine did not know what to say to these pilgrims. There was such a contrast as concerned this very Spital, where perhaps her own brothers would be found – oh, her heart beat quickly at that thought! – this very Spital with its tidy garden full of depictions and a fishpond, and these poor folk, with their scabs and dirty faces and bruised arms.

"Are you visitors as well, like we?"

"They will not let us in," said the woman with the bound jaw. She was not too old; she was more or less the age of Florentine's own mother, had she lived. "We cannot even peer in, as they have temporarily blocked the Leper's Squint."

The dirtiest of the men reached into the torn pockets of his cloak and removed a small golden bell, and rang it, loon birdsong and water on the air, a rivulet, and Florentine saw how Eglentyne flinched. The high sound was eerie, doubtless, but it was no more than that. The bell's peal meant nothing to Florentine. The bell man tucked away his ornament again. "Nay. Such transitions are not meant for us. No Canaic *eau* to vine." His throat was bittersweet. "No matter how many paternosters that we breathe out through our decrepit lungs; no matter the high count of our inhaled *ave* decades. Our affliction is considered troubling like syphilis, the wage of sin."

Eglentyne was restless, but Florentine trembled. She had understood almost nothing of what he had said. "But you are sick. Is it not a Spital where they do cure the sick?"

Eglentyne pushed past Florentine then that morning and battered her fist against the dark oaken door with the cruel filigree iron latch carved in the semblance of a fruit tree and a snake. "Let us in! Let us in!" She did not look to Florentine, not even to appeal to her to stop talking to the waiting pilgrims destitute.

Florentine, though, gazed at Eglentyne, with her dark blond braids and the freckles on the back of her throat. The pilgrims had wounds on their unwashed necks.

The latch with the fruit tree was pushed open, and the small iron man that reached for the fruit on the opposite lock-side saw it go further from his reach. It was difficult to see inside the Spital, for it was so bright outside the Spital. Florentine could still taste strawberry jam on her lips, raspberries.

The pilgrims behind them all began to ring their

golden and silver and glass bells at once, and to appeal permission to enter. The woman fell to her knees and cried most piteously.

The sister at the door – for she was a nun, in the same way that the Blue School sisters were nuns for nonconcordable gods – ignored the pilgrims coldly, though she let Eglentyne and Florentine step in, pushed aside the other rag-bound hands that were getting in the way with their grasping and entreating, and firmly turned the key.

Eglentyne took a step forward, wondering at the great chapel.

"Not so fast," said the nun.

Unexpected. Eglentyne and Florentine looked sharply at each other.

The nun grasped their hand each with her own outstretched. She revealed her neck to show a beard, for she was in addition a monk, it seemed. "I will hear your full and true confessions now."

As Florentine didn't know what a "confession" was, she looked to Eglentyne, who was muttering the same words Florentine had heard from outside the Spital gate, words of breads and family relationships and fruits and temptation. It sounded rather like their morning as so far.

"I have offended in thought and deed," Florentine overheard. Blonde Eglentyne had her fingers crossed behind her back. "I am heartily sorry for disobedience by drawing pictures in the dirt with a stick during Oak lessons –"

"Which lessons would those be? Never mind," said

the sister/brother, puffing up her short beard with her closed fist a little.

"And for deception by distracting the Blue Mother with inane questioning, and by disobedience again whereby we have gone withershins, in a contrary direction to regulations, and we have sneaked away here, to this holy house of healing."

"There is no sin in attempting to come closer to Jesu and His works," the grey sister/brother said piously, "you will be forgiven for that."

"And for stealing a strawberry pie that was setting out to cool."

"Fifteen-thousand *aves* and two hundred paternosters by the middle of next week," clipped in the underpriest.

"I am heartily sorry," concluded Eglentyne in a surly voice.

When it concerned the sister/brother, Eglentyne seemed to know all the right words to say, but then Eglentyne had lived in this strange world of houses, cobbles, pies, nuns and monks before.

The nun-abbé in question here was looking at Florentine expectantly.

"She doesn't know any of that, no examination or paternosters or anything," explained Eglentyne.

"A little heathen, isn't she," said the double-gendered cleric, "well, Spital rules, a few sins first I must absolutely hear, before I grant absolution and let you come in further."

There was the most glorious music coming from

inside the chapel, like all spring buds were singing at once. Florentine felt water run down her spine. She had only heard her parent's – well-loved – folk songs before, and birdsong, and the chanting from the Blue School, and a few more tunes there. But this was different and angelic must be what they called it; there were many human voices together; that must be one of the advantages of a town, the joining in multiple various vox. Rose hips in her mind, both sweet and sour-high, then compressing and soaring in complexity; the voices were singing the word *gloria* and it indeed was all glorious and perhaps even Christendom was all glorious if this was what Christendom meant.

Florentine felt uncertain in regards to her forthcoming confession, but she mimicked Eglentyne.

"I also stole the pie, or half of it, anyway. And I ran away from the Blue School this morning."

The cleric cocked an eyebrow, an act always envied by Florentine. "I have not heard of that Order."

"And I recaptured the tree, and hid it and grew it. But I do not know if that was wrong."

"Don't you?" The little pierce to the underpriest's eye was stronger now. He stepped forward, so close that his breasts brushed Florentine's own chest. "Little pagan," he said softly, almost as a form of endearment, "little pagan." He stepped back, gazing at her scalp. The word *magnificat* was being sung in flickering bell-voices by the unseen chorus ahead of them in the Spital chapel. Florentine thought the word close sister to *magnificent* or even liberating *magnacarta*.

"Almsgiving," he said with decision. "That is your penance."

Florentine looked with worry at her friend. "Shouldn't I be given chants about the bread prayer and the fruits, as with Eglentyne?"

"Oh, we decide, not you. It's either vestments or alms from you, wee pagan. And you do not look prepared for sackcloth. Now where are your alms?"

She trembled. This cleric was far more severe than the Blue Mother, and asked impossible things of her. "I have no coins."

The partial abbé was staring at her scalp again, where her braids had been wrapped round her antlers. "Then one little shave off the cartilage will do nicely for almsgiving."

"*What?!*"

"Unwrap your hair," said the Spital door-priest, "show me your puckish little demon horns."

"They're *antlers*," said Florentine defiantly. "Like on a *stag*, not on a *demon*."

"Unwrap them, sprite."

"Do what he says," said Eglentyne, under her breath. Eglentyne always had a sense for deciphering these types of occasions.

Florentine unwrapped her hair and stared the holy man in his bitter currant eyes. Each antler had been growing and now had a Y-prong as well. Florentine could use them quite easily to gouge the man's cranberry eyes in his pastry-doll face.

The cleric took out a carving knife from his cloak, much longer than Florentine's hidden jack-knife, and cut a long curling sliver off the left antler, an extended skinny toenail of a sliver – such an act hurt; it hurt! – and then deposited both the shorn coil and the knife back into his pocket and chuckled.

Florentine did not re-twist her hair to cover her animal parts and instead stared the man down. Her hair loose. Her mind, tongue loose.

"I grant you absolution, both; I wash away your respective iniquities, and with penance assigned and alms bestowed, you now may enter. And, please, state your business and/or infirmity."

"My brothers, Beaman, Eldritch and Percival. They are goats. They were brought to a Spital, likely this one as Eglentyne believes it to be the closest, brought by a ... by a woman with a hairy stripe on each cheek, but quite different from your own beard. My brothers also have beards, though. They would have been in distress."

"Ah, the saintly brothers! The little goats," said the man. "Yes, we do indeed have them here," she said, "they have been here for one year and then some nice weeks now."

Florentine burst into a smile: "Wonderful! They are fine; they are healed; I can see them?"

"Indeed you can. And particularly at this moment when you are free of sins venial. The absence of sins mortal is an assumption but, to be safe, absolution covers those too. Girls, I will lead you to them now."

Florentine and Eglentyne trailed after the nun-monk into the reaches of the sanctuary, which was shaped into a cross form, the same as churches often were, or so Eglentyne was telling Florentine. On one side were cots, where the sin-innocent poor and the paying sinful lay, and on the other side was a chapel wherefrom was coming the high arias and chimes, the bell-like music. It was dark in this chapel sec-tion and cavernous – Florentine had never been in a building other than her parents' cabin before – and, "Here they are; I take your leave," murmured the monk/nun, and left the two girls on their own, whereupon they ventured closer.

It was not at all entirely dark, Florentine saw as her eyes adjusted, there was in fact a great window through which pulsed sun, watering down pictures from coloured glass. It was not so different in conceptualisation from the Blue School in that the portrait was an enormous tree. The tree had cherries red and oranges orange and lemons yellow and plums blue and grapes purpure and green-apples green and white-peaches white and dates brown and olives black and even, Florentine spied them, greyfruits grey. All these fruits grew from one tree, a tree miraculous, for such a glass tree is not found in botany books, such a mixture of a tree.

On huge stone slabs whitened from foot-use poured these colours and, as Florentine and Eglentyne moved across the chapel towards the front, their hair, bodies, freckles and antlers were smeared with rivery lights, watery red and yel-low and et cetera. The music was coming from the front;

from a group of individuals perhaps forty strong. It was cold in the chapel, cold in the Spital overall, and it was warmer outside in the weather and very much warmer.

Florentine could almost see everything, as her eyes became further used to the darkness. She could smell stamped candles, the smoke and something like charred raven. How she had always hated the scent of burnt feathers. "What are they singing?" she asked of Eglentyne, who had shown herself to have more knowledge of Christendom's ways than Florentine had previously suspected.

"They are singing the *Opus Dei*, the work of God," muttered Eglentyne.

The music truly sounded like the work of God, or gods, so beautiful it was.

The iris expands; the eye sees at last. For there were Florentine's brothers, now castrated, singing of gods' work in the Spital chorus, with beautiful goatish and still human voices. Beaman trilled a solo, his castrato baying high as a snow's cloud. Their voices were prized. This was clear.

Florentine's throat closed, and she clutched Eglentyne's hand sharply. "Beaman! Percy! Eldritch!" She ran up to the choir, who were standing before the window of Yggdrasil, with all the glass fruits above them and glass animals, including a snake; and glass humans, including a naked man and woman at the window's downmost edge. The sun powerful, the music powerful.

The choir stopped singing.

"Florentine," Eldritch said in a cold voice. Statement,

not a question. And a statement without, unexpectedly, a sense of surprise.

"Yes!" cried Florentine. Eglentyne was more naturally brave and outgoing than Florentine, but it was Florentine who ran up to them, grabbed at their hooves and ruffled the stiff white hair on top of their heads, where goats like to be scratched and petted.

Percy, even Percy, drew slightly away from her.

"It is good to see you, sister," said Beaman, formally.

Florentine was faltering. She kissed them, hugged them. "It has been one year and six weeks. I have thought of you three strongly, every hour." She looked down at them; their wounds had healed to pink scars. But they were large scars.

Eglentyne and the rest of the choir, who were, aside from the brothers, all humans save a hawk perched on a woman's wrist and one dog soprano, now looked upon Florentine and her brothers.

"We are happy here," Beaman told her. "We have been Converted."

"You have forgot our forest ways?"

"We have been taught to remember the mysteries, joys and sorrows of Jesu innate in all once sin is flushed," Beaman corrected her. "They heal bodies here, but first they heal souls."

"We shall pray for you," added Eldritch, "and for the witch who brought us here, whose motivations were good though she was heathen."

"We believe in redemption for all God's sinners," said little Percy.

"The sinners of all the gods?" It was a heady concept to Florentine.

"One God," said the brothers in chorus. "Three gods. One God. Three in one."

"I am confused," admitted Florentine. It was as baffling as Mother Blue Cap's endless nature chants, and as equally contradictory. Florentine rallied, and looked Beaman straight in his yellow eyes, and she grasped his right forelock in emphasis while the others looked on. "I too have been to a School in this past year and six weeks," she told them, "a Blue School. It is perhaps similar to your lessons here. It is rigid. It is not so different in its way. And yet I have not swallowed every utterance as fact."

"Though you were not gravely injured, either," said Beaman, reasonably, looking down on himself, "and in need of succour both physical and of the spirit."

"I understand you; that makes sense," said Florentine, with a perception of desperation that she was again losing her brothers, "and I should have protected you much better. I never should have left you, or I should have accompanied you here to Spital-healing. I did not. But I am only a child myself."

"That is true," allowed Beaman.

"And I too have had loss and injury; I cut off my antlers and was left bleeding."

"And your antlers have grown back," Beaman

pointed out, "and our sacs and sticks have not, and never will. Do you begrudge us the only perks of that, our high, unearthly music sung, and our souls new-salvaged?"

Her antlers, indeed, were growing back.

"I do not begrudge your new happiness!" Florentine was weeping now, and the rainbow window behind Beaman and the rest of them was a blur. "But you are, all three, so churchly cold to me!"

Her brothers looked away from her, even little Percy, and the choir began again to sing the miraculous music, the most beautiful thing Florentine had ever heard, *gloria, gloria,* while outside the lepers tussled to get into the Spital.

In the walk back through the dark forest that night there were still the signs of spring, pollen and freshleaf scent in the hazy air, the twitter of courting birds long past evenfall.

Eglentyne held Florentine's hand in comfort and sang to her. "A hind, an elk, a roe, a fawn. Deep in the forest, and then beyond." The Spital pond had not been dangerous in the least. A small, toothy coil missing from her left antler. Disappointment did not diminish, but it was easier when shared.

It was a song chanted occasionally by Brigid in a prayerful state, and Florentine had heard it before.

Caribou, moose, havier, deer. Deep in the forest, where there is fear. Six extra weeks of winter this year, too. And now spring blossoms on the heather and vernal fungi, red with white spackles, in the tree crevices. Soon they would be home.

They received only minor punishment from Brigid for being gone a night and a day, some extra chants at fireside and kindling collection for a week of Moon Days. Florentine did consider this far more reasonable than fifteen-thousand aves and two hundred paternosters, or a peeled antler.

*

It was three years later. It was three years later. Florentine was thirteen.

She and Eglentyne and Ermintrude were now amongst the oldest in the Blue School. No one spoke of how a girl was to leave; one day a girl was there, and the next day a girl was not. One day Ermintrude with the black braids was there, and then she was not. And then it was just Eglentyne and Florentine, and the world became much crueler.

They thatched together rosemary and finger-spun fur fluff; it was an educated craft and their fingers were not too wise yet. They sat in a circle, fifty girls; for, as Ermintrude had left, so had come another to take her place at hearth, a younger girl wandering out alone in the forest, wide-eyed and talking of wars and decapitations, a young girl who screamed in the night. I wonder, thought Florentine, I wonder who left that I might come, and I wonder where she went.

They sat in a circle. The new child was ignored for the most part, which is a type of cruelty itself, but Florentine was not. The girls' fingers wove and knotted cloths from the weeds and soft rabbit fur and, rumour had it, the shorn hair of the girls who grew old and left the Blue School, being never seen again. So as she finger-wove, Florentine kept one eye out for dark strong hair that looked like that of Ermintrude, but was relieved that she never saw it.

"What are you peering at so closely, Florentine?" said a nasty girl called Alyssonne. Alyssonne was the leader of all girls, though she was only middle-aged among them. She had ringlets that were golden and tiny black eyes.

"Nothing..." said Florentine. She looked down at her hands, suddenly ashamed that she had so macabrely questioned Ermintrude's legacy and fate, even to herself. She could hear Alyssonne talking still, but she made herself look only at the soft fur twining through her fingers, as she used to narrow thread with her mother, back at home. Wool, fingers, then thread, then cloth, a miracle.

"*Nothing...*" mimicked Alyssonne, with Florentine's tone. The word caught Florentine's ears this time. She looked up just in time to see Alyssonne with both hands sticking up from her scalp, like antlers, and then Alyssonne quickly put her hands away, as did another girl who had joined in with the same gesture. Alyssonne and the other girl giggled, but said nothing.

"Stop it," said Eglentyne, in a loud voice.

Florentine looked down with shyness, and she looked up to see Alyssonne waggling her fake hand-antlers again, but the ringleted girl stopped in action just as quickly. All the little girls save Eglentyne did laugh, even the new little battle-scarred girl, though black-braided Ermintrude would not have chortled, had she been here.

"What are *you* looking at, Florentine?" Alyssonne asked again. "*Nothing...?*" She made her voice Florentine's voice again, on the last word.

Alyssonne turned to Katherine, the girl at her side, and loudly whispered that Florentine had horns because she was a cuckold, and cuckolds were cheats, and that cheats were not to be trusted.

Katherine whispered back just as loudly that on the contrary, Florentine's horns were because she was the devil's niece, for the devil had horns, and that Florentine had a tail too, though she had been hiding it from the others for the last four years. She was not here orphaned by the plague, but because the devil had no wish to pay for her babysitting anymore.

Alyssonne whispered back booming for all to hear that Florentine's good friend Eglentyne had been found clinging to her dead parents' sheets, abreast their corpses, and that wandering soldiers had had to pry her from the bedclothes while she cried most piteously, like a small kitten. This was in fact covert but true, Florentine knew, and was a confidence that Eglentyne had divested to Florentine practically upon meeting and to Alyssonne two years ago, when the other girl had been new and seemed particularly trustworthy and vulnerable herself after a greyfruit spring ceremony.

Eglentyne looked up sharply and saw Alyssonne and Katherine both making fake antlers again. "I said to stop your mockery."

"Come all and everyone," said Alyssonne, rising to her feet and smiling a pretty smile, "come with me and Katherine to wade in wells, though only those who have shed their antlers may come, or those who have shed their friends with antlers. And are you coming, Eglentyne?" Alyssonne stared down at Eglentyne with rabbit-dropping eyes.

Florentine watched as Eglentyne remained seated and thatching but stared steadily back, until Alyssonne became flustered and turned on her heels. She raced down to the nearest holy well, with all others following her but Florentine and Eglentyne.

They were still sitting cross-legged. Eglentyne's voice was warm to Florentine. "You've dropped a loop there, but I see you did there the same on the other side too, so the weave has evened out. It looks just right," she concluded.

That night Florentine crept out through the woods to visit her tree on her own, and once there she clasped the growing oak against her heart, and felt very sorry for herself. But then she stopped feeling very sorry for herself, for she had Eglentyne and things were not so bad this year, actually. Not so bad.

***

Bluebells, bluebells, everywhere. Jack nearly tripped over a nosegay on his WELCOME mat when he exited. Why would someone leave a little bundle of wildflowers there? It wasn't even a proper bouquet.

He discarded the small bunch of fresh bluebells into the recycling bin and, as he closed its lid, he noted that every single house along his road in the Haringey Ladder also had laid before it a similar, anonymous nosegay. So he wasn't even special. Not even to a potential stalker. This depressed

him further, and so Jack walked along his
road discarding into the rubbish bins his
neighbours' bestowed bouquets, so that no
one else would have to undergo a similar
depression.

When he'd finished doing his charitable
work, he paused for a moment. It was pro-
foundly hot and so he looked up at the sun.
Red ladybug. He'd heard of blood moons and
wondered if this was the same thing.

Finally, he stepped out onto Green
Lanes again, as was his pattern, and paused
for a moment outside his local corner newsagent's. The most current edition of the *Sunday Sport* for sale in the window was from
three weeks past. Not that Jack was a sub-
scriber, but it was relevant to note the
date. Several locusts fluttered by, hardly a
swarm. He wiped a sole bead of sweat from
his brow.

Several paces further down the high
street, there was a dead dog with its throat
torn out; Jack recognised it as one of the
pack that had been running stray last week-
end. The deceased dog's front legs revealed
strips of fat and torn muscle. It looked
like meat. In some countries, it *was* meat.
In all human pre-histories, *thou* wert meat.

Jack Sprat. Would eat no fat.

He reminded himself that he needed to go shopping today; his refrigerator was running on the bare side.

He walked back to the corner newsagent's for such groceries and combustibles. There was someone at the counter, a young individual of the female persuasion with a five-point set of deer antlers. She was probably helping her parents out at the shop; it was Take Your Surreally Zoomorphic Daughter to Work Day. Jack felt it rude to bring up the subject of the appendages; he kept his eyes on the floor, but pushed forward three packages of pita bread, two old oranges, some Alka-Seltzer and a ten-pound note.

"Thank you..." The stagged girl seemed equally shocked to be a shop girl in early adolescence. She looked at Jack very inquisitively, and far too familiarly. They had run into each other a few times in his roaming subconscious, but he was loathe to admit to it. "Perhaps you would also like to be taking notes on current world events on some... on some rectangular papyrus sheets the colour of urine, and bound with sappy glue?"

Jack pushed the proffered plastic-sealed package of Post-It notes back across the till counter space. "I don't need these at the moment."

"Are you sure?"

Jack wasn't sure at all. The change from the ten-pound note came to only two pounds, forty-seven pence.

Once he'd exited, he looked back through the newsagent's window to see that the girl was still observing him, as well.

***

It was the next year. It was the next year. She was nearly fourteen. On May Day, she went to her tree. Her oak had taken on the shape of a man, but whether a male man or a female man, she did not know. She was growing a green man or maybe a green witch. She was growing her own lover.

She had been thinking of lovers recently, imagining them, flicking at her or burrowing into her; how her body might stretch towards them, the dry ache in reference to them. And then she would wake into her leaf-bed and go into her morning, her mind haunted by these un-lovers, and she would think of their strokes on her all day as she practised the old processions, and everything took on a new angle; the processions seemed heavy with expectation; the chanting a preamble to something, she could not name it, a tight preamble that was something yet to come. Her heart had been beating fast through most of the Blue School duties these days. Though she had been rising towards the sky herself, growing breast blossoms, hair, staggered-interval antlers. Though. When she had last seen her oak tree in the quiet forest, the tree had now achieved a height taller than she was herself.

She returned in afternoon. She had red blood and brown blood on her thighs since the morning, but she had told no one, not even Eglentyne. She told the three sisters that she was feeling faint, and Mother Brigid had looked at her quite piercingly. But since it was a cross-quarter day and there would be revels into the night, they let her build her lean-to early in the afternoon already, so she could rest.

Once she was there, she stripped off her jerkin and saw the blood and clots run the length of her legs. She turned on her side, for she did not know if she welcomed the sight or no, and she went to sleep.

***

Florentine walked the Desert. It was a Desert; she had heard stories from her father, who in turn had heard stories from Venetian merchants when he had been a young man. There were lands of Deserts and blue birds called Peacocks. Florentine shuddered here without Eglentyne, for most adventures were better with Eglentyne, whose pace was steadfast.

A Desert was a place without growth, which was the cruelest of thoughts. There was yellow sand here, grime, but then there were no trees. What had happened to her trees? *What has happened to my trees*? whispered Florentine to herself. She would have been glad even for a dangerous lake. *What has happened to my tree, singular?*

Dream. *I am walking in a strange place. I am walking in the strangest of places.* She passed by the discarded shell of an enormous insect. The cocoon was light brown and feathery in texture, but bigger than herself. There was an exit to it, a hole as big as a human. She looked at it then walked more quickly away; she didn't want to meet the butterfly from that particular crisp egg.

Moments later, she passed another object – a huge plum, again bigger than she was herself. She looked up into the clouds, but there was no yggdrasil releasing seeds; there were no trees at all. There was, however, sweat on her brow.

She thought of her status here in the Desert, with her new blood falling dark down her thighs. No one observed her; she simply walked and simply dripped.

Evening chill would be coming; she hugged herself to keep her warmth within her. Like the cocoon and the fruit, her shadow was also much larger than she was herself; her antler-shadows could have been an enormous tree unto themselves, the branches. The oversized greyfruit was still there. As she stared at it, the greyfruit began to glow green. Soon the whole fruit mass was a bright spring green and lit from the inside as if there were a green candle there. She did not know what a green emotion was. She had always had problems reading the greyfruits aside from red (angry) and purple (anticipatory).

Florentine stopped walking in the Desert, however, when she came to a lake. A wish granted. It was her own dangerous lake, but in the middle of this Beach. The silvered breadth of it was encircled by sand. There were none of the growing things around it, no reeds or rushes, no pond scum, no trees (no *trees!*). But it was her lake nevertheless.

She looked down into it. She saw a girl of fourteen with brown hair and a stag's antlers. She saw with, and she saw, eyes grey like the fruit trees. She saw dry lips, a few freckles. A serious girl. She took her own eyes up again; not for her, the daffodil mirrors from her father's Venetian stories; not for her, mother-fables concerning the untranslatable languages of birds.

"Not for me," said Florentine, again to herself, or perhaps to someone else. She was bleeding again and she didn't like that, though she knew from the Blue Mother's talks and from the other girls that it was normal and eventual, though none of the Blue School girls had ever bled, that she also knew.

She kept walking to see that there were Easter eggs in the barren-sand landscape, decorated shells highlighted by the late-afternoon rays. And there were oversized sugar dioramas in the shapes of Easter eggs with one side an open window, a morality play as with the glockenspiel tableaux of Munich and Strasbourg, little dramas where Life and Death and Church play out their clockwork roles. Yet all these varying Easter eggs secreted by an inefficient Bunny were not at all well deposited. In fact, such were not hidden at all. They were nestled at erratic intervals throughout the desert as far as she could see ahead of her.

She turned around to see blood on the sand. And now she would always be able to find her way back to the cottage in the woods. Home. For as far as she could see behind her, whence she had come, she saw her eggs.

She swivelled and proceeded forward towards one of the Easter eggs. She saw that it was blue-green, and chicken-egg-sized when she got close to it, but it was not an Easter egg after all. Instead a turquoised bejewelled egg, yolk and white blown from it via a pinhole and then decorated to be frail; to be Fabergé. Florentine hesitated to pick it up. Florentine did not pick the egg up. She left the egg and continued forward in the direction that she had been walking before, walking through the Desert full of jewelled and sugared eggs everywhere, red menses behind her, eggs pushing from single nests in the sand dunes before her.

***

Florentine woke up into the holy day, with blood half-dried and still wet on her crotch, sticky on the green leaves, on her buttocks, on the backs of her thighs, like she were a bright glass of wine spilling over.

***

Martin walks the desert. He grieves Jack; he sorely grieves Jack.

Everywhere Martin looks, there are hidden surprises in the sand. These objects are the opposite of Easter eggs, if the opposite of an egg or seed – potential – is a corpse. Therefore the excising of potentiality. Martin sees the deceased nestled at uneven yet unfortunately regular enough spacings throughout the sand. Here is a plague-riddled likkerman; here is a swollen child of eleven years, dead of floods. *O, bring out your dead.* The body count includes radiation-, hurricane-, heatstroke-, malaria- and post-nuke-post-hoc particle emphysema-fatalities.

So this is not an Easter egg hunt Martin wishes to participate in.

Martin grimly sets his jaw and lo, he keeps walking. He is resilient even in the face of macabre holiday hunts.

It *is* a holiday, actually. It is May Day. Does Martin remember this? It is not clear. The perspective has changed; Jack no longer chooses his own adventure. Jack. Is. Dead. Martin chooses his own adventure now. The perspective shifts; the tense shifts.

May Day, three months after Imbolc, the bust-burst of shrub now, the spurt of cock and cunt now, pink silk hair-ribbons and fertile birdsong. The season is up and day-full, no funeral flowers today despite evidence contrary; nope, fresh bluebells for you milady, milord; drink cum and swap lusty spit.

It *is* a holiday, actually. Does Martin remember this?

If Martin remembers that it is May Day, then you and he both keep reading. That phrasing is used in the imperative sense.

If Martin forgets that it is May Day, and only sees these two-armed, two-legged exemplars of death, then you and he both return to Page 1 and start all over again. That phrasing is used in the imperative sense.

***

On May Day mornings, may-whistles are always made from sycamore. The girls are virgins, naturally, so also cherry-wood for those close to menarche (or secretly in the midst of it, like Florentine). O, traditionally from sycamore, but also ash and willow. O, traditionally sycamore, but also cherry-wood. On May Day, new women drink kirsch and eat cherries jublilee and marischinos. The sap in spring makes the bark slide off the may-whistles more easily. Eventually such may-whistle sticks dry out and they no longer work.

*

"Outside!" Strict hands and scattered, stained leaves; Florentine at fourteen was being pulled from her lean-to.

She stood half-dressed, with her shirt on and her navel downward exposed. She was still dripping blood. There was the trio before her: Brigid, Breesha and Bríg. Despite the awakening, they did not appear rough, nor angry.

"Where are the others?"

"There is no shame," Bríg said softly. "All of us are women, too. Holy wells and lady wells. But now you must leave."

To leave a home, what had become her home, where even its rigidity and stubbornness to the outer world had come to feel safe. Florentine felt panic rise inside her. Not death then, nothing macabre as that. When girls became women at the Blue School, they simply... left. "Where is Eglentyne? I must say goodbye to Eglentyne..."

"You are well equipped now," said the Blue Mother Brigid, and for once her tone was gentle. "You can eat of the woods and take what you need. You are kind. You have developed skepticism and comparative thinking, as we hope for all our girls. You are a success. You will survive." There were tears and pride-gleam in Brigid's eyes, both glittering in the afternoon sunlight.

Mother-aged Breesha took Florentine's hand and stroked its overside. Maiden-age Bríg, not too older than

Florentine herself but with her head shaved and shorn, looked on. "You will do better than survive," said Breesha, "you will thrive."

Florentine looked around wildly. "Where is Eglentyne? I must bid her farewell, at least!"

"The other girls, for they are still girls," said Brigid, "are in Glade No. 2 for chanting and root-digging."

"You need to go."

Florentine was not sure which of the three said that; or perhaps they all said it in chorus, for she wrapped a cloth between her legs, pulled on hose, and a cloak over her shoulders, and a pair of stiff-soled boots of cowskin, and a brown hood over her curls and horns. Her tears were streaking, running nearly muddy down her face. She turned her back on the Three Sisters and she did not look back even to her lean-to, a version of which into many years ago a blue bird had flown, and then flown out bright green.

She could not say goodbye to Eglentyne and that fingernail-scraped at her heart more than it was possible for her to utter out loud. She could go to her brothers, and attempt to cajole sweetness from their memories again. Or. She could go to her secret sapling in the forest. What she could *not* do, could never do again, apparently, was to return to the Blue School, or to be a girl. She stepped into the forest on her leather soles.

*

It was in the same forest two days later, near the creek, where from a distance, standing on the opposite bank and hidden by the willows, she saw them fish a body with blonde braids and freckles from the waters, and where she could overhear the other girls' voices carrying over the water, voices that said that Eglentyne had been searching for Florentine, and had lost her footing in the place where the waters were tricky, and that Eglentyne had tried to swim but could not do so, and that as her body was pushed through the waters rushing that her throat had been cut half through by a fishline, red necklace.

Florentine sat deeper in the forest hours later, dry-eyed, and tried to imagine an upbringing where one did not learn how to swim in lakes. It would have to have been an upbringing amongst towns and stolen strawberry pies. It was then that Florentine heard the bellow of a Horn, the trumpet that meant a Wild Hunt again.

She stood and faced the sounds in the dark woods. She could hear the dogs. Who was it chasing her, was it the Witch, the bird that she had taken five days to fall in love with, a hunter with a sharpened knife?

Her horns were strong this time, not the little girl-ish prongs she'd had the last time the Hunt rushed through. She thought of her mother and her father, the snow, the barbecued owl. Now it was summer; it was summer and she stood taller. The dogs – wolves? – grew closer and Florentine became confused. She smelled and sensed that there were other deer there with her. Was she Hunted or the Hunter? She was part deer, yet she raised an arm and waved it in the air through the gnats and dust and she felt obedience; she was controlling the Hunt. The dog sounds whimpered, and grew quiet. The keen of frightened fawns grew dimmer. Florentine sat cross-legged and raised both hands into the sky, up to her horns, and she felt the power of the trees and the deer and the humans and the dogs rush through her fingers, curling into her palms. She shut her eyes. The Wild Hunt would not come for her, not this time. The Hunt was in her control, this time.

She pushed the hunters away from the deerfolk. She stood to her feet. She would survive this. She would survive. She opened her eyes – Eglentyne would not survive, Eglentyne was gone, Florentine's parents were gone, her brothers were cold – she faltered, Florentine faltered, and she fell to her knees in the moss. The deer around her; they began to cry again, the bucks and the does. Deep in the forest, where the bad one goes.

The terrible Hunt was upon her then, and she did not control it any more, she could only squeeze shut her eyes, and the Hunt bit at her, and lunged at her, and snarled at her, and salivated over her, and she covered her face with her hands; she did not want to see it; she forgot that she had controlled it only moments before.

There was a terrible pain and she believed herself to be dying, that she was being eaten alive by the hounds and by the teeth of whoever their master was, but it was her head being wrenched, and she felt for the second time a loss of her antlers, only this time they were being devoured, bitten off.

When Florentine finally opened her lids, she touched what she already knew; that her antlers were gone; that she bled from atop her head, and from beneath her legs.

Florentine crawled to her oak tree and this time there was a variation; she used her birthday jack-knife and severed strong young branches to make false wooden antlers for herself, and she plunged those boughs into the two gaping wounds atop her head, and then she lay there, weeping, in the glade. The Hunt was gone. And she had failed. She had once again failed to control the Hunt. She now had harmed her own tree by carving off its two strongest branches, as efficient a gelder as a white bird on her brothers. She fell asleep there amongst the mushrooms and starflowers and, when she awoke in the middle of the night, her fake horns were gone; someone had stolen them from her scalp in the night and Florentine had not even felt that bad act.

As she lay there on her side, she saw that she was not the only one left behind by the Hunt, unclear whether that was lucky or nay. She saw that a small grown doe had also been left on its own. It had been ravaged too and one of its horns too had been broken off at the stalk, crumpled. It must have given suck to its first fawn only recently, and of that fawn there was no tell; the youngest deer had been swept up in the Hunt's cruel wake. Florentine crawled over to it, so that she was just within an arm's reach. The doe did not escape; it bayed in low, deep scratch of a voice. But the doe was engorged now; in pain, mastitis and grief all at once.

She stroked the hide of the doe. She saw that she had been mistaken; its antler loss was congenital. It was more than a doe; it should be called a stag too; it was a female stag. It had one short horn, malformed, as if it had not succeeded at being a male. Its fur was kitten-soft and glossy. Her finger brushed the fringes of the long-lashed animal eye, where a tear was forming. This caught at Florentine's throat and at her mind.

She wept, her fingers playing at the doe's teats. She wept for her parents, and for her brothers' manhood, and for the ache of missing all five of them. Her face turned swollen and the doe, the stagtress, whimpered, as Florentine soothed its head in her lap, forest unicorn. The doe with the crumpled horn. The deer called, deep in its female, wounded throat. Florentine wept with her, and clasped her arms around the doe's throat. Her tears fell on her pelt. Florentine wept and wept. Her tears ran down her throat and touched the tips of her breasts, and wetted her arms. The doe was keening, its dugs engorged; it needed to let its milk down, and it struggled to get to all fours. As her little brothers had struggled to their four feet the day they became goatly.

The dark pines and the evergreen sap scent surrounded the two of them, and the moon light meant that both doe and human read nearly blue against the dark-green conifers, a silhouette that showed this pieta, weeping girl, a weeping girl whose tears streamed as she milked the doe, and the stag milk spilled fruitless on the ground, absorbed. The teats squirted; the girl wept; the wind whistled with a cold, pursing breath. Eglentyne, she cried, and pressed her fingers sharp on the doe's small udder, and the only response, for the grimness of death is that it eternally gives no response, was the release of milk onto the soil.

Part II

7

Jack is Alive

It was the kind of dream that he would have liked to have discussed with his therapist, if he still had a therapist. A dream of an abominable snowwoman *née* Sasquatch. A hairy woman. The psychoanalytic elements were practically boundless.

Jack Candle lay in his good bed.

I'll tell you a story about Jack-a-nory, and now my story's begun. Jack be nimble, Jack be quick; Jack has jumped that candlestick. Jack is alive, and likely to live; if he dies in your hand, you've a forfeit to give. Jack again, Jack again, Little Jack Horner. Little Jack Horner, his bed in a corner. Aforementioned corner in the house that Jack built.

For this was indeed the house, and not the hound nor the horn, that belonged to the forest-farmer sowing his corn that fed the blue bird that crew in the morn that woke the priests all shaven and shorn that married the man all tattered and torn that kissed the maiden all forlorn that milked the doe with the crumpled horn that tossed the hound that killed the wife that ate the owl that lay cooked in the house that Jack built.

Because Little Jack Jingle, he used to live single, but when he got tired of that life, Little Jack Jingle, he left off being single, and Little Jack Jingle, he lived with his wife.

Jack-knifes, jackrabbits, hop-hop-hop. Jackhammers, Crackerjack, pop-pop-pop. Jack Mormons, a phonejack. Jack the Ripper, a roast-jack. Aceing-kinging-queening-jacking. Monterey Jack cheese. Carjacking. Jack Russell whelps, a jackass looking pretty. The Union Jack. New Jack City. A Jack-of-all-trades, a Jack-in-the-Box. Jackpot. Jack me off. You don't know jackshit.

He's got cold toes, Jack Frost, but he's full of magic beans. He's got a cold nose, Jack Frost, but he's full of jelly-beans. There was a man named and made of frost that day, and he called himself Jack.

I'll tell you a story, about Jack-a-nory, and now my story's begun. I'll tell you another about Jack and his brothers, and now my story is done.

Jack Candle lay in his good bed.

*

Back during the Ebola scare, which had
never truly come to pass as feared, Jack
had anticipated breaking into his tinned
goods just as he wished he could do now, for
supermarkets had stopped working at present.
Back during the Ebola scare, which had never
truly come to pass as feared, Jack had
planned out exactly what he had needed. And
he had ordered Tesco delivery-to-you a good
three weeks before anyone else would have
started panic-buying. The only one suspicious had been the disgruntled delivery man
hauling the plastic bags full of tins and a
20-kilogram rice bag from the delivery van
into Jack's flat.

That had all taken place a few years
back, a few years back.

Before Jack had started therapy to find
out who, in fact, was Jack.

This is the Tesco man unshaven and
grumpy, who toted the powdered milk that
always went lumpy, that lightened the
instant coffee whose texture was bumpy, that
was drunk by the man who called himself

Jack, with no daughter nor wife, ever the
lack, who read yellow Post-Its both front
and both back,

who dreamed of snowwomen who frightened
humans who grew big moose-horns who travelled with strangers who clutched at sticks
who half-drowned in cave-pools who flew to
the heavens who were harassed by cloud birds
who spat out seedlings that grew up flowers
that were bundled in posies that were left
on the stoop which led to the flat where Jack
lived.

Jack had foreseen that he would have to cook
and boil the food in stored pottles. After
his butane cans for his campstove ran out,
he would need wood. He could dig a firepit in
a quarantined section of the neighbor's back
garden. Jack had wooden furniture in his
bedsit. But how would he cut it? Jack had
thus ordered a small portable wire saw that
looked uncomfortably like a garrotte, a link
not eased by the fact that he bought it from
a military outlet website. But also insur-
ance if the neighbour proved himself to be
unamenable to Jack's proposals.

Jack had pasted into his smartphone, as
well, instructions for building a sanitary

makeshift latrine in the adjacent neighbour's back garden, which he believed himself capable of. He would trade the information for literal squatter's rights. He
bought multiple rolls of toilet paper.

O, he had been prepared; he had been
prepared for years. And now it all had come
to a head, though it seemed something different than a plague, something he could not
find out about even on solar radio because
there were no radio transmissions anymore,
and Jack (a) still did not know his past and
(b) was not even sure whether his neighbour
was still kicking, which might either complicate or simplify Jack's latrine plans.
But it was grim in Jack's flat. O, it was
grim in said flat. The yellow off the Post-
It notes cast a particularly sullen colour
round the room. Jack lay in his good bed.

There was a Post-It stuck to his nose;
that was where all the yellow was coming
from. He sat up in the dirty bed-clothes and
read the Post-It. *Look outside*, it said. He
went to his window and looked outside, down
onto the street. There was the little girl
with stag horns walking by, but not much
else. He shut and then, as an afterthought,
latched the window.

Don't forget your can opener!

***

Martin keeps walking that desert, doesn't he. He feels older than when he started. His stick goes in front of him, *hole-step-step, hole-step-step*. He looks up once into the sky. There is a huge white bird. Actually, it is a dinosaur. Actually, all birds are therapod dinosaurs. So when I say snakes taste like chicken, it's less humorous than you might imagine (dinos not technically reptiles; let's not get picky). Actually, that is not particularly humorous, anyway. Actually, I am less humorous and more capricious than you might imagine. I am your narrator. In less than two paragraphs, I am going to send you back to Page 1.

Up in the sky, when Martin cranes his neck, he sees a white bird. Though it is not a *crane*. The position is awkward. Though it is not a *Great Auk*. He jerks his head downwards. Though it has not been basted with the appropriate spices to make it *jerk chicken*. It is a winged dinosaur. It is white-hot like a glowing goddess, such as if winged Isis herself were a dinosaur. (Actually, there is/was an Indian dinosaur called *Isisaurus*, but it is/was not a therapod and therefore not a bird, white or no, big or no.) The white dino-saur-bird is carrying sticks in her mouth; is she your friend, Brigid-the-Cailleach, shown to be strict but well-meaning, or is she of her castrating and darker bent?

Martin ignores the white bird; Martin rubs sand on his bald head; Martin plugs his stick ahead of him in the sand over and over again and keeps trudging; Martin daydreams of violets and vaginas and lead-casting and green leaves floating in cave waters; Martin goes back to Page 1. *Chicken coop. Loop-de-loop.*

***

Florentine was dreaming of an odd world and walking in it, a world with high red brick houses and stone streets with large, brightly painted iron sculptures on the sides and with white painted instructions on the streets themselves that made no sense: BUS LANE. NO PARKING. This was peculiar to her but not astonishing, for, remember, all cities were odd to her. The most peculiar thing about this realm was its lack of folk. She noted happily that she was in posses- sion of her antlers once more and wandered downwards until she came to a thoroughfare. There was a sign above a window that said it was called Green Lanes, but she did not know if that was the name of the house or of the thoroughfare.

All the houses were stuck together

here, with no sky between them. She went
into the corner house once again. She
knocked first, but there was no answer. It
had huge glass windows so she could see
that, just like the last time she dreamed
this abode, there was no one home, just as
on the empty streets outside.

She quickly realised it was a shop,
as quickly as she had done when she had
dreamt this before. She always marvelled at
a dream's facility to populate its envi-
rons with details – who would ever care that
there were boxes marked GAVISCON here, whatever mysterious things those boxes might
hold, or bound parchments with the first word
of "Sunday" on them all. Those nonsensical details that not even the dreamer cared
deeply about. And that was saying something.
For she was the dreamer.

*

Jack sat at his bedsit table and took down a
few current-event impressions on the Post-
It notes, as the stagged girl had suggested.
He opened the window again and looked out,
but there was no sight of her. He had a
revelation regarding the Post-It handwrit-

ing, though he did not write that particular observation down on a Post-It. Far too meta for Jack's personal taste.

He looked over to the open window, and then had to close it, as there were stars and hailstones and blood falling from the sky, and he didn't want any of it blowing in and getting into his dehydrated hot cocoa (Ebola scare).

Item 1, yesterday out of the corner of my eye, while walking on the pavement bordering the High Street, I could have sworn that I saw four angels blowing trumpets.

Item 2, despite the odd locust and scorpion here and there, I haven't seen bees or wasps for a good two years now, and I believe this is an indication of what several well-respected newspapers refer to as "Colony Collapse."

Item 3, the matter of the newspapers. Judging by the date on the Sunday Sport *in the newsagent's, there appear not to have been any recent publications of any newspapers whatsoever in the last 2.5 weeks.*

Those were quite enough current-event observations for the time being. Jack got to his feet and stretched, yawning. He had filled up three whole Post-Its already, writ-

ing on both sides. But just as his stretching moment occurred, the whole world rat-
tled, pots clanging to the floor; the
entirety of the Edwardian terrace in which
was situated Jack's bedsit shook, as did the
terraces across the road. When the quake
stopped and Jack crawled over to his broken
window to peer out, he saw that the Earth
had been narrowly missed by an asteroid at
least five football fields wide, an asteroid
called Donna that was now floating blithely
off into the other half of its elliptical
space orbit.

"That does it!" said Jack aloud, though
he wasn't sure whom he could blame. He
decided to blame the little girl with stag
horns at the corner shop. In fact, he would
have a word with her right this very moment.
He stomped down the stairwell and outside,
where it was impossible to avoid the fact
that there had occurred a massive shift in
the Earth's axis, and Jack therefore was
forced to walk at an unbecoming angle all
the way to the newsagent's.

*

The girl with the deer antlers was still

there and she looked startled when Jack walked in, but smiled too, as if she had been hoping for his return. As she grinned, the earth's axis switched again, and Jack took advantage of the opportunity to straighten his back. He for his part did not smile and walked directly up to the till. He drew a blank Post-It note and a biro out of his jacket pocket and slammed both down on the counter.

"Write!" he commanded.

The deer girl blinked. She picked up the pen with a sense of wonder, and turned it round in her hand several times. "What shall I write?"

Jack looked at her meaningfully. "Write *Item 2, despite the odd locust.*"

The girl took the pen and slowly wrote that distinct phrase on the blank yellow Post-It note.

"Aha!" said Jack, and whipped out a crumpled Post-It from another pocket. He smoothed it out in front of them to compare the two Post-It notes. They looked at each other and now both blinked in surprise.

"Where did you learn to write?" asked Jack.

"At the Blue School in the forest,"

said the girl, "I could only spell my name before that schooling. I learned my letters with a charcoal stick on bark first at the Blue School, and then we graduated to quill on vellum."

"Spare me the gories."

"Where did *you* learn?"

"At some elementary school in North America, I presume. I can't really remember anything before the last three months or so," admitted Jack.

"I don't really understand most of what you're saying," the deer girl for her part also admitted. "I've often found that to be the case with dreams. For example, I have my antlers back in this one, and that is not at all the case in my waking life. But despite your nonsensical speech, I have to tell you that you do fit the description in a yellow note and highly accomplished master-sketch left by the shop boss, who has not shown herself or himself in this dream yet."

She took out yet another Post-It from behind the till, cleared her throat and began to read: *Watch out for a man called Jack. He is nondescript in appearance, manner, intellect and age, but he is a notorious thief of Post-It notes, which you will*

recognise as blank yellow pieces of paper
stuck together. He has been stealing the
packets from me for a good six months now."
Attached with a paper clip to the Post-It
was a colour copy printout, indeed, a secu-
rity-camera grab of Jack's face from that
very store's own copying machine (10p B&W,
50p colour).

Jack turned pale. Was this it, the
proof that he had been writing all those
Post-It messages to himself? Deflect, deflect,
he told himself, I cannot think on that now.
I will think on something else, for example,
I will think on this girl who has stolen my
handwriting!

"You are a counterfeiter!" he told her.

"You are a... purloiner!" She jabbed
her finger at her boss's note again,
emphasis.

Yes, this would be a good distraction.
He made himself look shifty and affected
a drawl. "It's tough times now, kid, we
do what we can. Don't pretend you haven't
noticed what's been going on lately."

"Why *shouldn't* I pretend that these
are normal times, that's been *exactly* what
you've been doing - I can see it in your
sneaky eyes! I watched you step over a dis-

emboweled grandfather lying in the street just before you came through the door, all the while pretending business was usual just so you could do a handwriting analysis – is *that* normal?"

She was a mouthy deer-antlered girl, that was the truth of it. Antlery. And mouthy. Unfortunately, he was now genuinely drawn in, and genuinely irked.

"Well, what am I supposed to do? Is it healthier if I say that yes, indeed I *have* noticed that lion meat is being served alongside lamb rotisserie at the North London Nigerian Suya of Berenstein Bears, or if I draw attention to the fact – not rumour! – that last month when there were still running buses, I saw ten Dutch tourists rise up in the air naked from one of the open-top red omnibuses, their clothes and belongings left behind on the bus. And the Dutch tend to be atheists, too. The recent, mysteriously opened mausoleums in the Abney Park cemetery, the plagues like Ebola five years ago and then MERS and then –"

"*We* have plague," interrupted the girl.

"– the whisperings I heard on the Tube, when the Tube was still running, that folks were turning up to work with marks on their foreheads – boils, sores –"

"*We* have boils and sores in our time too. In fact, as I just mentioned, the blue sickness –"

"Yes, you *do* go on about it."

Now it was the deer girl's turn. "In fact, in addition to the Pest, and aside from the fact that you seem singularly unconcerned with the actual victims of the plagues your realm endures, things are quite bad where I come from myself, and predicted to get much worse. All the soothsayers and even the Christendomers say so. A third of the ocean will turn into blood. A great mountain burning with fire will be thrown in the sea, killing a third of everything in the ocean, including ships."

"P'shaw. We've known about Fukushima contamination for years." (*Had* he known about it for years, indeed? Glory be – memories were coming back to him!)

"This will result in the death of every living thing in the sea, and a third of earth's waters will become bitter and poisonous."

"Japanese radiation, like I said."

"I don't know what the long word means. Rivers will turn to blood."

"Acid rain, common side effect."

"I don't know what those words mean. A great star will fall from heaven, burning as a lamp. It shall be called 'Wormwood'."

"*Je déteste* absinthe," said Jack.

"I don't know what any of those words mean. Anyway, it will poison the water from rivers and springs."

"Again, acid rain."

"The sun will burn so hot it will scorch people with fire, and scorch all the green grass."

"That's known in these parts as global warming. In process, but it takes a while and, you never know, things might sort themselves out in the mean-time."

"The sun, the moon and stars go out. Total darkness reigns, black as sackcloth woven from hair; the stars fall to earth."

"Global dimming," said Jack, "you get it sometimes in cities."

"A third of the sun will go dark, and a third of the moon, and a third of the stars."

"Eclipse," said Jack. "Bad moon rising."

"The sun turning red like blood."

"Well sure, like in five billion years.

I wouldn't worry your little Cervid-pronged head about it."

"And the shapes of the locusts will be like unto horses prepared unto battle; and on their heads will be as it were crowns like gold, and their faces will be as the faces of men, and their hair will be as the hair of women, and their teeth will be as *the teeth* of lions."

"Please," said Jack, disconcerted by the emphasis on the words *the teeth*. "Now you're straining belief. That's just too trippy. None of these predicaments – save horse-shaped golden hairy locusts with human faces, that's just too Hieronymus to countenance – none of these predicaments that you mention have caused the end of the world so far," said Jack to the little girl.

"And none of those events you mentioned to me have caused the world's end in my time, either," retorted the little girl.

They each stared at the other.

"Terrible wars, in fact World War Three," said Jack, testing her.

"We have had more than three terrible wars," said the girl. "We are still here."

"Space aliens attacking our planet, outsiders from other worlds."

"This we have had too," she said. "Saxons, Vikings, Normans, Celts, Picts. We don't know, anymore, who are the strangers and who are the originals."

"Hmm," said Jack, "dysgenic events, where gene experiments have run amok; extreme volcanism; insufficient resources to support current or future populations; the event of the singularity causing evil robots; total ecological annihilation; plain old mistakes."

"I don't understand a word you're saying, once again," said the little girl, "except for the word *amok* and the word *mistakes*. We have the word *amok* too, the Vikings gave it to us mid-invasion, like they gave us the word *window*. Thank you very much, Vikings! But I'm quite sure that none of the words you are saying matter anyway. And now I'm going to leave this dream. You only like to argue."

And she did. She was there one moment, holding a Post-It that tacitly accused Jack of chronic shoplifting criminality, and the next moment she was not there, and the Post-It note in question fluttered to the floor. Which was all very well for her, leaving a dream, forsaking it for waking up, or for switching to a dream about swimming through water lilies accompanied by secular medieval music, whatever she was inclined to do, but the problem was that it was not a dream for Jack. Jack was alive. It was his life, and in real life little girls with deer horns stayed in place, or they would if little girls with deer horns existed in real life, as such little girls with deer horns would follow the laws of physics.

He had the niggling sensation that he ought to dispose of three Post-It notes; first, the ones with the phrase *Item 2, despite the odd locust* in identical hand-writing, and he did so by ripping them into bits and eating the pieces right then and there, but for the life of him he couldn't remember why their disposal via the hydro-chloric acid in his stomach was so press-ingly important.

Jack bent down and picked up the final Post-It note that did indubitably seem of consequence – the accusation of shoplift-ing with attached mugshot – rolled it into a scroll and, *sans* paper clip, ate it to destroy the evidence. The Post-It tasted as sweet as honey in his mouth but, when he had swallowed them and the colour copy down, his stomach turned sour.

When he went out on the street, though, it
was the light of day. And then a flash came.
First there was one sun in the sky, then
suddenly three, then six suns in the sky,
then fifteen, then hairy locusts, then one
thousand. The light was white, then it was
yellow.

There was a pulse then, of sound but
also a wave of heat at one and the same
time. Jack lost consciousness immediately,
and perhaps seconds or centuries later
he awoke. This time the sky was becoming
lighter, and there were fires everywhere,
blooming tumbleweeds of fire rolling down
Green Lanes.

Jack was having difficulty breathing,
and his skin had started bleeding. He wanted
to be cold; wanted snow. *There was a man
named and made of frost that day, and he
called himself Jack.* He crossed the road to
avoid the nearest hoop of fire burning by,
and then another great white flash came, far
greater than the first, as moist and tangible
as a white lily, and this time he knew what
to expect.

***

She had been trodding the road for two years now. And the journeys had been curious. She wore the clothes of a hooded friar, so that her antlers were covered. She had her clothes bundled on her back, so that she was a hunchbacked friar, at that. Accordingly, she was sometimes given respect as a godly man, and sometimes opprobrium.

The roads were dusty, often, and when they weren't, they were muddy. She made her living with fake blessings in a low male voice, and her sex had never been questioned. There were just enough coins to go around to feed a free-lance priest, and a dissident one at that. For Florentine always seeded her homilies with a touch of anti-clericism towards the larger church, for she had found that that senti-ment frequently was welcome. Folk felt devout for tossing a few silvers in her direction, and at the same time could spit at one of the institutions that had forsaken them, an institu-tion that had had no real power when the corpses of loved ones had been pushed into wagons by the thousands, by the ten-thousands, by the even-more. The idea of a rebel friar satisfied something deep-rooted and vexing in the populace. Florentine was not the only dissident priest hiking the roads and making his coin.

Today she simply walked, step and a step, and wished that she had some sort of walking-stick with her, which she did not. The last two years had made her more comfortable with towns, with people, but there was an itch in her for her cabin home, and she often thought of it when she was bedding down, always alone, clerical celibacy being good guise for her maidenhood, in various inns, dirty and hay-filled, wine-smelling, drinking songs ringing in her ears long into the night. She would dream over her brothers, whom she assumed were still trilling *In Excelsis Deo* for churchly choirs. She would sometimes think of a log house, and a lake, and several rows of greyfruit trees, and papery spirches and evergreens. And the wildborn birds, boars, bees, martens, squirrels, fish, wolves, deer and her wildborn bothers and her wildborn self. There were no hints to guide her back home; unlike the fairy tale, she had no longer any brothers to speak of and she had left herself no trail, even though she knew well the direction. She found herself unable to turn round and follow back. When she woke up in the mornings, the same sounds and scents and sensations would still be there: ale, raucousness, rough beds.

(Only once did she bare her antlers for money, to a Belgian sailor leaving for his homeland. The next morning, rolling the coins round in her palm, she had felt like she had betrayed herself, and she gave all monies earnt that night to lepers that she met along the road. That morning, and always, the question came to her, the vexing query regarding whom it was who stole her second pair of strong good antlers, and their makeshift wooden replacements while she slept.)

Step and a step, on she walked the roads, to Spring Hill, to Waltham, to Nun's Head. She kept dreaming, and sometimes she dreamed of the desert world, but Jack's world had gone missing.

This morning, events had started peculiarly as she had hiked her pack over her back, making sure that her robes hid both her breasts and her antlers, and making equally sure that the crucifix round her neck on role was very revealed. Shortly after, she had made the acquaintance of another wandering friar, also of ambiguous gender. For she had met this friar many years before. It was she and he who had taken the curling off Florentine's left antler, and had pocketed it as payment.

Florentine was not recognised.

Indeed, they walked the day together and that night, the two of them shared a fire off the road, and dried fish and some cocket-bread. And the Spital friar, name of Ned, took out whiskey and shared that too, and Florentine took several swallows.

"I am not only a Christian cleric," the friar confessed, drunk in his-her boots later, whilst Florentine looked soberly on.

"What do you mean?" said Florentine, in her false deep voice.

"There are other magicks and other beliefs on this road, my brother," Ned had told her, "from Babylon to Rome to these very woods across the hay acres yonder."

He, or she, drunkenly took out a small pouch and emptied it on her, or his, palm. There were several gem-stones, several tiny pottery figures, some dried herbs and a long curl of something that looked like a toenail. Florentine blinked, but said nothing.

The cleric saw her looking. "What's that, you ask? Ah, well, that is a token off a very special magickal creature –" the words were slurred now, and the double-sexed priest was nearly falling off the log being used as a seat "– rarer than a unicorn... Six years ago, I came across a girl in a hood –" Ned peered closely at Florentine for a moment, the action jarring in the midst of intoxication "– wait, how old are you yourself?"

"Twenty," Florentine was about to lie, but the other friar, not as false as she but more corrupt despite sanction, collapsed down into a heap and began to snore.

Florentine intended to steal the pouch in the middle of the night, primarily for the piece that had been stolen from her, but also for the topazes and the garnet, but she too was tired and also fell into a deep sleep. When she woke very the next morning, the pouch and its owner was gone.

Her hood was down and she was splayed, exposing her horns to all who might travel on the road or look upon her whilst she slept, and she felt a jolt of shame, which she wished that she had not felt. She hurriedly tied the hood back up again. It could not have been this priest who stole her second antlers, or more than the trophy curl off them, anyway, for he had not purloined the full set now.

She met one more traveller on the road that day, a scribe named Will of Wychwood. They shared a canteen of her water and he thanked her, "though I am not often fond of clergy." She thought of the hungry sick outside the Spital, and of the abandoned girls of the Blue School driven wandering by poverty and plague, and she told Will in her false low voice, with her hood pulled tight, that she too was disenchanted, and that, though it was explicitly forbidden for Christians, that she gave more credence to dreams these days, and that they often taught her more than waking life, and that her mind often went soaring in such travels.

Will lit up at that statement, inexplicably, and began writing on vellum scraps. Florentine could not see what her fellow traveller Will wrote, but the act reminded her of Jack in one such dream, with his yellow paper remnants. Her head was suddenly dizzy. Her mouth went dry. She needed a place to finish growing, and not just her antlers: more ballast, greater structure, fewer wisps and dreams.

It was time to go home again, back to her family's cottage in the woods.

*

It was five years later. It was five years later from the Blue School. She was nineteen. It was one thing, the forest in springtime, and there was an entirely different aspect in summer. The hot pulse of it all; the leaves in green-ridged fulfilment and not just promise. In the creeks, there are necklaces of silver fish, which are sometimes trapped for food and sometimes not.

On just such a hot day, Florentine left her cottage and

stepped out into the morning. It was already warm and there was present the buzz of flies and honeybees. There was the cloying, sugar-scent of honey itself.

She stood over the for-many-years-not-so-dangerous lake with her hands full of wild-washed clothing, and she saw in its reflection a grown woman, and nearly a green woman with such a bounty of summer leaves in the foreground and her all amidst that forest. She was tall with adult antlers, as great as a buck's, the entirety of the rack shining and dark brown.

It was odd for Florentine, living solitarily, but it was also in its ways quite wonderful. She had the happy memories of both her parents and her brothers for comfort, and even though that was the past and not the living now, it made it no less real and so she enjoyed such memories. In time, she had been able to do the same with Eglentyne too, and Florentine found herself looking back on her general education in the Blue School with something akin to fondness.

She walked towards the greyfruit orchard, where the trees were naturally even taller and more busy than in her childhood. Her arms were heavy with the washing. She caught an image of drying the laundered clothes on her own antlers, and she giggled. She eyed the trees.

For a moment, she was snagged: for a moment, she was tempted to string the clothes along the branches of the greyfruits to dry, but her parents had never done so, and she found herself submitting to custom. Instead she targeted a spirch and a young willow, standing close together. The day was just beginning. She had no spirit for housework. The sun was beautiful and she should be battling mosquitoes or swimming the waters or running in the brush through the trees. She felt suddenly petulant, as Percy used to be at bedtime, and she knew that she was far too old for that.

Had her mother ever been petulant over housework? Florentine could not rightly recall at this very moment and this made her evilly sad. She could remember her mother humming tunes; she could remember her father whistling; she could not remember their attitude towards housework. A twig snapped. O, but now came a few chore memories – her mother a gentle chider whilst Florentine span wool; her father whittling for amusement after chopping wood all day, as if he still wanted the smell of wood on him just for a while longer in the evenings; her father's rough fingers carving at soft green soapstone and wood; her mother half cursing, half invoking sprites to help with the chores when faced with unruly children – aha! There it was! A memory on the subject she'd been faltering for.

(You may recall the wood pile for which said father was often a-chopping. Florentine's eighth birthday. What was the significance of the logs having both spirch and bruce sprouts? Hard to say; o, it is hard to say. Best to just accept. There are things in nature that we just accept, such as the fact that purple dye is made from snails in a barbaric fashion, or that the *puca* lure good men and good women onto deceptive forest paths with flickering fireflies and the mechanical use of echoes. It is best to take a Zen attitude to it all, and just accept. *"If a tree falls in the forest..."*)

Florentine looked up; the sun so yellow and the greyfruits winking green and, as always, she could not tell why. The greyfruits could read her, but she could not read herself. Even the years in the Blue School had not helped her with this particular divination.

So how did that spelle go? O, it went like this, it went like this. You were supposed to pluck one hair from head, hold it in your fingers, close your eyes, say the name of the sprite three times, and blow the hair away, with your eyes still closed. And then the puck would come and kiss you, and you'd open your eyes, and there would be the puck, to help you with your chores. Of course, her mother would only tease her children, and stop before the third mentioning of the goblin-name, for she and her brothers would be shrieking half in fear, half in delight, for Puck was not only helpful but also said to sour the ewe's milk on Imbolc, to blow out candles so he could kiss the maids, to pinch disobedient children (the type of unruly children that did not help their mother with her chores, Florentine's mother was clear to point out), and so... and so...

And so Florentine's mother would always stop before the final invocation of the good imp's name. "Ah, he usually comes at nighttime, anyway," would say their mother, with a wink in her eye and an excuse. Florentine and her brothers would all have to help with the house tasks anyway; they churned the butter; they hung the clothes; they carded the wool; they skimmed the cream milked from wild sheep.

It was not nighttime now. It was bright late morning. Florentine freed a hand and plucked a brown hair from her locks, and held it, the single hair shimmering in the day, day, day. She shut her eyes. She shut her eyes. She shut her eyes. "Puck," she said, "Puck, Puck." She blew away the hair on the breeze. No one kissed her. She opened her eyes.

Amongst the verdure, o so green, so green, there was a male. She wasn't sure if she ought to feel startled, and so she wasn't. He had no horns. He was a red man. Well, technically he was a white man with pale freckles, but he had red hair, and he had much of it, for red-blond curling hair covered much of his belly and his nipples and his legs and his arms. Around his middle he wore green leaves as the Witch had done; he was not entirely indecent. When he smiled at her, he was entirely indecent. She dropped her armfuls of damp clothing onto the forest floor. She did not run. She kept looking at him, as he was looking at her.

"Aren't you a pretty thing?" Was she? And if this were the case, was she not just lucky?

He moved in closer and picked down a greyfruit, split it and licked at it. She saw the pink flash of his tongue and his white sharp teeth. The act was such a shock to the greyfruit that it had no time to react by changing colours. Florentine had never in her life picked a greyfruit for sport; it seemed disrespectful.

"Ah, Pepys," said the red-haired man called many things, which was a word Florentine heard as "peeps," and so she saw that he was indeed looking closely at the open fruit that he held in his hand, and then at her. " 'Here I first saw oranges grow: some green, some half, some a quarter, and some full ripe, on the same tree...' "

"They are not oranges at all," Florentine told him resentfully. She felt some need to defend the greyfruit tree that he had just accosted.

He seemed taken aback, and thrown off speed a bit, but recovered. " 'And one fruit," he moved in just a little closer to her, not too much, but made sure that she noticed, "and one fruit of the same tree do come a year or two after the other.' "

He reached out and pulled a curl loose from her bun, and let it dangle in the breeze. She could not stop him; she was like a green bush statue in the Spital gardens.

" 'I pulled off a little one by stealth, being mighty curious of them, and did eat it –"

Florentine thought suddenly further on the Spital, and of its great stained glass window, with the light pouring through everything making colours, and with the naked humans standing by the tree with all its fruit, and offering the same fruit to each other.

She looked down at the fruit this man was offering to her. The inside of it, its fruitmeat, was indeed still changing colours even as it rested in his palm, red and orange and green and violet, just like the colours from the glass window, but there was something obscene and sticky to it, the fact that the colours still pulsed and the juice still ran, even though it had been severed from its bough.

He was whispering in her ear now; she felt his breath. " 'And it was just as other little green small oranges are; as big as half the end of my little finger.' Florentine, imagine that," the leafed man concluded, and he stepped back from her, and waited for her reaction.

"Are you a wild man?"

"Well, I am a *hairy* man."

Florentine blushed. "What is your name?"

"Call me Puck."

"As in, I want to *puck* you?" Florentine clapped both hands over mouth in shame; she hadn't meant to say that out loud. It was a bold thing to say.

Her mother had had many stories of hairy men and wild men who lived deep in the forest. There was something disreputable about them all, and that was something that had always excited Florentine, a flicker towards rebellion. His lips were close to hers now. He nearly kissed her. He then withdrew entirely, four steps back.

"I'm a Green Knight here to save the Angle-land, I'm a leafy Peter Pan, or at least a pan with a leafy peter – cognate cultural cousin to Pūṣan of wild beasts – I'm Father Christmas trailing both the holly and the ivy. My very real name is Viridios – Sylvanus when I'm feeling fancy. Do you think you are the first maiden to come creaming at me with your foliate fancies of green rutting in the bushes? You aren't."

No, of course she would not be, though it hurt to hear

him say it. Though why shouldn't she assume innocence as opposed to experience in him; he was assuming the state, correctly as it happened, in her; should she hold him by different standards?

"I think you are a hobgoblin, or possibly a woodwose or an *orco*."

"Names seem very important to you. If this were a proper fairy tale, I should be making you guess, but here I've given you seven true ones at least for free, already, a half-bouquet of long-stemmed woodwoses, and what have you given to me?"

She blinked at him. "My name is Florentine. Very well, then. What kind of thing are you?"

"All right, you can indeed think of me as a puck, a thing and not a name. My name can be something different. I can be just a puck to you." He winked, not blinked, at her, and she affected not to notice. "So call me Hrôdberxtas, Proto-Germanic Robert, and Robin for short."

"Robin is certainly less of a mouthful than Hrôdberxtas."

"What do you know of mouthfuls?"

She had never liked the name Robert and now she found she similarly cared little for its etymology or diminutives. It was a matter of taste.

He was indeed a beautiful man, with his red curls all aglow all over his body, from crown to crotch to calves, and she was a beautiful woman with her polished antlers and smooth hips and shy grey eyes. Or not-so-shy grey eyes, for it does depend. He was not shy at all and came close to her once again and flirted with his hands and her gaze. His beard was shorn short but bristly, bright red, and the sun made each hair catch at its rays, and the sun thus threw mysterious shadows all across his jaw. She looked closely all around his head and neck, but saw no evidence of growing leaves nor of seaweed nor of moss nor of mushrooms.

She looked up at the greyfruit trees, whose fruits were bursting with all possible colours, some even hanging from the same branches.

He kissed her white bare arm, and then the back of her neck, and then she shied away from him. He did not seem to have feelings in his heart for her, and if he did, he was not speaking of such feelings. Though he made her tremble and buzz, she was not sure she could accept this coldness. It was odd to sense such coldness in someone so full of life, with his Bacchic beauty and his smile now wickedly on her – there was an evil little truth, a hard small gold coin, to the force of his lust, and she felt it too. She felt a gold coin within herself, and it twisted and responded to him. How could he love her, or be warm to her, when he did not know her? Did she know him; she did not.

***

The desert is hot, then parched, then windy, then barren.

***

Jack sits in a firefly field and feels rapture. He has just drunk a strong cider, and made the acquaintance of a strange family, and now he sits on weeds in wonder. He could be his own ghost – Jack's ghost – because he has been travelling from a rather singular experience. There had been that blast, that many-sunned light, and perhaps he has been killed. But he's in the present, he's here, and Jack-visiting knows more than Jack-before. And lo, he puts his hand up to his head, now he has moose horns, where he had none previously except when he was dreaming. Dreams are not reliable.

The night air is strong, the fireflies irregular lit-matches between the dips and curves of his bull-moose horns.

8

The Holy Well

He was handsome and curly, and the following day he laid
a pattern of forest fruits on her doorstep, though she noticed
that he neither knocked on the door kept ajar in loose hot
summer, nor crossed the threshold.

There was a pattern in the shape of a star, but no
basket. There were canterberries and acorns and rose-hip
pellets, the tart ones, and mushrooms and the tough roots of
ferns.

In the centre of the star was the curled toothy trim-
ming off what had once been a young stag's antler. It was
stiff and slightly dusty, as if the curling had been kept in a
satchel for a long, longer time. Whereabouts did he discover
it; from whom had he acquired it?

Florentine could scarcely take breath. She parted the
door wide open and sank to her knees, taking the antler-twist
in hand. She pressed it down on the stone slab of the threshold very slowly and very carefully, so that it did not break,
and in this fashion flattened and coaxed it into its original
spiral.

When she had finished, she took it to the lake (dangerous or not, and fed by a holy well and not by Thames
Water Services), and lifted it up level with her horns. On
the water, she fancied she could still see on her the faint old

shadow of where the cutting had been taken from her carti-lage, though these were not the same set of antlers at all, and when she held the goblin's gift up she saw for a moment, before a blink, that it matched exactly, spiral by spiral, like a wooden box's lockpiece. Though in the end, again, these were not the same set.

She saw herself again on the water, and her mouth was dry, then moist. And her heart raced. And she thought of the puck. He knew her; he knew her totally – he had given her back this piece of herself. Her heart raced even more crazily, and she whispered his name three times and threw the curling far into the lake, where it sank slowly. His red hair, his bright mind. And she knew him too; knew why *he* knew it was important to give her such a thing. She clenched her fingers until the ripples ceased, spirals too in their own strange way.

***

So here we are again, or here we were again, in the present that yet takes the past tense. It's not timely, in any sense, to detail this realm at the moment. Where is Jack; what has happened to this world? you ask. What of the murrey rolling fireballs and the big white blasts?

Why have you wondered so little over

Jack's wife and poppet? They are in this world too, possibly. Or were, possibly. Have you filed them away in a witness protection program deep within the pages of this very novel? Maybe CIA? Stasi? Laid flat via arquebus? Am I asking too many questions? Between you and me, we may make it all the way to 36 questions exactly. Between the two of us.

Let's think up a name for Jack's wife. She's a person, after all. Keeping with Jack's Midas metaphor-cum-coping-mechanism, I propose Midas's wife's name, Hermodike. Are you okay with that? I knew you would be. It has the touch of the gender-bender about it, too. Nice.

Hermodike cried for Jack when he left. Her face turned a little tear-silver. *Do not forget me, remember me!*

***

Florentine stumbled upon him the next morning as she circled the lake, the lake that had always been thought too dangerous to explore in childhood. She stood by the spring that sourced the waters, her hair tumbled high and caught in her horns, and felt the hot sun on the back of her neck. Her family had called such a feeding spring a holy well, a well that nursed the waters, though the spring had none of the Blue School's accoutrements of ribbons tied prayerfully to surrounding trees and avidly selfied by new students, nor slithering, crawling groups of nine sacrificial animals. That was how the Blue School treated holy wells. Warm as she waded to her ankles, and as she closed her eyes to hear insect-buzz and water-rush.

She squared off to the imp once it was clear that he had seen her, too. "How did you procure the antler curling?" *He may know me; he may know me.*

He drew very close and looked at her left antler from which the curling had been stolen on that long-ago set, then stepped back. "I was on the road," he said. "Have you walked such roads?"

"I have," she said.

"There, just two months ago, I met a young woman. I will not say a maiden."

Florentine felt a spike of jealousy, but made no sign of it in her face.

The puck laughed at her and splashed his own face with holy water. "Oh, I generally prefer experience to maidenhood, but not on today's occasion, don't you worry."

Now the jealousy burned silently for the experience she lacked.

"She had wickedly black hair and she said her name was Ermintrude –"

"Why, I know an Ermintrude! –"

"She said her name was Ermintrude, and that she was off to join the fighters, for there are stirrings of revolt, they say, against the fat clergy and the wealthy squires, the decadent kings and snob-ladies who hold Dolce & Gabbana perfume to their noses and flee the cities and the Pest and leave the poor to shrivel –"

"Would not you have fled it too, if you had the means?

The puck laughed at her again. "All moot, my friend, I never die. Not in that sense, anyway. In another sense, I expire every year."

"Oh," said Florentine. Her mother, father, Eglentyne. She did not want to hear of it. "Tell me more about this Ermintrude."

"The dark-haired young woman, so spiky, so spirited, which I admired greatly –" he paused to gauge Florentine's reaction, then continued, "she said that she had learned to read, rather rare in a peasant in general terms and doubly so in a woman, despite the Education Act; she said that she had learned to read at a strange, strict school –"

"It certainly must have been my Ermintrude; it had to have been!"

"And she said as well that she had met a hedge priest, a man along the road name of Will, who was quilling a book of dreams –"

"I have met him, too!"

"Though, this book of dreams was instead a satire of the rich towards their poor. He said that he had shown some of his book to the roaming friar John Ball, who is a true and honest confessor, who also walks the roads and rails against the poll taxes and the Mother Church. And Ermintrude related to me that in hearing the very same stories from Will's book, she grew so enraged by the hypocrisy that, having met a true one such as Will the scrivener and heard further of honest ones such as Ball, she robbed the very next false hedge priest that she happened upon, name of Ned –"

"I know him too!" She shuddered a little inwardly, for she had herself been a false priest.

"And that Ned had in his possession an odd curled talisman that he had nicked off a human stag, a shape-shifting little girl, and that he had intended to use it not on shamanic rituals as most would guess, but instead would grind the curl down to powder, a process that stinks terribly –" Florentine was deeply insulted "– a process that stinks terribly, but results in the growth hormone IGF-1 insulin, a synthetic anabolic steroid for bigger biceps, an attribute which this hedge priest Ned confessed he had an affection for having precisely fifty percent of the time. And it turned out that Ermintrude had known just such a stag girl as Ned had described in her youth, and so it was that in addition to his opals and coins, for sentimental purposes only my fiery Ermintrude also stole the antler cutting off Ned, too. And that is the end of the story."

"No, it's not. You haven't told me how you then got the curling off Ermintrude."

"Oh, I traded her for it."

"With what?"

"Isn't it a beautiful morning and nearly, nearly

midsummer," said Puck. "The dew lingers late, does it not, though in a few more days past that all plants save the evergreens start slowly to wither, or to crypt themselves away, or do they not."

"Oh," said Florentine. She did not want to hear such darkness. "Tell me more about Ermintrude." Her friend with the black stiff braids; the tale of accosting false priests sounded just like what the always-prickly Ermintrude likely would be doing these days. She felt the sting for freckled Eglentyne then, who would never adventure forth from the Blue School and live on as Ermintrude and she herself had done. She had a fleeting impression of Eglentyne waving farewell to her but frozen, remaining ever-young as Florentine and Ermintrude grew older, waving through time but further and further away, lost through water-turned-ice, lost in a be-snowed forest. How kind the puck was, that he was trying to distract her from her grief. She understood his motivations. *He knows me.*

The puck offered his hand and she took a step further into the warm water; it was up to her shins.

***

Not long after the meadow, second time by his own dream-reckoning, Jack-in-his-horns shut his eyes, and when he opened them he had travelled back to the futuristic dream-desert where he had first met Martin. Well, life is full of surprises.

It was observed that the desert was dry and fruitless, as you might expect a classic desert, not dessert, to
be. Jack herewith exhibited a pathetic reliance on what is
said to be the lowest and most punishing form of comedy.
So there was no Martin and stick, no moustache manifesta-
tions, no wildly blossoming desert flora, and, Jack-in-his-
horns was relieved to see, no enormous white bird.

However, there did happen to be his therapist, walking purposefully across the sand towards him. The therapist
was wearing a jaunty hat.

"Where have you been?" Jack demanded.

The therapist looked at Jack with a great pulse of
curiosity. "Is that a question that matters greatly to you?"
He was a professional. The therapist sat down on the sand,
and patted the space next to him, urging Jack to sit down
too. "I've got a new one," said the therapist. "And it's good.
And you'll like it, since it's all about questions, too."

"Why?" asked Jack, reluctantly taking a seat in the
surreal dream landscape. It seemed a waste of good hal-
lucigenia. He had low-slung jeans; now he had sand in the
crack of his ass. Where was a cuirass when you needed
one?

"Nope, that's not it, either. No, these are the thirty-six
questions destined to make you fall in love with a person.
According to the *New York Times*. I get to answer them too.
Intimacy spurs intimacy. First, you can choose anyone you
want – who's your dinner guest?"

It was going to be one of those Proustian question-naires that the *Guardian* liked to run from time to time. "My family, if they in fact exist."

"I feel the same way!" said the therapist with delight. "My lovely sisters, quail-piped, who have rapacious appe-tites and rapier wit. The-rapists. Those in my profession are *so* tired of *that* pun, for the record. Now, would you like to be famous, and if so, in what way?"

"No."

"We differ there," said the therapist with no surname. "Personally I would like a School of Psychology named after me, the _____ian School. Yes, that sounds nice. Ques-tion three: before you make a telephone call, have you ever rehearsed what you were going to say?"

"Yes."

"Why?"

"Does that count as the fourth question?"

"What am I, a genie cheating you out of wishes? Of course not, it's still question three." The therapist was peeved.

"I suppose," said Jack slowly, stretching his mind to a past he wasn't sure he'd had, "I suppose because it gives me a greater sense of control concerning the outcome."

"A-*ha*!" said the therapist, rubbing his hands together. "Now we're getting somewhere. I really wish I could write that insight of yours down on a yellow Post-It note just now. Like the song from _____." He looked wist-ful for a moment. "Tisket, tasket," he added.

"I wish you could too," commiserated Jack. The musical *Easter Parade*, he concluded.

"Never mind," said the therapist, not one for prolonged sentimentality. "What would be your absolutely perfect day?"

Jack was having images crisscross in his head, angles trine at the most parsimonious appraisal. On one hand, he wanted to say a beautiful sunny day, waking up together with someone with whom he was deeply in love – his alleged wife Hermodike? – the therapist, after the next 32 questions? – making love, eating berries and drinking quality coffee for breakfast. A very good crime novel with, also middlebrow, Vivaldi's *Four Seasons* in the background. Then a swim in some nearby lake, then a nap, then dining *al fresco* on olives, fine cheeses, breads, strawberries and Prosecco, then perhaps more daringly another act also *al fresco* vis-à-vis his Chatterley fixation; on the other hand a simple cup of coffee that wasn't instant would suffice. Or, hell, hanging out with the best of pals – if he had them – in some bawdy Pacific Northwest dive bar all the Sunday, laughing, drinking, reading the papers, gossiping, arguing about politics, life, love, sex and the death of god until early evening, then stumbling along down to the rivers or lakes, knowing all sundry had spent too much time together and were in fact sick of each other's company but still staying on to walk the banks and swig shared whiskey: sarcastic, corned and mellow. A day well spent. On his fourth hand – "Well, I –"

"I'm not going to tell you mine now, and you've interrupted. Quit interrupting," said the therapist. "You might not have got into full swing, but you were about to go on and on. I could tell. We're going to skip to the next question as punishment. Part one, when did you last sing to yourself? Part two, when did you last sing to someone else?"

The therapist glared darkly at him, so Jack hurriedly said, " 'Salley Gardens', in the shower, with the dagger, first hummed softly to myself, and then warbled full-throat to the lovely Miss Scarlett, who dodged the prick of my knife."

"If you're not going to give real answers, then those are your puerile answers," said the therapist, sniffily. " 'My Sharona', also in the shower, as it happens. From my *100 Greatest Running Songs* CD. And then 'Always Something There to Remind Me', the Pet Shop Boys version. To my wife, over the phone. I am of a certain age, eschew Spotify and I love my wife. I am not ashamed." The therapist got to his feet and brushed the sand off his beige chinos and turned his hat upside down to shake it clean. "Let's take a walk, Jack."

Jack had only heard this phrase before in Netflix mafia movies and it made him very nervous. Robin Cook, Dr David Kelly, you know how it goes.

The therapist and Jack tread the desert sands. It was the middle of the morning and not unbearably hot. Jack missed Martin and his stick. Where *was* Martin? Jack watched the short shadows of the therapist and himself-with-bullwinkle-horns advance grey over the sifting dunes.

Martin would also have been making foolish enquiries, but not with the therapist's air of authority, with the implied smugness of secretly knowing the answers to thirty-six important questions. There was a flicker of movement overhead and a very small shadow on the sand for a second, and Jack looked up into the sundial sky. Had that been a crow? *Always nothing there to remind me.* There is nothing here, he reminded himself, nothing living in this landscape except melting clocks. In a sense.

Speaking of tick-tock desert time (and I highly recommend not just the obvious Dali or hourglass imagery, but also the underrated third L. Frank Baum Oz book, *Ozma of Oz*, published in 1907, which takes place in a desert full of clicking automatons), speaking of tick-tock desert time, "Speaking of tick-tock desert time," said the therapist, "if you lived to 90 and got to choose between the mind or body of a 30-year-old for the final 60 years, which would it be? Oh my," the therapist interjected, "this has to have been written by a young person. There are very few who would want their minds to stagnate at a mere thirty years of age. Body it is, of course."

"I concur," Jack said, but he bristled on behalf of the minds of himself and all his near-age-cohorts.

"And, while we're on the subject," said El Shrinko, "do you have a secret hunch as to how you're eventually going to die, when it comes down to it?" He stooped down to form and then cast an experimental sandball, but it didn't work as well as a snowball.

"I think it's possible that I've already died," said Jack. "That blast back in the real world, what was it?"

"Have you *always* had a fondness for the Narnia books?" asked therapist. "They're just not as good as the Oz books, I'll tell you right now. Baum wrote fourteen Oz books and they're far more imaginative and far less preachy. Anyway, that's not your seventh question; that's just a therapeutic question. Some Narnia characters, you see, find out they've been dead for a while in the last book after a similar 'blast'. Sound *familiar*? Also a therapeutic query."

It was Jack's turn to be annoyed. And not just for the spoiler. (Though to any un-Narnianed readers, please consider the fact that the therapist likely is twisting truth for his own ends. They do that, therapists. For any reading therapists, please consider the same for authors.) "Naturally, it sounds familiar, I just told you that that was how I felt. Do *you* have some hidden insight into how you will die?"

"Oh, absolutely pneumonia," said the therapist. "Though hopefully when I'm at least 95. Weak lungs. My lungs are my Achilles heels, but that suggests an unconventional anatomy. I'm actually practically perfect in every way."

Jack found it even more annoying that the therapist was quoting from the movie *Mary Poppins*. Oz, Narnia, Mary Poppins, *Choose Your Own Adventure* books; he diagnosed said psychotherapist with a clear case of arrested development. Jack determined to be an adult from hereon in contrast, and to answer each question as truthfully as he could.

The desert sand had taken on a high gloss in the morning light, and it shook and trembled like a creek. Ah. The word is shimmered. "Three things," said Jack's therapist. "Name the three things you and I appear to have in common."

This gave Jack pause. "Well," he said after some consideration, "I think that we both are attracted to mystery. The blankness of your surname and such. There was a reason I picked your intriguing, half-revealing/half-concealing profile from your website, after all. You secret away your surname; I concoct new names every time I visit Starbucks. I'm in therapy; you're a therapist. We are both wiggling out the answers together. We are both trying to find the _____ in things, even if it's from opposite ends, like a magnet. So there is that. Secondly, we both have a fondness for Post-It notes. So there is that. Thirdly, I once recall you mentioning in passing that you enjoyed the 2003-2005 HBO cable show *Carnivàle*, and I enjoyed it too. So there is all that." He took a big breath. He had talked a lot more than he had intended to. He looked up at the psychotherapist through his eyelashes.

The therapist beamed at Jack and, for the first time, Jack felt a rush of genuine affection for the man. He actually had quite a kind smile. There would be no Mafioso sting, Jack realised. This walk in the desert was just a walk in the desert, not a "walk in the desert."

"Thank you," said the therapist. "Thank you, thank

you. *Gracias*. Now, although I seem not to have my notes with me in this dream sequence, I do recall from my jottings – indeed, how could I forget – that you have an admiration – nay, obsession – with American CIA lore. I am myself a great fan of Tom Clancy novels. Secondly, you drink coffee not tea, and so do I. Thirdly, you are prone to disappearing, and so am I."

"Hmm," said Jack.

"Hmm," said the shrink, right back.

They walked forward in silence for exactly twenty seconds. *Tick-tock*. "What is it that you feel the most grateful for?" said the shrink conversationally, and for an instant Jack forgot that this question was part-and-parcel of a larger probing destination.

"My horns!" Jack said suddenly. He stopped walking and clapped his hands to his mouth in surprise. He had not realised that he felt that way. He carefully reached up and affectionately patted his left horn. "My horns," he repeated.

"My wife," said the therapist. "My kids."

"I should have said that," said Jack. He was wistful for a moment.

"Do you in fact have a wife or kids?"

"No."

"Moving on."

The next question concerned whether you wanted to change anything about the manner in which you were raised, and if so what would it be? The therapist muttered something about not being forced to eat liver as child, and no, Mater, no, he had in fact never grown to like it as his adult tastes developed and in fact as an adult even hated *pâté*. And he also wished he had called his mother Mater, which he had not.

This question was obviously a sensitive one for Jack, and so they both blithely skated past his lack of response about a past he could not recall, though the psychotherapist did look bright-eyed and hopeful for a few seconds.

Sand to the left of them, sand to the right, sand behind them and before them. No interesting objects to stop the sand monotony such as pyramids, sphinxes, green oases with dozing pack-camels. Nor even overgrown moustaches, sudden lakes, blossoming night-cacti, convenient metaphorical caves.

"Now, number eleven is where you take four minutes and tell me your life story in as much detail as you can. Good *God*, never mind, you already did it, twice," said the therapist, "that endless saga of ghosts and trees and birds and whatnot. There's no way I'm sitting through all *that* again, sorry, I have to draw the line somewhere. Here's me, though."

The therapist proceeded to tell a poignant tale of a lad brought up in Sutton, a shy lad, and perhaps a misunderstood lad, who went on to O-levels; university; two college romances; one girlfriend's abortion; City Lit qualifications at evening school; prenticehede; an eventual scandalous marriage to his own therapist, the former Frau Doktor Elsa Karolina _____, which meant her professional disbarring; the taking of his wife's unrevealed surname after their elopement, which meant disinheritance from his only middingly wealthy ageing parents; two kids whom were both named after his wife in different fashions (Elsie, Karl), now adults and working as a freelance street pharmacist and a lawyer, respectively; a succession of cats; living in St Albans where the commute was just fine. "Just fine," repeated the therapist firmly. "Now – any superpower, or talent, what would it be?"

"Are you perhaps 'messing up' our therapeutic relationship by disclosing? Or is that good practice? On the third hand," said Jack, with a flash of inspiration spurred by his recent decision towards earnestness, "wouldn't full disclosure be a better practice though, entirely?"

"We can't have therapists and patients falling in love all over the place," said the therapist, "so that is why it tends to be one-sided... Shades of *The Little Prince*. There you go. I believe there was a desert there, too."

Jack was trembling, and not due to the annoying fact that the therapist had missed the entire point behind that short book. He was trembling with insight. "Why shouldn't people fall in love; isn't that how true intimacy comes about?"

"Then we as practitioners lose our objectivity, and cannot truly instruct the client. This has all been thought out before," said the therapist. "Don't think that you're the first to suggest it."

"Don't you think," said Jack, and he solipsistically

tried throwing an experimental sandball too, which also failed, "don't you think it's odd that you're telling me all this, your Sutton life and your wayward child, but you still won't tell me your last name? Now, *that* disclosure would mean intimacy."

"That is your tenth question that is unrelated to the thirty-six questions at hand," said the therapist, "so please just shut the fuck up."

***

We're back in the world that Jack built. No, I'm still not going to discuss the fireballs and blasts. I suspect you have a good idea anyway.

Instead, I'm going to discuss the Palace of Tears, which once upon a time was a real place in this realm, not some long-past donjon with barbicans, allures. Jack likes his Cold War history, so this one's for Jack. Back before the Stasi shredded all their documents, necessitating so-called puzzle-women to be employed to piece together said papers like jigsaw-puzzles, like assembling torn-up Post-It notes (I reconstructed one recently; it had been swallowed, digested and shat out, but my inner puzzle-woman could still make out the historiated capital "I" and the words *Item 2, despite the odd locust)*, back before the wall came down, the Stasi had a building at the border-crossing between East and West Berlin, and this was where, after visits by special permission, West Berliners would say repeated goodbyes to their relatives who were still caught permanently behind the wall, visa-visit by visa-visit, forwelk, forwelk.

The Palace of Tears was found at Friedrichstraße Station. The palace was a fragile thing, for the architecture of water molecules holding up a structure is a delicate art. The buildings cried; the people cried too. Some people's faces turned silver from all their running tears: coins, argents, Midas. Some people had silver faces; some people did not have silver faces.

Some people are not old enough to have been CIA operatives previous to 1989 if they are only in their early thirties now. Such is the false house that Jack built, as fragile a scaffolding as palaces hoisted by tears.

***

The twelfth superpower question remained unanswered by both due to the therapist's outburst and they left it at that.

Neither felt particularly like they were growing closer to falling in love with the other person.

Twelve is a curious and beloved number. Jack has revealed its magic to you previously. They proceeded to the thirteenth question.

The therapist made both hands into a round O-sign and held them up, squinting, to each of the three golden suns in turn, as if trying to entrap them; or divine from them.

"Are you panning ore?" asked Jack.

The therapist lowered his hands. "If a crystal ball could tell you any truth – past, present or future – what would you ask of the crystal ball?"

"*You're* my chrysalis ball, said Jack, "that's why I went to you in the first place. You're my chrysalis and I'm your butterfly." *What other things do fly? A bird, a stone lion, a UFO, a balloon, a cloud.*

"That's your Freudian slip," said the therapist, "don't you mean *crystal* skull?"

"That's your Freudian *strip*," said Jack, "I think you meant to say... Oh... never mind."

The therapist smirked and pretended to write something meaningful down on an imaginary yellow Post-It note with an invisible pen.

Jack looked behind him in the desert. Where he had come from looked exactly the same as his future. Endless sand in retreat and in advance. You didn't need a chrysalis skull to see that. The therapist cleared his throat.

"Next question – *Da-da-DUM!*" he said with a sense of occasion. "Is there something you've always dreamed of doing? What is it and why haven't you gotten around to doing it?"

It was the oddest sensation. Jack saw, like a flash in his inner eyes, a cabin thatched with red-gold hair, peculiar enough to remind him of a dream he once had had. He who purported to remember so little. The cabin therein had been constructed in a glowing little green woods. Jack had always wanted to make a proper try at a garden, a little grass-time, grow some rhubarb and strawberries for pies, perhaps. But, at the same time, the image overlapped with his real home, the tiny bedsit off Green Lanes. Despite the street's name, the best he had done there in terms of horti-culture was an inefficient window box. Though once a bird had flown into the flat.

"Er, gardening."

"I *love* gardening." The therapist smiled widely at Jack.

"And how about you?"

"Why, I think it's gardening, too. I suppose I haven't had sufficient time for mine own little hundred up to now, though the rear garden's got a good 75 feet." The therapist seemed surprised by his own answer. "Or maybe it's just the appeal of eating the bounty of someone else's garden." The therapist giggled, which is not always becoming for his personality type (INFJ), but, unexpectedly, Jack forgave him it. "What do you consider to be your life's greatest accomplishment?" intoned Dr _____.

"My children," said the therapist, answering his own question, at the same time as Jack said, "My child." They both looked at each other inquisitively, but moved on to the next question with no further investigation, a question which enquired which trait it was that you valued most in a friendship. Jack thought suddenly of Martin.

(I'm bringing Martin back now, okay. I know I banished him to the beginning of the book, but I'm fetching him back to the desert. Though I'm placing him down some distance away from these two, like a chesspiece.)

Because Jack had inwardly vowed to be earnest, he answered honestly. "Like most, I value loyalty."

The therapist nodded. This answer seemed to have struck a chord with him. "Adventurousness," whispered the therapist. "I know it sounds mad, but Elsa is very adventurous. It's the thing I admire most about her, for she is not only my wife, but my dearest friend," he added.

The therapist looked down at the back of his hand, as if he expected to see the next question written down there on his sun-reddened skin, but its flesh was indelible and unliterary. "What memory is your most treasured?" he asked of Jack without looking up, still peering down at his fist in the desert light.

"I think what I told you before. It's me as the ghost in the trees, in love with the suns."

The therapist shook his hands a few time, waggled his head back and forth and seemed to rally. "So, you're saying real spook good, CIA spook bad?"

Jack sighed. "I don't know." He then thought to be polite. "What's yours?"

The therapist was staring at Jack directly in the eyes, disconcertingly. "I think..." The therapist faltered. "How strange! It's as if my recall is overlapping. I think it is when I met my darling Elsa, and we made splendid love in the more wild parts of the New Forest. There were no rocks and bad twigs to speak of either, which was fortunate, as this is not always the case."

Jack was terribly envious, because as mentioned in previous chapters, this was his "thing."

They both stopped suddenly in their walk. They had come to a wall in the desert, which Jack saw went up as high as he could strain his neck and to the left and right before them. They had not noticed the wall as they approached it as it was built from untempered glass, or possibly quality plastic, and was utterly transparent until you drew extremely near. It was ten feet thick, a bit over three metres for non-Americans. On the other side of the enceinte, the desert continued, exactly as unchangingly before.

Jack put his hand up to it. The curtain was ice, not glass or plastic. Unmelting ice, but ice nevertheless. His hand entire stuck there for a few seconds. His most terrible of memories? He shuddered, and unbidden to him came images of snowdrifts and carved-up snakes, of ash sifting through the air like cold flakes. He tore his flat hand away from the wall, and it stung him. Jack's palm was scraped from frost and bleeding in places, very shallowly.

"This is a fine to-do," said the therapist. He seemed to want to walk around the wall to observe it from all angles, as was his wont, but this of course was impossible. He turned back to Jack. "What is the most terrible memory of your life? Question 18."

Jack looked over his shrink's shoulder and saw both of their reflections there, merging in the desert sunlight forced onto ice so cold it would not melt. He gazed down at his raw hand and tried to ignore the circumstance that he had predicted that very question. He gazed down at his raw hand. Poultice. Meadowsweet, with crushed mint leaves.

For the first time in what the therapist claimed was several years of therapy, he felt certain that a real memory was emerging. It too took place in ice, amongst snow. There was the howling of animals, possibly of wolves. "Nothing," Jack first lied to therapist, but then he relented, feeling caddish for the deception when the shrink had been so vulnerable himself, and Jack told the therapist of those same, small, frightening details, of the white deep drifts and the wolf calls. The corner of the therapist's mouth twitched as Jack elaborated. Jack believed it could be read as either chiding over the initial lie, or as grace-and-favour. The flat of his hand stung forcefully. "You?"

The therapist sighed and placed both palms flat on

the ice wall, an act of seeming resignation that astonished Jack, for had not the therapist just seen the damage to Jack's own hand; did the therapist not learn from the mistakes of others?

The therapist, it was suddenly made clear, was trying to push at the ice wall. He eventually gave up and wiped his scraped and bleeding hands on his khaki trousers, staining them in a very un-therapisty style. "No comment," said the therapist."

"Comment is free."

Still the therapist deferred. "Moving on." He didn't look Jack in the eyes at all this time. "If you knew you were going to die in a year, what would you change about the way you live your life, and why?"

"If I could do it again, I'd pick and I'd eat more wild blackberries. Because nature is more important than Mazdas, et cetera, et cetera."

"Part of that first bit was a quote from Bloc Party."

"Yes, 'Waiting for the 7.18'." It honestly surprised Jack that the therapist knew of the indie techno group's back catalogue. But people always surprise us, always surprise us. "What of lemon fruits, then?" said Jack. He looked up at the clear wall that went on forever into the sky. "Do you know the land where the lemon-trees grow?"

"Now *you* are citing Goethe. Here I first saw oranges grow: some green, some half, some a quarter, and some full ripe, on the same tree."

"Samuel Pepys."

"Currants and gooseberries, bright-fire-like barber-ries, figs to fill your mouth, citrons from the South, sweet to tongue and sound to eye."

"Christina Rossetti. Are you feeling hungry?"

"Yes."

"Me too," said Jack. He reached for the therapist's hand and squeezed it for a moment. They beamed at each other.

"I told you I enjoyed other people's gardening work," admitted the therapist. "What does the word friendship mean to you?" the therapist asked shyly.

Again Jack experienced a disorientating blur of memory. "Colours gold and green. And ruby and sky-blue." Ah, it must have been Martin swimming through the green water, with all the flowers, and their rescuing of each other. Maybe the therapist was on to something. Jack stared through the ice wall. He wanted the suns to catch the reflections all up in a prism of rainbows, but the ice was too clear. Colours *or* and *vert*. And rubricated *gules* and *azure*.

"Hmm, abstract answer, but I buy it. Always was a fan of the painter Franz Marc." The therapist's face took on a look of wonder. "I think... I think... How odd, I am not sure that this is what I think at all! I think my friends are party-people, carousing all night. Yet they are sedate types who successfully solve the puzzles in *New Scientist* magazine. Maybe they have secret lives, and I have forgotten that. Yes, yes, of course, that's it; they must have told me at some point."

Jack smiled at the therapist in sympathy and then experimentally stuck out the pink tip of his tongue on the ice wall, where it immediately froze to it. "Erngh, raurgh!" he said to the therapist, meaningfully.

"No, no, don't do that, have you no concept of winter? Here, let me help!" The therapist retrieved a small canteen from his khakis and poured the warm liquid over Jack's tongue, melting the ice and releasing it.

"Thank you," said Jack, massaging his sore tongue. He licked his lips. "Grand Marnier.""

"As I told you, I've always been rather fond of oranges."

They both looked contentedly at the ice wall for a moment. Eventually the therapist enquired as to the importance of love and affection on Jack's life, whilst adding that both were of utmost importance in his own.

"Important," said Jack, tersely.

"Okay," said the therapist, taking the hint. "And we continue on. It's an assigned task, not a question. We're going alternate sharing five things we like about the other. I like your stubbornness."

"Your whimsy."

"Your fine set of moose horns. I always liked moose-meat sausage."

"Capriciousness."

"Your wise grey eyes. Your wisdom, actually."

"You've never forced me to answer one single thing during my therapeutic process. You've always let me continue as I am."

"You're brave."

"You're playful. These silly psychological mind games. I've always loved them."

"You're special. There's something different about you."

There was a wildness to the therapist, underneath the crossword puzzles.

"You're wild."

They stared at each other again, blushing.

The therapist cleared his throat and broke the awkward silence. "How close was your family? Was your childhood a happy one, compared to that of others?"

"I don't remember them, but I have to say that, yes, I do think that it must have been a close family. I think that it probably was happier than most. Up to a point." Jack was not sure himself what he meant by that last statement.

The therapist blinked once more in surprise. "Revealing. My answer is more like yours normally are. For some inexplicable *raison*, although I have the general sense that my childhood was happy, I cannot recall at the moment whether I had siblings or nay. It's all a bit nebulous. And how is your relationship with your mother? I'll go first," said the therapist. His face softened into brightness. "Now, *her* I can remember. She is pure love; I love everything about her."

Jack's face changed, too; he could see the shift in the reflection on the flat ice. And he could see a woman, as well, but she had the head of a large owl. Despite her beak, he had fragments of her: kindness, patience, pitched laughter, imagination. Quite a lot of imagination. "My relationship with my mother? Good," he said at last. "It was a good one."

***

A wild flight, in the sense of fleeing, a stag crashing Actaeon-like through the low trees and brambles harassed by his own hounds, the Hunt nipping at hooves, the dogs baying in a cliché fashion; they've got the scent, they've got the scent, they've got the scent. They've lost it. All is lost. The hunters release the tops from glass jars and all is won. The contents are crumpled fragments of crusted underwear, of piss-stained boxer shorts, of menstrual pads stolen from bathroom bins. The dogs have got the scent again; oh, they've got the scent, all right. The dogs distrainèd do their part; the hunters do the rest. The yolden hounds bite; they devour; they conquer; the stag is on its four knees, crumpling in the green roots of the deep woods.

We're here, not in the past at all, or not in the too-distant past, anyway. East Germany's Stasi had an elaborate "smell-jar" programme, where the most personal items of unlaundered clothing were, firstly, stolen in secret by the government from the homes of private citizens, and, secondly, bottled up in glass jars with impermeable lids and stored on rows of shelves and labeled with the finest, most officious museum tags a bureaucracy gone mad can afford. This was in the case that any such citizen were to turn to criminal acts, then said fugitives would be more easily traced by sniffer dogs.

The Stasi were also fond of hiding secret cameras and microphones in wooden stumps and trees in the forests. It is as if Hansel and Gretel and Snow White from the same German folk tales went a little nuts, if marzipan houses and the finger-bones of young male children and poisoned apple pieces in glass coffins weren't nuts enough already, yes. Bureaucracy. Its vines, they do twist and maladapt. Something to consider.

***

"Do you remember Simonides? Sorry, that's a bit of a joke," the therapist added abruptly.

"No."

"I assumed you wouldn't. You see, I know your little ways. Greek poet, used a method of memorisation called *loci*, also known as the art of the 'mind palace'. According to the 'brain-training' blog *Lumosity*, loci, not to be confused with Norse puck-a-like Loki, loci is rooted in the fact that memory takes place in an activated area of the mind linked with spatial navigation – chimps have far better spatial short-term memory than humans, by the way, but we won't go into that now – anyhoo, with the loci method, one populates a 'mind palace' with different rooms, and in each room is the object you want to commit to memory. So you make your object placed in the palace room memorable, and juxtapositioned imagery is even better. Say, for example, you want to remember a man with facial hair – a hairy man – and what that man did by a body of water. So you put a huge handlebar moustache in an incongruent setting – say a desert baking in your mind-palace – and next to the moustache you place a dripping water tap."

Jack blinked at the therapist. "What about the pineapple?"

"Pardon me?" The therapist laughed at him, but kindly. "*Your* pineapple, *your* problem." Jack looked crestfallen, and the therapist quickly clarified, "I do not have the capacity to crawl inside your mind palace and take a gander, though it's often been a superpower I wished I had in relation to my clients. Hey! *That* will be my undisclosed superpower."

"You're backtracking."

"Okay, question 25, then. It's actually a task. Similarly to how we did it before, we're each going to make three 'we-statements' that are true; for example, 'we both feel exhilarated and uncomfortable with the direction these 36 questions have taken.' That will be my first, to start us off."

"We both are hungry." Bellytimber.

There was a very long pause.

"We are both wondering whether the other person is someone else entirely," they both said at exactly the same time.

"Hey, not fair," said Jack, "we both had the same answer!"

"Tough," said the therapist. "And that observation, by the way, as I thought it too, counts as our third 'we' statement." He winked at Jack. "I rather wish I had someone with whom I could share the midnight."

"Huh?"

"It's a question, not a statement. The middle of the night. And I don't know why I said it anyway; I have Elsa. Complete the sentence yourself, 'I rather wish I had someone with whom I could share...' Dot, dot, dot," he added unnecessarily.

"I know what an ellipsis is and I understand when someone's voice is trailing off. Popcorn," answered Jack, "moving on." He mimicked the therapist, but in a rather flattering way.

"If you decided that you were going to be a close

friend of mine, what would be important for you to know?"

"I suppose... No, the ellipses! You answer first."

"All right." The psychotherapist took his time. "I would need to know," he said at last, "what you did last summer."

"Sub-par American horror film of 1997, based on a superior 1971 young adult novel by Lois Duncan?"

"The same. But also the truth. I would really need to know."

What an odd answer. Assuming they would be home, and not in a fictitious desert, summer was full of green park trees in London, not horror, as far as Jack's limited amnesiac experience went. Yet in such a perfect way the therapist was right – how *could* you be close friends with someone if you did not know, or want to know, what they did last summer or indeed all possible summers, be it horror or pleasure? "I also need to know that."

"For the next question, they want us to tell the other person something about them that we like, that we wouldn't say to someone we'd just met, and they warn us to be very honest, insultingly alluding that we might have been deceptive previously."

"I thought we already did this one?"

"They seem to want us to answer it again. I suspect it's a reinforcement technique."

Jack wondered whether it was possible for the ice wall to function as an enormous magnifying glass wielded by a child scoring high on the psychopathy checklist, in the glare of the three suns. The top of his head *was* getting extraordinarily warm.

"I like your shy glances when you speak of your wife, and you speak of her often," said Jack, taking the initiative. Extraordinarily, he did not feel jealous in the slightest degree.

The psychotherapist impulsively grabbed for Jack's hand and squeezed it in sudden affection, then disentangled as Jack's hand was sweaty from the heat. "I like your shy glances too. You have very long eyelashes. Like a 33-year-old white human male Bambi. Hold on, Bambi was male too. I get confused by the long eyelashes in cartoons. So sad about the mother."

"Now, we're supposed to share something embarrassing that has happened to us in the past," said Jack.

"Now, we have to share something embarrassing from the past," said Jack's therapist – "wait, how did you know that I'd say that?!"

Jack gazed soulfully at the therapist. The melting ice took on a romantic twinkle.

"Well, all right then," the therapist mellowed. "I once cooked an entire bread pudding – you make the posh ones with multiple *pains au chocolat*; they're quite extraordinary – as an anniversary surprise for my darling Elsa, but was I embarrassed when at her first forkful we discovered that I had in fact accidentally concocted said dish with three-week curdled milk! Gosh! We might have kissed the hare's foot that night, but we laughed and laughed and had quite the keak!" He smiled at his memory. "Then we developed a form of *lactobacillus* food poisoning and we had to go to A&E. Adjoining cubicles and E looked very fetching in her hospital gown. *Gosh!*"

In the ice was the reflection of the gold-and-red thatched cabin. Was the memory that Jack was going to speak of in just three seconds a true one? Well, perhaps that didn't matter. "My second grade schoolteacher exposed my moose-horns to the class at large by pulling down my Ace of Base hoodie, and the whole class laughed at me." That sounded right to him, but he wasn't sure if it was right.

The therapist nodded sympathetically.

The therapist finally spoke again. "When was the last time you cried in front of another person, and when was the last time that you cried by yourself? I cried when you left me. When you ended our therapeutic work together. Technically it was both *in front of you* and also *by myself*, after you closed the clinic door."

"Oh!" Jack had not noticed at the time and had no idea that the therapist had felt that way. He also had no recollection of abruptly ending therapy. By his recall, it was *he* who had returned to knock on an unanswered clinic door. "I… believe that I cried when my pet died. I don't remember if it was a cat or a dog. Maybe a guinea pig if I am allergic. In front of others? I have no clue. Men truly don't cry as often as women. I read it in *New Scientist*. You've mentioned that publication. I know you respect it."

"Like *Cosmo* for scientific minds. That you can recollect that fragment, however, is promising." The therapist approved. "We're on 31. We're supposed to tell our partner something that we already like about them."

"*Again*?!"

"I like that you said that."

"I like that you like that I said that."

"Now we're supposed to say what we find too serious to be joked about. I have a short but meaningful list. No rape jokes, Holocaust jokes or indeed any jokes concerning oppression of the vulnerable – *unless* the joke is on those who would hurt the vulnerable. And even then I am not obliged to laugh if it's not funny."

"You mean jokes about the-rapists?"

"I told you earlier I didn't like that joke. I mean that the joke would have to be making fun of the rapists themselves. Like *Football Town Nights*. Or the Nazis. Like *The Producers*. Or people who, say, stalk and kill the mentally disabled, if such people exist. I rather hope they don't. Wait. They do. I remember it from my clinical studies."

"I like your policy." Jack was actually pleasantly surprised at the therapist's insight. "That's my policy too, now. And, as I understand it, I have permission then to make a joke about the-rapists, because as the therapist you have the top-down power, and I am vulnerable?"

The therapist stared fixedly at the mole on Jack's left ear, not dissimilar to the one to the right of Jack's left nipple. Eventually a look of love came back to the therapist's eye, and he shook his head as if to clear it, and patted Jack several times on the back of his hand. "If I died tonight, I'd regret telling you that I have spent the most interesting days of my life with you. I think I've just been so scared of telling you."

Jack flushed and couldn't help being flattered. He had never known that the therapist had felt that way, or even enjoyed a single therapeutic session. It just goes to show you. "Hey, me too."

The therapist grinned a little, in relief. His eyes were welling up; Jack could see it. The therapist would have a new answer for Question 30 soon. Actually, so would Jack.

"Moving on. Question 34."

"What about Question 33?" asked Jack.

"The if-I-died-tonight *was* Question 33."

"I didn't realise." Jack felt a little shy. "I just thought we were saying those things and meant them."

"We did and we do." The therapist smiled widely at Jack. His teeth were very white. He brushed, flossed and gargled every night and every morning. Jack knew it without even asking. He knew everything about him.

"What if everything in your house caught on fire? After saving people and pets, what would be the one item you'd save?"

"I'd save my memories of you. Because."

"And I'd save mine of you."

It wasn't clear who spoke first and who responded, or if it was the thirty-fourth question, and it didn't matter. They stared mutually into each other's gaze.

The therapist voiced the thirty-fifth question in a low voice, and he turned his head to look downwards, now avoiding Jack's eyes. The question asked out of all your family, whose death do you think that you would find the most troubling?

Jack was about to say his parents, as the one thing he knew for sure was that he had to have parents, whereas having a wife or a husband or children was not a foregone conclusion. He was about to say that, but somewhere within him there remained a flicker of the fact that he believed himself to have a child. He could not separate himself from even the concept of this unconfirmed offspring; it was very deep-rooted.

He murmured something to this effect, and the therapist did the same. It was a terrible question and it seemed frivolous to merely ponder in a getting-to-know-you exercise, almost as if the price of love was imagining the death of your child. Quite sickening and cynical. Morbid. Jack knew that the therapist as a parent agreed with him, and he loved him for it.

The wall was melting into a hole in one place not too far to their left; the combined power of three suns had focused at one moment during the day like a magnifying glass, druidic, and was burning a narrow scar on the ice wall. Someone had not paid the murage.

"We're supposed to share a problem, a personal one, and ask the advice of the other person. And we have to ask the other person to reflect back to us how we seem to be feeling. Oh my. *Hwæt*, this is all very California even for a therapist."

"My personal problem," said Jack, hesitatingly, "is what it always is, and why I came to you in the first place. I cannot remember who I am and I cannot remember who I was." He reached for the therapist's hand and gripped it tightly, and the therapist gripped tightly back, and kept holding it.

"I'm sorry. I'm sorry that I haven't been able to help you yet."

"What should I do?"

"Keep trying. You're stubborn and you squeak out revelations from time to time. You're going to get there in the end. I believe in you." He squeezed Jack's hand so hard that Jack nearly yelped, but they kept on holding each other.

"How do I appear to be feeling about my 'problem'?"

"The right way," said the therapist. "Anyone would feel exactly the way you do, whether you feel bad or good or hopeless or hopeful."

The therapist released Jack's hand and they sat there before the ice wall for nearly five minutes. A tunnel had appeared through the wall where the ice had melted, but neither of them seemed inclined to do anything about it. The therapist seemed to have forgot(ten) his side of the question. Finally Jack prompted him with a joke about Lucy's psychiatrist stand in *Peanuts* and that spurred the therapist to whisper something in Jack's ear, then draw away just as quickly, as if he were ashamed of what he had admitted. Jack nodded.

"Then you need to wait," said Jack. "And you seem to be feeling impatient."

They both lay back on the sand, which felt warm now, not blistering, possibly due to the proximity of the ice. They did not touch each other but they looked up at the clouds. There's a bunny, there's a heart, there's a stegosaurus.

Once they were done, they got to their feet and they walked through the wall. The ten-foot passage glittered from above. It was like journeying through an ice-cube. The therapist had transformed into silver, like a kokological bird.

Once they had made it to the other side of the cocktail, the therapist turned to Jack. "I'm going to disappear now."

"Why?" Jack felt tear-sting. "Why?"

"I'm not real. I'm just a dream-therapist. *Poof!* Good-bye!"

The silver therapist vanished.

Jack looked forward, across the sands on the other side of the wall.

Ahead in the desert, but coming towards him, was a naked, smiling Martin. Martin carried his long stick, held like a threat or a very sweet memory.

***

"Do you know the land where the lemon-trees grow,
in darkened leaves the gold-oranges glow,
a soft wind blows from the pure blue sky,
the myrtle stands mute, and the bay-tree high?"

– Johann Wolfgang von Goethe, 1917

She bathed in the holy well, at its mouth where it was the least downsteepy and where she was for the most part hidden by soft low bushes on the autumn edge. The water was cold in an adventurous way on her breasts and belly. Her sex stung from the shock when she lowered herself into the ladywell waters, but soon the lake mouth felt cool.

Halfway through cleansing she felt him watching and she called out, she called out. There was no answer, was no answer. The water cold on the backs of her thighs was delicious, was delicious.

She saw the puck then. At first she was not certain there was a being amongst the verdure and believed him imaginal. Yet. He was then laughing and his eyes went up and down. In irritation, she splashed water at him, which he dodged. "Where's a ewerer when you need one? Are you Diana; are you going to turn me into a ten-point puck for spying? I'd look gorgeous with a stag-head, don't you think?" *Don't you think.*

She did not know all the varying stories of the blasphemous Roman gods like Jesus or Diana despite her years of fakery on the roads; she had only deeply known the

Blue School gods, and half of those she had forgotten. Had forgotten.

The water had turned warm now, heated by the bright morning sun. She felt it on her hips. On her hips. There were flowers on the spring edge, yellow ones with long snouts that had lasted their spring emergence into summer. They were fresh and the scent of them tickled her nose; and she also could smell the sexual, tangerine heaviness of the greyfruits; that scent filled her nostrils for a moment and she thought she could not breathe, but then she could breathe.

She could breathe.

He had disappeared.

The holy well fed the dangerous lake at the far end and she would get on her knees and drink from it, her breasts wet and splashed, her mouth dripping water like a wolf does blood. She did this three times and the last time she did it she saw her Green Man again.

He with his reddish gingery curls, ringlets really, twisted with barks and twigs and leaves, and such auburn coils were suggestive of an adult's coarse nether hair, for naturally as a woman now Florentine had this hair too. And his appearance caused in Florentine the disconcerting effect of staring at his curly ginger head and thinking, blushing, of hair otherwhere. All she had to do was lower her eyes. She did, and when she raised her gaze he was smirking. The Green Man had been stiff and his pubic hair had indeed been wild and wiry like his curls, but his smugness meant that

Florentine would not a second time give him the satisfaction of looking down. Then she looked down at him a second time and, while she stared, they moved towards each other so that they were stroking each other before their eyes even met again. There was something too raw and scraping about both their actions, but there was excitement in her throat now as their necks touched and she knew it didn't matter, that little pulse of time from something-never-happening to something-happening; none of it would ever matter again now that something was happening.

Her hands in the red hair that fell to his nape; his grind of stubble; he twisted her fat pink nipple and she twisted his small brown one in return. They drew their faces away from each other then, though they had already nuzzled and licked, and looked at each other in alarm.

She tossed back her hair over her shoulders and under her horns, bound it in a quick knot, and she looked at him and she trembled. Her hair was already becoming loose again and she saw that he shook too.

Their mouths, their lips met; they drank each other, clasping, both knees-down in the water, and they kissed and green candle like a lightning seared in Florentine's brain; she was enormously excited; down her spine; the flash made her wet too, sticky for him like a closed bud; the parts of her that had been protected from the water and from him. He was juicy, his cock stiff and dripping sap from its overgrown acorn tip when he reared momentarily out of the water and covered her body in his, like a pounce, his eyes with an indirect stare that meant he belonged to this moment only, and he kissed her and he bit her and she bit him. He put his tongue in her mouth and she liked it.

They fucked and the trees rained green leaves around their bodies, nesh; his limbs, lithe, turned at times to sinewy young oak branches, and then they would fuck closer, her lips squat down on him, grinding him into the roots, pounding him down with the wild red syrup of her cunt, like a heart thrust over his prick, and down he went, and down she went, and then from time to time the motions went backwards, and he caught hold of her horns and toppled her over so that she then was on her back and he ground down on her in this way, and the sap in him was green, and the juice in her veins ran a wild red, and they fucked like this, lost in sticky lust, grunting and churning and rubbing and poking, and swallowing, and licking, until the sun went down and they were fucking still by moonlight; they had become black and grey shadows tipped by a silvery golden moon at times, a tree and a stag, and a stag and a tree, and still they fucked.

*

It was during this interlude that a great tempest surged through the forest. The rain and winds tore through the alleys between the trees that only birds and honeybees use, and leaves and branches were littered down upon the woods floor, mere scrogglings left on the greyfruit trees.

There was a stick there on the ground, a broken

stubbed branch, sharp nubs remaining as if it had the beginnings of horns, and this storm detritus first turned green and snaky but then lightened, as if one dipped a pure green summer leaf into ice. The stick turned frostened white and grew wings; it knew the languages of birds. It flew off. It flew off forever or came back, who knows.

Other plants were left behind and active. *Datura stramonium* – the devil's trumpet, snare and tempting apple – that plant grew vines that twisted out and curled round the still-shaking trees, O jimson weed; once there was an antler beast, but it escaped, too.

Foxes and wolves twined round each other, and came purring towards the glade. Groups of nine animals came to drink wet-mouthed from the holy well. One set was squirrel, wasp, raven, beetle, ferret, hedgehog, badger, boar, eagle; another set was firefly, field mouse, marten, ladybug, toad, hare, robin, Churchill's black dog, the wildcat.

The storm was a crazed one, and at dawn when the thunder and watering had ceased, the forest entire glittered – bruces, spirches, cottonwood, oaks and greyfruits alike – and the ground mulch was covered where the various leaves and needles had rained down.

*

Something had happened while they were fused together, a part of her had split off forever, and a part of him too, and those parts had fused, antler and leaf. She was not sure quite when it happened: when they had been light and lusty, or when they had been caught inside the dark shadow plays. It had taken place, that splitting. She looked at him; she saw the sweat in his clavicle on the longest day of the year. The dim, short era of night had passed and now the songbirds called: nightingales, great awks, owls and Isisauruses. All birds were mating, or cooing for a mating, and the sun summer song at dawn meant leaves were at their brightest and greenest. Florentine caught her breath and looked at him again; he was not looking at her. Was he alive? O, he moves; the Oak King lives; he was only dead for a moment and now he lives to breathe and fuck and sing again. They could make love into the next afternoon; they could make love for days, and do not forget the nights...

She whispered one of his many names to him, and he turned to her, drew her close to him; kissed the tip of her nose.

"Close, but no cigar," he said, "the moniker is old plain John today." He looked sad, to some degree. "Ours is not to reason why – 'Which made them all to chafe and swear'. "

She lay her antlers gently against his arms in that embrace. "That is a harvest song. And today it is still a true and deep summer."

"Harvest, mudmonth, summer, what's the difference?"

"That's your fourth question now," Florentine commented. "How many are you going to ask me?"

"Druids or dryads," elaborated the puck. "Apples or

oranges."

"They were greyfruits, not oranges." She did not know why this mistake continued to annoy her.

"The point remains, birth before death before birth: that drunken, suffering old sod, how his mouth foams with ale and whiskey – Johnny B expires so that lushes might live to taste a swig of transsubstantiated high-grain alcohol. 'Do this in memory of me.' Apple, orange. Cider, Grand Marnier. Now do you see?" She did not nod, but he continued regardless. "Take Christ, that ol' bleeding-heart Mithras-wannabe, he too succumbs so that folks, those little acorns, might live to glop their tipsycakes; the Oak King burns."

The puck looked like he might say more on this last regent for a moment, but stopped himself and continued.

"Harvest follows, redemption follows, the holly leaves that prick your finger follow. And with it wheat, good or nay, and the clerics, good or nay, and the knotting down of nature, good or nay. Life, death, life. And so it goes, so *ad infinitum*. So is the way of the world."

"But you did not die; you are still here."

"So I am," he said, and he kissed her.

"Don't die," she said, and she kissed the puck back.

*

Puck, by the way, all his leaves tattered and torn, is known to sour the ewe's milk while still in her teats on Imbolc, so a fine fertility symbol he makes. Don't expect logic here. Or anywhere. Don't ever expect logic. But personally I always make an effort. The *puca*, Old English, they make lights in the forest and sounds in the forests and folk follow such beacons and echoes off the paths and lose themselves in the fairy-lit woods. Oops, there's a pretty red mushroom with white spots. Oops, I swear I heard Aunt Margaret calling to me. Oops, look towards the flicker off those pretty lights. Oops, now I'm completely lost with no compass and certainly no GPS. Oops.

The French, the Germans, the Dutch all have their *puca*-likes too, supernaturals who lure honest woodsmen off paths with white flickering Weihnacht lights bought at Globus supermarket, but these fairies are known as White Ladies. They are not so different from white birds, which are also alluring and dangerous. White Ladies love their lipstick and the woodsmen love their White Ladies, to be honest, and the Dames Blanches also are partial to entering farmsteads and spoiling the milk as it's churned.

Again, the souring-of-milk metaphor. And these are supposed to be our fertility icons, closer to the root in every sense? Never mind.

*

They had fallen back asleep and now it was very late morning, a day that felt like the morning the blue bird had flown into her twig hut. She lay next to the sleeping him, but she

did not know if it was he who was the blue bird, or if it was she.

She did know that when she looked down on herself after their night together that she had started to grow hair, not the pelts of puberty under arms and between legs, for those she had already, but red-gold stag's fur on her neck, arms, legs and belly.

9

Puck

Spring in the forest when the sun through the whole day
has cooked the woods and ferns down to the smell of licorice
by evening. They fucked in the trees and it was a beautiful thing. He held her hand and pulled her in there, and his
beard was bristly against her soft cheek. He held her hand,
and he pulled her into the crotch of the trees; he held her
hand and no one could see betwixt she disappeared.

*

The greyfruit trees sway in hot summer; hairy fronds twist
over the fruits themselves as on coconuts. Jungle even in
a northern clime, all ripe forest and lewd fruitmeat. Evergreens bake and vines stew and pine needles burrow into
Florentine's flesh and make her think about them even when
they're not really there. The winds blow but the feel on her
bare skin is hot puff; it does not distract her from the fruits.
She keeps thinking about them; she does not want to think
about them.

"Taste one," says Puck, "imagine how it would feel
in your throat. That crude red interior; the fruit-flesh sliding
down, slowly, the juice like musk and strawberry."

Florentine shakes her head no; Puck aside, no one
has ever picked a greyfruit tree to her knowledge; they own

themselves; they are not for picking, though her mother had gathered them fallen for cider. But now the idea is in her head and she cannot stop thinking of it. The tips on her antlers tighten.

Puck's hand is on her waist, moves up over the planes of her bare back, curls round her shoulders. Her whole body is itching, as when you sleep when it's too hot outside. "We could crack it off," he whispers in her ear, "I'd peel it open and pour the fruit into your mouth, your lips open. Think of how it would taste."

She is thinking of how it would taste.

"Your lips would be red." His voice in her ear. "You'd kiss it back to me, all that fire in your mouth."

She shakes her head no again, they cannot, no one harvests the greyfruits, they are free trees not slave trees, and Puck disentangles himself from her, his limbs just as sulkily purposeful in their retreat.

*

"You've grown more hair, you wild thing," says Puck to Florentine, and his hand brushes her thigh, where there is a pelt now, and fur over her toes and fingers.

Like his, like his, like his beautiful self. She clasps him to her and she does not ever let him go.

"I love your bark," she says, "your moss, your ivies."

*

There is bounty in summer. As summer drawled, he became distant in some ways yet intense in some forms, too. The bounty was there, wasn't there, was there. When she noted and duly informed him she was with child, as the sun dripped golden at Lughnasa, his lips went up and he patted her hand, but he looked left and right like a fox. It was at night when he became his churned-up self again, and they entangled each other in their fucks, the blood-drive in them both and the silkiness between them. It was good, but not *as* good. It was intimate, but not *as* close.

*

When she was pregnant she was bursting and yet she could not burst. She was endless spring that never hit summer. She would not pop like a bud trembling to expose its inners, its soft damp coiled leaves that did not yet take in space the form of a leaf. Yet.

*

Ewe. Yew. You. The best of stories are curious stories and so you understand that something once had been green and spicy in the woods, and then it was Autumn and not. The Green Man had been late for a fourth time now and, though she sat and keened for him by the lake, he did not come, and there was then a third promise broken.

"The beast hath root, the plant hath flesh and blood.
The nimble plant can turn it to and fro,
The nummed beast can neither stir nor goe,
The plant is leafless, branchless, void of fruit,
The beast is lustless, sexless, fireless, mute."

– Guillaume de Salluste Du Bartas, 1587

Dull thrills of sickness ran through her and she pushed herself exhausted to her feet, her grandest stomach with the drum the little one sometimes played. He had promised her that he would come and he did not come.

She said all fifty of his favourite names three times in the water as she had done before, and she remembered how they had hustled cloven to each the other, in spring when everything green would give a click and tremble into a flower or a grass blade. They had trembled onto each other and laid down in the shallow water. They had sucked. Now where was he, her world had become darkened blue, why was he a-change? She looked in the waters of the holy spring and there was she, great horns, great stomach, great breasts. There was not he.

There was a high keening pitch-sound in the bottom of her loins and she crawled up the bank and went to the cabin threshold where he had once left an ornament of forest gifts and she called for him. She screamed out to

Brigit, Áine and even Jesu for him; the deities did not interfere. She carved F + R on a tree as an invocation. She pissed
on starflowers and violets and called for him; he did not
answer. She cut her arm and squeezed blood onto the ground
and chanted *robingoodfellowrobinhoodpuckpanosirisbaphomet-
greenmanlokijohnbarleycorncernnunoswildmanhollykingoakking-
ludgreenknightviridiosgreengeorgeenkidufatherchristmassatyrsas-
quatchbigfoottlalocdergcorrafaceofgloryamoghasiddifaunuspashupa
tikokopellipangujacko'lanternjesusmaykinghernewoodwosepilosiye-
tisnowmandusiosinuusfig-gyschratsylvesterleshyorcojackfrostalkhi-
drsylvanuspeterpanjackinthegreen* and he did not come. Her
stomach lurched and she stumbled from the threshold into
the trees, calling for him, green bird, come back.

In the middle distance was the group of greyfruit
trees.

By the time she drew near to the glade, she saw that
he had indeed escaped her. As must have been his will; she
wept bitterly; he had planted himself and taken seed. A
large plant directly. Gymnosperm, the naked seed; it is well
known in Botanical Science that there are gymnosperms
with beautifully coloured cones: silvery, purpled, greenish,
marbled, such naked seeds.

When one walks the roads for years as a false priest,
as Florentine had done, one hears miraculous stories concerning vegetable lambs (*Agnus scythicus*), who grow from
melon-seeds. Some vegetable lamb-fruits, multiple, are
wooly in their pods, wet like the cruel skinning to make
astrakhan wool from unborn lambs ripped from their mur-

dered mothers' wombs; the very thought hurts Florentine and makes her eyes go blind for seconds with fury; fashionistas have their euphemisms and call it Broadtail Lamb or Persian Lamb, but we and they know how astrakhan is sourced in its sticky black coils.

The other type of vegetable lamb is singular, one lamb grows out umbilicular from the main plant, and its veggie self eats the grass surrounding its tether until it – the solitary vegetable lamb and the main plant too – like the astrakhan ewe and her astrakhan lamb, both die.

Some say that if you cut open an immature soft fruit of the first variety, that is to say the many-fruiting vegetable lamb, you see a little plant sheep already in there, complete in form but without its wool.

The other – singular – variety of vegetable lamb sprouts out from the stem itself to grow as high as your knees. It has hooves, bones, wool. Its blood tastes like honey. I said it already; if its plant-cord is severed, it dies.

"I will not die," says Florentine to herself, clutching her stomach. "*It* will not die."

This is the story of the Vegetable Lamb.

Vegetable lambs, also called borometzes, the perfect dish for your picky vegetarian college-aged nieces at Christmas, vegetable lambs are said to be mythologised from a type of fern with a hairy underground root (*oh-là-là*), technically called a rhizome. A rhizome with quadrupedal, ruminant qualities.

There are also stories told by peddlers who sell mandrake root: that the mandrake is a root off a vegetable man; that if you touch a mandrake you die; that the mandrake is a plant that grows from the corpses of hanged men; that it grows in the shape of a little man; that if you light an edge of its root it glows like a candle for you (do not touch it; do not touch it).

Florentine stares at the ground. He has sacrificed himself; he is mandrake; he is a vegetable man. There is a great green plant, taller than her. Tall as the greyfruit trees but not a tree. It should be an oak sapling, with all logic, but it is not an oak. It is not man-shaped; it is plant-shaped. It has huge pods spurting forth all over it. Ripe. It will soon drop its fruit; the scent doubtless heady. But Robin is gone. He has curled in on himself. She wishes indeed that there was a hint of his shape here; even a mandrake's hand, or a barnacle man like the barnacle geese which do not grow from beach driftwood, as rumoured, but instead grow like gourds as fruits on trees, even those approximations would do. But instead this huge plant. She touches her stomach; she touches one of the pods too, stroking both her belly and it. Will her child be a plant? Will it be green? Will her breasts spit out sap to nurse it?

There are problems concerning whether you are permitted vegetable lambs and barnacle geese during fasts; are they meat or are they frond? There are deep-set problems; fairy tales of the soft-skinned vegetable lambs with moist curls avoid the truth of astrakhan. Dried foetal wool does look vegetative, like a carrot left too long in the refrigerator, many months. Sadism. Florentine clutches her belly. Not a rolling pain, not this time. Masochism. Where is he, is he in this bush? Masochism. She knew he was always going to seed, and yet she had loved him anyway. You bake the ruptured ram in still-hot ashes: blood sweet and a taste like seafood. She clutches her belly.

She wept a bit and then, after further exploration, she saw that this vegetable he had become was of both varieties: there were the fertile pods as big as cantaloupes, contents unseen; but also there round the back, revealed at last, a vegetable man linked by a vine from his navel back to the plant. She had longed to see his shape in this plant and now she had found it. Robin, carding crones' wool for them before dawn, so they woke with their labours eased, but also sending night terrors to the old women to haunt their dreams. *Green-georgie-porgy, blows out candles with sighs. Kisses girls in the dark, and makes them all cry.* He had betrayed her; he had left her; he had gone to sleep on her and their fruit together; he had closed his eyes into Arnolfini vegetation eyelids and left her to fend the winter on her own, what could she do? She would bear it on Beltane, three months past Imbolc, three months past snow crashing through the trees and her eyes would burn at the memory of her parents and of Eglentyne. What would she do now, what could she do? She gritted with anger towards him; seeding and rooted, avoiding his responsibility. His vegetable head like a true jack o' lantern, scooped out with a candle inside, eyes glittering, but she did not move, just saw him for the turnip he was.

She did not in any way see him as a lamb of god, one who selflessly had sacrificed himself to Winter like a christ, not like the Blue School would have seen it. He had deserted her and ran away from her. He had grown from a plant called oak; now he grew from another like a vegetable lamb. Sheep are somehaps called lords of the field. He had retreated. Wolves compete with humans for the taste of the vegetable lamb; it is popular with them. He had abandoned her and it. The golden chicken fern, as the borometz sometimes is called, is starchy. Coward. His fingers were leaves, his subtle lips were petals, his prick a root, his arms and legs tough stalks. A re-greening, the Blue School would say, the transubstantiational return of man to nature, metaphysical, beautiful, symbolic. He had coldly gutted the animal that she was.

Florentine sat there in the woods, shaded by the grey-fruit trees, and looked at him. He was bound and could not run away, but he was gone to winter. Not far from here was the place where she and her brothers had dug a hole for their mother and father. It was late autumn; she should be burying apples as food for the dead, sustenance until all re-births. Coward. Soon the green stalks would toughen and unfallen gourds stiffen; soon the colour would stretch into brown, then be greyed, and the soft follicles on it creak into their wilt.

Curious bushes that grew bitsy sheep inside themselves, soft and tender little babies with their wailing; Florentine fancied she could hear their piteous cries even now.

The green was cooling all around the leaves and calyxes and pods now as winter came.

*

Three months later she came back in snow and looked at it again.

The cold calyxes, the buds of the plant. She had heard the stories. She was quivering; her body was quivering. Her womb was quivering. She touched the vegetable man again. Unheard lips. Shut eyes. In an odd way like the almost-child.

Florentine was suddenly dropped with fear. She could not do this on her own. She needed her mother; her friend Eglentyne; the Blue School matriarchs.

Numbly, she cracked off a hard gourd and cradled it in her hands. Her satchel was packed; the cabin boarded up; the greyfruit trees dead silent. Her shoes too dampened already in the snow; she should be dozing by fires, not having her early milk crust up in frost upon her bosom. Would there be a little lamb inside the melon, or a little man? She peeled the front of the plant and her fingers were raw in the cold. Inside there was no beast nor homunculus *per se*; there was a full-size adult penis, a facsimile of Robin's. She had once loved its texture and its smell, but now she looked at the summer penis with indifference before pushing the fruit back down into its nest again and peeling over again the shell. Were there recipes that made use of such fruits? She plucked two more such gourds and wrapped them all and she put all three gourds into her satchel.

Then she went round to the back side of the large plant and saw the green man, snowed over. He was still connected to the frosted stem by the fibrous root-vines that fed his navel, but he was no living thing. Florentine severed the stalk at the belly-button with her birthday pocketknife, let the frozen man-shaped plant fall over with a clumping sound in the drifts, put the knife back in her pocket, hoisted the satchel over her shoulder, shook the snowflakes from her horns, walked out from the glade and did not look back once.

* * *

Let's use a nature metaphor. If you were a squirrel, where is the coldest place of humanity in which you'd hide away your nut? Let's say seed. Squirrels love nuts and seeds, but what is not well known is that they chomp down peppermint candies like god almighty.

If I were some sort of cosmic squirrel, say that Ratatoskr who perches on the Yggdrasil Tree in Norse mythology – though I assure you, I am more the lockbox – if I were some sort of cosmic squirrel and I needed a denatured land – and why would I need a denatured land, and the answer is

that in a denatured land they no longer recognize the sprigs, the buds, the fruits,
the mulch, the seeds, the nuts – if I were
a cosmic squirrel whom we have endowed with
surprising powers that break all known
laws of physics and spacetime in all possible multiverses – if I were such a cosmic
squirrel and I was in need of a denatured,
inhumane time/place in which to secret away
my "nut" (potential, mind you, as either
tree or calorific energy, squirrel-wise), I
believe I'd choose East Berlin, perhaps a
year before the Wall came down. Not 1990s
Rwanda, 1970s Khmer Rouge, 1930s Nazi Germany, 1915 Armenia; hey, not even 15th-cen-
tury Aztec Triple Alliance. Those times are
purposefully cruel and easily recognizable.
No, I would choose a society mundane, des-
ert-grey and deeply troubled: peacetime. In
wars or leading up to them, folks at least
prepare for and expect bald sadism. In mundanity, we grow to accept our servitude to
the grey bossman, and the unusual becomes
unremarkable.

I would hide the green rush of life
triumphant and mischief bright-eyed and
subversive in a society where all trust is
gone. All friendship false. All involved

spy on each the other, and shrug shoulders in resignation. Perhaps I would have my nut just outside that society, depressingly observing it. Something ex-pat. So that all eccentricities are excused.

I wouldn't count on my nut getting amnesia or, worse, sudden recall. I wouldn't have wanted that. That would complicate matters. I would have wanted my hidden nut to stay exactly that, a nut.

Now who's the crazy one?

***

The snow drifts cling to the greyfruit trees; the orchard is silent. This tree cluster has witnessed murder and castratings and sexual congress; these fruits are glued shut and do not tell what they know. But secretly, the winter greyfruit pods are dreaming.

Not far from the greyfruits, the Green Man is asleep and dreams his vegetable dreams, fancies too weak for boys, too green and idle for girls of nine. He dreams of a snaky vine, perhaps his own, curling and growing and twisting. The vine is thick and uncut. Beneath his plant cocoon, in his shuttered mind, the vine is growing growing growing. He does not think of Florentine at all, for though she is flower, he is snout. He vines at any and at all: all flora quite certainly gorgeous but individual blossoms quite certainly unspecial; how could they not be, when all are special? That fights nature's very variety. Sap croons into his vine, makes it taut and pulsing, a secret river.

The greyfruit pods elaborate on such a vine in their own dreams; they dream of snakes themselves, crawling through their branches, unsevered. The snakes turn into birds; they break off and fly away; the greyfruit pods dream yet again of snakes, over and over again, their mouths teething at their own tails.

Florentine, walking hunched through the woods now, Florentine dreamt of a snake again last night, cooked as her mother would cook owl and rat. She tasted its flesh; she understood the languages of birds; her mother's own old story.

Simorgh the white bird dreams of snakes; Simorgh has once been a snake.

The Witch, remember her, the Witch dreams of holding a stick in her hand, and it turns into a green snake in her grasp: wiggling, unplantish and unplanted.

The deer dream of moving antlers, green from their scalps.

The three golden brothers, three suns, dream their hairy white dreams of snakes, who are then birds, who are then snakes, who are then birds; for the goat brothers it is all the same; once you have lost something it is all the same.

Florentine's mother and father dream of nothing, for they are dead. Eglentyne dreams of nothing, for she is dead.

Florentine's unborn child dreams of eglentyne, also

flowered, and of its stemming out, the sloth action of a lengthened offshoot sprout.

The abbess-priest dreams of snakeskin, peeled.

William Langford dreams of dreams, and in those doubled dreams an egg in which there is a little snake that sits the branch that shakes a tree that rains down nuts that feeds the bird who makes the nest where lies an egg.

The therapist dreams of ink blots with skinny, slithering shapes.

Ermintrude dreams of Robin and his tight green cock.

The lepers dream of shedding skin; their new and shiny selves.

The Blue Sisters dream of serpents.

Martin dreams of vipers.

Jack dreams of asps.

The Stick dreams of... Well, the Stick, now. Maybe I'm the Stick. Wouldn't that be something, a narrating stick?

* * *

Martin sees something and his heart clicks, a living human being in the distance, the first other breathing animal he has seen in twelve good years.

It's you.

"Hello, hello!" Martin runs towards you and hugs. Warmth in your heart in the desert, warmth from the cooking stars on your skin.

"Where have you been?" you ask Martin.

"I've been choosing my own adventure," says Martin, "and now I'm choosing you."

Nearly against your will, you smile. The same rush of pleasure as when you and the therapist fell in love. There is nothing more beautiful under the three suns than knowing that someone has chosen to fall in love with you; it makes you love them right back.

You hug, you hold hands, you keep walking that desert. After some time passes, and as the suns whittle down from their zenith, Martin says, conversationally, casually, "If you were to suddenly find yourself in a desert, and you were to find a fruit, what do you think you would find?"

Shiver and foreboding. A jolt of surprise that is nearly fear shakes you. "What are you citing?" For Martin's question sounds much like a canned quote.

"There's a psychological party game called The Cube," whispers Martin. "I don't remember who taught it to me. I travel a *lot*. And after the fruit, what type of disguise would you see?"

You blink but you are a little shocked; you have been hit by the suggestion that perhaps Martin is a disguised form of the therapist himself. Wearing a fake moustache over his Doctorate in Cognitive Kokology training. Now that you think about it, you have never seen them both in the same place at the same time. The fact that they inhabit different universes and realities notwithstanding. "I... Er... a pineapple. And after that, I suppose the disguise I would see would be a fake moustache."

"Ask, and you shall receive." Martin points ahead.

There ahead, in the middle distance, suddenly mate-rialises a large glowing pineapple, very Tiki-aesthetic, and some distance after that an enormous bushy, well-kempt moustache, dark-brown and oiled.

"Look, not really fair." (You sound like Tony Blair.) "I've already *seen* a huge fruit and a huge moustache here in the desert, so of course they're the first fruit and disguise that popped into my mind. I could have easily said a pome-granate or fake nose or a wig." But you haven't.

Martin looks a little confused, and taps his stick a few times on the ground, testingly. "Well, if you say so. Circles are hard to cut through and find the beginning point though, aren't they? I have been sent back to the beginning a few times myself, and yet it's clearly actually the end or the middle."

You stare straight ahead. You furrow your brow and shake your horns a little leftwards and snort mildly, but other than that you are determined not to let Martin know you are ruffled of feather or even of pelt. You have a surging need to protect Martin. From knowledge, from vipers. Martin is still, and always will be, you reckon, an innocent.

After walking for some time, you and Martin come across a small oasis. It is a topiary garden with any number of beasts and persons, evidently destroyed. Burnt bushes shaped like arms and legs and snouts and tails are strewn everywhere, and the odd leaf blows in the breeze. There is the drained cup of a dried lake that once was dangerous. There are some placards leftover where the vegetative statues have toppled and where tributes to these saints and heroes once stood in a grand orangery, as before a great church or Spital.

You lean over and see a bronze plate for a particular statue. Do you read it? You do.

"What does it say?"

You give him Martin a look of faint disgust. Perhaps Martin cannot read. He frequently makes mention of television. It is possible that apocalyptical education systems are not particularly good, lacking teachers and curricula and so on. You know very little about Martin: why he walks the desert; why he, unlame, uses a crutch. Perhaps – you clear your throat and then sink down on the leaf-spewed sand, gazing at the burnt-off branches before you and patting the space beside you in invitation – perhaps it is time *you* become the investigative kokotherapist, now that your love has left you. At the very least you, Jack, can use some of his techniques.

"I'll tell you what it says, if afterwards you answer a question of mine."

"Okay." Martin agrees in an open, childlike manner – innocent, as noted – and settles into the sand beside you.

You both gaze at the cactus destruction for a while until you turn your attention to the plaque.

"It's in honour of a Saint named Wiggle," you say. This is a little odd; you thought this Saint was named Kieran last time you were here.

"Who is Saint Wiggle?"

"My turn. Why are you here in the desert?"

"I am tracking you on foot."

You swallow, flush. Put off-foot. "And why would you be doing that?"

"It's your turn to answer." Martin was no guile-free wanderer, after all. "Who was Saint Wiggle?" Repetition.

You scan your brain, body and moose-horns for an answer and find none. You – and your darling (your therapist) – have previously suspected that you may have been raised a Catholic. You quickly devise a perhaps-false – though who can say it's false, only history's Saint Anselm by argument, perhaps, proving the truth of the Easter Bunny and the Flying Spaghetti Monster and God alike – you quickly devise a perhaps-false mental manuscript for mackerel-snapper – yes, you get to use that term; you believe yourself to have been raised Catholic, therefore intra-familial privilege; do you really think a Protestant would conjure up a sarcastic screed on the lives of saints; they probably have better things to do on Friday nights – you quickly devise a perhaps-false mental manuscript for mackerel-snapper bestseller *Lives of the Saints*; devise a saint biography regrettably excised from later editions.

"Saint Wiggle of Mornington Crescent –"

"What is Mornington Crescent?" asks Martin.

"It is a place name that gave rise to an extraordinary psychological mind-game best not played with lovers or therapists, regulations of which can be found with a cursory online search."

"I *want* to play it."

The dynamic is all skewed. You should never have answered him out of turn; you lost all your authority at that moment. Are you now Martin's therapist? How *can* you be when you are only Jack?

"Mornington Crescent involves exchanging names of London Underground stations until someone says the station-name of Mornington Crescent and ends the game. Both players have the power to end the game at any time. *Cockfosters.*"

"*Mornington Crescent.*"

"And game over and that's that." You clear your throat and continue: "Saint Wiggle of Mornington Crescent was known for his appealing set of fuzzy antlers and his dashing goatee. A controversial figure, only recently beatified, his eventual sainthood a posthumous tribute, as they usually are, it would be so gauche to have people suck your relics in your lifetime, his sainthood a posthumous tribute rumoured to have been a poker debt pay-off from the Vatican to the country of Lithuania. Saint Wiggle, my source papers inform me, led a life filled with debauchery."

"What kind of debauchery?"

"Questions for questions," you say. A wink of your eye and a twist of horned head soon gives Martin to know he has nothing to dread. "Why am *I* here in this desert?"

Martin blinked. "You are tracking *me.*"

You ingest that development and continue the hagiography. "The debauchery is not detailed. Saint Wiggle of Mornington Crescent led a life filled with debauchery until he turned to God in the last hour of his 91-year-old life – a deathbed confession/conversion contested by most people present on the night."

"Hmm." You're met with skepticism. "Shrine sites, miracles and notorieties?"

"Shrine sites include the Brothels-R-Us chain – both Lithuanian and Nevadan headquarters – and a small independent artisanal betting shop found in Finsbury Park, London, England. Miracles not detailed. Notable though miracle-skeptical for having made macramé plantholders in the 1970s using his own torn-out teeth. So that's it for Saint Wiggle."

Martin ignores you and Saint Wiggle for the moment, and peers out at the desert again. "In kokological games, it's all about the Reveal, which is also the most important section of a stage magician's trick. *The Pledge, The Prestige, The Reveal*. In kokological games, the Reveal is the legend interpreting the signifiers. You're in a desert. You see a vessel. What is it; what does it contain?"

"I... Er... I suppose I would see a faucet or a basin holding water." You don't point out that the faucet imagery isn't an original conception.

"Ask, and you shall receive." Martin points ahead. There ahead, in the middle distance, suddenly materialises an enormous suspended-in-air tap pouring water onto the dry desert. Yet you stay within your oasis. It feels safer there, amongst the destroyed, unsuckling cacti. Dry.

It's your turn. "What about your Stick?" you ask Martin. "You do not seem lame at all, my friend.

"*Saint* Stick. Please use its proper title, otherwise impolite."

"You're not answering the question properly." You had had the same problem with the therapist.

Martin draws a circle in the sand with his toe. "Saint Stick. That will do for now." This is the first time in many, many pages that it strikes you that Martin wears no clothes. Including no shoes. Martin draws the circle in the sand with his naked toe, around yet another destroyed topiary. He picks up another plaque and blows the sand-dust off and hands it to you. "What does this one say?"

The embossed bronze letters on the saint plaque actually say "*Item 3, the matter of the newspapers. Judging by the date on the* Sunday Sport *in the newsagent's* (etc.)," but as the shock of Martin's illiteracy hits you, you make up another story about a fictitious saint instead: "This fallen garden topiary, in the shape of an vegetable-man, like a mandrake or a borometz – one such vegetable lamb still being found at the Garden Museum in the London Borough of Lambeth – has a plaque which commemorates Saint Jezebelladonna of the Inky Flowers." There, a properly slutty name. Let him vegetable-stew over *that*.

"What's so special about Jezebelladonna? You have to let me know; it's part of your answer." Martin looks a trifle frustrated.

"What's so *special*? Three tits. What more do I have to say? Usually represented in Victorian garb cut low, so as to better mantelpiece her nipples three. She performed three – count 'em, three – miracles that posthumously hastened her path towards sainthood."

Martin is gazing up at the three (count 'em, three) suns in the sky.

You find you are talking very quickly, but Martin doesn't seem impressed: "One, Jezzabelladonna single-handedly diverted an asteroid from hitting Planet Earth by the strategic placement of nuclear detonations.

"Two, she invented the holy-water-and-vodka cocktail.

"Three, she found a missing contact lens in a full bathtub.

"That's it for Jezebelladonna, the auld hoor, though she's always been one of my favourites for three good reasons. Now my turn. Your answer regarding the stick wasn't very satisfactory, but let's try better: what was the first thing you remember when you arrived in this world? I suppose you're going to say that you remember nothing and that you've only been endlessly walking the desert."

Martin surprises you. "I have been walking naked in this desert for twelve long years, it's true, and I don't know much about my friend Saint Stick, except that we are fellow travelers, friends forever, bosom friends, friends with many, many benefits. Yet it may surprise you to know that I do remember that when I arrived, I watched a lot of TV. There was a great kokological television set up in the desert like a leftover university psychology party-game trinket, the morning after someone's brain must have magicked it up countless years ago and it just got lost in the spacetime. The television set was floating in the air, flatscreen and had Netflix, so I watched a lot of history programmes and scientific documentaries. Good stuff. Why," Martin asked abruptly, "why is it only the female saint sexualised here, and not Saint Wiggly?"

You feel simultaneously defensive and crude, and more than a little sexist. There is power in sexism and a delightful imbalance; the spite burns through you. "Saint *Wiggle*. That's a) not quite true and b) wouldn't you sexualise someone who had three bodacious ta-tas?"

"No."

"What's wrong with the three tits of Jezzabelladonna of the Inky Flowers; do they somehow devalue one's sainthood from the get-go?"

"No." Martin's expression reveals that he wishes he had never asked the question. Martin must hate you anew.

"Should all chick-saints be mewling little missionaries?"

"No."

"Check yourself, Martin and Stick, for the Madonna-Whore shame is all yours, friends, and it is recommended that you seek long-term couch-analysis for latent misogyny."

"No. I refuse to. Why the Inky Flowers?"

There are cacti that bloom only at inky night; that are flowerless now in day. There was once, now destroyed, a saint-like figure surrounded by smaller cactus animals, canine fellows the wolf and the fox; a boar, a stag, a toad, a badger. You lunge forward on your haunches for a moment to touch what had to have been Saint Francis.

"Ow!" Seminal cactus features have been retained. You sink back in the sand again. A few blood drops run down your wrist; you are the queen of toads.

"Ow!" Martin, never one to learn from the examples of others, has done the same. He too is bleeding. He is the queen of toads with ruby eyes.

"Why the Inky Flowers? Why not, amirite..." You are distracted. You look around at the plant detritus, and squint towards the sun, thinking. "This destruction," you conclude loudly and officiously, "these dead insects and burnt greenery, these remnants of the *saighir-sughaim-sine-saguaro* cactus, these spiritual relics like hacked-off angel and virgin faces on Ely Cathedral; like the ISIS-destroyed Palmyrian Temple of Baal: these are all signs of an advanced kokological game."

***

It was a bleak journey where the icicles whistled from the trees and the extensions of herself grew bitter cold despite bundling: belly cold, hands cold, feet cold, nose cold, breasts cold, lips cold. Her cloaks wrapped round her. At least no blizzardly wind, so there was not that sting additional.

In the snowed-over trees, as her footsteps left prints dark into the mush, just for a moment, she thought she saw a glimpse of someone, and her head swung back round. She thought she had seen that long-ago Witch. A pretty iced face and a smirk. But there was only Florentine now. The snow was surprisingly sterile; she had not been aware of how much she associated forest snow with blood, the fact of red slush melting into the drifts. The last time she had walked the roads, she had made best use of clerical mimicry observed on the travel. But now there were no horns severed but instead a proud pair on her scalp, balancing out her stomach, and no murderings of parent or owl. She was safe enough, the snow's whiteness was unblemished and she had someplace to reach by nightfall.

She approached the Spital before dusk. There were no lepers here in winter and five years later, and she hoped the best for whatever their leprous fates had been. She hoped many golden and glass bells for them, slow and painless wasting if decline was inevitable. Then there was no response to Florentine's knocks on the great iron door, and at last, more than half-frozen – far closer to three-fourths frozen – she went around and found that there was an unblocked Leper's Squint on this side of the Spital church, though she had been told otherwise, for the stained glass windows had been dark as Roman glass, the unrevealing sunglasses of the covered soul, and gave up no secrets, and she could hear no sounds either, no singing nor speech, behind the iron door.

When she looked through the Squint, she could see a circle of pray-ers, and the animal silhouettes of her brothers. There was no music coming from the altar in the cold stony unbright of this occasion. There was no sun cast through the miraculous window that previously had shown her fruits and beasts and glowing lovers. She threw rocks at the thick glass pane until the penitents looked in her direction, and then she went round the corner to the great iron door again and waited, clutching her stomach.

When the great iron door was unclasped and swung open, the hand holding it was Ned the abbess-priest-thief.

"You again!"

"Aye. I must speak with Percy, Eldritch and Beaman."

"And with babe soon, too," said the doubled-gendered cleric wonderingly, but he let Florentine pass into the Spital and trailed behind her to the nave. It was easy to keep up, for Florentine walked slow and her breath was hard to catch. She pushed memories of herself and Eglentyne in this same church with this same cleric firmly from her head, out through the tops of her antlers, away. It was easy to forgive Ned the inefficient shaman; she felt nothing from his old theft; he was as consequential as weak water, sifted snow that ran from boots warming by hearths.

The Spital cathedral was bleak and huge, hollow with no music to fill it. She heard now that the penitents were concluding a low sonorous prayer with an extended amen, one as self-righteous as the Blue Sisters' pre-dinner invocations to Daddy Dagda always had been. Once finished, the churchly drifted away from a smoking brazier, red-pearled with coals, until there remained only three goats, and Ned who whispered in goat-ears and then fell away back into the greater space himself, leaving the four of the siblings alone. The brothers, all three, wore rood-charms round their necks on chains (not collars, though perhaps it is the same).

It was Beaman again who took sour, cold appraisal of her state, while Eldritch and Percival looked sorrowful on. "Sister. Our minds have not changed in these five years and we will be staying here with our Mother Church."

This is not your mother. Your mother is dead in the snow. "I guessed as much." She shook out her snowy robe and stood closer to the brazier, so that it melted the cold off her in the stinging pains that always roll over a near-frozen life as it warms up again. The ice water slid down her now-burning cheeks like tears. Her feet squeezed and erupted in hurt; the babe in her belly kicked.

"There clearly is no father and you are nearly at confinement," Beaman said assessingly, "leave the child with us," said Beaman, and the others nodded, "and we will give it a Christly life."

Florentine saw, as a burst of light under her lids, her green childhood with her brothers, their foursome laughter under sun and trees before they became white goats and before she became part stag, and even after too. That life had been a gift from her parents, she now realised; therefore she could not in good conscience in turn give her child a shivery stone building and strips of sorrow lashed upon one's own shoulders, no matter the music and the coloured panes that would, come daylight, warm into beauty once again.

A good life even after her brothers had become goats, up to a point. They had been children. Perhaps if the bird had not been there, her parents might have even done the act themselves eventually; such goats had been in her family for a long, long time. Was there no way to pick choice scattered seeds as a green bird does, to pince fruited glass and god-arias and green childhoods and firefly meadows all, and disdain every pod of grief? They had all three been sweet boys, and then sweet fluffed-up goats. Such goats and even stags, all horned beasts, had been in her family for a long, long time. Percy always had been her favourite.

Its blood tastes like honey. She unhitched her satchel, and took out the scarf wrapped around the three large gourds. The brothers watched in wonder as she unwrapped the material wound tightly round first pod that she had opened, then re-sealed. She unclasped it like a clamshell jewellery box. There was no tiny ballerina figurine rotating on satin to wind-up musicbox strains, but there was, against the lush red softened fruitmeat, the unsoiled and unplucked penis. She offered it to Beaman, while the other two goats looked on jealously. "I am sorry."

Beaman took the opened gourd in his hooves and looked closely, but then pushed it back and turned his nose away in disdain.

"Please," said Florentine, "it is still fresh; I think it will attach."

Beaman had grown so cold in the Church years; there was very little of her brother left at all. "You think this is sacrifice enough? We know of sacrifice through Christ's great grace. From which three small goats did you plunder these?"

She fumbled, her words spilling. "From a plant; there were many such fruits; the individual concerned still has his stick and rod aplenty it is and he will not miss these." And it was the truth. "These gourds thrive still; you three can have your own sticks once again."

Eldritch and Percival drew closer, tempted.

"Stop!" said Brother Beaman. "Do you not see the corollary with the glade of Eden and the female offering tempting fruits?" Beaman turned his back then and stared dispassionately up at the darkened stained glass window that showed that very scene.

Florentine could only barely make out the image of a woman holding a gourd. The woman was smiling and surrounded by many animals.

Her brothers were wethers now full-grown. Had they been bucks, they would have been stinking of piss and musk with shaggy fur dagged and trailing. They were instead clean-shaven and clean entirely; she would be giving them back their dirty buckhood.

She began to speak. She spoke beautifully of the rich

reddened fruit she held in her hand and the fine strong cock within in. She argued that the man and woman in the story lived lives in nature free of strictures and could not sin, for they had no knowledge of it. She parlayed for fertility and for the lack of it and for the Adam-and-Eve right to fuck and rub and bury their faces in between the other's legs and take pure aria-singing, stained-glass *gloria gloria*, life-affirming joy from it.

She held out the fruit to Beaman, but he did not sway, choosing his stone castle, and tears began to fall down Florentine's face. The baby did not kick at all and perhaps had died within her. The church was cold, the only point of heat in it was the brazier, just as the only point of heat in the cold cabin that long-ago day had been the pulses of her snow-white brothers, hidden in the trundle box.

Percy stepped forward. "Thank you," he said to his sister, "you are sorry but were then only a kid, a kit, a fawn yourself. Thank you, and I will accept, O sister."

He was the smallest, though a triplet, and the prick, smelling of violets now and ambergris, would be big on him, but no the matter. He stuck his snout into the base of the gourd, sticky, oozing sap and cum, and chewed it swiftly off. Whereupon Florentine thrust it plain between his back legs where the healed scars were, where the white bird had done its work, and oaky curled horns like dirty fingernails burst from the top of his head and in his hindquarters the prick grew suddenly into him, veins and folds attaching like unfurling plant fronds and it reared up proud and her hand fell away.

Percy was an adult, a masculine buck, but he still retained his sweetness of spirit and his gentleness; Florentine understood this was the case already.

Florentine left the two remaining bundled fruits at the foot of the brazier. "In case you change your minds," she said to Eldritch and to Beaman.

Then she and the living babe in her belly and her brother Percy left the church and Spital, following the route she and Eglentyne had once taken long ago returning to the Blue School.

And so it was then, a month, more, after Florentine and Percival looked back to the Spital garden, where the topiary of saints and heroes and trees was entirely covered with snow, forcing celebrities to be as anonymous as the common man and common woman, which perhaps they should be anyway. There was no sign as to whether a bush was Diana-Huntress or John-Baptist, though every new snow tree began to flicker with sunlight off the stained glass window fruit, reflected colours skimming the snow-drift surfaces covering the branches. She thought only once of Robin when she gazed at the snowy statues, detached from his stalk and now vegetable-prone.

Florentine was recognized from a distance by the Blue Mother, who hailed Florentine and Percival closer. The Blue School, that school with the roof of sky and door-corridors through tree trunks, so completely different in winter. She felt rolling cramps spool through her and she gripped for balance at the white hair that ran down Percival's bony spine. The branches held up tents of snow, lending an enclosed and covered quality to the glade. Florentine remembered it well from her years here, and there were the same shivering little girls as she once had been, grouped round the great fire.

"My Florentine." The Blue Mother spoke first. She stretched out a hand to her Florentine, and Breesha took Florentine's other hand, and young Bríg, her head shaved near like a monk's, laid a hand on Florentine's belly.

Florentine recalled that first Imbolc. How she had stood there with Eglentyne and how they had watched the seeds pop in the fire. Now, Florentine would find it impossible to catch a seed that contained all her thoughts; she felt so many things at once. She and Percy stood there, unmoving, and the great fire cast their odd shadows onto the deep snow: a grey buck; a grey stagged woman swelling, both frozen in place like trees who were tethered.

*

What is the significance of *My Three Sons*? A popular 1960s

American television show watched in re-runs. An obvious indicator of a parallel world. Not our known cosmos. Therefore foreign. Three billy goat-brothers gruff. My three sons, would say Florentine's father, my three suns. But their father and mother too were long gone now.

Florentine and Percy were left with only cod-mothers, god-mothers. Brigid looked beadily at Percy. ("Don't lock eyes with her!" Florentine suddenly hissed at her brother, stepping in front of him even in her advanced state, remembering multiple goat sacrifices at Beltane, at Litha, at Lughnasa, at Yule, hell, at any ol' time.)

"Aren't *you* a handsome thing?" commented Breesha, stepping past Florentine to stroke Percy's buck-fur. Percy looked nervously at Florentine.

"This goat is my brother," said Florentine loudly enough to make sure everyone, from the three sisters to the fifty blue girls, heard her. "No stews tonight."

"What a shame," said Breesha, who was looking longingly into Percy's yellow eyes. "We could have made you a god for a night. Danced round you with all the naiads spilling forth from the river –" Florentine thought joltingly of Eglentyne, and clutched her throat "– and ourselves in the trees, and the bonfires burning high, and the juice running wet, and the wine in your belly–" Percy was looking extremely tempted, even though he had led a devout and saintly life up to this very moment.

"Stop!" Florentine clapped her hands, and the three sisters reluctantly drew themselves away. Percy looked torn between buckly attraction to Breesha and a disinclination to be eaten, so Florentine would have to decide for him. Florentine pushed his rump away from the School glade. "Go," she hissed in his ear, "go back to the glade and the cabin. Don't get church-tangled all over again. You want to live – so, now: *live*."

Percy looked alarmed, but first he bit off from his neck the chain with his rood-charm. "Take this," he nosed it onto her, the small vial now strung round her neck, "it is the wood of the one true rood, a thousand, three-hundred and sixty-seven years old."

The dry little piece of stick was in a diminutive silver chest that hung as a charm and the chest could be unhinged but then the wood was locked in with a thick – but still transparent – green glass, making the relic look eerie, like something seen at the bottom of lakes.

"Wear it," said Percy to Florentine.

She glanced uncertainly at Brigid, who gave a slight nod. "I will," said Florentine.

"Take care of yourself and your little one," said Percy, "may it fare well for my niece."

"You don't know that it is a niece."

"I know that it's a niece. And she shall have stubborn horns in some manner, that I know too. Such horns run in our family and have done so for a long, long time."

Away Percy ran in the blue-shadowed snow, through the trees, towards the greyfruit orchard and towards the frozen plant, away.

*

The sisters brought her cypress to soothe her pains, *eileithyia,*
eileithyia, and when she screamed out one archwife each
held a hand and the Blue Mother held her head. Florentine
saw a woman with a bow and arrow before her eyes and
heard a crackling like old coals and pushed that image back
in her head and the sounds back into her ears from whence
they had come. She screamed through the night and no time
passed at all and yet it was so fast all the same, the world
was red and fast. It was wind and ravage and bonfire, it was
bonfire time and she had forgotten it with her great belly and
she screamed as no animal should have to scream but yet
only human women do, that splitting price for too-big skulls,
and then it came, then *she* came on the morn of Beltane Eve,
soft and wiggling and bloodied and crying she came, and still
hinged to Florentine, still connected to her like a vegetable
lamb, but when Florentine's legs coughed out the afterbirth,
Brìg bit through the stalk and the infant kept on living. The
infant stayed alive. Her vine was cut but she sucked hard at
Florentine's dugs and she lived.

Florentine stared up at the familiar green ceiling and
saw how the sun lightened just the edges of certain trees,
before it made its large reveal. The babe, the sweet babe, was
nursing at her chest and yet Florentine saw only the morning trees, with the sun soon to warm them. A bird was crow-

ing forth the morning just within her sight. The blue bird crew, and the whole world began to wake up.

Not so far away from where she and the babe lay, and it sucked, sweet milk on strawberry tongue, its eyelashes so perfect and skin, despite the blood, so plump and pure, not so far away from where she and the babe lay and the three sisters crouched, a green man was walking toward them, rubbing scars on his arms where the pods had been plucked, but otherwise entirely whole.

*

"How did you wake up?" she asked.

"A goat was nosing around for onions, and he smelt so bad that no one could slumber with buck-stench such as that. Not even I, and I'm a rutting, horny thing." He kissed her neck and his fingers brushed over the silver rood-charm she wore, and he grinned for just an instant. She did not know if she should let him kiss her so, but their argument seemed so long ago – what was it now, he had led travellers astray again, or not shown up on time for her – and she could scarcely recall why it had mattered. She felt rivery honey love for him. It was nearly springtime and the daffodils already were honking and the breezes already carried spores. He felt dirt-churned, farmer lust for her.

*

They were wed by the sisters in the cool groves, leaves
bursting on branches as they pledged their troths a year and
a day – purely ceremonial: they would be wed forever by the
grace of the tripled goddesses.

He looked at her with love in his lips and eyes, and
stroked her face. Then he was stroking her everywhere and
then they were down there amongst the leaves in the dirt,
while the others looked on. He took her, and she only barely
gave herself. She could not catch up with him; her heart was
racing, his hands tough branches holding her down, and
she felt her own pulse inside her, but it was far too late, and
what's more she was torn and bleeding, child-ravaged, laid
there on her back while he looked down into her eyes, rough-
smirking, and she'd been sundered again. The leaves, the
onlookers. The sun through the cooled trees.

*

She, who took everything in her stride, was already in love
with it. There were little nubbins of horns already growing
from her tiny scalp between soft dark hairs, from Florentine;
and one hand was curled into a cloven hoof from her father;
and there, a necklace of birthmarks on the babe shaped like
leaves that stretched across her tiny collarbone, a series of
marks as pale brown as autumn, from Eglentyne. Florentine
thought of the red necklace round Eglentyne's neck that had
killed her. The babe was perfect.

Florentine's horns could grow bigger than anything,

like branches across the world protecting her little daughter. She'd be a mother. A provider. A Horned Goddess, the archetypal Protector. Yet Florentine could not allow herself to be this thing. She shut her eyes looking down on the baby, so she did not have to see it.

"My little jewelled egg," said Florentine, "my progeny." She raised her lids. The infant looked piggish at birth, as all infants do, but also impossibly lovely, a delicate animal of flesh and miniature human fingernails, shocking that such hard surfaces had been inside her just before. Now it was pink and squalling. The Sisters had to take it from her arms and soothed it, for Florentine had no mother left and no knowledge how. The Three Sisters would be good to it, at least until womanhood, and many things could change before that. They could give it the life that she could not. And in some ways she could not stand to look upon it, to see the pieces of himself that he had left stained on her babe. But then she would coo down, and see herself in it, and sometimes even Eglentyne.

She could not care for such a little animal. The Blue Sisters would watch out for it, and be too strict but also wipe its tears, and hopefully there would be no Alyssonnes or Katherines. Yet there always would be cruel Alyssonnes. She would never come back for it, just as her parents never did for her.

Her sex hurt from the birth and still she bled. Her nipples leaked. She was a mother and woman wed at Beltane Eve and now a divorcée and barren already by Beltane Day.

She could not find it in herself to weep, for it was all her fault already and had she been wiser, she would have guessed that it would play out this way again.

She kissed her baby daughter and took the basket up in her arms, walking towards the fire. She was overcome with an irrational fear that the sisters would, once she had left, dash the basket to the coals as with their seeds, but the thought was just that, irrational. They were not on-purpose-fully cruel women: severity was functional and prescribed. They would take good care of the littlest one; they would will the very milk from their teats to nurse it; she knew it to the tips of her antlers and yet it was very hard to let her poppet go.

She gripped the wicker basket.

Goodbye to the Green Man, you cruel thing, goodbye forever; we shall never meet again.

We shall, says the green man, whispering in the trees, calling from where she had once saved it as a sapling, *I shall find you.*

"You won't," said Florentine, and she meant it. She would hide herself away from him forever. She would never heed his soft sex-calls knavish over lakes and streams. She would never melt to him when he came wooing in the shapes of animals. Again, his whipping up of nightmares whilst innocents slept, but also his midnight kindnesses in carding crones' wool, so that old women awoke delighted to find their tasks completed. Her sex ached. Her self ached. *Goodbye, green bird, goodbye.*

She was bleeding herself between her legs again. She still held her nineteenth-year antlers up. This splitting from her poppet far worse a severing than that from mere horns.

She placed the babe with its infant antlers and cloven hand and birthmark necklace in the basket that she woke up early to stud with eglentyne flowers, and her breasts ached, and she handed the babe over to Brigid, Breesha and Brìg. *Goodbye, my jewel, little egg, goodbye. Goodbye Eglentyne, goodbye.*

* * *

He's flying flying flying, trailing green smoke, all clouds look like snakes, cool forests, in love with suns that shine through trees, he's flying flying flying off of her and into someone else, adhering to this new person like a barnacle goose. I'll make an attempt: His name is Jack Green. He was born in 1967 in the state of Alaska, studied statistics at University of Washington, Seattle, recruited young and by 21 was living in West Berlin, listening in on train carriages, watching footage of the ghost trains circle round the city, the ones that never picked up passengers on the East Berlin side. There were some stowaways, whom the U.S.

was always keen to offer assistance to
in exchange for information; there were
some stowaways but usually the East Germans discovered their escaping compadres
first. The eastern side of the Berlin Wall
was painted white precisely so escapees'
shadows were seen more easily against it.
The moving spiked grille grate in the
moat sluiced through the water, silently,
and escapees never knew until it stuck
them and held them underwater, underwater
where there also was found a bed of nails.
Jack Green found both the aural experience and also the transcripts he typed of
discovery and subsequent confrontation
extremely depressing. The hopes dashed,
the greyed return to interrogation and a
worse threat, chilly Siberia (same tem-
perature as Alaska, technically, presum-
ably the same wild beauty). Then there had
been his wife, shared a department, and
memories of her both scratchy and blurry,
and he believed himself to have loved her
though the memories were brittle brandys-
nifter glass, and their little daughter,
born 1989, just as things were crumbling,
and he knew for sure that he had loved
that one.

Though this cannot be, the times don't work out at all. Let's try again. Jack Green, born 1974 on Alaska's Kenai Peninsula, surrounded by wolves and feral humans and moose (*Alces alces americanus*). So there we recognise both the wildlife and coastal watery motifs. Exchange student in France, recruited young at 15, emancipated from parents that same year, lived in Berlin squats in the heady days of the early 1990s, rutting environmentally-minded young dreadlocked white girls and reporting back on them in precisely typed memoranda, yellow Post-It notepads transferred to electronic typewriters, betraying every Nelke, Cornelia, Anja, Claudia all over again as he revealed their tastes in techno music, dabblings in vegetarianism, starry worship of Baader-Meinhoff. Then there had been Erika, code name Lavendel, and love. And he had kept on lying. And their little baby. And by then he had found out what the East Germans had found out. And he had kept on lying.

This scenario is much more plausible. You always have to work out the details first. That's what good spies and also effective pathological liars do.

So how about this version, a child born in 1347. A bad year all round for the continent. Some deep tragedies in that life, loses parents growing up, loses only friend, for all practical purposes loses siblings, etc., etc. Grows bumpy bits, grows hairs, grows horns, grows up. Takes a lover, sex so good our hero disassociates, churning, green magical fucking, red rutting horny fucking, the kind that makes you pussy-dazed, dickmatized. Our little flower get knocked up. His name is Jack Green. This is the house that Jack built and now he's going to have to live in it... His name is Jack Green. He is 33 years old. He is dying dying dying. He is flying flying flying.

Where does such a spy fly to? He is spying spying spying. Mister Spook peers through trees towards sun and smoke; it's summer, and now it's winter. False stories, fake people constructed with quick-frozen tears, O jack frost. He had flown in; he had glued himself to someone else; now there were consequences to pay.

***

You're sitting there with Martin, and you remember something. The memory has not been implanted. (A verb never so apt, amirite?)

It happened before that forest dream you spoke of to your therapist. Now it is *you* who is likely a ghost, as you have accepted that your world has exploded. Starbucks. Traffic lights. Bedsit. *Sunday Sport* in the newsagent's. All gone. What you're remembering is this. Before your CIA assignment. Before your adulthood. Before your childhood. Before the dream in the forest where you hung around a while as a ghost. Before then, an infant. It's the sense-memory of it, the way your fingers curled round the swaddling. Now you're playing mind games in a hallucinatory yellow desert with the bald man and the stick.

The sensation of holding the baby fades in the heat of three suns that, however fictional, are extremely authentic in every way that matters. Sunburn risk, basically. *Ya gotta buck up, Jack, ya gotta buck up and be a man.*

You're annoyed by your own subvocalisation. You clear your throat. "Let's take a walk, Martin."

He looks wary. He's heard that one before. (If Dear Readers wish to take that walk, go back to the beginning of the book.) "A kokological game?" He's surprised. He muses for a moment. "Well, maybe. It could work. That was rhetorical. So my turn for a question. While you're walking in the desert, you come to a cave. What do you see?"

As it happens, you and Martin have just come across

exactly the same cave as before. You're repeating your mistakes. You're repeating your best decisions. It's frustrating. You monotonously intone to Martin: "I see a cave." Actually, you *do* see a Cave.

"*Oh-là-là!*"

"The entrance is open."

"*Oh-là-là!*"

You *do* see a Cave. You're seeing one right now. "The entrance is open and I assess that the interior is blue." My god, this is pointless. He already knows this. *You* already know this. It's your turn for a question. But he's still jabbering:

"What do you do when you see the entrance to the Cave?"

"I go inside."

"*Oh-là-là!*"

"Please shut up." Martin is silent. "I've changed my mind," you decide. "We *both* go inside."

"*Oh-I–*" You give him a dirty look (not in that way, oh-là-là), and Martin shuts it. You are standing outside the Cave with Martin. **Go back to page 17 or page 109 or whatever.** What would your beloved therapist do? He would use metaphor and *trick* out the answers. *The Reveal, The Prestige, The Pledge*, all reversed. Martin knows something. What it is, you dunno. You're gonna *trick* it out. Metaphor is fiction is parable is story.

"There was, by the way, another Saint, whom I neglected to mention."

"Yeah?" He looks marginally interested.

You casually stare at the cave in the hot desert heat, clasp your hands behind you, conjure up and then recite: "Saint Malabaster of the Diphallic Urgency was a polarising figure. The Patron Saint of Idaho. A popular-slash-unpopular guy. His proponents, well aware of this tension, pre-emptively push his celebratory festivals like there's no tomorrow, his Feast Days being February 30, April 31, June 31, September 31 – Malabaster's birthday – and November 31."

"Now hold on a minute..."

"Malabaster's image in contemporary paintings is fertile with symbolism. You should like that, Martin, for all kokology is symbolism. The only two questions remaining are, who creates the key; and who holds the key."

There is an uncomfortable silence. Is that a buzzard overhead?

"I'm waiting."

"Hold on." Martin is nonplussed. "*That's* your question? Those are two questions."

"Not really. They're practically the same thing. Who *creates* the kokological key; and who *holds* the kokological key."

Martin is faltering, and in his faltering you are confirming your recent suspicion that he is not a shaven-headed young *naïf* with wooden cane after all. He's someone else. You used to do this all the time, breaking Stasi double-agents. Deprive them of their ego, and see what's left afterwards. You used to do this all the time. You love doing this. Good-bye to Martin. Who's Martin.

Martin's someone who is answering your question, albeit slowly, just as you enter a blue-tinted cave with ouchy stalags and stalacs. Stalag 1347. "The... answer...to... your... question... is, of course, y –"

A ewe has just rushed along the studded cave corridor past you towards the exit, a vegetable lamb. A yew tree has sprung up in your path, which you both duck around. Will you always be ducking around, avoiding the yews, avoiding the – oh, hang it. Back to metaphor. "Thank you," you say stiffly. "Back to the story."

The cave is getting darker; you have been crawling through now for nearly a week.

"Back to the story," you continue. "A former altar girl and Boy Scout, Saint Malabaster is one of the Church's most enigmatic canonisations. He is best known for his pet bumblebee, Malachi, whom Saint Malabaster was said to have led around by a flimsy silver thread on halcyon late summer evenings, re-baptising with Holy Rites a new Malachi each time his pet passed away. Once rumoured to have been born with literally two faces, Saint Malabaster was doubly blessed *down there*," you whisper coyly, scanning the darkness in the blue bioluminescence of the cave walls for Martin's reaction, "until an unfortunate encounter with a temperance-movement schoolmarm –"

"Internet darling and *Little House on the Prairie* star Nellie Oleson!" interjected Martin.

"Why yes, or at least her mother," you agree, surprised to have a co-pilot on your airship of lies (fictive and inventive metaphor to others). "Because his second penis was cut off – I've had to spell out his diphallism for you, Martin, due to your incomprehension of subtle allusion –" Martin does not look insulted "– due to that occurrence, Malabaster is often depicted carrying a large, phallic baguette on a plate. Perhaps even you will understand that particular imagery."

Martin nods his head and thumps his stick on stone. "I do."

The Cave is even narrower this week. "Ciabatta, for the record. Fusion bread. Malabaster cloistered himself away for many years in the late nineteenth century, a time during which he penned 'On Beauty, Spirit and Bumblebees: Meditations on God's Smallest and Sting-y-est Creatures'. During his frequent prayer sessions, he often wrote of an experienced sensation of a large, luminous, spiritual presence emitting from the underside of his mouth – as if someone had stuck a candle underneath his chin. Patron Saint of flashlights – torches to you Brits – and, once again, the 43rd State of the U.S.A."

"Damn," says Martin, "dang and darn it. What happens when you come to a point in your journey when you can no longer turn back? You see a body of water," he adds, unnecessarily. Has he heard a d___ word you said?

The two of you are standing before a massive underground lake that blocks your mutual path.

You find yourself a little bit scared. You can't remember if you can swim or not. What was the outcome last time? You start to babble about saints once more. You're not quite sure where the saints are coming from. "We come to Saint Penelope Pongo. *Hoo-hoo-hoo!* Both pig, both orangutan, Penelope survived the unusual flaunting of pedestrian bioresearch restrictions to reign triumphant, more beautiful than before the knife –"

"Jack," Martin says gently, "are you going in the water or not?"

"More beautiful than before the knife. Note the medallion round her neck in all her portraits, the medallion saying 'One Smart Pig'. O Charlotte, and your thousand spiderling babes. That's a *Charlotte's Web* reference, you see. I loved that book. Just like *Mary Poppins* and *Ozma of Oz* and *Choose Your Own Adventure: The Adventure of the Serpent Cave*. And *Dinosaurs: The Reference Book*."

"Jack." Martin is trying again, but you don't see him. All you can see is the enormous blue-green lake in front of you that you will never get past; all you can recall is the books of your childhood past but not the childhood itself. You feel *extremely* petulant.

"Note on Penelope's portraits, too, the reddish fur for all good reasons on all knuckles of one of her hands."

"Jack –"

"There is not one itty-bitty chance that you don't know the reason why peeps have hairy hands, so why the metaphorical bashful eye-swoop down to the asterisks line-up?"

"I'm going in the water now, Jack – look –" Martin is hovering on the bank.

You shield your eyes. "Note on the other hand and on the other hand a cloven hoof holding a glass jar of pig embryos. If you look hard, *real* hard at her *Pongo pygmaeus* features, you might spy the hint of a sow snout. Penelope died at the hands of an angry mob after the soft-opening week of her 'longpig' restaurant."

But Martin is gone. Martin has gone under the water.

"Humans can get so protective of their in-group. Tajfel *et al.* (1971). Social categorization and inter-group behaviour. *European Journal of Social Psychology* 1 (2): 149–178. Oh, fuck it."

You dive in as well. You konk your head. The lake is shallow. It only comes up to your knees. You stand up, shaking. You're walking on water. Martin is on the other side of the lake, waving. You're walking on water. It's a miracle.

"Saint Penelope Pongo performed miracles," you shout across the water to Martin.

"I know," he shouts back joyously, "we all do, hurry up."

"Saint Penelope Pongo was beatified in 1948," you yell back. "Rumours are rife that Penelope in 1948 re-staged as applied performance art the Loaves-and-Fishes miracle and fed the masses with endless supplies of Spam and fried eggs."

You're wading through the water. There are leaves

in it and frogs in it. It's so shallow. You're nearly there. "She was canonised in 1952! When a small boy found the imprint of a juvenile pig's trotter in the Minnesota snow that looked like Jesus Christ. She is the Patron Saint of stem cell researchers, Big Andy's Pork Smokehouse, cannibals and –"

"And Biruté Galdikas," says Martin. He's beaming. You're on the other side. "You made it."

***

Jack doesn't know how to tell you the truth here. But I'll give it a shot. The scientific mavericks got it all wrong with multiverses. That was the conclusion of Top Secret East German Cosmos Laboratories, knowledge also extracted sneakily by U.S. intelligence in 1988. Multiversical splittings – exemplified ironically by East/West nationhood – may well result in evolutionary-tree-type bifurcations, splintering off into realities into realities where in one you have a cake with blue frosting and one where you have a cake with yellow frosting (cf. Hadhazy 2012). Never to reticulate or hybridise again. Multiversical splittings may well result in this. But existence is looser than the dichotomous essentialism forced by our limited ingroup-protecting chimp brains (Bryson 2017). If sets are leaky, overlapping, Wittgensteinian (1956), or even simultaneous, same, reticulate (can remerge, can half-merge, can minimal-merge), then we are in fact only *believing* that dichotomisation is complete, distinct, equal and real. Belief is nothing, and multiverses are leaky, blurry, shared-setty and non-binary. Leastways that's what the East Germans say and I dunno about you, but I have always found the East Germans, like Vladimir Putin and Donald Trump and the reactionary Giuliani-loving subset of the FBI, super-trust-worthy.

Jack's present, when he is not found in an apocalyptical desert fever-dream of ragnarokstars, is a present filled with Starbucks decimations. O, the humanity.

Perhaps long ago, Jack *did* discover that said East Germans had for their part discovered that binaristic quantum theory is the wrong divergent track. Then, perhaps, many splits *began* to merge. East and West became Weast. The Iron Curtain melted down and the river of molten capitalist ore flowed out to eager, grasping hands (ouch!).

In London, where Jack was indubitably "transferred" and cajoled to forget both mate and child through the gentlest of brainwashing techniques, necessitating serious therapy a mere thirty years later in the urban village of Crouch End when blips fizzed into connections despite such tender mind-control, in London, the underground rivers that flow through the city also start to merge. They have been bifurcated and dam it if these rivers aren't getting rather frustrated. The Holy Well under Shore Ditch, where the Blue Mothers dispense waters in glass vials to pilgrims, the tributary from this holy well flows into the River Moselle, that mossy hill in Wood Green the Green Man once danced down, and the healing creeks of the Moselle pour into Pymme's Brook, whose streams have a secret recipe and are dotted with floating strawberries and pieces of cucumber. The River Flēot meets all anticipated tides; the Hackney Brook bursts its culverts.

William Langland, dreaming, has this to say on the subject of all rivers being

one river, and on the subject of looking
straight into the sun:

> Under a brood bank by a bourne syde;
>
> And as I lay and lenede and loked on the watres,
>
> I slombred into a slepyng, it sweyed so murye.
>
> Thanne gan I meten a merveillous swevene --
>
> That I was in a wildernesse, wiste I nevere where.
>
> As I biheeld into the eest an heigh to the sonne

Part III

10

John Barleycorn

"they sweep through forest and air in whole companies with a horrible din. This is the widely spread legend of the furious host, the furious hunt, which is of high antiquity, and interweaves itself, now with gods, and now with heroes. Look where you will, it betrays its connexion with heathenism."—Jacob Grimm, 1883

Don't look straight into suns, but you can look straight into stars.

The stars were layered thick in their constellations behind other constellations, so many that one truthfully could only guess at patterns, with the lights white and near milky, and the sky in between dark and unguessed.

The magus's old finger pointed out zodiacs Florentine did not see. "There is the Egg, jewel of the spheres. And its Bird, not so very far away, the former not the only infant. For baby stars, according to *New Scientist* magazine, can make their own playmates. Baby stars such as L1527 IRS 450, which whirls round till the dirt in its orbit creates worlds and more worlds. Wondrous."

Florentine, 24 years of age and admiring, nodded. The stars were indeed *wondrous.* She had met the magus in the inn earlier that night, and a few friendly words had led to the revelation of his astronomical profession, even at the

Nebuchadnezzar age of 60, and the invitation to observe the celestial heavens under his good instruction. A country inn meant light was dim, and there was only the purity and softness of the meteors falling, which Florentine swore out loud she could hear crackling on this August night, which the old astronomer swore could never be the case, and which Florentine then swore inwardly to herself could never be anything but that case.

She wore a wimple with high eaves that covered her horns, her story now that of a journeying novitiate. The fetch a more dangerous guise than that of a male priest, for though her godliness dissuaded some so did it actively attract others. She travelled by day; bade sanctuary in churches by way of the cross on the chain presented by her goat brother, a glimpse of the relic as payment. On the rare occasions that she crossed paths with those travellers she had met before, they would each turn the other way, recognising correctly the other as a grifter, and no business of theirs.

This old man had been different. He had no sensual motive for her wimpled self; she had grown wise and could spot those chancers before they even asked to rub her rosary or sought private spiritual counsel. He had not told her his name. He had seen instead something else inside her. He was not Christian, nor Forestish like the Blue Schoolers; he spoke of spheres and planes and Plato and swans. It had been in the spirit of sheer delight that she had stepped out into the night with him and in the spirit of recklessness that she had whipped off her wimple and shown him her horns.

Florentine stared out at all the baby stars again, with her hair free in the wind. Somewhere out there was her own babe, calling to her. Somewhere out there were her parents. Somewhere out there was Eglentyne. Somewhere out there, though she never wanted to think of it again, was the Green Man. They had once been wed, but he had never come back a year and a day later, and so now they were not wed at all. She touched the roodwood secreted away in the locket round her throat. Wood, trapped and locked up. She felt a pang for all baby stars.

As she and the magus watched the skies, a glow lit up the heavens and the glow was green. Phosphorescent. "Will-o'-the-wisp," breathed Florentine, for she had heard of this before. She turned to her wrinkled friend. It was her turn to educate him. He had a half smile on him as she explained that a will-o'-the-wisp also was known as a *fata morgana* or jack-o'-lantern. "But what you *may* not know, grandfather, is that these green glows in the sky are a substance known as a gas, which is a vapour or a fog. Will-o'-the-wisps rise up when vegetables rot towards death."

The small meanings such as "Jack" and "death" and "vegetable" made her throat click and cough, but she kept her eyes on the stars as she awaited the magus's response.

He only smiled wider. "A *fata morgana* also means an illusion. Perhaps what you see there queer and luminous is instead the *Aurora borealis*. So how will you test your theory?"

"How will I... test it?"

"How will you test your jack-o'-lanterns, your will-o'-the wisp of the swamp? It is 1371, the world is new-budding, you shave yourself to fit the world –" she blushed, she had not told him it was necessary to shave fur off her visage and corporeality to appear human and not-beast "– the light is coming back now, where is your science?"

Once upon a time Florentine walked into a room. It was high up in the inn's small third storey, high up via the staircase, a rickety frame of chipped board, fine hair and dust caught in grains. This staircase was interesting to her, as it said so little, straightforward and were no vice, sufficiently parsimonious that she would never know whose hair had settled amidst the dust-motes upon which she ascended. Continuing on from there, she came to the room. The magus waited for her just beyond the door-frame and gazed at her in a grave manner. Florentine blinked. This formality was not what she had expected staring up at the stars. Yet here he was.

"Who are you?" He did not answer. "Who are you?" she said again to the magus. "But your name, what is your name?"

"What is *yours*?" he countered, and so she told him. "Well, it is probably only right that I tell you mine. I am Gerald."

He was an elderly man, but his eyes were bright. They were bright like hers. They were bright like Eglentyne's.

"Gerald," she said, "Gerald, you are very old; you are

nearly sixty."

"I am old," said Gerald, "but I am not sixty. I am thirty-six, only twelve years older than you," Gerald said to Florentine, "I am thirty-six long time ago and my real self sleeps, underneath the weight of a lake."

He was an extremely old man. "How very dangerous is that lake?"

Gerald ignored her. "I sleep underneath the lake. Underneath the lake I'm dreaming underwater. My real self was stolen by a swan maiden."

Florentine found it shocking and did not immediately know why. She thought of the white feathers on swans. Swans had grey feathers, too. "If your real self sleeps underwater, then who are you now?"

"I am Gerald. I am not from now. I'm not from now. I am actually not from now. I have been traveling through the years to you."

Florentine thought for a moment's breath. "Do we not all travel through the years?"

"Not in the direction I do walk."

A many-years-ago memory, the man with great horns who rapped on the cottage door; the tremendous city with panes of glass and on the other side of them yellow scraps of paper.

"I have been traveling backwards while my real self sleeps under the lake, but here is now," he said, "I have only been here since this morning. What year?"

"It is 1371. You know that well. You just said it

yourself."

"So," said Gerald, "so the wall has been built around Moscow."

"No, no," said Florentine, "that was several years ago."

"And so the plague rages on and on and on for the Franks, for Rome, for the Turks."

"No," said Florentine, "that was, I think, three years ago."

"And that beautiful music of stargazer John de Dunstaple?"

"I do not know of what you speak."

The magus finally permitted her to cross the threshold of the door into the room. He locked the door behind them both with an old iron key, his crepe-like fingers, the wrinkles on them, her teacher, and she thought, I will always remember this moment in the room.

There was indeed an antechamber. She had conceived already that there would be another far locked-away space and she stood there in its foreroom. Illuminated books stained with murrey and verdigris and saffron, the alluring handiwork of medieval monks. Gerald appeared to take some pleasure in watching Florentine's eyes dart across the books.

"Interesting," he said to her, "do you read?"

"Yes," said Florentine, "I do read, Gerald, I do read. I was taught at the Blue School."

"Oh, child." He began to laugh. "We will show you

this book." He guided her towards a small table atop which there was a scroll well splayed. "This book is called the secrets of women."

He already knew her secrets. He knew her horns and now her name.

"A crypto-translation of the Devil's own tongue. Kippered, with parsley and small wild onions. *De secretis mulierum*, where the pseudo-Albertus Magnus lets us know exactly how females scrape evil from the manly silver fleece we call Life. How their lust, as Tiresias puts it, grows to ten times that of men. Do you find this true, Florentine, a wimple such as you?"

It was the first time he had used her name.

She thought for a moment.

"Do I find chiromancy, charms, potions, baths to be true? Who is Albertus Magnus and how was he faked?"

Gerald did not answer. Gerald did not answer. "In this book," said Gerald, "you will find how women are the currying creatures that we feel they are in this book. Such logistic reflexivity is taught to all priests."

Florentine felt offense. "I do not think that women are evil creatures," she said, "nor do I think that priests should be taught such things. Where is the proof of it? From mine own travels, it is more likely men. But even truly wicked men are rare. Most folk are both. I go only from mine own eyes, and ears, and antlers, and hands, and my past."

Gerald began to laugh again. "What past can you

have? Are you not a nun? You wear the habit. Perhaps a nun of the repentant type. But your science is good, after all."

"You know that I am not. I showed you my horns and you saw them and you saw them. And I have never told you that I shaved off my pelts and yet you understand this."

Florentine looked around the room. She had never seen so many books together: in scrolls, in piles, in rolls, on goat parchments and rabbit vellums that the scriveners and scribes had illuminated and rubricated until they'd become exasperated with their inkhorns. In such books, one finds knowledge: one finds musical notations and charms involving throwing flowers into water and instructions for baths that requires one is overcome with befuddling vapours bubbling up from tests and stories of women with hair consisting of venomous snakes that swallow small animals and stone statues alike and travel tales of la Barbe and Mister Chicken and those types of spelles one finds in grim waters calling for tansy and bishopswort to stop quickenings and recipes to cook heathencakes and angels' curds and riddles and leechbooks with medical secrets –

"Do not read the leechbooks. The leechbooks are not for you to see."

He understood her pelts. He understood her thoughts. "What is in the next room, the postern," asked Florentine, "this is but the vessel room before the room of all the rooms." She fingered the cross of dead trapped wood. The necklace of birthmarks round the baby's throat.

Gerald began to laugh again. "This little life is just

the little life before the rest of all the lives we can see. It is we who are in the antechamber, my dear."

But suddenly Gerald's face grew somber as something flashed over his expression.

"What do you think of?" said Florentine, for she could see that he was far away.

"I'm sorry. Sometimes I dream again that I am my real self, sleeping under the water, and I forget that is I now who lives the dream. It is very confusing for me," said Gerald.

"I understand," confirmed Florentine. "What were we saying? Regarding what one wishes to see beyond the antechamber."

This time he did not laugh. "I leave you." And so he left and then Florentine heard the unmistakable sound of the iron key turned in the lock, so that she was in fact the prisoner and a caged stag while his footsteps echoed down the staircase, trodding on old hairs and dust.

At any other time this likely would have bothered Florentine. But this was not any other time. She straightened her nunly headdress. Her heart was beating quickly. And she advanced towards the red curtain that separated the small room from all the other rooms of the world.

Before she had a chance to push away the red curtains, someone else parted them. A woman's hand. There was a flash throughout the room then, a lightning flash as with the great city with the yellow scraps of paper. There was no woman, only Gerald parting the curtains, but Florentine could see nothing in the darkness inside. Gerald was back. Had he not retreated downstairs?

"There is a match," he said. "The cards match." And he parted the curtains further and this time he showed her a woman who was older than Florentine and she had a set of cards laid out. She stood up, smoothed out her dress and beckoned.

There was a lightning again, and again Florentine stood before the curtains in the antechamber, with the world waiting on the other side. Gerald was downstairs. The hand she could recognise. The woman who was the Witch. She was silver.

There was a woman's hand parting the curtain. The Witch stood up from her cards, smoothed out her dress and beckoned. There was a lightning and then the Witch stood by the curtains again, far away from the card table.

"Hello, Florentine," said the Witch.

"I don't know. You know my name, but I do not know yours."

The Witch ignored Florentine's implied question. The Witch was disguised as a harlequin, a checkered costume. "Come here, come here on the closer. I want to show you this very curious card suite made up of a sweet of birds."

"Suite?"

"Sweet science and the prints on them are each hand-painted and they are quite beautiful."

"What is this game?" called Florentine. She never seen anything like this before.

"This is the Tar-Road," said the scrywoman. "Which is, of course, the Royal Path."

Although walking the road as a priest had meant that Florentine had become moderately proficient at certain games such as chess and knucklebones, she did not set a-playing cards and never had and especially not now, for it was not seemly for a novitiate to be laughing and gaming and ale-ing. Many nuns did, but their reputations were questioned and gossip followed them. Florentine had not wanted gossip.

"Now I will tell your fortune," said the Witch. "I am a great admirer of Trocta of Salerno. And I find her medical treatises found in this library very useful," added the Witch, as if to explain her presence. "Very useful, without the poison dripped by the pseudo-Albertus. But I am here for the cards and not for the leechbooks. I am here for the birds and not for the john-cages."

Florentine had no idea where Solano was or who was Trocta. The Witch saw this on her face. "*None* of us know this forgotten knowledge, but never *you* mind," said the Witch.

The Witch was disguised as a harlequin disguised as the goddess Diana. Florentine now saw it, but it was mockery-puerile-Pierrot-clown. The Harlequin romance is upside-down, you charming devil. The Witch had fake arrows made of paper slung as if jokes into her belt. The world as represented by this enclosed library shimmered and felt silkish, not entirely opaque. Florentine could not tell if that was a good feeling or indeed a frightening feeling. The world was a joke. Books with recipes for tansy, bishopswort. She remembered things comparable. Her mother, speaking of herbs in leechbooks. *Taste the white snake and you will understand the languages of birds.*

"I have been waiting for you to come through the years."

"Here I am again," said Florentine.

"Yes," said the Witch, "you were old and now you are young again."

"But I am young. I am still young." She did not know of what the Witch spoke, but unnerving it was that the Witch knew her name. This talk of sleeping underneath lakes. She herself was sleeping underneath a dangerous lake. The Witch's lips were very ruby. Florentine could see a moistness between them as the Witch sat down at the table that was in the centre of this larger room.

On the table were a number of triumph cards. They were forced, like a magician's trick from the Witch's slight hand. "Sixty of them," the Witch told Florentine. "We have fixed the odds. I see you for what you are." The Witch was pretty and her hair was silver, her skin young and her lips rent and reddened. The table low and so the Witch knelt before it.

"Here we are," she said to Florentine. "Here we are again. Sixty," said the Witch. "And from the stack of sixty we have four queens and forty in number of birds – six suits each – and five hearts, each of honest words and yet too artifice; and sixteen trumps: Diana and Actaeon and Faunus, called Figgy; and thirteen more. *O ludus trumphorum*, you game of games, our medieval passion plays out the way it's dealt. I do not need to continue. I know that you know, that is all."

Florentine looked at the playing cards, which were a deeper beautiful; and backed with a grey colour called coyote. *Triomfi*, she saw upon them right-side-up the beautiful hand paintings. *Very* beautiful, she thought, five speeds with six kinds of birds. Five speeds with six kind words. She saw a little painting of a juggler and then she saw a little painting of a harlequin, and then she saw a trickster, a trickster she saw; and then she saw a medic, a medic she saw; and then she saw the birds; she saw birds. What color were these birds? They were blue bird, white, burnt gold, red bird, green bird, black bird, six weeks, six suites.

The deck itself is lost. In the *carte da triomfi* of the Royal Path, the Queen of Hearts is upside-down. This is not unlike the Red Queen Hypothesis of evolutionary theory (Van Valen 1973), where the strategies and counterstrategies in the battle of the sexes and more serious skirmishes with pathogens mean that we are not only upside-down but run in place, like *Alice in Wonderland*'s Red Queen. Red is a blood colour, love colour.

"I see you for what you are," said the Witch. "Take off that castrating cloth winded round your horns."

Florentine untwined her horns.

The Witch laid out the cards and she dealt Florentine

more or less cards and she had Florentine touch her narrow fingers and Florentine had the Witch touch her own fingers. Florentine's mouth felt what Florentine felt. The room was hot. She could smell hamburgers, something else. The murder of beasts for meat. She could smell on the witch boar-musk and vanilla. There we go. Gold, frankincense and murder.

"This is the last day in the world," said the Witch, "this is the last day in the world."

They touched the cards together and their fingers intertangled and as the Witch slipped through the birds' taxa, as the Witch flipped through, so did Florentine's fingers follow those of the Witch. It was not mockery; it was only admiration.

The Witch told Florentine's fortune, blue bird, white bird, gold bird, red bird, green bird, black bird. It is elliptical. "I cannot tell you more," said the Witch.

Finally, when all the cards had passed and started, there was but one card remaining and it was, it was, the green bird that was the suite and it was the card that was the cup. The aced cup from which poured out the streams.

"These five water streams on the hand-painting," said the Witch, "of this vessel..." She touched Florentine's face and Florentine trembled. "They are your senses; touch," the Witch clarified, and she looked at Florentine's eyes and they looked in each other's lives, into Florentine's cloudy-grey gaze and into the Witch's strange silver eyes with fringed long, thick lashes. And the Witch's beady intelligence; it pierced Florentine down between her thighs. That pull of the Witch drew even closer to Florentine and she whispered in Florentine's ear, "And your sight to you here," she said in an unquestioned answer, "it is your hearing and so it is your touch, your sight, your hearing –" Florentine was so close to the Witch she could smell the murder scent, muck and smiles.

"I can smell you," said Florentine, "I can smell you." Green bird. That act that uses everything: sight and smell and taste and hearing and touch.

Florentine felt only compassion, but she stood there trembling with her new goals. Her new role raw and stiff. Her nipples raw and stiff. She could not stop shaking and her heart felt as if it were dropping further down her frame. There was one still yet one sentence that the Witch had not said. For she had seen her heard her touched her smelt her and yet one sense to remain. The Witch told Florentine's fortune. Blue bird white bird gold bird red bird green bird black bird. "It is elliptical. I cannot tell you more. I cannot tell you more."

Sweet, painful dreams underneath lakes. Florentine could barely breathe. The breezes that skimmed such lakes in springtimes. The Witch pulled even closer and then the Witch kissed her. And then Florentine tasted her.

The Witch was a real person. She was a grey witch. A silver.

"There is a branding on me," said the Witch, "come closer. You have no pelt on your back and arms either."

"I've shaved it. Needs as must. I have travelled the world. Now I am so –"

"Those who refuse to work at cheap rates, the pay as before the blue sickness came, we all have been branded." The Witch showed Florentine her brand on her upper back: a snake biting its tail. It was ugly and the dark brown crust of it. "They have started branding." The Witch laid up the very last card of all. It was a red bird card. It was plain nothing else. The card was entirely bad. "We can see redder reds if researchers add proteins to our eyes," the Witch told Florentine, "we absorb new reds otherwise unseen. According to *New Scientist* magazine, soon we shall see all the red lights on the visible spectrum and even more than the colours that truly exist for us."

"Yes, I mean to ask, what is the *New Sci* –"

The Witch stroked Florentine's breasts. "You are bald here, too." Hand on her leg. The return of the Witch. "Florentine, where is your pelt? I thought you were a stag. I thought you were an animal."

No one had told the Witch that.

"What is your name?"

"My name is Cyprine. If you removed the estrogen from the centre of a bird, then male plumage results."

"No, no," said Florentine, for she had learned this at the Blue School, where the curriculum had been very insistent on female primacy, "it is quite the other way around. The female bird is the default; the male is the divergence *post-hawk*."

The Witch merely shook her head; they were on their knees now, holding each other. "Cyprine," she repeated. "*La cyprine est le liquide sécrété à l'entrée du vagin de la femme lorsqu'elle est en état d'excitation sexuelle. La cyprine est une variété de vésuvianite'*," quoted the Witch from Wikipedia. " '*If these proteins were present in the eye you would be able to see red light that is invisible to you now, says co-author James Geiger, also at Michigan State University. But since objects reflect a mixture of light, the world would not necessarily always appear more red. "Something that looked white before would now look green with your new super red vision," he says...*' That was *New Scientist* again."

Birds can look white and then they can look green.

" '*The Snowball Earth hypothesis proposes that the Earth's surface became entirely or nearly entirely frozen at least once, sometime earlier than 650 million years ago.*' Wikipedia. '*This secretion, called cyprine, was produced by the clitoris.*' French Wikipedia, *encore*," continued the Witch. "And marital instructions from the Holy Roman Catholic Church, as cited in the 'Anatomic Study of the Clitoris and the Bulbo-Clitoral Organ' by Vincent Di Marino and Hubert Lepidi, 2014: '*Before the sexual intercourse, the husband shall delicately rub the button of love with a finger moistened with perfumed oil, in a circular motion.*' Do I need to quote more, Florentine?"

The Witch no longer looked silver; she looked green. Florentine was still trembling. "No."

And then the Witch took Florentine to bed, or took her to the floor, for that is more accurate.

*

They stretched on the wooden slats of the library, holding each other. The room was enclosed. Outside, the last hour of ink played out. There came no light into the room, but all skins were luminous. "Do you wish to see the last star of the night?" whispered the Witch to Florentine. "The last star. And then tomorrow the first star in the world."

Down they toed, balancing the staircase. Florentine felt jealousy now over every hair-strand, over all who had visited the Tar-Road before. But of course if one is wise, then one always keeps such thoughts silent.

The sky was dark and the trees darker still, silhouette. It was August, so not too cold. They each held the other's nude fingers, right hand to left. And Cyprine was correct, one star left in the sky, the empyryean sphere having already enfolded the others, the nest within a bird within an egg. The star a bluebird, sparked and glitter, and Cyprine squeezed Florentine's hand. There was wildness in the woods; Florentine much preferred it to a house. A bird was calling, this time real and not star. *Gavia adamsii*, the loon with the fractal chessboard on its neck. It was calling from a tree quite different than the other spirches and bruces. Curious.

"Come," said Florentine, pulling Cyprine after her, and the stones tore in small ways at their bare feet and the air healed in small ways their bare bodies as Cyprine followed Florentine onto the edge of the glade.

They stood before the forest. Florentine held her breath. Everything was silent and there was only the rustle of Cyprine's breath. The sky was changing, becoming lighter, but Florentine clung onto night and would not let it cease. She held all the night in her heart and it did not change. In the dark night she saw the outlying tree from which the loon called. It should not be growing here. The loon high up, invisible, and still it warbled. A partridge in a greyfruit tree, checkerboard neck. Cyprine asked Florentine how the tree came to be here, but Florentine did not know. She had heard of a process in plants called selfing, self-fertilising. Perhaps that was how this singular greyfruit had come to be off a distant country-inn path near the forest, far away from the only greyfruit trees she'd ever known.

The sky, the sky was lightening. Florentine was letting go of night. She gave a small cry. The last star in the world was gone. Cyprine pressed close to to Florentine, her breasts against the other woman's, and held her hand so tightly. "Let the day come."

The sun opened up in red, blood red red queen red red bird red, blood on snow, eye-proteins detect the redder reds than ever you have seen, or so says *New Scientist*, detect reds beyond reds and golds, red-gold like hair-strands caught in stairs and thatched for cottage roofs, gold like locusts and gold like gold molasses and gold like the gold coin between Florentine's legs, twisting. The sunlight hit the trees and made them green and the Witch called out with joy, and her call was a more beautiful sound than even the *gloria gloria* in churches, *gloria, gloria*, they were fucking against the gnarled wood of the greyfruit tree, the witch's hand rubbing at Florentine's bud until it purred into *gloria gloria* itself. And then she grabbed at the witch's hips with both hands, her fingers sinking into soft, night-milk flesh, subtile, and Florentine cracked open the charm round her neck, bit the glass open and let the wood free, spat it out and she fell to her knees and licked at the witch with passion, quail-pipe, while the sun poured hot over them and the green leaves spilled out with their colour and she swallowed the cyprine and choked on it and wanted more, the Witch trembling and thrust back against the bark, yolden, eyes closed, hands gripping. They were wild girls, not careful controlled card artifice in ordered rooms. They were animal animal animal and wanted to drink, to ravage meat; the witch smelled like meat and tasted of cold, sun-warming leaves.

Then they were tumbled into each-the-other down in mulch. The bird had been calling but they never heard it. Their ears were roaring and they never heard any of it. Over them the Wild Hunt went by, just before the near-circle of the sun became a low disc and cast pink and clarity across the whole wide world, with the Witch's cunt in her mouth and the Witch's finger dripping wet sap from Florentine's own sex, rubbing, obscene and *gloria*, no other word for it, *gloria gloria*.

They fuck, the Wild Hunt rushes by with horns bellowing, with a male horned god that they don't even look up for.

Florentine looked up some, wet and near-ashamed, but trembling and happy, never ashamed at all, her hands full of Cyprine's flesh, and she saw that in the sunlight that the bird perched atop the greyfruit and watching them voyeuristically was changing colour from chessboard to blue, and it was time; the blue bird was crowing... She raised her head further, but Cyprine covered Florentine's eyes: don't look up, don't look up. Florentine had heard this tale, but her breath was still ragged in Cyprine's ear as their passion turned to caresses, and kisses, and embraces, Florentine's neck naked of the rood-charm, trying to get close to each the other, trying to get closer still; Florentine had heard this tale and knew that if she saw the Wild Hunt she'd meet her death, or so the story goes, that crowd of Herne's and his arrogant self and his huntsmen and the blue bird crowing the same song the hunt-horns were playing. Florentine was kissing Cyprine, and Cyprine's tongues were deep and soft in her mouth, but she wanted to tell Cyprine that she could control this Hunt. That she nearly did it last time.

She tried to look up entirely, but Cyprine held Florentine's jaw down violently so she could not, and Florentine spat in her face, and then they crouched there half-sitting and naked, glaring at each other. "I said that I would find you and you said you would not forget me," said the Witch.

"You left us by a dangerous lake," Florentine shrieked back, "and the owl and my parents and my antlers in a tree, all before you came back!"

The Witch was screaming now too, still wrestling with Florentine's skull, so that Florentine still could not look up at the Wild Hunt. "I tried to call you from the forest; I had no choice; it all happens all at once!"

"You are a coward; let me look!"

The Witch was far stronger than Florentine, perhaps not so surprisingly, and Florentine settled into this force but she shut her eyes and disobeyed therein the only way she could: she thought of the Wild Hunt. *I am the Stag;* she thought, *you are chasing* me; *I am controlling* you. The Hunt faded. Her horns remained. The blue bird stopped calling. It was daytime.

"Due to me; I did that," Florentine told the Witch as they rose to their feet, each brushing twigs off their bodies and glaring at the other, distrusting.

The Witch did not answer that comment, but stared half tenderly, half spitefully into Florentine's eyes. "Let the day come," said the Witch.

*

Here is an Egg and here's how it works. Peel off the shell, Fabergé-jewels *or* matryoshka Russian nesting dolls *or* sugar castings doled out by fertility-cultist Easter bunnies, candy moulds you peek inside to see all the dioramas of the world playing out. Peel off that eggshell in whatever form you like best and you uncover a forest. A silver woman and a stagged woman fight, then fuck together on the woodland floor and over them the Wild Hunt rushes, but then the Russian do cease, the rushing do cease.

Next, they do walk up the stairs of a rickety inn all the way to a distant room. The Witch and the stagged woman stand there in that room together, and next they are licking and touching each other. "Cyprine," whispers the Witch, and the stagged woman tastes cyprine. The Witch is a grey witch. She is a silver egg. The goose that lays the silver egg.

The Witch shows the antlered woman a brand on her back; the antlered woman shows the Witch how she has betrayed her animal self.

Black bird, green bird, red bird, gold bird, white bird, blue bird. The cards are already laid out, and only afterwards does the Witch tell Florentine's fortune.

"This is the last day in the world," said the Witch, "this is the last day in the world."

The Witch plucks up all the cards away from Florentine's grasp. The witch is standing by the curtains. Florentine is standing by the antechamber curtains. The witch is standing by the card table. Gerald is standing by the curtains. He removes a key from the lock and he and Florentine retreat into the antechamber. The witch no longer exists.

Gerald removes a scroll from Florentine's grasp. "Not for you," he says. "Not for women. *De secretis mulierum*. The Devil's own tongue. Kippered, with parsley and small wild onions." He puts the book down on a table. Florentine does know that the room contains books that have not yet come to be things, the future books of the preacher John Wycliffe

who writes in his Bible of the woodwose when he stretches
for a word; Wycliffe is predetermined just as Gerald under
the lake dreams of future selves. John Gower's own copy
of *The Secrets of Secrets* – كتاب سر الأسرار – is found in this
library. She knows that Gower knows Chaucer, whose
ponderings on nuns and friars also will be found here in due
time; she knows that Geoffrey in turn knows her friend Will
Langland, who dreams before rivers if not under lakes.

Inside the library, in both the antechamber where
stands Gerald and the larger room where sits the witch,
where she hand-paints cards of Taraux and Tarocchi with
a cyprine tinctured blue by copper; inside the library are
written jokes and secrets as well as wisdoms. Of particular
importance to Gerald tonight is the palindrome, where a
word reads the same way both from start and finish, though
he says nothing of this to Florentine, whose name he has
remembered. Gerald is trying to remember when he is, a
difficult feat when all happens at once. Perhaps it is the year
nobles fear Frankish invasions more than customarily, for
their branded serfs are becoming far too restless. Gerald asks
his questions to determine his placing.

The magus is already waiting in the room that pre-
cedes all other rooms of the world, underneath the dangerous
lake, but Florentine is not there. She is walking backwards
down the stairs. She is walking on eggshells.

Florentine is outside the inn on a starry night with
her antlers shown full to the wind. There is an old man with
her. Him again. He has called her *venatrix*, but she has not

told him her name yet.

And now they talk of will-o'-the-wisps and jack-o'-lanterns and swamp gas and red stars, things that light up from the inside, and now Florentine loosens the grip on the rood round her neck, and thinks of her own lost babe.

Red Queen somersaults and runs in place; words read the same way both from start and finish. Jewelled eggs look like Russian nesting dolls and in each doll is another doll, and in that doll there is an egg, and in that egg you'll find a seed, and from that seed will grow a tree, and on that tree you'll find a branch, and on that branch there is a nest, and in that nest there sits a bird, and under that bird there lies an egg. An egg in which there is a little snake that sits the branch that shakes a tree that rains down nuts that feeds the bird who makes the nest where lies an egg. And not so far away is the house, and not the hound nor the horn, that belongs to the forest-farmer sowing his corn that feeds the blue bird that crows in the morn that wakes the priests all shaven and shorn that marries the man all tattered and torn that kisses the maiden all forlorn that milks the doe with the crumpled horn that tosses the hound that kills the wife that eats the owl that lies cooked in the house that Jack builds.

*

Florentine awoke; she awoke in early afternoon. The autumn sunlight still high and she lay unmoving in the heap of rouged autumn leaves, also some orange, some bronze: near-mercurial as greyfruits of whose pale leaves were also present a few.

Her limbs ached, for she and the Witch had stopped bickering and fallen asleep tangled each into the other, affection being the child of spite.

There passed a moment for Florentine where all time hung in the afternoon sun, and there was the physical ache of limbs and satiety between her thighs of a good night's work, and no knowledge further.

But then it was like she had tasted the white snake's stew; as if she had put one wet finger to her lips to understand everything all at once, for she certainly understood that the Witch was no longer there with her, but for the first time after an encounter with the Wild Hunt, the third set of antlers atop her own head still were.

It's time I fess up. I am a stick. As your narrator, I am omniscient. I am the Stick in the Machine. I'm going to stick it to you. You and Martin are hugging. You feel twinkly all over.

"We've forded the lake. But how," Martin whispers in your ear, "how do we escape this cave?"

You look at the lake. You could go back the way you came. Or you could try something different through the tunnel that continues on the opposite wall of the cave-enclosed lake. You have not noticed this before. Perhaps water levels were higher. "We keep going. We're halfway through. We follow the tunnel through to the other side of the mountain."

"What if the tunnel continues for ever and ever? What if there's no hole on the other end? What if there are more lakes in our way like this one?"

"You've asked *three* questions, Martin! And you just had your turn, as well."

"We're still playing the game?"

"Grab your stick! –" (There we go! At last! I have been ignored for pages.) "And we're off into the wild blue-black yonder. It doesn't matter what transpires; at least we won't be stag-nating here –" you pause for a moment "– *stalag*-nating here, going back the way we came. It doesn't even matter if we have a real choice or not; what matters is that we think we do."

"Doesn't it?" huffs Martin. But you are correct. Or maybe you're not.

As you walk and more frequently crawl through the continuing tunnel, you confide to Martin your reasons for detailing a hagiography in the first place.

"I cannot help but think," you tell Martin as your knees scrape and your heads bump, "as I metaphorically finger the minutiae of these holy lives, that I could make a fine argument for memorialising another individual, one of many deeds and sufficiently serene demeanour."

In the darkness, you can hear Martin snort. You let a dramatic pause lengthen then, to punish him before resuming.

You continue. "Allow me to elaborate. I was born in a snowstorm – Alaska – my uncle was born in a snowstorm – Southern California – my grandfather was born in a snowstorm – Colorado – my great-great-aunt was born in a snowstorm – Massachusetts – all on December 6. Four near-Christmas miracles on the exact same day of the month in the exact same weather conditions for four consecutive generations in the exact same family."

"What happened to your amnesia?"

"I'm halfway to a cure. Remind me to tell you some time about my former surveillance work at Friedrichstraße Station. It was much admired." You have a different tone about you. Arrogant. And officious. You sound like someone you know.

"You're starting to sound like your therapist."

This telepathy stumps you for a half-second. "How do *you* know I have a therapist?"

"Only the Californian snow would have been unexpected."

"Needlessly petty, Martin. And avoidant. You're not fit to kiss my therapist's snowboots."

"Didn't you once say you were Catholic? If you count nine months forward from the whiskey libations of Saint Paddy's Day, you reach, roughly, early December. So, also unexpected."

"Saint Patrick. Hmph. A real kill-joy who outlawed *sughaim sine*, the native Celtic practice of homoerotic nipple-sucking practised as publicly performed obeisance to new clan chiefs. Never liked Saint Patrick. December 6 will be my Feast Day."

"Isn't that Saint Nicholas's Day?"

In the cave gloaming, little Tannenbaum flickers return to you. Children-and-shoe traditions. A toddler laughing. "I will boot jolly old Saint Nicholas, Santa Claus, Sinterklaas, Saint Nick, whatever, never liked him, off of it. It's like the boardgame *Sorry*; once I land on his square he has to go back to the beginning and start again. So that's the Feast Day covered."

Far, far ahead, there is the proverbial light, end-game, tunnel.

"Let's get back to the miracles." The two of you scurry forward on your knees toward the light. "The repetition of snowy seasonal birthdays being only the first miracle. I frequently in my youth, misspent in rural wilderness, I frequently in my youth took it upon myself to actively avoid the killing of mosquitoes."

"We're nearly there. Are you truly claiming to be a saint?"

The thought still far away, the glimpse shows only blue sky and puffskydaddy clouds. The tunnel drilled through the mountain must be very high up. You had not noticed an incline, but there you go.

"Yes, I ate fish, chicken, beef, lamb, shellfish, bear, squirrel, moose and pork, but such is not the point. It caused me true psychological distress to snuff out their little mosquito lives as my parents bid me do –"

"It caused you true psych-ological distress because you are now talking like a psych-ologist yourself."

Perhaps you have incorporated your beloved thera-pist's persona a tad *too* much. Transference, a terrifical task.

"It caused me, a potential saint, true psychological distress to snuff out their little mosquito lives as my parents bid me do even when the creatures were biting me, and so I had the spiritual acumen –"

"You really are plodding along here arguing that you are a psychologist, a spy and a saint? Do you not consider that hubristic?" Martin has become very eloquent of late. What's up with that.

"The spiritual acumen to merely wave them away, hoping perhaps that they would bite my younger brother instead, and yet avoid the torture at which many Alaskan mosquitoes were at risk, that act whereby a human child holds tightly their arm's blood flow to allow a mosquito to suck until it is a red roly-poly balloon, only to release the finger-tourniquet to observe said red-ballooned mosquito blow up like a little bloody bomb."

"You had a little brother?"

"I had three little brothers." You find his interruptions annoying and distracting, even though escape is nigh. It has become very light in the cave. "No, as an ascetic I avoided such acts and such sights, and would wave the insects towards open doors. You can see here already that I had the animal-loving inclinations of a more self-determined Saint Francis of Assisi. Goody-two-shoes with hippie hair and an alarmingly wafty spiritual philosophy. Never liked him. Nor did my wife, Frau Doktor W–" You clap both hands over your mouth in shock and sneak a look at Martin. He is politely looking away.

The two of you exit and you're standing on a natural stone ledge high up on a cliffside. It's like walking through the window. Through the looking glass.

"But one sub-Arctic summer day everything was to change," you mutter. Martin is no longer listening, for he is looking down open-mouthed on the forest canopy directly below. This betrayal, despite your effort to keep the hagiography topical: "Everything was to change. I had once again unlatched the window screen to let the indoor mosquitoes fly free, shooing them as one does houseflies with their ugly gemmed eyeballs. Yet at that very moment the mosquitoes hovered *en masse* in the window frame and then, as one accord, formed a perfect letter 'J' –"

Martin, crouching, appears to be distracted. "Er, for Saint Jezzabelladonna? The second one you mentioned." He looks like he's about to take a leap.

"No! For Jack! This was the house that Jack built."

"It doesn't even feel like it's you talking. Who are you?"

"I could say the same of you. Again, the house that Jack built. Or at least the window frame. I was using third person."

"You certainly were."

" 'J', my first initial, a 'J' which shimmered faintly garnet from the blood-infused mosquito bodies, a 'J' as if to thank me for saving the lives of so many of their conspecifics at the risk of mockery from my family and friends, and all this before the horde dispersed and lightly flew away into early evening, the faint paper-scent of spirch trees in the air, the delicate hum of insect buzz as well –"

Saint Malabaster of the Diphallic Urgency would have appreciated this vision too, with its manifold sensory aspects – tears filled your eyes; it was as if you could still see the afterimage of the 'J' hanging in the air, as if you, Icarus-like, had stared too long at your magnificent Sol. You cleared your throat to vocalise such thoughts.

"Or, perhaps, stared with unforeseen but not unwelcome introspection at my magnificent 'soul' and the effect my good deeds had had on approximately 413 synchronised mosquitoes. This was the second miracle, and the impression it made on me, and my religious sentiments at the time, was not inconsiderable. Good-bye, little blighters, fly free, fly free."

You rather wish Martin could have stuck around for the *dénouement* – beatification requires a minimum of only one miracle, sainthood three, and there was still a third to go (count 'em, three) – but he had taken a jump two-thirds of the way through the mosquito speech.

So it was to be the fourth and final miracle, then. You spread your arms and leap, too. You land brusquely on the tree canopy, alongside Martin and a blue-mouthed white bird. Miraculous. From time to time, the white bird with the blue mouth changes colour to a blue bird with a white mouth. *Très* kokological. You ignore the implications. "Anyway," you say, addressing Martin alone, "anyway, that last Icarus leap of mine –" there, you've verbally shoehorned the metaphor in after all "– that last Icarus leap to join you here was not the third miracle to which I alluded."

Martin groans and buries his head in his hands.

"Both the stately Jezebelladonna and yours truly initially performed three. Inevitable for Jezzy though, wouldn't you say? Mine own miracles were, though I blush to say it –"

"You're not blushing at all –"

"It's sunburn. That third final miracle was more the result of a raw talent-slash-propensity. A simple healing of the infirm elderly, though such *largesse* is hardly simple in *realen Welt* terms."

386

You say this meaningfully, while secretly congratulating yourself on concurrent German and French etymological flourishes. Martin is pretending to ignore you and is looking in the far distance, but you know him better than that.

"Just as I suspected," says Martin. "We're trapped in a loop. Look over there –" In the far distance, you can see the tiny figure of a bald man, carrying a stick. "Now there." And approaching him from the opposite direction, walking away from the cave and forest, a tiny human with moose-horns.

You feel a little uncomfortable with this. "Should we… join them? Introduce ourselves?"

"Absolutely not. Something different. The situation craves it."

"Situations can't crave anything; they are subjective abstract summaries."

"Shut the holy fuck up." Martin has at last found his spine, and it's not solely the stick propping him up. You bite your lip, guessing correctly that this newly empowered version of Martin would find that voiced sentiment patronising.

You stand up, teetering on the treetop. You can see everything – ignoring the doppelgängers – the forest and the desert too. You see an oasis of cacti. That's where you're going again.

"In this case, Martin, whilst out motoring, I happened upon a man in his 70s doubled over in leisurewear clothing (sweatpants, such as one might wear at a senior citizens' residential community), breathing heavily, doubtless due to a weak heart. Speaking of hearts, Saint Valentine's price for curing a little girl's blindness was the destruction of all 'idols' in the household; that is to say, destroying representational art the religious provenance of which and with which Valentine took issue; the fine-art equivalent of burning books; never got any valentines myself; never liked him."

"Okay."

Martin is looking at you. You can't read his expression. He has to accept what you're saying. He has no choice. You draw close and hiss in his ear: "I immediately pulled over and helped that old man to his feet, despite his protests that he had just finished a 10-mile jog, and forced him into my car, only releasing my charge when I drove up to the local senior citizens' home and deposited him on their doorstep. The wondrous thing –"

Martin shakes himself free and wants to interrupt you, but you put a finger to his lips.

"Shhh. Shh, darling. The wondrous thing was that he was entirely cured and actually rather sprightly for his advanced age, though his manner remained cantankerous. I drove my Volvo away with good haste before the orderlies arrived, leaving the poor old gentleman, now healed, first cursing on the residential doorstep, though his cure was so holistic that he rallied and then pursued my vehicle for some time, pounding on the trunk and windows, a rather pointless exercise and lost cause.

"Have you ever read the multiple pleas to Saint Jude, the Patron Saint of Lost Causes, from his followers?

Such last-ditch prayers break your heart; Jude must be interceding 24-7; have always felt ambivalent about him due to the terminal illness associations; I hope that Ol' Hey Jude is up to his afterlife duties. Another rather pointless exercise and lost cause, as the horsepower of Sweden's finest far exceeds that of an elderly man, no matter how recently rejuvenated. Herein, however, I completed a third miracle towards sainthood, as I cured the frailty if not the disposition of my elderly subject."

"Okay, then."

You look meaningfully at Martin. "Exactly. Okay, then. You're obviously uncomfortable with my miraculous flying prowess. Let's climb down now while we've got the chance." You're still avoiding significant eye-contact with the bird. You go down hand under hand, foot under careful foot as you descend the tree, pausing occasionally to take breath to inform Martin above you.

"Thus, I thought it only right that I submitted my good self for papal sainthood consideration. There is that pesky little detail of requiring individuals to have been dead for five years before sainthood applications and I am drawing healthful breath, and also nominating myself, a maverick and unprecedented move – unchecked ambition and perhaps even narcissism (not in my case, to be clear) has been observed in aspirant holy ones before, particularly amongst attention-seeking martyr types such as Saint Joan of Arc, with her steed, and her armour, and her being burnt alive by fire, and her humourless, po-faced self-righteousness;

never liked her –"

You're on the ground. The forest floor. You're on your own. Martin hasn't followed you down. This has never happened before. You're on your own. What shall you do?

You leave the lip of the forest for the dunes and your vista expands. You're treading the sand, muttering to yourself. You reach up to ascertain your moose horns are along for the ride: still along they are. You look all the way up. Martin and his Stick are still standing next to an extraordinarily, preternaturally handsome man with bull-moose horns. You check yourself a second time: yep, horns.

"In consideration of my great service towards the Church community," you shout upwards to Martin, the Stick and the singularly, devastatingly good-looking man with the bull-moose horns, "in bringing to light four forgotten saints (count 'em, four) – still extant, in a buy-four-get-one-free spirit of things – Wiggle, Jezebelladonna, Malabaster and Penelope Pongo – I request that the deceasal requirement be summarily dismissed!"

"What?" Martin shouts downward. "We can't hear you!"

"That I might be accepted as Saint Jack-a-rine, though I would prefer my actual surname to be honoured as opposed to being just another cath-a-like to my quasi-homophone Saint Catherine!"

"What *is* your surname?" shouts down the ganemydally gorgeous man with the bull-moose horns.

You shout it up to them.

"What? We can't hear you!"

"And speaking of first names, I've never liked the name Catherine and if one really wanted to pay tribute, she is a woman best commemorated for the beauteous flashing fireworks display of so-called Catherine-wheels, and not by the sadomasochistic torture-wheel apparatus by which she met her end and a machine towards which the aforementioned fireworks device doth grimly nod, and I've never liked the name Catherine due to the fact that I consider Catherine's stubborn lack of saving her own spine by refusing to convert back to pagan ways to be a character fault, and due to the fact that I therefore find her death all a bit depressing and wasteful, to be honest; never liked her. I would therefore additionally request the general patronage of mildly blasphemous apostates, and also the general patronage of those who bake delicious fudges and distribute them to friends, such individuals being a true gift from God if ever there was one."

"What?" shouts down Martin.

You sigh. You shield your eyes to the glare. In the desert's far distance, two men – one with a stick, the other frighteningly intelligent yet compassionate with horns – are coming towards you. You look up again and still see your kind and charming trippelgänger with Martin. You dutifully lower your head. Across the sand come the charitable and insightful man with the bull-moose horns, and Martin and the Stick.

"Dear Jack!" the two of them (plus stick) shout

across the desert. "Thank you for your letter to the Holy See. We regret to say that your application for sainthood does not suit our needs at the present, or indeed any other, time, including *post hoc* to your eventual demise. We will be reviewing your baptismal records at Holy Family Cathedral in the Archdiocese of Anchorage, Alaska, with the slight possibility of ex-communication on grounds of blasphemy. Yours in Christ!"

On your way to meet them, you stumble across an oasis. It isn't much to speak up. Someone has trod through the palm trees and kicked out the camels and left it rather messy. A hollow where perhaps a spring or puddle used to be. There are cacti statues and new brass plaques before each saint-cactus: *Saint Jackarine*, reads one brass plaque. *Saint Stick*, reads another. *Saint Martin, Saint Bird, Saint Pineapple, Saint Mustache, Saint Froggy.*

From the middle distance now, Martin and the man with bull-moo se horns (you, let's face it) are still approaching. You have just enough time to gaze around more purposefully at the saintly cacti. How many times have you been here now? Do the plaques change every time your brain shifts anew?

You stare particularly at what was mere seconds ago Saint Froggy. It's not an amphibian anymore: it's a reptile. The plaque now reads *Saint Snake*. You jerk your head up. Martin and Jack are nearly even with you. The snakes are rising. You stretch a hand out to your righthand horn, a maidenly gesture, as if adjusting a hairdo. The Jack approaching you does exactly the same with his lefthand horn, a mirror to your movement rather than a replication. A left hand is very different to a right hand, you see.

The couple reaches you and there is an awkward silence, a social discomfort apparently quite common in doppelgänger rendezvouses. "Whatever did you do to these poor cactuses?" asks Martin. "Jack, please meet Jack."

"Hello."

"Hello."

You look up to the tree. You see another, tiny Martin and Jack waving down. You avert your eyes.

Martin-down-on-the-ground sighs loudly. "Don't be pretending you're all shocked. You've re-started multiple times and it was inevitable that sooner or later one of you would be running into the other."

You sneak a look at your fine self. Gorgeous fellow, with stalwart horns. You wonder if he was from the return trip to Page 3, or if he had re-started at the cave pool, or from some future trajectory you have yet to experience and choose.

Gorgeous fellow. But he's got to go. You lock horns with the other Jack; a fight to the death: go back to Page 1. But if you prefer, you can go back to the tree canopy where you're squatting with the first Martin and the Stick and the Bird. Okay, then. Keep reading.

This time when you look down on the oasis, however, once you've miraculously materialised on top of the trees, you see yourself still arguing with that bull-headed

Jack, and see also Martin and his stick. And when you shudder and check, yep, sitting right behind you are copies of Jack, Martin and the Stick, just as Jack, Martin and the Stick are also sitting right in front of you. Oddly, there is only one unreplicated bird present.

You count on your fingers: including yourself and the two down below, five Jacks, one for each finger. Both Martins are silent up here; so too are both other-Jacks; sticks for their part always silent. That said, you can only conceive from your singular brain to yourself; you're the only thing that exists. Thus reassured, you ignore the other humans up here (likewise the sticks) and take vantage of this vantage to look further across this desert, across this desert.

In the *near* distance down below, you see yet another Martin and Jack marching towards the oasis. But this Jack has no horns.

In the *middle* distance down below, yet another Martin–Jack couple approaches. This Jack has got horns, whew, but the Martin has no stick.

In the *far* distance down below, Martin and Jack are both trotting across the sands, and both of them have bull-moose horns. Mutations slightly differing each time, genetic sand-drifts.

You therefore shimmy down the tree again (the doubled Martins, Jacks, sticks and bird are impolite and do not respond to your courtesy-*adieu*), and then you half-fall, half-stumble the last few feet onto the sand. You look forward: nearly at an undestroyed oasis. This version, this time, its shoots form an *orchard of pomegranates, with pleasant fruits. A fountaine of gardens, a well of liuing waters, and streames.* Yes, *thy lips, drop as the hony combe: hony and milke are vnder thy tongue. Let my beloued come into his garden, and eate his pleasant fruits.* The lake has been replenished. There is no one here but you. Certainly no beloveds. (*Its blood tastes like honey.*)

Up above, the trees are unpopulated, though a shadow crosses the sand and flits above it, almost pterodactyl in cast.

Ah, there we go. Martin naked with Stick, but otherwise solo and therefore normal, is approaching. For the first time perhaps ever, he appears connected to you, unquestioning. Indeed, he recognises you.

"Where is the Witch?" asks Martin.

You do not know what he means. You runs through all the witches of your mind, your hybrid English/German/American mind: Witchfinder Generals, witch balls, witch's milk, mistletoe, covens, clusters of deformed twigs in trees called German *hexenbesen*, the Würzburg Trials, the Water Witch incident, jinxes, hex signs, witchhazel, Samantha from *Bewitched*, Halloween green noses, that cartoon witch from the *Archie* comic books: Sabrina.

"Cyprine?" *Oh, he can read your mind, but mutations turn up anyway; it is the party game of don't-drink-the-witch's-milk; it is the party game of evolutionary theory.*

"Truth or dare?" asks Martin, additionally.

"Oh, you with your games."

You and Martin look into each other's eyes, an eye-gazing exercise down on the sand. You fall in love and slip into each other. You become one person. JackMartin. The House that Jack Built. In the words of British 80s synth band The Housemartins: "*Build a house where we can stay/Add a new bit everyday.*" The housemartin bird, blue on top but white from below. When seen from the other side of the looking-glass, white all over, with the blue unseen. Sometimes the bird is Housemartin and all blue with unseen white, and sometimes the bird is Martinhouse and all white with unseen blue.

She turned up at the inn door bedraggled and sullen. She knocked once, and then she knocked twice.

Gerald the old man, Gerald the somnomancer answered her call and pulled open the inn's wooden door.

*

There was mist that fluttered over Lough Gur, whence Gerald had taken her and where now she stood upon its shore.

"Over there, seventeen feet down." Gerald indicated a centre point of the left quadrant of the lake. "Since you were doubtless wondering."

He was an old man whom Florentine took now the opportunity to carefully examine for the verisimilitude of sleeping beneath waters. He did not look like a ghost; his beard was of a genuine grey shade; the folds of his skin, whilst aged, were no less real than hers and he was of a substantive property altogether. "Teach me how." She whispered this at first, but when she said it the second time she said it full-throat.

*

To dream-travel is a science and it is an art. There are no swan-maidens involved: that was one of Gerald's lies. The science involves the reconfiguration of dream molecules in a precise teleportation that makes use of Flanagan's Third Principle of Carnivorous Wormholes as well as extract of frankincense.

The art, for its noble part, requires learning over many seasons the talent of self-spectral projection. An apprentice first learns to self-project in terms of space, as this is much easier, and when they near the *niveau* of master-craftsman, nearly ready for their mortarboards and diplomas, they have thence become adept at temporal self-projection as well.

At some of the best dream-travelling academies, you will often find twenty, thirty persons sleeping under the lake all at once, whilst their selves go travelling in 1) Bosnia Herzegovinia; 2) the outer reaches of Ursa Major; 3) late Aztec period; 4) Berengia. And very learned doctors, such as Gerald of Fitzgerald, son, son, son, etc., can project *others*, bodily and spirituous, just as he was now showing off to her his hometown Irish lake.

"I will show you *this*," he said. "I can teach you quickly."

"Thank you," said Florentine, equally quickly. She knew this would be necessary.

"You have had this ability longtime," said Gerald to her, "as do we all. As when you see burning cities littered with yellow scraps of paper, as do we all, you have had this ability longtime."

That said, and towards which has been alluded, most non-sexual and non-disease-ful spontaneous ejaculations of self-projection in the common person not involving spectral arts and sciences in their essential nature involve extreme reactions to trauma – very occasionally joy – and subsequent dissociation.

*

When they began, Florentine would tentatively tiptoe into the waters towards her aqueous bed, sometimes thinking of Eglentyne, who had never learned to swim, but once Florentine had learned the ancient technique of human gill recapitulation theory, and newer techniques of suspended animation, she grew adept at dreaming smoothly underneath the lake, and sometimes when waking would look up, for a few moments before paddling herself to the surface, look up towards the blue-green sheen of brightness, seventeen feet above where the sun shone strong, and would feel quite content to dally a few seconds more.

One day Gerald woke at the same time, and he touched her wet hand in his fatherly way, and when they had swum to the surface, he said to her, "Today has begun the time."

When they went back down again and slept, on this occasion their selves, parts of their seeking selves, floated to the shore while their other selves stayed anchored.

The next week, they went further, to the lake of Loch Finne, to the wood of Coill a Muc, to the castle of Caisleán Bhaile Átha Cliath.

"Sometimes," said Gerald, "sometimes there is a danger of splitting, so that you grow a new human off yourself, like a thumb. You must be mindful of that. Of that must you be mindful."

And then three months after that, they slipped into a few seconds forward, and then into last week, and then the future of three years and also this time too in Tráigh Lí, both time, both space, Gerald holding her hand all the time, and then one glorious day Florentine travelled by herself to a yesterday at the Spital, where she saw that it was, for that time at least, dark and abandoned, and she wondered where Eldritch and Beaman were. She did not test her reserve or emotions or talents to journey to a long-ago winter with an antler-set a-hanging to a tree, and she avoided the Blue School altogether. Gerald had warned against such travels based on extreme personal emotions and experiences on the same splitting principles he had mentioned earlier, and she believed Gerald to be right.

"When we travel, when we connect to another body, we change form, or colour – or even sex, as with Saint Perpetua when she flew into another part of her mind and became a martyr and before that a sudden man."

The soar of fingering the stars as your brain rushes past them to your destination.

"Sometimes," said Gerald, "sometimes there are those talented few who can take their pulse and bones, as well as their spirits; who lift themselves bodily as well for that soar through the Astros, that moment before one's mind rests like a small robin in a new environment, a new era."

The mind becomes a bright blue egg itself. An ostros plum, set down in landscape. This fragile blue Egg. Inside there may be just yolk and bilum. Inside there may be Schroedinger's chick, ready to peck its way out.

A blue like the robin's blue-egg gates of Ishtar, beautiful beyond belief, with funny, furry hybrid animals stalking the lacquered bricks for their blue-winged goddess, paw after paw. What type of egg does a god lay?

Sometimes when Florentine went soaring, she envisioned her horns carrying precariously such a blue Egg, balanced in her horns, and then at her destination this image would fade, having safely guarded this Egg all the way to the journey's end. Sometimes in the sky the sun glows as a cold blue Egg; it is a sun and not a daughter. Sometimes we drop our Eggs in our egg-and-spoon games no matter how carefully clutched amidst our sometimes-heavy antlers, no matter how careful and caring we are. Sometimes Eggs come back; they grow again and they may have traits of their sisters or brothers: birthmarks that continue generationally through the force of love.

*

Sometimes such children remember their previous lives; they say: Oh, I remember when my previous mother did that or my father went to market, when I fell in love and when my house burnt down. I remember it all.

And then all such children forget. In fact, it is

required that we forget ourselves in order that we once again, like John Barleycorn, can live.

*

Gerald and Florentine existed together in this paternal, top-down association for many months: twelve months, ten-plus-two fingers-full of *luna*, a year. This learning process of trial and repeat, test and hypothesise, was qualitatively different than her time at the Blue School or her autodidactic years on the road, in that she felt the same soar of creative pulse she always had, but now in a differential response she set herself tasks to test it and improve it, not just swallow it whole via ritual or social cunning. Always Gerald wore the cowl of a leecher. And each day by day, Florentine's skills grew greater. The Pledge, the Prestige, the Reveal. Now she knew the pledge to be the insight, and the prestige dream-travel on its own. She remembered frequently William of Langland with his book of reveries – prophecy or trick? The curious green dreams of *merveillous swevene wildernesse*; they too seemed less trick and more precognitive. She wanted to ask this of Gerald, but she had always held her tongue on this matter; she was never sure why.

Complementing this, she also frequently considered Elijah, that green man, who from her clergy-travels she had gathered had forced choices of either/or upon his populace: Yahweh or Ba'al. His water-splitting and verdigris aside, he did not seem to embrace that flow of *merveillous swevene wildernesse.* In this particular case that particular green man seemed, therefore, much more trick than treat.

*

On one occasion, Gerald took her to a large English *polis*, an incredible one that she took to be Lunden, a different time when people shouted and blood ran over cobbles. Sometimes you find yourself in a place you have never been before, or perhaps a time, and Florentine often found herself in both. She was never clear on these occasions whether she was experienced by others herself; she knew it could happen, but without direct caught gazes it was difficult to know if she was in turn observed, and so on this particular summer day concerned, full weird sunlight, smoke in her nostrils, she followed Gerald's lead and did hang back.

"There are different ways of shedding one's annual antlers, the tines *beam, palm, bez, trez, royal, surroyal* and *advancer*," intoned Gerald insouciantly, looking on upon the mayhem, "sometimes by stealth, sometimes fate, sometimes choice. In this way one becomes a 12-point don't-give-a-fuck buck, my dear."

*

On another occasion, they travelled encapsulated (for Florentine had turned out talented), spirit-flesh, to a hot land with people who had dark skins where there was also much shouting, and also blood. And here they were seen, but their white skins were not exceptional, as for the onlookers the circumstances of necessity for one's survival trumped, as always, casual wonder over strangers. Amongst the hot sticky trees ("*les vodouisants*," murmured Gerald, perhaps naming such fronded trees), Florentine heard other Norman words, but could not understand the meaning.

"This too is a revolt," said Gerald, full-voice.

***

A child was born in 1974. It was a boy. Let us call him Jack. Jack grew up in a house his parents built. When he began to speak and express himself, he began to tell his mother about another mother, another time. He pointed to a set of antlers growing on his young head, but his mother could never see them. She laughed with him though, and hugged him tight, and, since they were in Alaska after all, she told him "Mother Moose" stories rather than "Mother Goose" stories. "My little moose-boy," she said, and she chucked him under the chin and patted these invisible antlers.

Such fantasies of former lives of imaginative children usually fade by age 5, as stated in the famous child psychology book entitled *Stop Talking About the Other Mommy!: Strategies for Time-Travel-*

ling Children and Their Present Parents by Frau Doktor Elsa Karolina _____.

***

That cold blue sun, that egg Gerald, took Florentine with him to an unusual location at the end of those twelve months (two hands' worth – plus two – of moons).

In the middle of the cold blue lake, a lake silky like a loon's call, a lake blue like a solemn greyfruit, in the middle of the cold blue lake there streamed up a red fire, *fata morgana*. Florentine and Gerald stood on the shore to where he had guided them both, and gazed at the hot red flame and the curl of smoke, its reflection like rain-nipples reverberating all the way to the shore.

Florentine turned towards Gerald, asking him why he had brought her to this distance, if he indeed wished her to gaze solely at the flames. The shore seemed a long distance from which to do it.

Gerald gave her a look of faint disgust. "We must have some sense of ritual, don't you think?" Yet it felt so strange to swim waters after so much time spent dream-travelling, that shortcut of intentionality. The bonfire set amongst the blue, like Imbolc fires at the Blue School.

They stripped, even Gerald of his braies, then swam past halies and pickerels to the fire in the middle of the lake, skin flickered by fire-leaves, and then paddled with their feet stepping up and down to hold themselves up on this staircase of water.

"Past the blue lake; look into the red," said Gerald *fitz* of Gerald *fitz* of Gerald *fitz* of Gerald ∞. There in the fire was a reddest point, redder than a blood spot and redder than a baby star and redder than a three-sunset. "Look on it," said Gerald. But when Florentine looked on it, it was no longer there: just a thumbprint-sized absence, blue again in the fire. But she kept awatch. A red point was born again, and grew, and then the colours joined the main shades of the fire and one could not tell the difference.

"What you see in the fire there is called a cell," said Gerald, "I have travelled to other times far future and I know this is the name. And I have travelled many thousands of years past those times, too, to when they discover and confirm that each cell –"

"Soul?"

"That's what I said. That each soul can replace another, but yet it is the same soul. We are changed, but we and our children – our *adams*, made of neuters and electricities and proteins – our adams and eves are *always* reborn. All things are born again."

"Oh, yes."

"The green trees from the dead trees, the Jack from the plant, the fruit from the womb, the Egg from the white bird, and John Barley from the corn."

Florentine was suddenly struck by an unexpected pain. The point of the fire that had disappeared reminded her of points on her that had disappeared. Antlers. Babyflesh.

For some time they watched the rise and fall and re-rise of the souls, the cells, and then they swam back. As they clothed themselves, it was then in the fire's light that she saw for the first time, released from its leecher's cowl and bruised onto naked skin, the ring of birthmarks around Gerald's neck.

***

So how about this version, a party guy, born, like, a really long time ago. No computers or even fast typewriters. A good-time guy with *molto* girls. He knocks one little flower up; he has feelings for her but it's obviously not going to work out; does the slow fade on her, but now there's the little sprout off the old tree, and what's he supposed to do about the baby? Child support payments shall bore him, let's face it. He hides himself away, avoidant-type of personality on the Strange Situation Classification (SSC) psychological test, dead man in a tree waiting for spring or for Excalibur or a prince's fair kiss to make red apple fall from his lips or for rising sap or for ... His name is Jack Green. This is the house that Jack built and now he's going to have to live in it... His name is Jack Green.

```
He is 33 years old. He is dying dying
dying. He is flying flying flying.
```

***

We have Pret-à-manger sandwiches and Prada shoes and
Campbell's Tomato Soup Low Sodium and Spud-21 missiles.
We had the people's princess and then Facebook and we've
had printed advertisements for quite a long while. We're not
so different, you from my future, and me from your past.
We have 1970s horror films where the pantlers bake John
Barleycorn into loaves of wastel and pain-demain and we eat
him that way. We have corn dollies. We have guy foxes all
Novembers; their tails turn red flame as we heap the bodies higher. We have ol' John Barleycorn, the name for evil
booze in the Big Book for alcoholics of an anonymous bent.

*

She had dream-travelled to a field, set back. A field fringed
by her forests. In her nose stung the smoke; in her lungs
reeked the air. The sky was black with ash already. Although
it had been twelve months, she could still feel Cyprine's fingers on her. Their sex stain might last even longer that that
of Jack. Just as with her Puck, however (who had never paid
his childwite), she pushed these antler-nubs of thoughts back
down deep into her scalp, for the Wild Hunt was no use to
her at all. She was tame; she was Tame Hunt. Her horns

honest signals. She had dream-travelled to a field. Where was Gerald? He was sleeping beneath the lake. He was stolen by a swan maiden. He was lain by a gigantic green bird.

Once upon a time men and women and their boys and girls lived in forests and sometimes jungles sometimes plains. But then came wheat and then came barley and then we were cast out from the paradisiacal garden where we had doves' eyes and our beds were green and everything smelled like fir and cedar (Christmas, basically), in our now-inequality our wages thus became whiskey and beer and meadowsweet-mead, bucks to build pyramids and wall up the new spaces called cities. But we remember trees, we remember animals, we remember animals called humans, we remember all our sacrifices necessary to retain good crops rather than being reliant on our two good hands. Agriculture takes away personal responsibility. But let us remember good goated grandparents. Harvest festivals. We plough the fields and we do scatter. *Wir pflügen und wir streuen. The good seed on good land. But the land is watered. By the Green's good hand. He sends the snow in winter, the warmth to swell the grain. The breezes and the sunshine. And soft refreshing rain.*

There was three suns come out o' the east their fortunes for to try. And these three suns made a solemn vow. John Barleycorn must die. To everything, burn, burn, burn. There is a season, burn, burn burn. A time to be born, and a time to die. A time to plant; a time to raise the harvest high.

The barleycorn man was burning, the wicker figure a donjon twenty feet tall. For this was indeed the barleycorn man, and not the hound nor the horn, that belonged to the forest-farmer sowing his corn. The flames peaked, orange and red spit in the sunset, pain and bite were in the fire. There were three suns rise in the east, three suns great on high. And they have sworn a solemn oath. John Barleycorn should die.

The men advanced towards the burning effigy, and Florentine watched half hidden behind a cypress, some distance away but still her heart in their advance. Her antlers had been lead-heavy for months now. Was there a man amongst the wheat sheaves of that herce? Did the fire crackle and the singing drown out screams? Two steps more advanced the three men towards the bonfire. Two steps more advanced Florentine towards the three blue sisters, carrying her babe thrust forward in her arms. We will take care of her, do not worry, says Brisha, and she looks up to the sky. *And they hae sworn a solemn oath: John Barleycorn should die.*

An anonymous blackened man in the cage amongst flames, she saw it now; she could see the silhouette formed by him against the thatched cage inside the barleycorn man. He was sitting cross-legged and he was indeed screaming, but the singing of whiskey muted him to others. But she saw him. She saw his eyes: he looked straight at her, and she was not saving him. The flames were curling around his face and looked almost green for an instant, like a will-o'-the-wisp, ivy curling like a silver carving, foliate. But the flames were bloodened all again, no peter-panning.

People, men and women and children, approached

the fire and sprinkled it with alcohol and still it was not quenched. The children, already corny on posset and mead, drank down the whiskey, and whiskey always burns like fire. They ploughed, they sowed, they harrowed him in. They throw-ed booze upon his head. And these folk made a solemn vow. John Barleycorn was dead.

We will take care of her, do not worry, says Brisha, and she looks up to the sky. *And they hae sworn a solemn oath: John Barleycorn should die.* That moment when the baby left her arms. *Sir John Barley-Corn fought in a Bowl, who won the Vic-to-rye, which made them all to chafe and swear, that Barley-Corn must dye.* That ring of birthmarks around the babe's good neck. *When she kissed it last good-bye. For I will tell you once again. That Barley-corn must die.* Its eyes screwing shut, Brigid patting at its head. *For I will tell you one last time. John Barley-corn is dead.*

> *From the gloaming of the oak-wood,*
> *O ye Dryads, could ye flee?*
> *At the rushing thunderstroke would*
> *No sob tremble through the tree?—*
> *Not a word the Dryads say,*
> *Though the forests wave for aye.*
> *For Pan is dead.*
>   – Elizabeth Barrett Browning, 1844

Seconds before the bulk of the fire crashed in on him, she

saw that the man in the fire had stag-horns atop his head, the shadow of them stark against yellow flames for a hesitated moment before the whole bombfire crumbled and flamed green with the burning of new wood.

*

In the ash twists a green snake, a serpent born from hot ash that becomes phoenix that gives a jeweled egg that births a snake that evolves to birds that lay those orbs that split to snakes to birds to eggs to snakes to birds to eggs to birds to snakes. Seeds thrown into Samhain fires, pop and pop. In the ashes, there are burnt seeds. Some seeds, some gymnosperm, some say that plants grow more easily from ash. The bones that sprout (then egg, then snake, then bird, then egg). A sower went to sow his seed, and he sowed in the dead; he sowed it on the old white ribs, he sowed it on the head. Some seed fell upon the path, as he sowed from his cup; seed mixed with bones, bones mixed with seed; the birds ate it all up.

There is no one to observe the grave of this fire at dawn, no time-travelling antlered woman, no somnomancer, but in the sky, in the sky, flies a huge bird, white then blue, blue then white, cloud, sky, sky, cloud, in the sky flies a huge bird. The phoenix picks out seed pods to eat from the ashes and thus stops such germination, at least until its cloaca shits out gemmy dung. Scattered the corn. Scattered the corn. This is the blue bird that crew in the morn.

***

N.B. There is a heretical sect of kokology, a syncretism between kokology and the psychology game called The Cube Game, full of imagery of green flying birds and melting desert ice-cubes and forest shelters thatched with hair.

Many of these variants are later *hereticisms*. Take the desert game, for instance. What follows as detailed shortly below – here is your map's legend, your magician's reveal – is the *syncretic response*. This is what occurs when splits begin to meld and hybridise again. No green birds exist in pure kokology, the forest party game does not require oneself to knock on one's own door, and the cubes are certainly not *ice*-cubes in Cube Game fundamentalism.

We're basically dealing here with three *sects*. Games that have mated and joined in unholy congress. The you-are-walking-through-a-forest game. The desert/cube variations on that same game. The bird-changing-colour game.

These are a few. In many, one; in one, many. In between, you may tell truth, or dare, fall in love, end up in Mornington Crescent or regress yourself with caution.

You are in a desert.

You see a disguise. What does it look like?

You see a fruit. What is it and what does it look like?

You come to a vessel lying on the ground; what is it; what does it contain; what do you do?

You put down the vessel and continue walking across the desert. Eventually, you see a cave. What does it look like; do you enter it?

You enter the cave and come to a large body of water that blocks your path. What is it; what do you do?

You escape the cave; how do you do this?

You see a tall tree in the desert on which sits a bird; what do you do?

You keep walking across the desert; you come to an oasis of cacti. What do you do?

Everyone on the planet dies in a nuclear blast; what do you do? ("That seems oddly specific." "Just answer the question.")

You pick yourself up and keep walking. The snow comes and you keep walking, like the bad winters in Little House on the Prairie *with internet darling Nellie Oleson.*

The sun burns and you keep walking.

You come to a wall blocking your path. What does it look like? What colour is it? How tall is it? What do you do?

You are in a desert. You've come full circle. You're a snake biting its tail. What do you do?

***

The snakes are rising.

***

```
The snakes are rising.
```

***

The snakes are rising.

II

The Bluebells, The Wild Hunt

The bedroom is lit by near-midnight sun. On the bed, amongst the *Star Wars* bed-sheets, a boy of eleven sprawls, reading intently. The shades are up; the dimming daylight of 11pm means he squints only a little. Summer Alaskan children have no need for flashlights. Torches. Flashlights. In the book the boy is reading, everyone carries real torches with fire on the ends.

In this non-canon *Choose Your Own Adventure* book, called *The Adventure of the Serpent Cave*, a boy and a girl have fallen through a time loophole into an ancient Mayan temple. Guarding the temple entrance is a god covered in green quetzal feathers.

Do the two of you speak to the god?, the heretic *Choose Your Own Adventure* book asks. *If so, turn to Dresden Codex Serpent Series of the 13 B'ak'tun, page 2012. If not, keep silent.*

The Alaskan boy, disobediently reading what his mom calls trashy juvenile fiction at night, turns to Dresden Codex Serpent Series of the 13 B'ak'tun, page 2012. There he reads that this green feathered god is the Maker, the serpent that fashioned the world. The illustration from the *Popul Vuh* scares the Alaskan boy a bit, and so the boy quickly turns the page.

You find yourself in a bluebell sward – sticky matted grass and flowers, the book states, *surrounded by fireflies.*

That's better.

***

Florentine walks through a meadow. In a far-flung meadow, *glossopteris* grows, a fern with fronds of green tongues, one of many disappeared plants from dinosaur times of the Flirtaceous–Paleogene. Through the meadow lumbers a woman. She is sasquatch, she is yeti, she is antlered. Full hairy now too, due to her deep exploration of the 0th Law of Submersibility by which Juliana of Verulamium discovered the equation for proximate hirsutedness after repeated occasions of underwater manifestation-kineticism due to the Eighteenth Principle of Fast-Time Dilation. In layman's terms, it means that due to frequent lake-based spacetime travel, Florentine got furry.

And so Florentine stumbles.

She stumbles over long flowing stands of her own hair, luxuriant from her legs, pubis, palms (!; we mentioned this bodily phenomenon previously), etc.

Florentine has a serious look to her face. After many travels as well as conversations with Gerald regarding the nature of fate she has come to a decision, and so she now gathers glossopteris; she carries a bushel of it, a bouquet, in her shaggy arms.

*

A small boy walks through a forest. A small boy clutches a book and he walks through a forest. It is a wonder to him, but he chose to skip ahead to this page and here he is. He passes a glade with silver trees; he passes deeper into the forest. There is a sudden roar overhead; he watches a white airplane above dropping bombs that never hit the ground, glittering dung pellets; there is a sudden roar overhead and he watches a white airplane above him in the sky through the branches, but he tells himself it is a white quetzal or a white pterodactyl from his childhood *Dinosaurs* reference book. Now he hears scurrying up ahead; hears sounds that indicate a fair bit more than a mere burrowing animal.

When he parts the trees, the little boy sees a hairy beast, human-formed, female-formed, trapped in a wooden cage. So he knows it is a girl bigfoot – and how angry she is. She's covered with red-gold hair like his friend Jackson's golden retriever. The bigfoot fights with the wooden bars of the cage, but she can't get out. Her hair grown so tight over her own lips in a horizontal hairy band that she cannot speak. She bites lips behind the pelt-gag and redness trickles down at each its corner.

This is a different path from the choice he made in the bluebell field, a different path. Choose your own adventure and hers, do you release the hairy animal, or do you keep her in a cage?

*

Florentine wanders through a field. She finds herself in a bluebell sward, sticky matted grass and flowers, surrounded by fireflies. Florentine is wandering through a field, a bluebell field where the underwater streams that sometimes appear, rear up into mossy springs, and then disappear again, *elijah, elijah*, the running spring.

All around Florentine this sunrise, after midsummer White Nights, all around Florentine the tongueless sound of bells warbling. As they had done for the lepers at the Squint, now so did the bluebells now for her. She has abandoned glossopteris for the blossoms of Blue Bell Hill; her hands hold purple-belled stamens. The rivers meeting and merging under this childhood memory of a firefly field; the rivers pulsing up like orgasms, like cum, in holy wells amongst the bluebells, amongst all of Florentine's good own flowers. Such holy wells fed by lakes often appear for Saint Kieran, the wild saint who preached to the animals, the saint whose name no longer sits engraved atop a brass plaque in one timeline's oasis. Such holly wells are ringed at the edges with Christmas, red pearls and dark-green leaves, father christmas, that is another name for him, Figgy, sprite, Jack.

The sun pours out radiant. It is dawn, a White Sunday at Whitsuntide, when do appear the White Ladies, but the ladies are all birds. One bird. One lady is a bird.

Florentine walks naked in the field, and she tears the hair from her body as she farmer-walks to sow it in the soil. She strips the hair from her sex, from her arms. The bells are calling like flutes, no they are birds, no they are bells. William Bell compiled the folkloric story of Puck in 1852, two volumes. Florentine was naked as you always wanted her to be, prototypically female, less casually beast, but she is never who she wanted to be. The bells are calling, Whitsuntide. Her discarded hair glows red-gold in the sunrise. She leaves it there. She does not leave it there. Which page? You choose.

Florentine climbs the distance up the hill. In the sky overhead swim entirely hairless white ladies, caw-cawing; in the air overhead the birds are calling: *kent, cunt, hunt.* The Kentish forest quakes and heaves. It spits out wickered things – straw bears and wooden bird cages – it spits out wakened Jack, but Florentine covers her face with approvable hair, her head's hair remaining, so that she does not have to see him. (She is aware that he will be seeing every part of naked her.) She glimpsed one small straw bear in the seconds before she covered her eyes and lost herself to the world around her; one of those small straw bears had winked a cranberry eye. All such wickered things had been thatched like roof-tops. This is the house that Jack built.

****

Gerald also makes his way through a forest. Gerald has his instructions from his *protegée*, always an interesting dynamic. The forest piney and wild; the bruces pungent and the scent of their needles makes Gerald's mouth water for the retsina he had learned to appreciate during month-long scientific expeditions to the beaches and sun and nightclubs of Naxos, Greece. The forest encompasses the old man and he enjoys traversing it, and so he is discontented when the brambles and evergreens give way to sand dunes sifting through the trees, even though Jack had told him that this would be the case.

On the edge of the forest now. He takes stock of the landscape. An interesting vista he gazes at, more or less as Jack had described it. The dunes that spill into the forest become dominant in the landscape, they turn full-desert, a sandy expanse in an evergreen forest (this natural phenomenon also can be observed in the southern part of the State of Oregon, USA). Though, at some distant point in the desert, there does seem to be an unnatural glittering wall. Gerald additionally observes large floating objects in the membrane of the air from the *middle* distance: a moustache, a water tap, a pineapple. A mountain (or at least some protruding stone clusters) with a cave far away; an oasis fairly close; a bird – a vulture? – gliding over it all.

Gerald on a mission. The old man steps onto hot sand that slips painfully through his sandal gaps, and then soon enough he reaches the oasis. No camels, but trees of the palm variety (recognised from scientific expeditions to the Caribbean resort of Kokomo Island). A wading-pool of a puddle. And there too cooling his feet sits the individual predicted by both Florentine and Jack, a young man with luxuriant hair and a wooden walking-stick. Gerald sees immediately that this young man has a glint to his eye: clearly Jack's brother or cousin. The long flowing locks of the younger man are admired for a moment, and then Gerald taps him on the shoulder.

The young man, who had been watching a PBS nature documentary on a far-seer screen, turns around and introduces himself as Martin. He makes his walking-stick nod respectfully towards Gerald, too.

Gerald takes out a razor blade from one of his deep wizard pockets and explains carefully to Martin what he needs from him.

Martin stands up and nods.

***

This one took place once before, when Florentine came across a structure in the woods (it was her own home). Early evening. Outside the cabin, her father used his fingernails to

gear up rich sod so he could sow the corned seeds. He did not
see her and was humming whilst he pressed seeds deep into
soil, each kernel cluster dropped with a small dead fish from
the lake (the dangerous lake) to keep seeds happy and to
make them grow the better. She watched him for a while.

Late spring, with the cabin door ajar. She entered.
Hurrah, dinner time! Her father joined the family. The
family sat to sup. Florentine smiled at one brother, a little
boy named Eldritch, second in a litter of triplets, neither
buck nor gelding. The boys had had their sixth birthday
celebration just last week, and her father gave each a wooden
carving of a different little man, painted blue, red, yellow,
and her mother gave each good boots for their feet, leather,
leather, leather, and Florentine gave each a sapcake she had
baked secretly with her mother, sugared, brucey, crispy. She
had already spent the day amongst honeybees in the bluebell
field, and after this dinner the four would go outside again,
running each on their fine two legs, and try to catch fireflies
in their collective gourded hands (not one of them ever succeeded).

Yet before this spring adventure, her firefly impulses
momentarily controlled, Florentine sat down at the wooden
dinner table with her family, gaze flickering up to the small
portrait a tinker once had painted of her paternal grandfather. Grandpapa had yellow eyes with horizontal pupils and
a long white beard and perhaps he even wore a bell around
his neck. Grandfather, Uncle Pan, Cousin Billy, Nanny –
such goats had been in her family for a long, long time.

A baked raven in a sixpence pie that Florentine wrinkled her nose over; she never liked bird but Beaman, Eldritch, Percy enjoyed darkbird well enough. Four-and-twenty corvids baked in a pie, but here only the one. The savoury sauce, the stringy good meat, her parents smiling at their children's arguments, and later the chasing of fireflies. Already this summer she had eaten fox, wolf, snake, crow (humiliating), rat and boar. Groups of nine strange animals, and now with raven seven of them eaten already this summer.

"Eat up, Florentine, don't toy with the flesh," said her annoyed mother, "taste the holy meat portions, *papyrus oxyrhynchus*." (*Idolothyte*, meat sacrificed to idols. But this is only the seventh odd meat. There are yet two meats to come, some other afternoon.)

Her father spoke passingly of having heard then seen a snowy owl the night before, and her mother spoke of spinning flax and how she might dye the colours this season.

Florentine thought of tree-coloured, sky-coloured kirtles and dutifully took a bit of the broth, with a piece of the carrion. It did not taste bad. "Do you remember when we lived at the other place?" asked Florentine. "When I lived there with my other mother and read all the books? It was a cold place, with many mosquitoes." Her mother and father looked at each other and her little brothers giggled.

"You've never lived anywhere but here, poppet," said her mother. "I was swollen with you when we retreated. You were born in this house. Your *father* was born in this house, many years before the Loaf-Mass day I met him berry-picking."

Her parents' conversation turned to other matters. "I will have to sow them again," vowed her father, "I swear the owls have bitten all the seed sacks, or else it is the mice."

*

I swear you have said all this before. The White Bird is a dinosaur. *Reptile volant*, says naturalist Georges Cuvier in "Extract from a work on the species of quadrupeds whose bones have been found in the interior of the earth," noting that its long finger supports a membrane that forms a good wing. Or perhaps the White Bird is a white former dinosaur. It soars over prehistoric T-rexes, bounces its beak against cheeky mammals like you. It flies straight out of the *Dinosaurs* reference book; it's bobbing in the trees now: it's gone green now; it's a canary in a coalmine now. It will survive the poisonous gases of miners just like it survived the poisonous gases of the Flirtaceous–Paleogene extinction event. Like those who endured apocalypses or plagues, no one ever gives birds enough credit for emerging mostly unscathed from extinction events. This dynamic is always due to lack of eyewitnesses. The White Bird not dissimilar to goddess Ishtar, who wears feathers like the birds do and look, the Witch has survived. (If Florentine had bothered to look closely on her own good back after her night on the tarot cards, she would have noticed that the Witch herself had owl claws.)

***

Top, bottom, up, down, strangeness, charm.
Not as far back as a cosmic egg, wham bam
thank you ma'am, just as far back as Jack
the ex-spook, complete in London bedsit
but before the bright light, before the
little stag-girl, before the black helicopters appeared in the sky. But after
recruitment, after the East German assignment. Now we have a standard Jack Candle
of where to place our specific vantage in
time. Perspective is always highly important. Yes, a temporal standard candle, if
you will, be sure to look up the scientific
definition when you feel like it. An era of
known brightness. Here we go.

Jack walked down the narrow North
London alley that cut through the Haringey
Ladder neighbourhood. The alley had been
conceived in Victorian times as a pretty
pedestrian footpath, but now might be more
properly described as a mugger's paradise. He clutched his plastic Tesco shopping bag close to his frame so that no
teenagers rushing by on bikes could tear

from him his purchases of one dozen eggs and Fair Trade coffee. Not too much on his mind. It wasn't therapist-day, after all, and things had gone smoothly at Tesco's. He always paid for both in self-mined gold and silver.

He first observed a few droplets of water in the cobbles, which he followed further (Gretel, Hansel), as the stains on the rocks became larger and large, puddles. The little lane, sectioned at regular intervals by the neighborhood roads that crossed it perpendicular, did not reveal who was dripping and, as Jack continued to walk with his shopping, he realised that it was, in fact, impossible to name a source, for the puddles had become huge along the pathway, flooding it. There had been no rain.

Jack whirled around to see if someone was following him with spilling water balloons, though this was not a logical direction to turn. Jars, faucets, no one was there. When he circled back to his initial trajectory, there was indeed someone there. Jack dropped his bag and thus his eggs. Irritating.

An old man standing in front of him,

dripping water, smiling.

"Who?"

The old man continued to smile and pointed to the crescent moons and constellations on the magisterial kirtles he wore. "I am the starry messenger. I mean, technically when I spent some time as Galileo, I fancied mself the starry messenger. I mean, technically I spent an entire *lifetime* playing Galileo Galilei, a pleasurable *rôle*. I had a lot of leisure hours under house arrest that I spent spacetime travelling. I spent much of that time as Merlin, mind you."

Odd old flickers of his amnesia troubles sprinkled Jack's mind. Whichever life of his that he could not remember had had just such an old gentleman carrying exactly such a starry message from that place, that time. Jack thought of his dream of the ghost crying in the treetops, of the place with three suns. Which were technically three stars. Were they not.

"It's good to see you again," said the starry messenger. He had a ring of star-shaped birthmarks around his throat; Jack had noticed it at once.

"However, I have never seen you

before," mentioned Jack.

The old man winked and held both arms low and water poured out of each sleeve making two lakes (dangerous lakes), which perhaps made Jack think of faucets in deserts. For a brief moment, he recalled something important. He drew near to the old man, whispered to him, into his ear.

Jack nodded goodbye, picked up his bag of crushed eggs, and continued on his way.

Several years of intensive psychotherapy now according to the therapist, though Jack could recall only several months at most. Apparently the first year had con-sisted of uncomfortable silence as per the therapist's unique method. Today Jack wanted to discuss the ancient con-cept of dreams being souls drinking from the waters of Lethe, of how such waters flow like a Langland river, of how Pan had had his male lovers too, of a Lethe-drunk dream from the night before that involved a snaky/winged temptress (the therapist always seemed to be interested in Jack's peculiar brand of erotic somnolescence). Or perhaps Jack could cite the quote he had read in *Metro* newsmagazine and written down the other day, something the therapist would appreciate: "Waking consciousness is dreaming – but dreaming constrained by external reality" (the neurologist Oliver Sacks's work *An Anthropologist on Mars*).

It was a boring and sunny day, a different day. A hint of unrest via the fact that most people's mail slots were spilling over onto their doorsteps. But nothing more serious than that. Besides, it just meant Royal Mail were doing their job. Oh yes, and that passenger pigeon with a scroll written in blackletter German tied round its ankle doing its job too. Jack ignored it. It turned green and flew off.

So all in all a boring day. The No. 29 bus to Finsbury Park, the pleasant walk down a grimy high street to Crouch End. Knock on door, hello hello, armchair, uncomfortable silence again. This time, shockingly, the silence broken by the therapist, who had started weeping. Jack was unsure of therapeutic protocol, whether he should offer a pat on the shoulder or a kind word or do as the English generally prefer to do which is to

simply ignore, but as the therapist was
glaring at him between sobs with a fer-
vency that seemed quite personal, Jack
reasoned that solace was neither required
or desired.

Jack instead concentrated on the
small leaf that was growing out of the
therapist's right ear, and a veritable
small bush emerging from the therapist's
good hair.

* * *

The Witch soars above, but this cosmology is confusing,
because you also state that Florentine was once saved from
the bird by the Witch. Well, maybe Witch-the-saviour was
from one time, and Witch-the-bird from another. That'll
learn ya. Actually, that solves the whole problem. The
Witch sifts down the wind on wings covered with milky
way, we are all made of stardust, see you in the stars. Her
lover is the hairy man who descended to the underworld
house of such dust. Or she is the hairy man. Or Pan is
the hairy man. Or Pan's *eromenos* is a hairy man. But you
initially said that the Witch was hairy too. Silver hair, I
remember it, from back in the chapter where Florentine first
met the Witch in the snow, I distinctly remember you saying that the Witch had a hairy stripe of hair on each cheek.
And then later you say that Florentine grows red-gold hair

like a deer. I remember you saying it. And Jack Robin, he of fifty names or more, he is hairy too. You can find a representation of the Witch in the British Museum; her breasts, her beauty, her owl claws, her feathers. You can find dinosaur representations of the Witch in the London Natural History Museum. She has been separated into two museums. The Witch, most importantly, has been separated into two selves. Then she kept dividing. It is simple atomic theory, a chain reaction. You know how this goes. You know how things go when dung drops from warplanes.

*

Or even this, or even this. It is a day-after-a-birthday dinner; a day after a day when three little boys turned into goats, and a day after a day when the birthday girl grew horns. Yes, that very morning. That is when we find ourselves.

"I don't want breakfast raven again," grumbled little Eldritch.

"Bite your throat," said Florentine's mother, "it doesn't matter to the oak tree if a wild boar rubs its arse all over it. Regardless, we are having griddlecakes upon yesterday's especial birthday-request."

The griddlecake in Florentine's mouth, fried, oiled, was a good thing. Seasoned with crushed evergreen needles and rock salt, and she and her brothers jostled and elbowed each other to reach for a second one. She had the advantage; her brothers had trouble with their newly quadruped joints in terms of manipulation, but Florentine's sense of bodily self had not been similarly awkwardly transformed. She touched her new horns, the weight of them, of course, and she could reach up a second time and touch them, and she did, but her general shape had remained that of a girl – albeit a stagged one – and *this* was satisfactory to her.

The morning sun filtered through the small glasses of the windows. Her father was drinking the greyfruit cider, but speaking wistfully of a type of zooplankton known as alewife. Florentine glared up to the tinker's small painting of her grandfather that she hadn't noticed since earlier that spring: goats, *indeed*. Her mother, and likewise her father too, appeared unperturbed in regards to their offsprings' transformations.

The fire crackled a little in the hearth. There was a knock on the door, but Florentine was the only one who heard it. She rose from the table, and the others stayed chattering. She saw a naked man with a walking-stick, just his back and backside, retreating from the cabin. She wondered whether she ought to interrupt the breakfast, whether she ought to point out and then correct their mutual inhospitality, but then the smell of griddlecakes lured her back to the sibling rivalry of breakfast, and she chose to say nothing (we always choose our own adventures). She shoved a cake in her mouth, tasted bruce trees and pitch, and she remembered the taste from the other place with her other parents where the seasoning sap was called something else instead. She didn't think more on such a shift, and she certainly didn't say more on it.

The fire crackled a little in the hearth. There was a second knock on the door.

It was you.

*

Oh yes, and back in Jack's world, when Florentine was visiting, did you not mention Labatu, the horse-headed demon of Ishtar herself? Or something like it. I swear you mentioned something like it, something you saw through a looking glass, *speculum regale*, the king's mirror, the green king's mirror, and you saw back in Jack's chain reaction nuclear exploding world those harbingers straight from Revelation 9:7, biblical ugly, biblical beautiful, horseheaded locusts and the uranium kept dividing and reforming and dividing and reforming and dividing and reforming and through the speculum you saw the wild being as described, with a long mane – coarse, as you have described it, coarse like the mane of a horse – the wild being, man or maiden, the wild being has long hair over its human shape, the sticky hair trails the ground. When you look up from the ground into the sky, you see baby stars, the horsehead nebula, nuclear fusion but then fission and then fission and then fission and dividing, did you not mention such things? No?

*

Father Eldritch and Father Beaman were in deep conference. Vespers had been sung and strawberry pies were waiting hot in the larder and yet. Father Eldritch officious, his brother more circumspect, their evening chats consisting of regularities and small rituals, such as the way Father Beaman would modestly check twice the grooming of his fine white beard (a goatee) in the gazing ball as they passed it each evening.

It was insane springtime, buds aburst and pollen staining the air yolk golden, but such carnal matters were never truly discussed at the Spital. Still, the pollen made both Eldritch and Beaman nostalgic for the moment.

They passed the pagan statues of Diana and Actaeon and then the more decent ones of Paul and Veronica and circled round again, intending their habitual loop. Father Beaman stopped then, looking down at the garden soil and a long-ago memory. There was a shoot of perhaps seven thumbs tall, a green shoot with tiny branches. The sap, ejaculate, dripped down the shoot. The two priests stared at it. The spring air smelled of chlorine, bleach, pear trees.

"I buried them here," said Eldritch in reference to the gourds. "And now something is growing in the churchyard. One of the pods has clearly taken germinating root at last, after many years."

They both stared at the baby plant.

*

A monk-abbess travelled down a road freckled with spring. Father-Mother Ned Bituminous called to everyone Father-Mother Ned Bituminous did pass by; Ned whispered that the blue sickness was coming back in this early section of the year of 1381. The monk-abbess had had a hard time of it so far: threatened with literary pastiche by the scribe Geoffrey; thwarted in a quest for synthetic anabolic-steroid IFG-1 insulin mass production; humiliated in some senses by the stag-girl who had in fact grown a source of said steroid.

And then, of course, after the ascent of her goat brothers, Ned's career at the Spital had not worked out the way Ned had hoped, and Ned eventually had been demoted to assistant-priest/postulant and by then, of course, as Ned did have a modicum of self-respect, Ned had taken up his/her old profession – hedge-priest and part-time grifter, carving wooden curse tablets for gamblers. There was a market for religiously sanctioned antiquity, for merely the wearing a holy sign did not always allude to a sign of devotion. Just as the enemies of the Egyptians carved cats with women's bodies on shields so that the Egyptians would be afraid to attack out of fear of blasphemy, so did anti-Christians sometime adorn themselves with roods, or those opposed to Forestish ways array themselves with the holy white bird of the Cailleach crone (O Cailleach's wethers, the wethered brothers of Florentine!). A twisting of one's superstitions gainst one's self.

But now, nearly seventy, he had grown sympathetic to his congregation. Ned had taken it upon herself, in her dotage, to warn the people:

"The blue sickness returns," Ned told a passing man with seven wives as the season blew over them all, "avoid the population centres of Lunden, Canterbury, St Ives; get thee to the countrified places or, if you're that way energetically inclined, and it looks as if you might be, to a nunnery."

"The babes and crones are coughing," Ned informed the five sackcloth-clad members of a heretical sect on a pilgrimage.

"We never *see* the sun; we always *saw* the sun," the sect answered in chorus. This made sense to Ned due to the eight-minute delay before the Sun's good light hits the earth, and such a Sun that geocentrically circles the noble Earth, *bien sûr.*

As Ned walked along the grey road doing what she felt was his good duty to warn what had been observed, perhaps most frightened were those of a oldmotherly or oldfatherly age, for like Ned those travellers could remember the first time the blue sickness came. The bitterness and riots in cities, and that grief felt especially by clergy, for had they not cared for the sick until their own buboes had come, the spookraven masks and the incense cups held up against cats (oh yes, cats had been killed *en masse*), a cure that never seemed to work (oh yes, Levites had been blamed and killed *en masse* too, there had been spitting on Jews as well as cats).

We neglect Ned even as Ned's thoughts turn charitably to others. So! As Ned walked the grey road, felt zephyrs push spores past his face and as Ned cautioned others, he ruminated over a long-ago trade he'd once made, a bargain and a raw deal. Oh, in those halcyon days Ned could still pull a pretty girl with good effort, but these days effort accounted to naught and coin was required and he had frankly given up on the very idea, the tempting idea though it was, the silky sweat-lunge of limbs and tongues, of blinding lust that made her prick a rock, his clit a wet pebble in a stream, she had frankly given up on the very idea and indeed never ever gave a second thought to succubi stroking his shoulders and chest with delicious fiery tongues as they bared their tempting tits, never gave it a second thought at all.

But it had been a raw deal for Ned even long ago back then. The girl with raven braids had beaten Ned in a game of hazard dice, made him drunk on barleystuff and then thieved Ned's pouch whilst Ned had slept.

And even though Ned (a false priest *then* but a good priest *now*) had himself as good as stolen the carved-off spiral from the stag-girl via tricks of the confessional, and indeed when coming across that same beast once more in his road travels had intended to thieve once again but relented at the last moment whilst the stag-girl had aslept, even with his own chequered past Ned had regardless felt outraged at this fresher slut's theft a mere two days after he had the moral strength to decline a good theft himself. And due to this betrayal, Ned had tracked the dark girl as hounds do hare, or perhaps more as cats do mice, for the girl with black braids never realised that Ned had traced her. Ned had hid behind

a mulberry bush and witnessed her seduction and then abandonment by a ruddy young man.

"How night your braids are," had commented the
young buck, fingering one braid, and the girl had blushed
fierce. "I'll play a game with you," had added the young
man, who had not yet let go of the dark girl's hair and indeed
was still stroking it, standing very close.

The smitten girl had nodded; Ned had seen that even
from the bush.

"Guess my name, and I'll give you a kiss, and guess it
not, and you'll give me your purse." He clearly meant metaphorically, for his eyes glittered.

Ned in his spy-bush, accustomed to using the art of
cajolery and at one time adept at sensual flattery, had seen
that the deed was already done, as the girl's smile indicated
she was well pleased by the uneven terms.

Naturally, she had not been able to guess correctly,
and clearly her desire was to be a poor questioner.

Ned had watched their congress and been stirred, but
then Ned also had watched how the buck whistled in the
early morning gloaming whilst the girl slept and took the
young girl's leather purse, too, and took her heart, too. And
Ned began to change that very day, for when Ned, voyeur/
voyeuse, saw the girl wake up alone and realise tearfully
her abandonment, when Ned observed her horror that her
money purse was disappeared, Ned full understood her fury:
the buck had spoken literally when she'd thought metaphorically, and that she'd therefore allowed him her unfigurative

snatch for free.

Ned had interfered with neither the figurative nor literal acquisition by the young man (stopping an act of congress as dangerous as stopping a theft-in-progress), but, like the fairy tale of the green Grinch, Ned's heart had grown soft over the sound of the girl's sobs and that very day when Ned had continued along the road Ned had vowed to become a better priest and that he would no longer purloin stag antlers for the concoction of growth hormone IGF-1 insulin anabolic steroids for bicep enhancement for, as Judith Butler points out, all such masculinity and femininity may be performed, regardless. From that point forward, or perhaps ten or fifteen years later, Ned was a changed man and woman. As part of this spiritual work-in-progress, Ned had in fact returned to the Spital and indeed had flourished there for many years until the terror reign of the two goat brothers, who in their deep adulthood had become too much to bear, though they irritated primarily through dental habits.

Now, on the road, a tinker walked by, a very old woman with a wrinkled smile. "Paint your frown for a half-groat," she told him.

"Thank you, mother," said Ned. He gave her three angels and she, with berry dyes, charcoal and papyrus, produced shortly a fetching caricature reflecting both his femininity and her masculinity. Ned was well pleased. Before he made his leave, he took care to warn the tinker of the Bristol deaths, which surely came from a ship sailing out of far-off Araby.

Ned thought of many other tales as he walked the roads warning of the return of the blue sickness, but the recollection of the girl with the black-haired braids is the tale with the most relevance to us.

"Go to the country, the forests," warned Ned to all humans she passed along the road and to some stray dogs as well, "avoid these towns..."

*

This one took place before, too. A hypothesis had been in her head for what seemed like forever. It had perhaps been there since she dreamed herself into a world with yellow scraps of paper and tall buildings, but it had become a burning thought and sprigging hope ever since her first lesson with Gerald. There was an urgency Florentine had never felt before, something spurred on by the barleycorn field. Men burn fields to yield greater crops and now she'd take that lesson to heart and to horn.

The day was calm weather on the lake, a goodly week after she had witnessed the wicker burning in the field. Gerald, something on his mind of late, was singularly untalkative. Florentine watched the rise and fall of birthmarks on his clavicle as he breathed; now that she knew that they existed on his old flesh she would always be looking for them; she watched them under the slits of her eyes.

The very next afternoon she tried to go to the glade. She had the talent; Gerald had said so, that moment of bleed-

ing and greened grief; she could recall the breaths between
holding the soft miracle, and then the transfer to the Blue
Sisters. Everything after that moment was black and unrec-
ollectable for months.

Gerald was whispering in her ear. Merely his remembered advice. Gerald himself had just jettisoned off on a scientific expedition to a university library called the Maldives.
Centre, cell, soul, whispered Gerald's memory.

Florentine stood, centred, started the process of travel
both corporeal and *spiritus*. Her heart raced and she could not
do it. Despite her talent, she could not take herself back to
the green bridal glade where the plants had cooed best wishes
and all things fine had melted into sadness. Florentine fell
to her knees, covered her eyes with her hands, and began
to weep. *Dream*, said Gerald, *Transfer*. But she could not
transfer.

Some days passed. Florentine spent them walking outside
the inn. At nighttime she looked for stars, or the Wild Hunt,
or even for Cyprine, but due to mist or fate she never saw
any of these. She slept in a hay bed on the grounded floor,
paid for it in scullery and made avoidance of the provocative
library.

Finally, one evening she stood first before the sole
greyfruit that grew outside the inn, then lay prone in the
grasses unseen, closing her eyes. Her goal a different season
and a different place. The thought of this destination made
her heart beat just as quickly as when she had attempted the

glade.

She was white snowed, amongst hounds with red muzzles that gave no heed. Florentine caught her breath; this being worse than she could have ever conceived: she moved amongst the *mêlée*; no one felt her. She called out then and her mother turned her head in Florentine's direction, but this just served to terrify her mother more, who now believed her unseen daughter to be in danger, too. Florentine invisible to her parents, to the hounds, to the sensed-but-not-seen hunters. *She* could not be seen. She tried to interfere, but she was helpless to stop the teeth on her parents. She could not touch.

She shuddered out of the dream, sobbing, and then she cried for a week. She had never experienced the full violence on that first occasion; now she found herself in receipt of terrible knowledge involving the specificities of her parents' deaths.

Tanned Gerald said nothing when he returned and she informed him; he squeezed her hand and never said I told you so.

At the inn a week later, when she had dragged herself from her straw tapet and Gerald had persuaded her to down some stew and cocket, long after Gerald had taken his leave, she sat at the wide hewn-log table and peered out at her fellow humans. Generally they avoided her eyes, feeling guilty, no doubt, over the scrutinising gaze of a nun. They were no different on this night, and so Florentine moved on to her small flagon of beer and posset, served in a surly manner by the inn owner who was aggrieved by Florentine's free habits over the last seven days.

"The serfs are ridiculously vexing," one outraged merchant was telling another over his mug a few tables away, "they mutter of Eve spinning and Adam digging and then of gentlemen, some rhyme they have taken upon themselves as children do 'Little Jack, Jack sat on his gate'. And then these cotters *spit* on the ground."

"Though not yet at you."

"Aye."

"*Dum flagrat vicina domus, ibi proximat ad te,*" said the second merchant, omniously, likely pretentiously, but his friend did not understand Latin and was frequently frustrated by authors who do not provide translations directly below in the footnotes.

And there was such dark chatter. If the subject was not the great mortality, a fifth pestilence like that which had murdered two-in-three even in Lunden, if the subject was not the great mortality and that folk in Bristol arguing their wastage had been spied once more with buboes underneath their arms and sooty freckles, if the subject was not that the child king was weak – if the subject was not these grim topics, then the talk turned to the tax of the year before and the cruel increase in the leasing of lands.

Florentine covered her head with her hands; the innkeeper, assuming Florentine at prayer, retreated. But Florentine was in fact remembering Eglentyne, and Eglentyne's account of her parents' bad plague deaths in their beds.

Spring was here, Beltane bells, and on the day itself she set herself a task. It had taken her longtime to re-summon courage. The road she paced that day had been full of harbingers and travellers that whispered their forebodings that peasantry was refusing to pay taxes, that cats were dying in heaps and that the great hairy and fiery star in the sky several years past would be returning yet again to bring doom. She should try now Eglentyne. And this fine spring day she did, and this fine spring day she failed. Just as with the loss of her parents, she did succeed in transporting herself. For this third attempt, she stood on the riverbank and called to warn Eglentyne, but when her voice was heard this served only to distract, and Eglentyne did slip.

Florentine's hands passed like air through the water, like a ghost's. She could not alter the stream or change it or support Eglentyne's head as her friend was carried down the current towards the line that would cut her throat. Florentine had no real effect on this world in matters of real consequence; that is to say, Matters of Life or Death. And she grew to understand that not only could she not change the past but even worse, that by calling out she had caused in some sense Eglentyne's fall. In her more cogent moments, depressive nights that followed when she wept in her pillows with great distress, she would remind herself that Eglentyne had *had* to die first for Florentine to attempt this thwarted rescue, and so philosophically Florentine could not have caused this then at all. This was the coldest comfort, river-cold. She could not continue to journey back to these instances; she could not change them and she could only make them worse. Gerald's advice had been right.

Gerald was gone more and more often. And when he returned he was not tanned and rested these days, rather stressed and uncertain. One day he had a blue streak of paint across his face, with no vocal reference to it, and Florentine did not speak of the mark either.

The following day, though, she turned to him as her mentor, and addressed him directly and formally. "I went back again to the painful times, and the efforts were not functional."

Gerald sighed and turned to her. "Yes, I knew that you would try this." He looked down at his hands. He appeared weary.

"You're my teacher."

"Yes."

"You taught me this skill in the first place. Teach me how to change these happenings. How to best Death itself. It *surely* must be the deepest motivation for all who journey in this manner."

"For some, the deepest motivation is an ice-cold White Russian cocktail in the Bahamas." Gerald rose and brushed off his magisterial robes. "Come with me." He climbed the stairs to the library and the antechamber, and Florentine followed him. Her heart thumped for she knew that soon she would solve this, and fix everything that had happened before. Perhaps he would lead her to the great hall of learning that was the Bahamas.

Her teacher lead her to the far right corner of the room. There was a large collection of dusty scrolls and bound books there. "Open them."

She opened one. *A Grimoire with an Ayme.*

"Another," said Gerald.

The Munich Manual of Demonic Magic.

"Another."

It was a bundle of pages from a Bible, Deutoronomy: *"There shall not be found among you any one who maketh his son or his daughter to pass through the fire, or who useth divination, or an observer of times, or an enchanter, or a witch, or a charmer, or a consulter with familiar spirits, or a wizard, or a necromancer. For all who do these things are an abomination unto the LORD,"* read the page when Florentine smoothed it out on the shelf.

"And another."

She unrolled a scroll called *Tractatus de Nigromatia* and looked at this book, too.

"Do you see a pattern in these books of shadows?"

Florentine placed the scroll back on his grubby shelf and looked up. "Necromancy."

"Yes."

Florentine raised her eyebrows. She wanted a far better answer than that.

"So many scholars and yet we cannot reverse it. Death and poll taxes, so the saying goes. There will come a time when we can make gold, just as the stars do fuse, chrysopoeia in a particle accelator such as the Spallation

Neutron Source and *voilà*, just as the alchemists foretold for us, but though that fine alchemical day will come for us, we have not been able to reverse this other thing called death. It may be that entropy is so strong it prevents the putting-back-together of such a consequence. The second law of thermodynamics. Although we once thought this too about backwards time travel, and yet here I am."

Half of Gerald's words she did not understand; he was always mixing up scientific expeditions he'd attended with other eras, and jumbled too his nouns and and philoso-phies (worse, of late Florentine had noticed a trend for her to do this, too; it was as if the more one dream-travelled, the more the language mixed),

Florentine nodded.

"I see you are crestfallen. But understand that many scientists before have gone insane via this very quest, and in addition it is not too good an idea to overconcern ourselves with the dead, no matter how we loved them. We have this life to live here too." He paused here, and took a close look at Florentine. "If your experiment is to bring back your mother and father, or your baby, or your friend, and yet many wise persons and their own experiments did fail, what step would you take next, as a fledgling scientist yourself?"

"I would reformulate my hypothesis and try again."

"And with the same results?"

"I might try to figure another way around the prob-lem. I do not know."

"Then think about these words I have said, and think

too of those who have tried fruitlessly before, as I vouchsafe to you that they have, though science should not take too much on authority. Good thinking to you." Gerald looked even more drained than he had when they met to start this conversation this fertile spring day. He retreated to the staircase and descended.

Florentine stayed staring at the jumble of grimoires. She was a scientist, taught by the great Gerald *fitz* of Gerald *fitz* of Gerald *fitz* of Gerald ∞. She would figure a way around all this.

It took a week. Eventually the itch became too coaxing. It was necessary for Florentine to go back to the library. Eve with her apple (*Eve did spin*). She'd developed a taste for knowledge. Gerald, for example, had so much knowledge in his head that he had not been willing to tell her where or which book would give her the wisdom she sought. She stared at the whole library. Though she might find the necromantic spelles in such books that dealt with deep sleep, she reasoned. The answer would be here though in this red-lacquered room, and here it most definitely was, underneath six dusty manuscripts halfway down the fourth shelf in the room before all rooms.

The book was called *The Juliana Treatises*.

The page in the book, once found, looked like this:

Magick Spelle that derives from the 0th Law of Submersibility,

In order to corporeally change the wicker-weaves of spacetime,

In association with Trocta of Salerno's original references on necromancy, adjusted for dream-sojourns,

In order to initiate the temporal process to spur death towards life. 5 measures of IGF-1 insulin synthetic anabolic steroid, at least three Human-Stag antler sets' worth. Wer-Stags (inclusive of Wer-Women) being like the Wer-Wolf very rare; however, Unicorn horn can be substituted for this property, which was required in antiquity by the Old Ones, but of which make note that we have discovered since that Unicorns do not exist. Just the teeth of Whales, and therefore, while miraculous enough, the ocean ingredients are no help to us; therefore use Wer-Stags. Full-Stags cannot be substituted; if fully animal, the concentration is not the same and would involve too large a cull. Due to its so-called unnaturality, a Hornèd Doe can be substituted in a pinch, but this is not encouraged.

Once attained, the horns must be pulverised and powdered; we recommend the fine work of a Heidelberg apothecarian for this process, Doktor Schneeball.

Additionally 13 measures of human hair, wer- or not, washed and plaited. Once wickered, this agent can be post-spelle sown into the soil OR thatched into a roof.

Ferns, glossopteris (2 bouquets)

Borametz blood, that type that tastes like honey. 5 jars' worth; let the blood distill in a bubble glass beaker until the honey turns blue. Pour out into 5 jars, so that the blue honey is phosphorescent, and then use such bait to catch at least 413 fireflies. You catch more flies with honey than you do with vinegar, as the Americans say in their annoying quest for perpetual friendliness. Mosquitoes may be substituted.

As with the recipe work of every great cook, there were additional annotations in the manuscript, hurriedly scribbled:

Bluebells? Violets?

Greyfruit cider???

(immortality tree of life found in utter Blackness?)

Signed, *Juliana of Verulamium*

*

Florentine set to work growing as much hair as she could. She drank plenty of deer milk and ingested calcium pills imported from Frankish merchants to make it particularly profuse, strong. Soon curls began to sprout from her nose, her ears. Her eyebrows grew shaggy and the inn regulars gossiped regarding her within her earhearing.

She paid it no mind. She would fulfil Juliana's treatise. Florentine went walking in the forests, by rivers, and she let her hair grow. She tripped over it, and one day the strands fell over her sight to such a degree that she saw not the hunter's snare, the cage that caught her, and there she would have remained had a little boy not seen her passing by, and freed her, and she had continued on her way.

Her hair grew fast now all over her skin, thanks to the deer milk, thanks as well to frequent follicle stimulation through currying, a simple dollop of Rogaine and the sheer power of will. So much so that that every day she shaved it and tucked the hair loops away in a leather bag stored under her bed, and thought of her infant in her arms the green day, and still her hair grew, even faster.

It grew dangerous to walk the roads except in the hours directly after shave-times, for all folk were a-flutter now with plague news and angered by it, and her hair made her a target. On several occasions clots of small boys threw pebbles at her. If she wasn't directly spoken to, she was still directly glared at, suspect as she was under the hang of hair, from which her antlers did push through. All the anonymity she had enjoyed as a fake nun was cut short, and folk travelling would even stop their gossip over plague or taxes to curse her.

And yet, with this urgency and lack of being the recipient of the customary selective blindness she had experienced as clergy heretofore, Florentine found herself liberated by her own ostentatiousness. Her whole adult life had been purposefully avoidant in others' eyes and now her body, its horns, its hair, called out *Look at me, look at me*, and they looked, and all the while she grew herself for another, for her lost egg.

There is the importance of using a standard candle for time travel, writes Juliana of V: "*Yes, a temporal standard candle, if you will, be sure to look up the scientific definition when you feel like it. An era of known brightness. Here we go."* That's what Juliana of Verulamium writes.

*

There comes a woman to the forest, deep in leaves, dark, and the group of deer there have sprung at her arrival. The tree leaves settle and the night bird crisp again; the forest is as before but the herd itself is gone, save one. One of the deer had given birth, wrongly, and the fawn is longer gone, likely to wolves, likelier to foxes. This transvestitely hornèd little roe whines softly, but the woman is heartless, hartless. A knife to one horn and it's gone and in her bag, and knife to the second and it's severed too, but not before a crowing call in the woods and the cutter turns her head in distraction. It is not a clean cut, the horn crumples, it is not a kind cut, the doe weeps.

And yet the gelder, she is tracking something else. And eventually she finds it, too. She looks down on a sleeping girl, perhaps better said the youngest of women, with tear-stains dark and swollen on her cheeks still, slumbering directly where she fell exhausted in the bracken. She cannot be allowed the comfort of humble ersatz antlers, for that might mean changing the story and the woman in the forest cannot afford that risk right now. The standing woman waits for herself to feel emotion but she cannot touch it; she is only cold for the greater good, the ends manifested by the means (this act will be doubtless mean).

The very young woman sleeps through the loss, an insane and improbable occurrence in itself, and later the gelder walks through the woods with both a crumpled horn, a wooden set and a full young set, pearling on the coronet, all three thefts dropping blood alongst her travels.

*

Florentine made one additional visit to retrieve something lost. She could have walked in real-time all the way from Kent, two days' walking to Haca's Ey, or two and a half to Camlet Moat, wherever the cabin stands; its position is nebulous (like much in life). She could have walked there in her real life but now she pressed hard on the 0th Law that meant the ever more she dream-travelled, the ever more her skin follicles responded juicily. Much hair was what she wanted, and so via dream-transport she found herself in her *time* but in another *place*. In front of a tree full prime-life and gnarled.

Up in the branches was her first young pair, though covered by leaves she knew it was there. When she crawled hand and foot up the branches, she saw that her horns had done more than passively hung through the years: they had grafted onto the tree itself and indeed had leaves growing out of them in this fine light season. Well, life is about severings. She took out the jack-knife, her long-ago birthday gift, and once again hacked at these horns, this time axed not from scalp but from tree. A similarly painful act full of remembrances, but she set her jaw and gritted her teeth to her larger purpose. The sap that showed was rose-golden drops.

She held them triumphant in the air at last, twenty-two years since she'd touched them free, and the winds whistled through them as if through a barred cage; she felt the breezes on her face.

When she got down from the tree, the Witch was waiting. They watched each other, unsmiling.

The Witch looked pointedly at the antlers Florentine held in her hand. "A paucity of synthetic IGF-1 insulin powder?"

"What do you know of it?" Florentine clutched her old horns to her furred chest defensively.

"Let us walk together," suggested the Witch.

Florentine could see no motive, either strategic or romantic, and so she found herself following the Witch along the same route that led towards Florentine's old childhood home. She held tight in one pocket the half-harvested doe horns; she held tight with her arms one pair of werantlers, and tight with her crown yet another. Uneasy lies the head, etc., etc.

Halfway to Florentine's family cabin, the Witch paused, then stopped. "Come sit here," said the Witch, descending to the ground, patting a space beside her on the grass, "come sit here and tell me how it goes with your ingredients."

In the library, the Witch would have had access to

the same spellebook that Florentine had had. Knowledge is democratic; there was reason to trust the Witch, and reason not to trust her. "I have sourced the antlers and most of the glossopteris, and now I shall walk back to my childhood home and dig up the borometz."

"You sound cut-throat."

Florentine stared down the Witch. "I am adherent to the recipe."

"Good cooks improvise," said the Witch, "never mind, though. May I follow with you?" The Witch got to her feet.

Florentine sighed. "You may as well."

But when they arrived at the cabin, at the glades where the greyfruits grow, they saw that the jackplant had indeed become uprooted. They then sat on the shore of the lake (dangerous) and Florentine tried hard not to think of all that happened here, of the sorrow that leaked through the happy days. The borametz gone and Jack had not returned here after the Blue School after all; Jack could not be rendered. She had steeled her heart for the act of julienning him, but now her coldness towards this compromise, even this had been in vain. She began to weep.

"Why?" asked the Witch.

"I do not know where I will find a borametz again. It is required in the recipe."

"Hmm." The Witch did not appear inordinately sympathetic, but appeared to take Florentine's predicament seriously. "Well, there is rumoured to be one such vegetable lamb at the Garden Museum in the Lunden Borough of Lambeth in the century of 2000, and, as I'm sure Gerald has taught you, you could journey there and then. But I can tell you now that you will find only a rhizome root. You will find neither mandrake nor borametz lamb."

Florentine began to weep all the harder.

"However, you also could journey to your Spital friends, for there in the statuary garden is a new borametz sprig, a mere colt, right there."

Florentine was shocked but relieved. Of course! Those long-ago gourds, left behind with her brothers. "Why do you help me? You and I, we have attraction but still animosity between us."

The Witch shook her head, smiled and looked at her own fingernails for a period. She drew down her cowl and showed Florentine again the top section of the brand upon her back. "I have my own reasons."

"You have read the treatise, too? How do you know the specificities of these ingredients?"

"*Who*, exactly, do you think is Juliana of Verulamium?"

"I, we..." Florentine fell silent and her eyes grew wider.

"Why do you think I was in Gerald's library in the first place, painting and then putting my tar-road cards into place? I am, of course, a scholar."

"This does not surprise me." Florentine nodded.

"And I wish to help you. Your mother told you fairy tales about a snake and the languages of birds," said the Witch. "Let me tell you quite a different fairy tale."

This did, however, surprise Florentine.

"In the beginning, in the very, very beginning, there was being and there was non-being and there was none but the clear force of the universe, nowhere and nowhen, long ago and once upon a spacetime, and all that, there was a primeval egg. We can call this the problem of beginnings, or we can think of it instead as a solution of beginnings. But anyway, there was an egg.

"A primordial pangu seed, smaller than an atom, tiny, very hot, then quick expansion via energy joules and eventually a cooling." The Witch looked meaningfully at Florentine. "Uniquely then do quirky quarks turn up – forward to top, backward to bottom, up, down, strangeness, charm – only to annihilate each other. This quarkocide means only the billionth of all matter created remains, and what remains are the electrons and protons and neutrons, and these then form atoms.

"Only a few minutes after the big bang and the seed has germinated, now bigger than a galaxy, hot plasma, all sub-atomic particles charged and glittering. Everything cools and then glows. Everything gets lumpier in the universe. Positively charged protons capture negatively charged electrons and form simple elements of hydrogen and helium. The universe is not perfectly uniform, and few eggs are, especially in a big-bang scramble. Nature is not about fascist perfection, but *change*. Astronomer George Smoot's model of the early universe shows an uneven green-blue egg, and indeed the Universe is blue-green generally, but has redder and hotter and therefore lumpier spots; it is, as said, imperfect, and that is why we love this joule-ed egg so. These ripples are magnified via gravity, and become galaxies, 'clusters of galaxies, and the great voids of space', according to Smoot. Baby stars in 'star nurseries': horsehead nebulae, 'like eggs in a nest'.

"This relationship between the micro of quantumnicity and the macro of Newtonian physics does a dance we call the Cosmic Serpent: any change in the tiny produces a change in the huge. The serpent moves through matchy-matchy rungs, honey, oh sugar sugar, the five-carbon DNA sugar called deoxyribose, undulating moves like Jagger, wiggle, wiggle, there we go."

Florentine was unimpressed. "What use is this against the horrors of this world when it comes to exterminating plagues, or to cruelties such as brands like yours or impossibilities such as quests like mine?" *The baby with its pink fingers, its green heart.* She blinked. She was crying multicoloured tears, globes rolling down her face as she thought of the baby, coloured sugar tears, blue, pink, green, all the colours of the fairies in the Disney film *Sleeping Beauty* plus plum-purple for one so-called bad witch, DNA; all the subatomic particles charged and glittering.

The tears were rolling but the sun was shining and

she smelled the greyfruit trees. She sat there crying until she felt good. In all of this time, the Witch said nothing. Though she sat there with Florentine and she did not leave.

When Florentine was able to speak again, she said merely, "A cosmic egg."

"Yes," confirmed the Witch. There was a long pause over it all. The near-midsummer pollen was sparkling in the sky, a lacy yellow veil. "One of the Grimm brothers has referred to gifted children being able to laugh roses, and of a rare few who can cry gold. Have you ever heard of candling an egg?" added the Witch, conversationally. *Jack Candle. A standard candle of known luminosity.*

"Yes," said Florentine, for she had.

"Think on it now," advised the Witch.

And so in this way did Florentine imagine holding a candle behind a hen's egg – though why must it be a chicken egg, let us say instead a dinosaur egg, an ishtar-egg – in this way did Florentine imagine holding a candle behind a blue-green egg so that one could see the life growing within it. An old wife's trick. The embryo-snake, the ouroboros begins. It all begins. *Jack be nimble, Jack be quick, Jack jump over the candlestick.*

"Let me tell you another story. I will re-relate to you that motherly fairy tale," said the Witch. The Witch's comforting of Florentine was not smooth, but then again it was not entirely clear whether the Witch's intention was to comfort Florentine.

"A fine lord, such as the type who do not pay taxes in

this year of 1381, a fine lord plotted to eat the crest of the king of snakes. Heavy lies the head that wears the crown. Let us say queen of snakes. I like that better. A fine lord plotted to eat the crest of the queen of snakes, the queen of pomegranate sauces, red garnet seeds spilling from her ovipositor every season after she emerges from her sleep (cf. Giambattista Basile), the queen of snakes."

Bluebells began to ring at this point throughout the forest like churchbells; Florentine and the Witch both heard them. There were wonderful moments of silence between the bell musics just as when churchbells sound, the silences every bit as piercing as the music itself. And then the bluebells chimed again, all through the forest.

"A fine lord plotted to eat the crest of the queen of snakes," continued the Witch when the bells had faded, "because in this way he understood the languages of birds. You see here the way that snakes and birds are the same. The lord is having problems collecting taxes this season and requires the distraction of a hobby: learning a mysterious new language not found in the online Berlitz language series. The lord, with an admirable craving for the numinous, comes to a clearing in the forest. Here all the snakes have congregated, and there is their queen. The lord takes out his sword and cuts her to pieces; he guillotines her head and now has her crest. The forest revolts: other snakes attack, trees fold in on him and small birds swoop, but it is too late.

"He escapes by taking off a piece of his clothing, one piece by one piece, a form of high-stakes strip poker. Each time he leaves a garment behind, the snakes stop to investigate it and taste it with their flickering tongues. (This is rumoured in Alaska to be an effective method of distracting a pursuing bear, as bears too will stop to sniff each discarded garment – do not try this in your home forest without corroboration.) And in this manner the fine lord makes good his escape, though by the time he leaves the forest he is entirely de-frocked. The lord goes commando. No matter, the serfs are well cowed and do not comment; the emperor has no clothes.

"Nude," emphasises the Witch, "*naked*. The fine lord summons his best cook and bids her make a stew from the crest, but forbids her to taste it. Yet while simmering the soup this curious Eve licks a finger absent-mindedly, and at once she too can understand the languages of birds, and she too hears the gossiping of a flock at the window sill – feathered blue, red, gold, black, white, green. They speak of bird matters: Hegel, precognition and the formation of vegetable mould through the action of worms, with observations on their habits. The cook keeps the matter of her new talent private from her lord.

"For some purpose unexplained in the original story, the lord and his cook go out riding the next day. The cook hears the forest birds say that the lord's horse will break its leg and throw the fine lord to his death, but the cook says nothing. And so it comes to pass."

This was, as it happened, more or less the fairy tale that Florentine had often heard from her mother, but in her mother's version the lord survived the fall from the horse with the broken leg; the cook was discovered to have illegally tasted the stew; the cook was killed.

"In autumn, in quantum," mentioned the Witch casually as the two of them sat there and listened to the return of the bluebells in the silence that ensued, "in autumn, in quantum, snakes lick stones in the forest, and then they retreat to caves and they sleep through the winter like bears."

Florentine was not sure that this was a correct recounting of natural history; it seemed more like a euphemism for fellatio, but she did not challenge the fact voiced by the Witch.

Florentine rose then, and stripped. She did not look at the other woman. She walked out into the waters of the dangerous lake. She dove under to a swim when her feet touched nails and pieces of broken glass at the bottom. She held her breath and swam under the grille studded with spikes, saw nothing in the blue-green bracken but lily roots, and dodged the grille again and swam up to gasp for breath. She had become an accomplished swimmer during her sojourns with Gerald, but his lake was not imbued with memories of bleeding brothers or white-bird terror, dung-gem pellets falling. She treaded water, and through the water pouring over her eyes she saw the figure of the Witch standing on the beach, watching all the way from the shore.

Florentine dove again into the water, and ran her hands along the bottom, muck. Nothing. She rose again and looked towards the shore. The Witch was gone; she was no longer observing. This put a spike of fear into Florentine, but she had no time to think of it now. She gulped air and went down again, skimming her hands in the deep mud until this time she found what she sought. Up again, and there was the Witch again. Where had Cyprine gone in the seconds Florentine had been down? It would have not have been possible to step away and then come back so quickly, but yet Florentine swore she had seen such a thing. On the other hand, she was, after all, a witch.

So where is that house that Jack built? While Florentine is underwater, seeking a long-ago antler, the Witch does a spelle of sorts. She must hide Jack, and keep him safe. She is a cosmic squirrel obliged to hide her nut.

Jack, split off, has been wandering the ether for a while. It's time. The Witch turns into a stick. She becomes an entire forest, a glade, an Amhurst Grove.

Jack goes crying in the trees for his lost love (his own damn fault), his lost child (his own damn fault) and most of all his own lost self (unsurprisingly, his own damn fault). He's a faded ghost of his old self, you know.

Jack, drifting through the trees, wasted away millennia in this fashion. Now he glances up to the clouds. If he could skywrite clouds, he'd see an alphabet there. The puffy letters would spell out F-L-O-R-E-N-T-I-N-E and C-Y-P-R-I-N-E. And R-O-B-I-N, J-A-C-K. And M-A-R-T-I-N. And B-A-B-Y, E-G-L-E-N-T-Y-N-E, B-E-A-M-A-N, E-L-D-R-I-T-C-H, P-E-R-C-I-V-A-L, E-R-M-I-N-T-R-U-D-E, N-E-D, G-E-R-A-L-D and P-A-R-

E-N-T-S dear.

"Time to go, Floren-jack; time to go, Mar-tine," says the Witch. "We'll make sure you get a good childhood. We'll get you a profession – we'll make you a spy. We'll get you a wif, and call her Hermo-dike. You can build a home in this time. No green but, that said, Martin has no horn. But we all change from such split-tings. This indeed is the house, not the hound nor the horn. Build your home, Jack. Thatch it with red-gold threads so the rain doesn't come in. You'll be safe enough."

And thus does the Witch cache her nut. So Jack is Florentine. Hardly a shock, no? **If so, go back to page 1 and start all over again.**

Epiphenomena: a secondary phenom-enon. Jack's splitting off is the second for first, as you recall, first came Martin. Florentine is Jack is Martin. Or maybe that wasn't the first. **If this troubles you, you know where you can go.**

The Witch has been gone only a few seconds and now she is returned and wait-ing lakeside. And Florentine is swimming back to her.

✷ ✷ ✷

When Florentine reached the shore, half-paddling to dodge the nails and glass, and once Florentine had stepped out not at all Aphrodite-like but rather pulling dark muds of leeches off her skin, she then met the Witch again and unclenched her fist and showed the Witch the long-ago curl she had once thrown deep into the lake; she was full of luck to have found it again at all. The branch antlers, the severed antlers, the roe antlers all still waiting on the grass. Florentine nodded toward her palm. "Every little bit will help."

The Witch had an odd expression when Florentine showed her the long-sunk antler-curl. "Goodness, such platitudes. I thought better of you. So you've reversed the old spelle," murmured the Witch.

"So I have," said Florentine, and she intended to say more, but right then blustered in a great yellowed buck.

"Ah, Percy!" Florentine hugged her brother tight, for some time had passed indeed.

"You again," Percival said to the Witch. Then he nuzzled his sister, remarked on her fine strawberry-blonde pelt and told her that upon bidding her goodbye he had in fact returned to this, their old house. He had married happily, as a matter of fact, and was now bringing up three kids of his own. "Two little does and a buck," he said proudly. "How is mine own niece?"

Florentine's eyes fell. "She is gone."

"I am sorry," said Percival.

The witch Cyprine merely stood eavesdropping.

"Do you have news of Eldritch and of Beaman?" asked Florentine, for any other talk felt more soothing, and in addition it vexed her still that her parting with the other two had not been good by any measure.

The Witch stifled a yawn, but Florentine and Percival ignored her.

"I have, indeed," said Percival, "from time to time a travelling mendicant who also journeys past the Spital keeps me informed. They are well, and have risen in the ecclesiastical ranks."

"And..." Florentine was not sure how to phrase the question. "Has the green man ever come back to this glade?"

The Witch rolled her eyes and Percival shook his shaggy head disapprovingly. "And what do you want with a cad like that?" He pawed the ground. "And no, he never has."

"Well, then," said Florentine.

"Well, then," said Percival. "Shall we go to meet my family? And where, by the way, is the keepsake holy rood I once strung around your neck?"

"*Well, then,*" mimicked the Witch. "That charm round her neck has clearly been popped." She winked at Florentine, who stared straight ahead.

"I've sadly lost it," Florentine lied gently to her brother. There were many things she could not tell him just now, but he was her brother and he understood.

He chuckled. "Never mind. I have not believed in the healing power of magickal roods for many a season. If it brought you comfort for a while, it did its intended duty."

"It certainly did that." Florentine smiled and scruffed up the white hair on her brother's neck.

The Witch followed with them but continued her enigmatic soliloquy as was her wont, though no one had requested it from her. "Quail-pipe, and then a good hart's tongue," she said insinuatingly as the three of them made their way across the meadow grass towards the wooden cabin.

"The hart's tongue fern is a rarity," said a glass-frog – family name *Centrolenidae* – much lower. The trio abruptly stopped walking.

Florentine and Percival blinked and peered downward into the grasses, but the Witch was unruffled by the amphibian intrusion. "You've both as children tasted many strange animals," said the Witch. "And there is always a pattern: you taste snake, you understand the languages of birds. You taste rat, you will understand the languages of wolves. You taste fox, you will understand the languages of bats. You have both tasted owl, and so naturally you understand the languages of frogs; it is merely that neither of you have ever bothered to listen before now."

"That's right," said the frog. "*Asplenium scolopendrium*, aka the hart's tongue fern," it added.

Florentine could scarcely breathe, and felt excited despite the frog's rude botanical clarification. "And to understand the languages of snakes?"

The witch shook her head. "Dark things. The ninth animal. Holy meat sacrificed to idols. Let us not speak further on it."

They did not.

*

Florentine and the Witch sat outside in the meadow where the fireflies twisted in the air.

"I've been here before," said the Witch. Florentine didn't comment. Inside the cabin were her sweet nieces and nephew, already sleeping in early evening, and inside the cabin too were Percival and his wife Rozamunda.

Rozamunda had winked at Florentine and Cyprine. "Have a drink and a kiss out with the fireflies," she had said, handing them a flask of greyfruit cider. "Only from fallen fruits," she had assured Florentine.

"Of course," Florentine had said.

Florentine hadn't felt much like kissing. Yet they drank the greyfruit cider and felt it giggle up through them as they watched the fireflies in the twilight.

"So." With no warning, Florentine upended the flask and let it drain to the ground. She was already quite drunk. Cyprine raised an eyebrow. "Now I'm going to the Spital." The fireflies trembled.

"On foot?" The Witch raised the eyebrow on the other side of her face.

"No, and for two reasons. The first is that the roads

have become dangerous for me, with so much hair and such a wealth of antlers. The second reason is because I can still force more hair out by use of the o$^\text{th}$ Law of Submersibility." She was still unsure whether she trusted the Witch. She looked in Cyprine's silver eyes and decided she would try to. "I will leave these antlers, which I have harvested from the tree, from my sleeping innocent self, from the animal, from the dream-moose walking, from the stolen shaving, I will leave them all in your safekeeping, leave them with you."

The Witch smiled. "What if I turn steal *them*?"

This was exactly what Florentine was hoping the Witch would not say. She ignored the provocation. "You could instead deposit them all in my room for me, in the Kentish inn."

The Witch looked thoughtful. "Yes, it is technically possible for me to do that."

Florentine was on her feet, whisking grass bits off her skirts.

"I was branded for non-compliance to the old serf rates," said the Witch abruptly. "Since you never asked." (But Florentine had indeed thought of the Witch's brand very often.)

"The snake symbol?" Florentine was duly shocked: she had never conceived that the Witch would be the type who could be *forced* to work. Though of course that is the very tragedy of forced labour: without consent, whether one is stubborn or strong of heart or no. "That depiction seems more of a choice, like a tattow."

"It was originally a circle. I had a smith re-brand me later to my taste to modify the loop-de-loop. *That* was my choice, but the initial act was *not*."

Florentine put her fingers to her own lips and felt the past pain through thought alone. "Cruel."

"Yes. I pity flagellants, who hurt *themselves*, when there are so many only too willing to undergo the sadistic role."

"It's not quite so," protested Florentine, standing thoughtfully in the field, but itching to journey. "It is more that flagellants such as my brothers feel that by punishing themselves with whips, that their God will see that they have suffered enough, and so then any new plagues sent by God will never hurt them."

The Witch nodded, then got to her feet, too. "Gods can do terrible things."

"The Christian one, anyway," said Florentine. There was something blue that she was trying her hardest not to think about, but the Witch was not allowing her to avoid the subject.

"Quit beating yourself up about it," said the Witch. "Children were often sacrificed to the God Molluck in agricultural sacrifices in that valley outside Jerusalem. What was its name?"

"Gehenna. It was, and is, a hell."

"Ah yes, Hel –"

"I said, 'Hell'."

"Ah yes, Hel, the Norse crone who bellows the bonfires to char the green man. Norse, *hel*, the hidden place; Protogermanic, *haljo*, the one who covers up or hides something; Protoindo-european, *kel*, to 'conceal'; concepts of hell as a hidden underworld may well be because humans were often buried underground. Be sure to bury apples for your beloved dead," advised the Witch, "hell fires, *pfft*. I've been burned at stake many a time, and look, here I am. The 'eternal fire' as mentioned in Matthew 25:4. And yet the worm never dies, the snakes always come back, eggs born in wood ashes, Mark 9:49. The eternal flames, the ever-living John Barleycorn. Phoenixes, ouroboros, the snakes bite their tails and in that egg you'll find a seed, and from that seed will grow a tree, and on that tree you'll find a branch, and on that branch there is a nest, and in that nest there sits a bird, and under that bird there lies an egg. And on and on we go."

"Shut up," Florentine screamed to the Witch, "you cruel, cruel thing!"

"Was it *I* who was cruel? Did *I* summon up Molluck? Children were often sacrificed to the God Molluck in agricultural sacrifices in that valley outside Jerusalem. What was its name?"

"Gehenna," answered Florentine, "it was, and is, a hell."

"Ah yes, Hel –"

"I said, 'Hell'."

And on and on. The snake bites its tail. Go back to Page 1 and begin all over again. Go back to the egg; crack out pho-

tons again. But sometimes, nevertheless, despite these rondel loop-de-loops, due to mutations despite replication, we sometimes arrive at a different day.

"But you encourage such patterns," shrieked Florentine, "you don't allow for these changes. Fundamentalist!" (Can Florentine read the gentle narrator's mind? Has it come to this?)

Florentine was aware that she was far more drunk on greyfruit cider than she had believed herself to be. She took a breath to steady herself. "Come with me to the Spital." She wanted company, even the bad company of the Witch. There was something that linked them and it was something different than spit and soft red lips.

"No," the Witch decided, "I will take these antlers to your inn-room instead. It won't even take me much time: as I'm sure you've gathered, I too can dream-travel. Thus resulting in my dashing cheekbones." The Witch turned her head proudly so that Florentine could see the narrow hairy stripes on either side of her face.

She was infuriating. Florentine was not sure the Witch would even fulfil the errand for which she was volunteering. *Coloured sugars, DNA sugars. Ostara Easter eggs. DNA, coloured sugars.*

"I certainly do not mind plagiarising Whatsapp and Creek since they stole it from Frankincense anyway, and so I will tell you a third fairy tale of truth unless you wish to hear a suggestive dream I had last night concerning kabuki-faced females dancing violently on stilts to loud trip-hop. The third story goes like this, the bases are on the inside of the helix and the honey on the outside. The configuration of the coloured sugar and the atoms near it is close to standard configuration, the coloured sugar being roughly perpendicular to the attached honeycomb," said the Witch.

Florentine stared at the Witch for a moment. Then she stepped forward and kissed her, tasting coloured sugars on the Witch's tongues. Close to sun, white, light yellow, orange, orange-red, cherry-red, dark-red, glow, far from sun.

The fireflies echoed the colours, fireflies Florentine could remember all the way from childhood. She pulled Cyprine close to her; their kiss was sticky. Florentine's cunt was wet, but she needed to get wetter. She pushed the Witch away.

"Florentine the Wild," said the Witch, admiringly.

"What?"

"Not yet, but one day you will be."

Florentine turned her back, but three seconds later when she turned around to check, the Witch was gone. *Glossopteris means tongue. Coloured DNA sugars. Casting forget-me-not flower seeds in springtime to tell the future from them.*

On Florentine's fingers where she had touched the Witch were the crystal grains of coloured sugars, pink, blue, green as in *Sleeping Beauty* and violets for the witch. Florentine could still feel the violet-flower taste on her tongue.

479

To transport from the cabin to the Spital, Florentine didn't even need the medium of water these days; travelling had become as natural as, if not quite breathing, perhaps swimming itself, which is why she guessed Gerald initially had made use of the water analogy in her apprenticeship period.

Now she shut her eyes. The white shoots pushing up the new greyfruit sprigs and the splitting-up of the acorns; the cottonwood sweet stink on the air, a fragrance that was the same as when one smushed one's nose up against a still-sticky aspen bud seconds before the leaf pushed out.

Now she opened her eyes. No lepers. She was outside the stone gates of the Spital churchyard and she could smell pear trees here, mayhaps even something more erotic if it were not such a puritanical place. She pinched at the hair growing freely from her left arm. A thumb's-length more from this most recent trip. That was good. Every little bit would help, platitude or not.

The plant-smell became more fertile, even foetid. Florentine rounded the corner of the stone fence and stepped over it into the statuary garden. There was no question as to where the borametz would be growing: on the far side from her, past both the Oklahoma Capitol Ten Commandments monument and the satirical Baphomet statue response, was a garden section where bees and insects buzzed hard and where pollen was thick like the air had been buttered. Near the sterile and tame Spital lake. And then that green scent too, that growing scent, both alluring and repellant all at once, enticing her forward.

There were two figures standing near this lush corner that she approached, and at first she thought them hounds, though with pleasure and recognition realised soon enough that their four-legged quality was of a goatly bent instead. The goat monsignors wore each a red velvet cape fastened round their neck with tiny polished obsidian buttons. Both of her brothers were staring with wonder at the two small plants that had sprung up erect from the ground. Florentine believed for a moment that she could actually see the slow but assured growth of these plants, and then she believed it more. From these penis-seeds will grow a tree will grow a fruit will grow a seed will grow a tree.

"Brothers!" The cardinal and the archbishop had not heard their sister approach, so entranced were they with the addition to their garden.

"Ah, sister," said Cardinal Eldritch, and he greeted her with far more affection than he had done on their last parting, and Archbishop Beaman followed suit. The three of them stood in an embrace for a moment, while the scent of the new plants swanned over them; pollen was everywhere. "Have you word of our brother?"

"He is married to a fine Toggenburg doe named Rozamunda, with three kids kicking up the greyfruit grove and woods." Both her brothers smiled.

"And you are well, even if a woman, even if a hairy one at that, even if a pagan one at that, unchristened?" said

Eldritch. He dropped his gaze, a monsignor of the cardinal rank. "Please excuse me," he mumbled.

"Where is your own babe? You were near full to term when we saw you last," asked Beaman, somewhat timidly.

"She has left us. She was gone a day after her birth."

The brothers bowed their heads, and Eldritch murmured a quick prayer for the dead.

"I am trying to reverse all of that."

"Hush, Florentine." Beaman's eyes were alarmed. "You musn't speak of necromancy. We are within the garden and by a very safe lake adjacent to a House of God."

These wells are holy ground. Take off your shoes. Florentine glanced down at her bare dirty feet. Though their motives were good by their own churchly standards, she could not speak her aims. Even Gerald had balked at the subject, and he was a Forestish swan-lover who slept under lakes. The pollen still sifted through the air; it had not settled anywhere. Florentine would be very careful from hereon.

"The delicate matter of your hair," ventured Eldritch, "can we speak of depilation? We have here the finest tonsurers in the land, of which you may partake."

"I shall," said Florentine, "make the argument that woodwoses are found even in the Christian Bible in Genesis 27:11: *'Jacob answered her: "You know that my brother Esau is a hairy man, and I am smooth."'*

Eldritch considered this. "That is true. But Esau was not a good man," Eldritch mused thoughtfully. "Still,

Saint Chrystostom was said to have been so hairy due to his asceticism that he was indistinguishable as man or beast. I suppose there is also the tale of King Arthur and his hairy prophet Myrddin. And Geoffrey of Monmouth tells us too how Myrddin – Merlin – crawled into the woods, ate blackberries and grew hairy, sleeping under ash trees."

" 'O Holy Ash, yggdrasil, we suck juice from your leaves and elixir from your fruit,' " intoned Florentine, with an element of mockery.

Her brother blinked, not used to interruptions of a non-christly bent. "After this longtime vegetarian blackberry lifestyle, Myrddin took to the deepest forest, and he also took to eating human flesh so that he could understand the languages of snakes. Only later was he bestowed with the gift of prophecy. It is claimed that he knew when humans would go extinct. Though of course this is all very blasphemous and worldly, since we will all rise up on the judgment day."

"Other than knowing when their next lay comes, the only kind of prophecy that matters to humans is knowing the date of their personal extinction," agreed Florentine. Eldritch blinked again, nearly a tic this time.

"Yes," Beaman added eagerly, "and Sweeney, the Ulster king, the one who attacked the priest, he was cursed with madness and tore off his clothes and ran into the wood where he too began to eat human flesh. And only then did Suibhne grow hair and feathers and talons, once he had retreated to the woods to compose limericks –"

"To compose *poetry*," interjected Eldritch, under his breath.

"To Compose a Great *Limerick* to God," continued Beaman, "in order to be forgiven and then he is cured of his hairiness. Perhaps something like, 'There once was a great king from Ulster, who elected to sing *paternoster* –'"

"Cease –" said Eldritch.

Beaman continued babbling, but ceased the godly limerick: "And the barley hero Beowa is hairy too –"

"Indeed!" interrupted Florentine, "barleycorn itself is significant. Goddess Isis fucked Osiris with his dick of gold in a barleycorn field of dreams." (She was a well-educated young woman. Both the Blue School and Gerald had taught her well.)

"Yes!" said Beaman excitedly, "just like Christ, the barley hero Beowa suffers, dies and is resurrected, and peasants celebrate this resurrection by the drinking of his blood! So perhaps being hairy is not always bad, but it usually is."

Eldritch glared deeply at his brother Beaman.

Florentine cast down her eyes and made her voice of a penitent strain. "In truth, I need this borametz to cure myself."

"Ah." Eldritch nodded sagely. "Pray continue."

"It is said by good, churchly people that eating a borametz stem will be the cure for hairiness and I think we must all three agree that my hairy state itself is now quite entirely obscene."

In the end and with their permission, she took out

her jack-knife and cut off the small but perfectly formed borametz. The borametz looked exactly like a miniature doll of Robin and it winked at her before she cut it, which she found unnerving. She did not expect it to scream like a man when she cut it, but it did – this had not happened previously in that severing in frozen winter. When it was fully severed, though, it lay there like a limp poppet.

When she had completed the act, she saw how her brothers flinched.

She left the second plant behind with her brothers. "In case you ever change your minds," she said, "and wish like Percival to fuck."

" '*Those who, hearing the Word, hold fast to it in an honest and good heart, and bring forth fruit with patience*', Luke 8:15," Eldritch quoted sanctimoniously, "not such carnal fruits as these." Eldritch looked uneasily at the phallic fruits already rearing up from the remaining adolescent plant. "There additionally may be a problem with the other priests plucking the fruits too unripe," he murmured.

Beaman, however, looked interested at the mere thought of retrieving his bollocks once again and frigging other grown bucks in the sunshine free of this Spital, of being rid of this Church. Beaman would not be long for here, she reasoned, but Eldritch, she suspected, Eldritch would never prove susceptible.

*

When Florentine returned to the inn, she saw that the Witch had kept her promise, but the Witch was not there. The Witch has stepped out for a moment. The Witch has returned to a firefly field; in this long-ago past she is there to locate Jack. Jack lies on his back wondering up at the stars, admiring the moonlist cast of his brand-new moose antlers. Via the Eighteenth Principle of Fast-Time Dilation, the Witch transports him to a dreaming, therapeutic desert.

***

Once born by bifurcation, Martin noted a lack of green, for he had ended up in a different dry desert only sporadically lush. We always choose our own adventures. If time ran regularly for the intervening fourteen years – actually twelve due to time-dilation – this makes Martin 33, Christ being another fellow who hung out with a stick.

Sacrifice and guilt are aging. Do a fair job on wrinkle accumulation. *Jackrifice; don't jackrifice. Choose your own adventure. If you jackrifice your poppet, turn to another page and become a mourning ghost oft-recounted in therapy sessions.* Jack aged and Martin did not. Time goes differently in interim environments. Also, it's generally stressful and aging to have your new world blown up by a nuclear bomb.

Even if every springtime she had remembered to cast forget-me-not seeds to tell the future from them, Florentine never could have predicted Martin's desert. Pineapple consumed on a Hawaiian scientific expedition. The hairy pelt of Gerald's grey moustache. A water faucet pouring in a London bedsit. My three sons. Oh, it's funny how mutations stay with us. DNA transcription errors are only one base pair per 100,000, but they still occur despite the best efforts of proofreader DNA polymerase. Copying is *often* perfect, but it is never *always* perfect.

* * *

Gerald travelled to Jack. A West Berlin neighborhood, a street magician. On this bifurcation his real age, 36, his real young self sleeping under water. But Jack is nineteen.

Gerald waited just outside on the pavement when Jack exited his headquarters and then doubled back as he had been trained to do. The street magician performance blocked his path.

"I know your name," the hairy street performer told Jack. He spoke with English with an unusual Irish accent. Jack panicked over his blown cover before recognising that this flamboyantly dressed wizard was just another Kreuzberg crazy. Likely of an environmental Green Party bent. Most of them were. "I'll tell you now. Your name is Martin."

Jack laughed, relieved. "What tricks can you do?"

"I melt lead in spoons to tell fortunes." Jack smiled. "I also undertake the erasing of cold stenograph machines so that transcribed memories do not stay fixed." Jack shivered. That was a little too spy-like for comfort.

Though Jack felt inclined to be kind. "You have a bit of blue paint on your cheek," he tells the street performer in English, "*blau*."

"Ah yes, excuse me, a Celtic expedition, back home to visit a great-aunt for her Milkmonth birthday in 1292, you know how these family things are, formal dress required. Nevertheless, I am now the starry messenger, and so I want to remind you that at some point in the future, even though you'll be harnessed by amnesia, to do your damn best to pay attention to Post-It notes and passenger pigeons."

***

There is an old hornèd woman humming by a cabin in

the woods. She is picking fruits up from the ground; she is famous not only for her fine set of antlers but for her greyfruit cordial. Perhaps there are one or two mischievous grandchildren giggling behind her in the cabin. A witch comes knocking on the door, selling apples. ***Do you taste one?***

*

There is an old hornèd woman swimming in a lake. Behind her is a cabin made all of marzi-pan. Soon a small boy will knock on her sugary doorstep, lost in the pages of a book. ***Do you let him in?***

*

There is an old hornèd woman in a library reading books, and another old witch. From time to time they pause to smile at each other, and read further. ***Is this your chosen page? Do you disturb their tableau?***

***

Pseudegraphica, oh those writings falsely attributed to previous authors. That is why the authorial voice here has been mercurial. I have been pulling your leg all along. I have cheated on you multiple times, with nymphs, with satyrs, with dry-

490

ads. Trust me.

Oh yes, and that passenger pigeon with a scroll written in blackletter German tied round its ankle doing its job. And you ignored it. It turned green and flew off. *Jack Sprat, he ate no-fat. His wife, she ate no green.* A mistake on your part, ignoring that message intended for your eyes. I will reveal what the message said; it read that the future borrows green energy from the past and that we all recycle, re-use, reduce. That time is eternal inside black holes, where the true eternal tree of life is found, and that for this reason it is not just cancers that are immortal. *Maybe.* Hox genes, I've put a hox on you, you're breaking off into Okazaki fragments.

The message said that limestone is a graveyard and that the first bacteria were purple bacteria and that purple dye comes from snails. That people and plants alike descend from algae - a tiny, single-celled green alga called *Chlamydomonas reinhardtii*; that humans are more closely related to fungi than plants (we practice kin selection to save particularly the red toadstools with white spots that cause

jinxing visions in small goats on Moon
Days), that mushrooms themselves are connected with small threads like the internet, mycelia that link unrelated plants:
greyfruits to bluebells, glossopteris to
borametz, bruce to spirch – everything
is connected, just like I told you. That
trees have been observed sleeping, and
moreover dreaming. That poplar is a form
of aspirin. That a Japanese flower called
Paris japonica has the most complex DNA of
any organism, far more many genes than any
mere human. People once believed in spontaneous generations – maggots from meat,
crocodiles from logs – but DNA is destiny.

DAZL, the spermatogenesis gene. Come
on and dazzle me. Adenine green, thymine
violet, guanine blue and cytosine pink.
Sex is invented. Have you ever noticed
that bees have hexagonic eyes as well as
hexagonic honeycombs? Similary, humans
have roundish wombs and roundish eyes. Sex
cells and eggs were invented. Oh DNA, you
gorgeous thing, you CATGuT thing, vio-
lins made with catgut strings plucking on
your mnemonics, cars in garages, apples in
trees, cytosine, guanine, adenine, time
– again, we were once via our last uni-

versal common ancestor a form of *Chlam-ydomonas reinhardtii*, my name is LUCA. Then bivalves known as devil's toenails, crouching stones, small shelly fossils. O DNA, and how those rates of duplication and inversion accelerate 100 mya after the dinosaurs appear, as the dinosaurs went on to vanish once again during the Flirtaceous-Paleogene Event of 66 mya. O fish, amphibians, reptiles. We are descended from a near-reptile descended from an amphibian descended from a fish. Amplexus, dick to cunt, amphibian sex. Glass frogs, translucent so you can see their inner organs. O mammals, knots of pigs, xy-goats, the male deer called buck, puck, buck. Nonsense mutations, mis-sense mutations. To every thing there is a season. Disappeared and forgotten concepts of *Triceratops*, *Ramapithecus*, Pluto, the steady state eternal universe. Paradigms change and mutate even within science.

So then I put it to you. Is fusion a form of blasphemy? Say, if we re-fuse multiverses? Such fusion contradicts entropy in terms of energy expenditure required and therefore the second law of thermodynamics that states that entropy increases and fusion does not. It may be that entropy is so strong it prevents the putting back together of such a consequence. Once the supercoils of DNA have passed into protein, they cannot get out again. And that is blasphemy. Necromancy is blasphemy. Reincarnation is blasphemy.

But the Green Man is a tree. He becomes Martin's walking-stick. Florentine becomes Martin becomes Jack who was Puck. The stories fuse. Mitosis is blasphemy. Mitosis vs meiosis dividing and dividing.

The anabolic steroid energy of antlers adds to the spelle. The sex within green energy recycles her in present-day; the love within green energy recycled the new baby in medievalia. She's kick-started reincarnation on her way to save her child.

We are all the green man. Or green woman. You know what I mean. O, Florentine wrote this all to Jack in blackletter German letters in order to communicate on his terms, wrongly guessing an East German spy affiliation when he was merely a hidden nut squirreled away by her own subconscious. And as we know, Jack had a pattern of ignoring passenger pigeons.

***

Florentine stood on Blue Bell Hill in Kent, her feet scratched with troubling rocks and her hair filled with colours, her knife glistening. *Elijah, elijah,* the running waters. She took her jack-knife and it caught the sun; her face reflected was not upside-down as in spoons, her face reflected was already properly there in the dangerous lake of the knife. The sun glittering on it; she tasted the turquoise blue of the universe, the symphony of the colour red, *we are all synaesthetes, touch the knife.*

A succession of slaughters went through Florentine's mind as she raised that blade, of her own sacrificing ancestors: nine animals, women in blue robes, men in white robes, serfs branded by irons. It was summer now, nearing Litha. She banned such kinfolk from her mind. The sun rained down; she heard it. She shaved her mons pubis and her feet and under her arms and her limbs and finally her head: Florentine the Egg.

Florentine's hair murmured approvingly to her from the bundle on the ground, but she ignored the flattery and added to it Martin's locks. The hair-stuff all laid flat now on a spread bruce-branch, threads catching in the needles. She cross-hatched it and wove it together intertwined with green leaves, too, a skill taught by mothers and fathers. This took all of early morning. There was no tapestry *pattern* to speak of, but when finished the mat glittered red-gold in the

sunlight. Good enough to thatch a house, and hopefully sufficient for the broth. *This is the house that Jack built.*

Next she placed upon the newly woven mat the two
bundles of glossopteris ferns sourced from Antarctica itself
in a time when the land was not frozen but where now
snakes should freeze, once upon a time glossopteris (so fun
to pronounce!) there grew. O, once a upon a time we were all
united on Pangaea. Now Florentine gave these flowers to the
magick spelle. She added a few bluebells to boot.

Now for another ingredient. O, on the top of Blue
Bell Hill the sun called to her; her fingers tasted the insects
she had gathered just last night on a dream-sojourn to
Alaska, where she had stood and watched 413 mosquitoes
perform a synchronised swim through the air and then shut
her eyes to her own cruelty (for every spelle requires a sacrifice enforced on others: consider here the sadism the scientist
Weismann inflicted by cutting off 68 mice tails to prove cell
differentiation over generations). Thinking of the greater
good, thinking of a small infant who wept green tears, she
clapped. She smelled the texture of their annihilation on her
own hands and she was as culpable as her murderous ancestors now. Four hundred and thirteen tiny lives snuffed out.
The greater good, though not by the perspective of the individual mosquito. She placed the mosquitoes on the mat.

Next she placed the dead little borametz on the
woven hair-sheath. From some angles the little doll looked
like a lamb, and from some angles it looked like a man.
Mostly it looked like a piece of dried root; cook it with pars-

ley, sage, rosemary and spacetime. So she added parsley, sage, rosemary and spacetime for good measure. All good cooks improvise. It is the truth.

The sun spoke. She heard the flavours of it, top, bottom, up, down, strangeness, charm, the turquoise-flavoured ice-cream cone of the galaxies, the jumbled-up jellies of musical symphonies; her fingers smelled the sounds of the wind on the top of Blue Bell Hill. It was all there, all there but the antlers. She gave to the assembled heap her childhood set, torn from her with the death of her parents, and then she offered the antlers of her adolescence, bleeding in a forest, and then the crumpled doe-horn and even the wooden set too, for good measure. She added too the wer-moose horns of multiple Jack-mooses from an infinite number of Jack-moose dimensions. To gather these wer-moose horns she had travelled as recently as that very morning, through deserts, through caves, through dangerous underwater lakes, *I have cut off your moose horns, go back to the beginning of the book and begin all over again.* Alces alces was the largest extant member of the deer family and therefore a man-moose was a wer-stag qualifier. Yes, indeed. She added the oft-stolen curling, too, *beam, palm, bez, trez, royal, surroyal, advancer, monarch, imperial*, that very curl off the third pair she still now wore.

And now that knife, that we mentioned right from the beginning. That knife and its duty.

Bluebells, and that sour gummibear taste when you looked straight at them, and the sun roaring, Florentine's mouth hearing it all in a deoxyribonucleic acid trip. Florentine took the knife.

For the third time in her life (for the second time in third person), she severed her own horns. Her bald head rapidly became splattered with blood. As she was bald, so could one also see the wounds in more stark prominence, compared to when she had her fur.

Now she was hornless. The sun. The bluebirds. The rising snakes. Her hairless, hornless body. A rock was sufficient to break down her own antlers, and powdering the others took through the night into the next afternoon. She was thirsty and she smelled the dark colours of the night; she could see the rustle of the darkness and her arms ached from lactic acid, not just deoxyribonucleic acid. She did not sleep. No one stayed with her. She was alone. She undertook too the distillation of borametz blood cooked by bonfire in the murky hours, borametz blood bubbling up in an alchemical beaker until the honey turned blue. She did not need the death of fireflies, for she had been complicit in the death of the good mosquitoes. Once the borametz blood was honeyified and blueified, she returned to pummelling the horns and antlers to pulver.

The powder complete, she poured it over ferns and flowers, over the thatched hair. The borametz honey she also poured into the mix, a slow and stately languorous pour by which honey so often shows off. She set it all alight. All ingredients – the hair; the fern; the flowers; the mosquitos; the parsley, sage, rosemary and spacetime; the boiled borametz honey; the anabolic steroid IGF-1 insulin by way of the antlers – all the ingredients burst into a bonfire, and the flames were turquoise, hot pink, green, violet. Yet the spelle lacked a ninth animal. We all know what animal that is, but she could not bring herself to kill another human; it had been bad enough with the owls and mosquitoes as of late and bad enough for sure with all the sacrifices, big and small, that she had made in her life between those points.

The spelle did not go. And then it did. As luck happened, the mosquito-bodies carried human blood in them themselves; she understood now why they were allowed as a recipe substitute, for their vampiric little selves had sucked up blood from a totality of nine different animals: owl, rat, crow, bat, wasp, frog, toad, snake and _____. She had been waiting for the ninth animal. We all know what that animal is. The ninth animal found sacrificed in the mosquito corpses was burnt and the fire flew up and she tasted it all in the smoke. Enough human blood to kick off the languages of snakes. Now the snakes, they all came slithering. *Do this in memory of me.* Human. Florentine was 33 years old.

The serpent in the stew. As Eve tasted it from the tree, as the cook tasted it in its broth. Intoxicated with life whilst living, as the Gnostics theorise. She could not see eternalism, but that did not mean it was not there. And not just the snake. From the sacrifice of the ninth animal, she understood at last the *languages* of snakes. Knowledge, all knowledges, the languages of snakes all the way back to Eden, knowledge coursing through her, knowledge of the world, of DNA, of evolution, of science. She was the split-off pieces of the Divine.

Florentine stood up, resplendent, the air whirling in fractals around her, the fire flowers blue, green, pink and violet where she stood in the middle.

This magick spelle of Juliana's, would it ever work? Oh, it ever would. Florentine grew a pair of spectral antlers. She was whole and furred again, pronged lightning from her skull. She remembered Cyprine's kisses. She remembered Robin's kisses.

Things calmed. She stood balanced on a steady hill and she wore a steady pair of imperial horns. Her red-gold pelt was back, not just spectral, but all over, and she patted it approvingly. She was Florentine the Wild and she was ready to begin.

Or this, or this. You can choose now a different adventure. You have been waiting for the ninth animal. You can take up the sword, but it's not clear whether you are Sir Gawain or the Green Knight.

You can kneel before a stone to remove a blade – perhaps it is the snake-witch stone of Gotland, Sweden of circa 500 AD, which depicts a female figure with a snake in each hand and over her floats an eagle, a wolf, a boar. In fact, your spread-leg position also is quite similar to the horned shaman on the Kelto-Scando Gundestrup Cauldron of Himmerland, Denmark of circa 250 AD, a cross-legged individual who also holds a snake in his hands while surrounded by bull, stag, boar, lion, dolphin, ibex, hound; you see how it all fits together, it all fits together. A snake in each hand is worth four in the bush.

With your treasured jack-knife – the knife you used to cut off your horns hanging in the tree, the knife you used to sever Jack the Borometz, and the knife you used for all variable antler cuttings – you will now finally ultimately completely lastly use to cut the throat of the snake (the bird). You put it all together, you do the spelle. You purposefully kill the snake (the bird) at the climax of the spelle. Now you will understand the languages of birds. Is this what you wanted? Is it worth going back to the beginning and doing it again?

You know what? It doesn't matter. What happens next is what happens next.

Over Florentine's head, as she stood there on the hill was a roar entering her ears that she had heard before. Here comes the Wild Hunt in the skies. Here comes Cernnunos, horned like Florentine, or perhaps he *is* Florentine on another bifurcation. Here comes the Horned One called Herne the Hunter; here come his huntsmen, too, all drunk on angel shares, whiskey evaporations; all using Lush Angels on Bare Skin cleanser full of ground almonds, rose, chamomile, clay and lavender. He has his full throng with him – the boars, the birds, the snakes, the bugs, the bears, the wolves, the hounds, the minks. Their muzzles are bloody. Even the mosquitoes, even the mosquitoes' mouths are bloody. They have torn her, they have bullied her, they have terrified her, they have ravaged her.

But what happens if Florentine looks skyward? She stretches her arms wide, snakes invisible in each hand, and she tilts back her head. The weight of her antlers drags her head back, heavy lies the, etc. She meets the eyes of the Hunt full-on. She does not bow her head. She knows the beasts and they know her. She can heal their pain, for she is stag. She can heal their pain, for she is tree. She has tasted frog, so she speaks the languages of boars; she has tasted snake, so she understands the languages of birds; she has tasted human, so she understands the languages of snakes; she has tasted bat, so she understands the languages of bees; she has tasted wolf, so she understands the languages of bears; she has tasted rat, so she understands the languages of wolves; she has tasted bees, so she understands the languages of hounds; she has tasted lizard, so she understands the languages of minks; she has tasted egg, so she understands the languages of humans. Such transference is well known, just as when sickened folk nail their shorn hair unto a tree, and as the tree heals so do they. The tree of life and the leaves of the tree for the healing, Revelation 22:2. She hears the tableau of their claws and beards and fangs; she listens to this sight of them as a painter hears her painting. She smells their ruddy complexions, their greenness and the bloodlust in them as a scholar smells his language, as we dream of glossopteris with many tongues. Perhaps a dream where you have the turquoise ice cream of the universe all over your face, and where your mother walks into the room, sees you and then laughs. You have gone down on the lush creamy cunt of the universe, the pussy of the universe, the turquoise pleasure of its galaxies is there for all to see.

Florentine guides the Wild Hunt, Wild Hunt, Wild Hunt. She's the only one with horns now; it's always only been her up there in the sky. Jack the little boy in the *Choose Your Own Adventure* book watches Florentine release herself from the wooden cage. And her freedom causes an explosion, a singularity or a multidivisibility. Now it is the time for all the horns in this spelle to release their power. She has saved their potency for this future, recycling her animal self in a closed system, and now this loving future gives birth to Gerald the egg. Phoenix, ash, egg left over from the spelle. Everything divides again and somewhere in the world Gerald is born.

Florentine is Jack is Martin is Ghost is Green Man is Stick is Witch is Therapist is Hermodike. Egg is Bird is Simorgh is Snake is Dinosaur is Baby is Eglentyne is Gerald is Merlin is Galileo. It can blend together even more, fusing personalities into a tight dense cosmic seed. Florentine is Snake. Witch is Bird. Jack is Baby. Parents are teachers. Three sons are three suns.

The blue-green egg cracks from its singularity.

A mysterious blue-green egg begins to grow...

12

Green Woman

The Wild Hunt rumbled across the clouds, thunder, sunshine, and Florentine flew strong within the gang of animals.
She held in her left hand a serpent, which periodically turned
into the Green Man's prick, and she held in her right hand a
serpent, which periodically turned into a wooden staff. All
animals equals – bees, hounds, minks, boars, birds, snakes,
bears, wolves – not beings over whom she had dominion.
She spoke their languages, and those who spoke hers (those
who had eaten of the blue-green cosmic egg, whether scram-
bled or fried) translated for others, and those others translated between them.

"I am Cernnunnos. The Horned God. Or the Horned
Goddess, if you're nasty," Florentine told her fellow lin-
guists. "Maybe a Stagtress. I am not some middling female
opposite without the power, but the original cosmic egg.
Since the vestigial state for reptiles and therefore mammals
is female, the male organ is in development rather an over-
grown clitoris, as it happens, as noted by Kilchevsky *et al.*
2012."

"*Buck, puck, phuck, fuck,*" the white birds called, far
above the Wild Hunt.

"*Kent, cunt, hunt,*" the white birds called, far above the
Wild Hunt.

The bells are ringing. People-beasts and other beasts,

the million split pieces of the divine. The taste of the serpent in the stew.

The Lady of Wild Things (where the wild things are) is born at Yule, marries at Beltane, dies at Litha, born again at Yule once more. Just as Solomon Grundy is born on a Monday, is christened on Tuesday, marries on Wednesday, takes ill on Thursday, grows worse on Friday, dies on Saturday, is buried on Sunday and that is the end of Solomon Grundy. Except it isn't really, because Solomon Grundy was born on a Monday, and so *ad infinitum*.

There is an egg, and in that egg you'll find a seed, and from that seed will grow a tree, and on that tree you'll find a branch, and on that branch there is a nest, and in that nest there sits a bird, and under that bird there lies an egg. This was indeed the house, and not the hound nor the horn, that belonged to the forest-farmer sowing his corn that fed the blue bird that crew in the morn that woke the priests all shaven and shorn that married the man all tattered and torn that kissed the maiden all forlorn that milked the doe with the crumpled horn that tossed the hound that killed the wife that ate the owl that lay cooked in the house that Jack built. And this was indeed the house, and not the hound nor the horn, that belonged to the forest-farmer sowing his corn. *Cernnunoswildmanhollykingoakkingludgreenknightviridiosgreen-georgeenkidufatherchristmas*

There was three suns come out o' the east their fortunes for to try. And these three suns made a solemn vow. John Barleycorn must die. To everything there is a season. A time to be born, and a time to die. A time to plant; a time to raise the harvest high. And on and on we go.

In the end, it doesn't matter. The Wild Hunt continued with Florentine triumphant. She led it whether hunter or hunted. The winds grumbled on.

"I hear Jack has built a thatched cottage house of red-gold hair," said the lefthand snake conversationally, "do you know the reason why?"

Even in the midst of the roar of the winds and the clouds, Florentine tilted her head left.

"I wasn't addressing you," the snake said rudely. It looked pointedly toward the righthand snake. Despite her irritation, Florentine relaxed her grips so they could talk without effort, for she was curious. She was the disobedient fairy-tale cook, eavesdropping on birds. She eavesdropped on the Cailleach, flying screeching through the sky.

"I do not know," admitted the snake in Florentine's right hand as the Wild Hunt moved across the skies, screeching, bellowing, braying, the world beneath them all, beneath all nine of animals. *Satyrsasquatchbigfoottlalocdergcorrafaceofgloryamoghasiddifaunuspashupatikokopellipangu*

"To keep a version of his self safe, they say," said the lefthand snake. "So whisper many. I once ate salamander, and so I understand the languages of trees, and they are certainly gossiping. Shouldn't we, the trees, have a ruler, that's what the olive tree said to the palm tree. I suggested the Green King – I suppose a Green *Queen* at present – but the trees were having none of it. At least not the palm tree, who was a communist and declined the general idea of a monarch overall in every way."

"That's the way trees are," the righthand snake mused. "I wouldn't know on palm or olive ones, for they are southern sorts, so I can only speak for the bruces, spirches and greys up here. But so far as I've seen that is the arboreal socialist *modus operandi*."

"Ah yes," said the lefthand snake, "I forgot you were from around these parts. Tell me, was that you on the Gundestrup Cauldron..." And on and on they went. Florentine wondered whether the king who killed the crested queen of snakes to understand the languages of birds had found avian as well as snakely conversations to be of a superficial bent. Likely not, for the Witch had said that birds knew Hegel... *jacko'lanternjesusmaykinghernewoodwosepilosiyetisnow-mandusiosinuusfiggyschratsylvester*

If Florentine could have glanced at her watch, she would have at this point, but as it happened she owned no watch and was airborne above all trees with eight other animal types and her hands were busy grasping a snake in each fist.

It was at this point, however, that the conversation of the snakes finally got interesting.

"It's rather obvious," the iconic righthand snake was saying, "that in the double-slit experiment we see that light can act both as a particle and a wave. And further quantum experiments have quite explicitly suggested that we can change the outcome of an electron's path merely by observing it, that such electrons can go back and change the past based on a future not yet experienced, and that pairs or groups of particles can become entangled with each other, affecting each other though not connected in any Newtonian sense of physics. That is, at least, how I understand it."

"Don't doubt it," said the former Apep, snake god of the Egyptians, now known as the lefthand snake, "have you seen the chops on the Midgard serpent? Norse legend, mate. Now I'd like to get entangled with *her*."

The winds continued lifting up the Hunt amongst the clouds; Florentine reckoned they still were somewhere over Kent, but was not sure. The snakes chattered on and despite their alternating inanity and complexity – pretty much what you'd expect from snakes, admit it – she listened to them. One of them was now propositioning the other, whether male or female she knew not in either direction. Snakes such as the golden lancehead snake can indeed be hermaphroditic. Orisis himself would be fond of such golden qualities applied to such phallic qualities. Brigid the Cailleach herself is the patron saints of serpents and of holy wells. The lefthand snake continued chatting up the righthand. Lefty had claimed to be a former lothario; this was now proving to have been an accurate self-assessment. Florentine stared straight ahead as a stately Lady of the Hunt, god Cernnunos, Stagtress, etc, etc. *leshyorcojackfrostalkhidrsylvanuspeterpanjackinthegreen* But she was listening.

"We could entangle and merge right now, even," the lefthand snake was saying brazenly.

"I don't know," said the righthand snake, blushing, shy. Or maybe it was just a copperhead, genus *Agkistrodon*, species *contortrix*.

"Don't be coy," Apep said in a coaxing voice. "It's really easy. Just bite my tail, and I'll bite yours. We'll be a double-ouroboros."

The righthand snake fluttered its lidless eyelashes. "You're very convincing. Was that you in the Garden?"

"It was," the lefthand snake said modestly.

"And as Kaa in the Disney movie *The Jungle Book*?"

"The very same."

"Well..." The righthand snake considered the matter at hand. Florentine held her breath but pretended to ignore them both. Was that some fire down below? Something was happening down on the ground. "Okay!" The righthand snake decided at last. "Let's entangle!"

And in this manner did the two heraldic snakes form a double ouroboros, a loop, a wheel, a doubled snake, an entangled pair whirling, and Florentine attempted to hold this great circle, this burning shining loop within her hands, rotating brilliant white hot heat like from the sun, the snakes spinning faster and faster... In the ash twists a green snake, a serpent born from hot ash that becomes phoenix that gives a jeweled egg that births a snake that evolves to birds that lay those orbs that split to snakes to birds to eggs to snakes to birds to eggs to birds to snakes. An ouroboros, a circle spinning –

"Stop!" cried Florentine. "What's that happening

down below?"

"It appears that the peasants are attacking fields," Lefty remarkd again, "how unusual. Of course in the Middle Kingdom, we had slave rebellions from time to time, so I recognise the signs."

Florentine held the Hunt within her horns, and she also held tight to the idea of a new Egg called Gerald. But she looked down anyway.

She could not see. But birds' eyes were keener, and they told her and, after all, she understood the languages of birds.

"Down below," said an eagle, "down below the tax offices do burn most purposefully."

"Yes, I see the fire in the scarp," Florentine remarked with irritation – the winds did blow – "but who is there? Who is it that does the burning?"

"A-ha," said the eagle again, "I recognize the individual in question. I came across him in an anti-secular lobbying group previously. The preacher John Ball. He whips them into a frenzy."

This, for some reason, irritated Florentine even more. "Should they not be whipped up into a frenzy, then?" She found it hard to hold the Hunt; hold the thought of the growing egg; hold her anger.

"Pay the eagle no mind," clarified a hawk, "conservative leanings. Default symbol by U.S. Republicans for years. I was too, come to think of it. 'Hawkish' leanings. But I assure you I'm a pacifist."

Birds were as conversationally tangential as snakes, witches or frogs. "But *who* is down there; what is their aim?"

"Do you not pay attention to national concerns?" The hawk at least was more to the point than the eagle.

"I have been preoccupied with other matters, such as reversing the inevitable destination of death. And also metaphorically as well as literally enacting the entire story of our being from the first cosmic singularity egg of the cosmos to its rebirth."

"Okay, since you've been napping –" The hawk was unimpressed.

"I haven't been napping –"

"Since you've been napping, you should be informed what it is that all others know by now, and that is that as even teenage vassals have been outrageously coerced for coin, the serfs have been refusing to pay their shillings as far as Essex; that the lords have been accused of bringing in plague-ships to stop the rebellion – actually, I can see it now, the bright little ball in the distance, yep, they're burning Essex, too, good riddance – and that the tax offices have been torched and all books as well – "

"All books?" Florentine thought of the library at the top of the inn – *I was branded for non-compliance to the old serf rates*, she heard Cyprine saying in her head – was this for the best?

"And if you had been listening properly to the whispers, Florentine," her righthand snake now chimed in, its tail coiling insinuatingly round her wrist, "the whispers throughout the forest, by the bees, the snakes, the swine – if you had been genuinely listening instead of pursuing some esoteric resurrection-*cum*-birth angle of your own, you would have known all this; the signs were there. Now the craftsmen have joined the serfs, and some officials and soldiers too, all following the mad priest of Kent, all protesting the tolls of pavage, pontage, cheminage, scutage, haulage, wastage, murage, stallage, pannage, scalage and tronage, sake and soke. So the rumours have it –"

Below the Hunt, the smoke twisted, a campfire seen from a great distance. Florentine yearned again to know the actions within the smoky underneath. "Psst," she said to her ally the hawk again, ignoring eagle and snakes, "describe for me who you can see on the ground." The clouds were icy cold but below them Kent was burning.

"There is a great number of people," the hawk reported, "I see a man in a cowl, perhaps a monk, perhaps it is a nun, perhaps a monk, perhaps a nun, it is difficult to say; I see a family setting barns alight, mother, father, children, all laughing uproariously; I see the tinkers all infuriated; I see a maid with black braids; and a reeve of all things; and there's the sendal torse of a Forestish Blue Sister too amongst them all, maiden, mother, crone, I cannot tell; I see a woman with horns like yours, my Lady, and with her an old wizard watching; I see a building under siege, perhaps a Spital, for it seems most manor and religious houses are targeted; I see a good deal of farm animals making their escapes since their fences have been burnt – how odd, there seems to be two goats staying within the throng and not escaping, goats dressed up in little red outfits mocking priests, how odd, but then all good folk enjoy blasphemy, I suppose; I know we birds of prey certainly do. We are great friends of Rabelais as well as Hegel; we are very enlightenmenty educated. Moving on. The mob grows close to Savoy Palace, the smoke's becoming thicker, and I cannot make out anything more due to this obfuscation. I am CE Thomas Hawk reporting from KHOK nightly news, signing off," the bird concluded triumphantly.

"Well then, we must go down," said Florentine, "and we must help them. Not right that they force pay. Or that they brand. I have thought it for a while. Anyone with a conscience or reason would think it. My brothers, my friends – "

"We cannot interfere," all the animals said in chorus. "We have never interfered before."

"What can we do?" Her hands started to shake. She could drop the snakes. She could let the spelle that concocted Gerald dissipate. Let the snakes fall from her hands, power leaks out, the fall to earth.

"I'll tell you how it goes," said the double-snake. "I've been here once before and now it loops around again. Yesterday the prisons were opened and today the palace burns, and then tomorrow the child-king will meet the rebels and agree to all they ask. And then the next day the powerful break all their promises (though just as the rebels would, too); the child-king appeals to to the peasants with a populist

"*I am your king, I will be your leader. Follow me into the fields*"
and they buy it, they all do. Meanwhile there is chopping
of heads, severings of loops. I never said it was pretty. And
then by midsummer most of the rebels are dead. I've seen
this happen before, loop-de-loop. It all comes round again."

"But those people-beasts below as well," protested
Florentine. "It is not just the people-beasts who are queens
and kings and bishops who matter, but the front row of
the chess game, too." The stag-girl vomits coins: shillings,
angels, groats, nobles, ryals. She does not weep gold and
roses. This depiction of a stag expulsing capitalism is seen
on the antiquitous Niederkorn-Turbelslach seal but, ah,
never gives a nod to the other bad isms, does it; there's the
rub; it's not enough. Florentine recovered, wiped her mouth,
though the winds and cloudstuff still pushed through horns,
between her fingers. "We must bifurcate. Mutate. Change
the story." She spoke desperately. "I'll go down in disguise,"
vowed Florentine. "Participate. I'll wear a hood over my
horns."

"Humans are prone to removing both hood and the
horn. And besides, you appear to be down there already,
observing." (Ah yes, that long-ago lesson with Gerald.) The
two snakes, now a circle, spoke in unison and their mouths
were full of tail, but they mumbled dark in a duet: "I know
whereof I speak."

"We cannot just watch." It was the same as when
she'd impotently seen her parents slaughtered, the cutting of
Egentyne's throat. The same as when she'd viewed this fiery

scene unfolding on the ground, whilst on the ground herself. She could watch, but she could not interfere.

Those who refuse to work at cheap rates, the pay as before the blue sickness came; we all have been branded. A snake biting its tail. The ugly dark brown crust of it, but also the false, self-satisfied scar of populism. The Witch's smooth back, lovely in its strength before the red iron crushed down.

"Second chances, new lives and the same people," said Florentine, "the cycle of seasons and nature, new fresh eggs. But what of different paths –"

"Would you break the loop-de-loop?" Not just the snakes looked shocked; the bears, the bees all paused in astonishment. The Wild Hunt, previously driven by mindless wanderlust, by clouds, hovered in the air. Time was frozen, like the whole universe was an ice cube around which we walk to observe. And then it wasn't.

"I think," said Florentine slowly, "I think the witch inside me whispers. The trees inside me whisper."

"The languages of trees," the lefthand snake, muffled, said in a knowing understone.

She was falling from the sky; she spoke blasphemy against the second law of thermodynamics and so she lost her Hunt and animals; she was falling into brush, into moss and into a tree. There was one tree now before her. The Greyfruit Good. She could taste it as she beheld it. *Your sap can cure our dead. Your late-budding leaves slap poultice to our wounds.* A memory, Blue School litany. It perhaps once was a sapling she saved. It perhaps once was a borametz she severed. It perhaps once bore a fruit that a serpent tendered.

She fell from the sky. The rebel angels fell from a rainbow, you know, Lucifer the shining morning star shamed just for seeking knowledge. All bees are angels, yet also messengers from gods. All bees are split-off pieces of all gods. All insects are beautiful, all insects are always beautiful. They followed Florentine as she fell, starry messengers, they turned into fireflies and Post-It notes. The bees accompanied her for most of the fall until she was inches from hitting the ground, then they abruptly flew up to the Hunt again. By the time the bees had lifted and she had hit the ground, she had tasted their melodies; smelt their black-and-gold stripes. She heard the colours gold and crimson. Florentine could feel a golden torc around her neck like the necklace that killed Eglentyne. It was not visible, but by the time she landed stricken near the tree, she could feel it, cold, golden. She had eaten bat, and so she had understood the implications of what the bees had sung to her.

*

Florentine stood before the tree. She was naked but she wasn't really naked. She didn't feel naked and that is important. She was covered with a stag's glossy, fine-haired red-gold pelt. She was only naked if you consider animals to be naked. If you insist on putting trousers on Mickey Mouse. Bipedal, with her fine strong horns. She was not as resplendent perhaps as she had been when leading a bestial throng all-powerful, but there you go.

Overhead the Wild Hunt roared on. Well, she had chosen her own adventure. Yes, she had. She had kickstarted the growth of the egg called Gerald in some other time, perhaps hatching underneath a swan, perhaps dreaming underneath a lake. Yet Gerald was different from Eglentyne was different from her baby. They were all quite surprisingly unique. So she had not cheated death as she had hoped. We always begin again for sure. Yet though we may persist, the stories change. Florentine stood before the tree.

There is a custom, you know. I will tell you of this custom. Many humans undertake to transfer their sickness from human flesh to trees. They do this by attaching pieces of cloth or their fingernails or even hair – they tie onto branches these bits of the diseased humans, or they shove thatched hair into hollows so that the tree in effect "eats" the symbolic human parts. Sometimes they nail up the clothing pieces. Injured, the good tree oozes its version of gore: sap, blood. As the tree heals, and heal it so often does, so does the human heal, slowly, incrementally, with the tree. All in good, good time.

Florentine had her jackknife, once labelled with her name but now missing letters and showing F - E > T - E, tucked up deep inside her. That was always where she kept it. *A cached nut.* She removed it now and, once again, for this second spelle, she sheared her hair and her flensed skin now too. She nailed her whole animal self to the tree to heal the world and change the story. It was clear then that she was no tree. She stood there oozing red, no skin. She was a snake who shed but had no endodermis underneath. Never was there a more vulnerable small bird than Florentine de-skinned. She had coldly gutted the animal that she was. You know how this story of sacrifice goes. They nail us to trees; it causes us to tremble.

Slowly, ever so slowly, the world tree quivered. A little pale sprig pushed through on one of its bruce ever-green branches, more yellow than the old needles, and a sticky leaf was born on one of the spirch boughs. Healing sap gathered round the nail that staked the stag-pelt to the greyfruit trunk, and a borametz-shaped fruit began to stir on yet another. Florentine was healing the world, the narratives pulsed and then shifted, but she was a flensed being, still standing dying, bleeding out. The tree continued its surge to heal the pollution-choked streams, the radiation-soaked meltdowns, the dioxin-clogged air, the lonely dark wound in the ozone, the poverty, the toxic bad-isms too. It pushed out the green energy it had captured up from futures past and borrowed from the present. Florentine had powered herself into it. $F = T$, but $F - E > T - E$. Blasphemy.

The red two-legged stag was bleeding so profusely now from the body shock of losing its organ called skin that it was soon to fall over, but as the loving green sap coaxed a scar from the tree, so did a leaf sprout out as a balm over one of Florentine's bald palms, and then a leaf upon another. Her body grew more foliage, not just fig-leafs over genitalia, and the healing leaves and vines and moss grew over all her shape now, salvaging her. She took a breath and it was the most gorgeously green, photosynthesised breath in the world. The air shuddered beautifully throughout her body. Her hands were leaves and evergreen needles, her mouth was white bark, her limbs were gnarled branches, her blood was pine cones, pollen, cool green sap.

13

The Stagtress

In a black hole, if you go down deep enough, you find a tree. Here time is eternal, according to Einstein's citing of the Schwarzschild solution. A tree grows there in the dark. But in utter blackness, an immortal tree does not grow. Under a bell jar, never branched out. This would break Newton's second law of dynamics and Newton's law of gravitation. Some argue that this is an idealised tree, and therefore exempt from Newtonian law firstly due to the eternal tree's idealised nature and secondly due to the great gravitational pull within such a black garden. But people always make excuses.

Split split split *green man florentine jack martin cernunnos stagtress juliana cyprine hermodike therapist elsa karolina* Split split split, they find each other through the different eras, genders. All the missing elements of the periodic table of elements are filled in: florentinium, jacquesium, martinium, etc. Now, beginning with elysium, the unstable transuranic elements are steadying. Stars now suck up all the galactic helium so that star-voices are high-pitched, peculiar. Radiocarbon dating now shows us that once there was a series of earths on this very same spot where now tugs a black hole. Inside which is a tree. A good tree. The universe is hesitating, indecisive. But now the tree starts to grow again. Some theorise that even in black holes, there must be entropy according to Newton's second law of thermodynamics, i.e. eternity cannot truly exist.

Bluebells, violets and greyfruits grow on this tree, and the lapis lazulis, ultraviolets and silvers shine in the dark. And now things start to join. You can choose your own adventure. *figgy sprat robin green king lady of wild things* Nuclear fission but then fusion and then fusion and then fusion and joining. The million$^\infty$ split sparks of the divine reunify under the Twelfth Arboreal Theorem of Gnostic Eternalism. All knowledge ever known or suspected, all the google$^\infty$ sparks of it is reunited (and it feels so good). For knowledge is the only hint of elysium you've ever known. All the serpents in the stew can be tasted all at once. That's what I call *amore*.

Yet in this version of this world, Florentine pushes together the revolt of peasants, the toxic bad-isms too, the nuclear bomb, the split world. She was healed by the tree that now she helps. Leaves in her mind and leaves on her flesh. She is clit the cosmic egg. This egg reheals its embryo, its albumen. Its shell is the turquoise of turquoise, and sometimes the blue of lapis lazuli. Florentine is quaking, her antler-horns shiver; she is starting.

Florentine is licking at the cunt of the Witch, the turquoise universe ice cream all over her face again; and the Witch's kisses are of violet honey, blue, green, rose on Florentine's tongue, reciprocal altruism as well as reproduction. Florentine's tongue is deep within the Witch's mouth; the Witch's tongues are licking coloured sugars from her lips. Her hands caress witchy creamy tits and the Witch's back – well, the Witch's back is scarred still, because scars tell us we're still alive and healing. A witch's finger is on Florentine's clit, the cosmic egg, the double-slit experiment, and Florentine lapis lazuli-ies at the world, and the world is trembling, earthquaking, nearly there. Soaring into something else, something that smells like rapture, now Florentine is there. And the green man's prick is up inside her, he's shooting out the tree's green sap inside her; the Witch sucks her nipple; the green man kisses her ear; it's rising, it's all rising, it's joining. Jack caresses her breasts and she's caressing herself and Martin is sucking the witch and the witch licks at the green man.

Florentine fucks all the trees; the redwoods of the world inside her sticky tree-sap, dripping dew, dripping waterfalls and rivers. Her head falls back so she can feel the sequoia, the hills; her hands stroke the she is you

Your hands stroke the soft-lilied petals of the world's skin, its violets, its camellias, its soft baby animals of tender wools, soft fur; the world writhes against you, pleasure building up inside it. The leaves come fluttering down as the world peaks (mountain) and continues, sheer climbing bliss, green leaves joy falling as rapture shocks right through you you're him

As rapture shocks right through him, lightning, campfire explosions, the rain, the giddy sex of it, fucking the spirch trees, fucking the greyfruits, the bruces. The tree inside the black hole, the tiny trapped tree bursting into leaf now. It's the same tree he's been making love to, it's you and her and him. The world is orgasming, he'd you'd she'd like to teach the world to sing.

The stars are tickling down his your her arm and he she you are going supernova, bigger banging, quarks gathering again, the singularity over and over again (yes), the icicles of comets heating up (yes), the cosmic eggs hatching, see you in the stars, we're almost there, bees, questions, numbers, DAZLing. Glossopteris is found in Antarctica, for everything was once united on Pangaea. This art whereby you use all your senses all at once, taste, smell, sound, sight, touch unifies the million$^\infty$ split pieces. But yet the tree is fruiting and moving within the black hole. It should be static, blocked-out, eternal. But instead it's growing.

Florentine you he gasps, the final painted tarot card of the aced cup in the act of being turned over and pouring out, kokological birds flying everywhere through the air, all colours, green and gold, blood red, black for sorrow, their feathers pointing upwards like angels, their trajectories branching out like a bomb.

***

Got something to tell you, so oyer and terminer. If mutations show up in linear time as we march on to a never-ending end, eternalism cannot exist as a purity itself. In the words of Mark Twain, history does not repeat itself, but it does rhyme. Unknown syntax, revelation. *Apoca-*

lypsis means "hidden." Each bifurcation is nuance; each merging is nuance.

And saying so, you must have been aware that Florentine has hung on as did the others even when reborn. This suggests lumpiness, not the undiluted uniformity of gnostic eternalism. Perhaps it even can point, like a witch's gnarled admonishing finger, towards free will.

Apocalypsis means "to reveal, to uncover." But I just said it meant "hidden." I never claimed to be a reliable narrator. Yes, it's me. It's been I, the Witch, who has been weirdly lecturing you, the Sceptic, throughout the book. Also at times in the form of a stick. Didn't you ever find the capricious (how Florentine's kin are so fond of that word!) tone to be familiar? You would have been right.

In the Christian biblical text of *Revelation*, the limbs of the tree of life are cut off. The ones who testify to such things say this is coming soon. *Hallelujah*, the most beautiful-sounding word on earth, a word from the tongues of the gods, a word heard only after you have swallowed the full circle of the white snake-segments and tasted wisdom and understand that all the birds are singing *hallelujah* all the time. Come, all gods. Come, one god. One all, all one, multiples joined. The Abrahamic cults got it so, so wrong. One, but never singular. It was always one made up of multiples, and multiples broken free from ones.

And thus said, how on earth shall we heal this tree ravaged by those blinkered by such tunnel-vision? We may not be able, as Florentine did, to nail ourselves to it. But there are other things afoot. Aplant.

The tree buds in the black hole; its limbs have their fingers out, almost touching the event horizon, creeping over that lid that keeps time solid. Almost there. The tree has been growing for 13.8 billion years and it is already much bigger than the Milky Way. It is no longer just a world tree – our own tunnel-vision again – but a galaxy tree. No, a universe tree. No, a multiverse tree. Other things aplant.

yeti jack frost robin goodfellow jack o' lantern cernunnos jesus sinuus john barleycorn attis green george snowman

Bluebells that wear snake sauces. On

the tree inside the black hole now come
the morning leaves. Through which dart
bluebirds. All said, this one shorn moment
of the universe whilst all others rode
the winds of a great Hunt outside this
diorama. Juliana says naught in her spellebook of the crumpled house, that the
cook ate of birds. Naught of that plotted
attack as the snakes fold into the universe. That tax-office priests of colours
gold and blood lie tattered in borametz
honey.

For inside the black hole, by the
tree, there is a cabin, further, a lake,
further, a forest, further, a land, further, a globe, further, a galaxy, further,
a universe, further. The house is built;
ring the bells. The May Lord is shaved
backwards as we move towards our summer.
It is midsummer day. The forest inside the
black hole is sown early with flowers; the
leaves change.

***

Florentine sees a living babe on the ground amongst the
mosses and the roots. She runs to it and it smiles. It was
once her newborn in the glade. Once a girl who died young.
Now Gerald is here, though she thought she lost him with

the Hunt. The greyfruits sway around a cabin, fireflies buzz and play between her antlers. She takes the baby up in her arms, and he coos. Her nipples leak milk. One day he will sleep beneath a lake. But not yet.

She holds the baby. Her begifted leaves have returned to thick russet stag hairs across her body's skin. No pattens, no aketon. One day soon her lover will come, a cool young witch with a literal spring to her step. Once a sapling that grew in the woods. Once a walking-stick. The Witch's kiss will taste of coloured sugars. But for now Florentine holds the new baby safely and tightly; walks away from the cabin until she reaches the shore. She looks down into the dangerous lake. In her reflection she sees Martin, and then Jack. All three of them are horned. All faces, all times crunched into eternalism. You'd think. But the tree in the black hole somehow is still growing. Florentine must blink hard to view just herself and the babe. It takes some will, but finally she sees herself and her fine stag-antlers, holding a small Gerald. The infant gurgles. Perhaps already he has taken to the environment of lakes.

***

Jack walks a modern London street, straight past his therapist's clinic. Jack remembers everything now, so he has no need of therapists.

pan derg sylvester is that the same

doe who sowed Martin is that the same doe
who married the figgy who horn-tossed the

Nope, Jack has no need of therapists
per se. Instead he is intent on meeting his therapist the *person*, Herr Doktor
Jimmy von Schneeball. For it became clear
to Jack at some point in the fantasti-
cal dream desert that while Jack might
have lost his wife Hermodike - codename
flower Lavendel, and lost his little daughter, too, lost them both to the vaga-
ries of spacetime interference - that the
therapist also was pining for his wife
Frau Doktor Elsa Karolina Schneeball, and
Doktor Elsa was most likely equally fictive, Jack reasoned, lost in quite similar
crypto-medieval phantasmacosmomagicali-
therapeutagoria. Furthermore, even if the
wife was real, Jack could always attempt
Jimmy's no doubt amusing, meaningful and
most importantly narcissistic seduction.
The therapist and Jack just had so much in
common. They were two sides of the same
coin. Three sides, if Jack thought about
it too much, which he didn't. *oak king*
that lay cooked in the house an undevoured
owl a new owl is unexplained

Jack will remember this time to tell

Gerald when he sees the old man dripping
water in an alley, and Gerald, many years
later, will tell Florentine all that Jack
knows. And now this world changes. Jack
has made note. Jack has made Post-It note.
His act may have wobbled matters. No black
helicopters in the sky, they've flown off
everywhere through the air, their feathers pointing upwards like angels, and he
hadn't even got(ten) to the day when he
meets the little girl Florentine in a
newsagent's yet.

Jack's date with the therapist in a
dingy North London Starbucks breaks all
laws of client-based therapeutic practice-
dynamics, but Jack smiles to himself, for,
let's face it, Jack may love sincerely but
Jack has remembered that he is cocky cock-
robin at heart.

Just now, for instance, right at this
moment, Jack can see the therapist-cum-
love-target through the window, seated
above the salt on a banker eating blank-
manger and frumenty. The therapist taps
his triple-sunned watch. Jack grins cheek-
ily, and makes sure to duck as he passes
the door-frame's threshold. Today he'll
call himself "Saint Figgy." Everywhere the

white ladies call from the skies and the
seasons do crest. Jack Frost, king of big-
bang, this world with its wounds and trajectories, the cuts and corroborations.

$$* * *$$

That this is the house, not the, that belonged to the corn
married the man all that fed crumpled horn the blue bird that
crew in the morn that woke the priests all shaven that tattered and torn that hound nor the horn kissed the maiden all
forlorn that milked the doe forest-farmer sowing his with the
that tossed the hound that killed the wife and shorn that ate
the owl Jack built.

     Martin chants that this is the house to himself as he
walks the bright desert hides and hundreds, holding a tree
in full summer-bloom. For Martin's never been happier. He
has his old friend the stick. He has a fine set of goat horns
atop his head. This is a good thing because he always felt a
little left out *vis-à-vis* Jack and then Florentine *white ladies*
forest-farmer ishtar isis viridios bigfoot basajaun simorgh
popol vuh pixie homme sauvage goblin peter pan pilosi
dusio And Martin's even got a mission. He's been tasked
by an old wizened version of Florentine to ring the bluebells
of the recovered oasis to get young Florentine's attention
through the centuries as she stands on a lakeshore with the
Witch sometimes called Juliana, discussing the properties
of the cosmos but still has yet to do the spelle. She's hesi-

tating. Through the aeons, multiverses and carucates, Martin will remind her. His message will arrive with this sound, apocalyptic bluebells, leper bells of glass. When he pushes the stamens of the bells together to make their voices call, guillotines and high-stakes flocks of birds escape. Martin has eaten glossopteris, and so he understands the languages of bluebells.

The holy night-blooming cacti are everywhere. The holy night-blooming cacti are holy day-blooming cacti. The desert is almost entirely an oasis now; the vista turns lush in bloom, but he knows where he's going. To the saintly oasis with a holy well fed by a lake, and he'll be turning a cold shoulder to saints such as Patrick who drove out the snakes. Such personalties are a distraction, a nothing-burger, as the Americans say. Martin has a job to do. And that job is to ring the bells.

Call Martin to come in with the doe, should the forest require a snakey sauce with its egg, should the Oak Lord require an Eve with his apples. Soups and honeys, my goodfellow. Call Martin to come in with the honey. Call Martin into this house, the cuts and the owl. Only the Oak Lord can hear via bluebells; call Martin to ring the bluebirds louder. The white ladies are brooding, squatting down to give lay to protons, gravity and bluebells. Call Martin in this with sound, the apocalyptic bluebells are ringing, the priests of the universe are riding

***

little girl carving her name

*****

man with no memory

*****

youth walking burnt sands

*****

goats screaming in mudmonth

*****

nine – eight – seven –

*****

stripling walks with sapling

*****

old horned woman with old scarred witch

*****

hermodike maia gaia fange holzmoia ostara fauna lamia pela hamadryad ishtar isis and now traffic-signal green man helps thera-pist across street, perchance to bed

*****

horny Martin beds down with stick after fine day's work of
bell-ringing in the green world

***

the boars, the birds, the snakes, the humans, the bees, the
bears, the wolves, the hounds, the minks nine animals three
sacrifices times three the coloured greyfruit joy and sorrow
and surprise and anger and glow the kokological birds break
free from the tarot game and all such cages everywhere
through the air, all colours, green and gold, blood
red, black for sorrow, their feathers pointing
upwards like angels, their trajectories branching out like
an explosion the colours gold blood branch green
break

*

Florentine stands, baby sleeping on the grass besides her,
witch coming to her someday soon between the leaves.
Those lost and loved still beside her and the wind's flute
music across, between her hands and horns. Her babe on the
ground, safe enough to leave him giggling and sticking fingers in the mouth; he's only a gesture away. And so Florentine purposefully closes her eyes, stretches her fingers, feels
her limbs and her horns, her nursing teats. There is a flicker
of shadow-play from an interrupting sun and her eyes flash
open, but nothing there. Soon now.

She keeps her eyes wide. She is clothed by pelt and a ring around her neck not of blooded wire, not of birthmarks. The torc is made of leaves off the great tree itself. Golden leaves from autumn, pale yellow-green teenagers from spring, dark-vert summer beauties and the absence of leaves from winters many, the spectral gaps that allow us, as with music, to relish the pauses.

This colourful leaf torc hangs from her neck and extends to her antlers. You may observe such a necklace on the Cernnunos sculpture of Étang-sur-Arroux, the hornèd Gundestrup cauldron and also on the Pillar of the Boatman in the first century of our lord.

The bluebells are ringing. Do you act?

The birds are flying. Do you restart the world?

The Witch has arrived. The coloured sugars of DNA on her tongues absolutely will stain yours if they do touch: wild rose, blue violet, forget-me-not, forestish.

Do you kiss her back? If so,

THE END.

THANK YOUS & ACKNOWLEDGEMENTS

Thank you to the *Under Trees: The Germans and the Forest* exhibition. I spontaneously visited a friend in Berlin in the New Year of 2012 and loved this art show. Though the anachronistic Heptarchic forests in *The Stagtress* are Celtic and Angle-ish rather than continental Teutonic, the idea of a little girl with stag antlers was kickstarted there and I began making notes for *The Stagtress* in a hipster Kreuzberg café that very evening of New Year's Day, aware I was taking part in a pretentiously situated act both environmentally and temporally but cheerfully inspired nonetheless.

Thank you to my fine editor James Chapman and to the fine Fugue State Press. It is amazing that a truly experimental press has existed for so long and I am honoured to take part as its alchemy bubbles forth into the future.

Thanks to antlered early readers: Liz Barnes, Conor Gibson, Matthew Gwynfryn Thomas, Veronika Thiel, Liz Fitzsimon, the Hackney & East London Writers' Circle.

Thank you to the following written works and one musical work for inspiration:

Medieval People by Eileen Power (1924),

The Golden Bough: A Study in Comparative Religion by James George Frazer (1890),

Penguin Dictionary of Religions by John R. Hinnells (1984),

The Jutish Forest: A Study of the Weald of Kent by Ken P. Witney (1976),

Life Before Life: A Scientific Investigation of Children's Memories of Previous Lives by Jim B. Tucker (2005),

The *Choose Your Own Adventure* book series of my early adolescence (1979-1998).

"The Blue Bird," © Tadahiko Nagao and Isamu Saito, founders of kokology, I.V.S. Television Co., Ltd., and Yomiuri Telecasting Corporation, 2000.

"The 36 Questions That Lead to Love," © Daniel Jones for *The New York Times*, 2015.

The Medieval Society's Feudalism and Manorialism Vocabulary List.

The Great Hospital's article on medieval hospitals (http://www. thegreathospital.co.uk).

Haque magazine no. 3 (2014) and no. 4 (2015), the bi-annual magazine by the Hackney & East London Writers' Circle, published earlier versions of chapters 1, 9 and 10 (the latter two in a vastly different form) under the titles *"The Stagtress* — excerpt" and "The Hagiography." I read the former aloud at North London's Mascara Bar at the *Haque* launch in 2014. I read "The Hagiography" twice in 2015 as a slide-based performance piece at London's APT Gallery and Brussels' ZSenne Art Lab as part of Teststrip's *Need & Error* visual art and film exhibition (thank you, Seeta and Iffy).

[Post hoc: an unusual and moving 2015 dream and the issues raised for me in writing *The Stagtress* regarding eternalism and quantum entanglement later led me on an intellectual adventure in 2017, after I was done writing *The Stagtress* earlier that year. This excursion meant I read about some of psychologist Daryl Bem's psi experiments (previously I had only known Bem for his evolutionarily sound sexual orientation theory called the Exotic Becomes Erotic theory and as the husband of gender theorist Sandra Lipsitz Bem), as well as a book on eternalism called *An Experiment with Time* by J. W. Dunne (1927) — I mention these inspirations in a time-moving-backwards sense, rather than just time-going-forwards sense, in the spirit of both *The Stagtress* and Bem and Dunne's hypotheses.]

Harry Christopher and the Sixteen's beautiful, soaring *The Rose and The Ostrich Feather: Eton Choirbook, Volume I* (1990) and their amazing version of "Magnificat" kept me sane (along with the help of good friends) in the spring and early summer of 2015 when I was simultaneously recovering from my father's sudden death and my own subsequent pneumonia and a miscarriage, and inspired an entire chapter of *The Stagtress*.

Further to that note, thank you to all my lively friends and family. You're wonderful and I love you.